ALSO BY CARL HIAASEN

FICTION

Squeeze Me
Razor Girl
Bad Monkey
Star Island
Nature Girl
Skinny Dip
Basket Case
Sick Puppy
Lucky You
Stormy Weather
Strip Tease
Native Tongue
Skin Tight
Double Whammy
Tourist Season
A Death in China
(*with William Montalbano*)
Trap Line
(*with William Montalbano*)
Powder Burn
(*with William Montalbano*)

FOR YOUNG READERS

Wrecker
Squirm
Skink
Chomp
Scat
Flush
Hoot

NONFICTION

Assume the Worst
(*with Roz Chast*)
Dance of the Reptiles: Selected Columns
(*edited by Diane Stevenson*)
The Downhill Lie: A Hacker's Return to a Ruinous Sport
Paradise Screwed: Selected Columns
(*edited by Diane Stevenson*)
Kick Ass: Selected Columns
(*edited by Diane Stevenson*)
Team Rodent: How Disney Devours the World

FEVER BEACH

FEVER BEACH

CARL HIAASEN

ALFRED A. KNOPF
New York 2025

A BORZOI BOOK
FIRST HARDCOVER EDITION
PUBLISHED BY ALFRED A. KNOPF 2025

Published by Alfred A. Knopf, a division of Penguin Random House LLC,
1745 Broadway, New York, NY 10019.

Knopf, Borzoi Books, and the colophon are registered trademarks of
Penguin Random House LLC.

Library of Congress Cataloging-in-Publication Data
Names: Hiaasen, Carl, author.
Title: Fever beach : a novel / Carl Hiaasen.
Description: First edition. | New York : Alfred A. Knopf, 2025. |
Identifiers: LCCN 2024037195 | ISBN 9780593320945 (hardcover) |
ISBN 9780593315477 (trade paperback) | ISBN 9780593320952 (eBook)
Subjects: LCSH: Florida—Fiction. | LCGFT: Thrillers (Fiction) | Novels.
Classification: LCC PS3558.I217 F48 2025 | DDC 813/.54—dc23/eng/20240823
LC record available at https://lccn.loc.gov/2024037195

This is a work of fiction. All names and characters are either invented or used fictitiously. Most events described are imaginary, except for the assembly line stealing of adult novelty items, and the random throwing of bagged pro-Nazi leaflets from moving vehicles in Florida. Also accurately represented is the Proud Boys' peculiar membership rule regarding self-gratification.

penguinrandomhouse.com | aaknopf.com

Printed in the United States of America

The authorized representative in the EU for product safety and
compliance is Penguin Random House Ireland, Morrison Chambers,
32 Nassau Street, Dublin D02 YH68, Ireland, https://eu-contact.penguin.ie.

In memory of Jimmy Buffett

FEVER BEACH

CHAPTER 1

On the afternoon of September 20th, dishwater-gray and rainy, a man named Dale Figgo picked up a hitchhiker on Gus Grissom Boulevard in Tangelo Shores, Florida. The hitchhiker, who reminded Figgo of Danny DeVito, asked for a lift to the interstate. Figgo agreed to take him there after finishing an errand.

The distance to the highway wasn't far, and the hitchhiker would have walked if not for the pounding thunder and wild lightning. As a boy he had witnessed a neighbor's gelded llama struck to the ground by a bolt that lit up the small Wisconsin pasture like Lambeau Field. The llama had survived the shock, but from then on yipped day and night like an addled collie. The hitchhiker shared this anecdote with Dale Figgo, who agreed that lightning was a thing to be avoided.

Soon they entered a manicured subdivision called Sanctuary Falls, where Figgo eased his Dodge Ram 1500 quad cab to the curb and told the hitchhiker what was about to happen. The hitchhiker placed his backpack on the floorboard and pivoted warily toward the back seat, where he saw an assault rifle, a can of bear spray, a sex doll made to look like the lower torso of a woman, and a pile of clear Ziploc bags. Each bag contained a handful of what appeared to be beach sand and a garishly printed flyer. Reading upside down, the hitchhiker saw that one of the words was "JEWISH." Figgo began sorting and stacking the bags on the console.

"I'll drive," he said. "You throw."

"Do what?"

"The sand is for weight. Also, so the baggies won't blow away."

The hitchhiker said, "I'm pretty sure 'Holocaust' isn't spelled with a *k*."

"And I'm pretty sure I didn't tell you to proof-teach my business."

Slowly Figgo began driving up and down the tidy streets, the hitchhiker reluctantly lobbing the slur-filled Ziplocs onto driveways of multimillion-dollar properties lush with bougainvilleas, black olive trees, and hybrid palms.

When the hitchhiker noticed a shamrock painted on one of the mailboxes, he asked Figgo if they were in the right neighborhood.

"Never question the mission," Figgo said.

"What mission exactly?"

"Community outreach, dumbass. To enlight the motherfuckin' citizenry!"

"'Enlight'?" the hitchhiker said. "For real?"

Figgo reached across and popped him in the jaw.

"What the hell?" cried the hitchhiker, rubbing his chin. It was the first time he'd been slugged by a driver. Propositioned? Sure. Robbed? Too many times to count.

But never once punched—and he'd thumbed his way from coast to coast.

Figgo said, "You want a ride to 95 or not?"

The rain was falling harder, the thunder more ominous.

"Why'd you hit me? For Christ's sake, I'm old enough to be your dad."

"Just keepin' it real," said Figgo, grinning. "That's what I do. My top forte, you might say."

What's wrong with this fuckwhistle? wondered the hitchhiker.

After all the bagged tracts were distributed, Figgo made a phone call to somebody named Jonas and reported that the run had been completed without incident.

But then, as Figgo was navigating an exit from Sanctuary Falls, a gangly, middle-aged blond man stepped into the road. He wore orange Crocs and a terrycloth robe, and he was clutching one of Figgo's baggies. Heatedly he waved both arms, signaling for the pickup truck to halt. The hitchhiker perceived that this particular citizen was rejecting Figgo's version of enlightenment.

As soon as Figgo hit the brakes, the man in the robe lurched closer. Figgo grabbed the can of bear spray from the back seat.

"Aw, don't," the hitchhiker said.

"Self-defense. You're my fuckin' witness."

"Seriously, the dude's wearin' a damn robe."

"So did Mike Tyson!"

Figgo rolled down his window. The man in the street was cursing in a wheezy, irate voice. He called Figgo a lowlife racist and scumbag Nazi. Then he reared back and hurled the plastic bag, which, because of the sand, made a *thwap* when it bounced off Figgo's forehead.

"Game on!" Figgo crowed, aiming the nozzle of the bear spray at the maniac.

But when he pulled the trigger, nothing happened, not even a squirt. The hitchhiker reached over and snatched away the can.

"It's empty, bro," he said.

"Viva," Figgo muttered. "That stupid bitch."

The angry homeowner was now endeavoring to spit, through a slanting sheet of rain, at Figgo's prized Ram. When Figgo stomped on the accelerator, the man tried to jump out of the way but ended up splayed across the hood of the quad cab—robe unhitched, Crocs airborne, the back of his skull spidering the windshield.

"Stop the truck!" the hitchhiker shouted.

"No way." Figgo sped up and began to weave erratically.

"You killed him, man!"

"He ain't dead. He's hangin' on like a damn gecko."

Figgo made a screeching swerve and the pedestrian slid off the hood, landing in a heap on a bike path. Figgo sped away, nervously checking the rearview.

"How come that asshole got so pissed?" he muttered when they were back on A1A. "He sure didn't look Jewish. Do they even make blond Jews?"

"Let me out," the hitchhiker pleaded.

"See what he did to my truck?"

It wouldn't have been necessary for Figgo to hit-and-run the man if only the bear spray had worked. The container was empty because Figgo's tenant, a woman named Viva Morales, had in a moment of panic mistaken it for Raid and blasted the blinding contents at a cockroach, rendering the townhouse apartment she and Figgo shared uninhabitable for thirty-six hours. Thrifty by nature, Figgo had saved the bear spray can, trusting it was good for another shot or two.

"That shit ain't cheap," he groused to the hitchhiker.

"Seriously, I'll get out now."

"Chill, brah. That old geezer's fine," Figgo said.

"You need to call 911."

"No way. He flipped me the finger when we took off."

The hitchhiker, who had observed no such gesture from the man crumpled on the bike path, fell silent. Soon the fleeing pickup truck got stuck in traffic, inching through the downpour.

"So, where you headed for?" Figgo asked.

"Austin, Texas." The hitchhiker gathered his backpack onto his lap, prepping for departure.

"What's the woke situation down in Austin? I heard it was bad."

"Austin's cool," the hitchhiker answered. "Great music."

"But mostly country, right?"

"All kinds of music."

"That rap shit, too?"

"Hip-hop, sure."

"See, that's what I'm gettin' at. The rotten libtards, that's the whole crust of the problem."

"Ah." The hitchhiker stole another worried glance at the big gun on the back seat.

"Sorry about the punch in the face," Figgo said.

"Yeah, I'm not sure why you did that."

"Wanna make some money?"

"Thanks, but I'm set," the hitchhiker said.

Traffic had come to a stop. The hitchhiker figured there was an accident somewhere up ahead.

Figgo said, "It's easy work. I'll pay ya fifty bucks cash."

"To do what?"

"Stuff more baggies. I got the carpy tuna bad, so I could use some help." Figgo extended one hand for inspection. It appeared totally functional.

"Plus there's some people you should meet," Figgo went on. "Good dudes. Colleagues of mine."

He pronounced it "collig-yoos."

"We're workin' up somethin' so freaking big it'll blow your mind. You can crash at my place, downstairs on the sleeper sofa."

"Sweet," said the hitchhiker, a millisecond before he flung open the door, rolled out of the truck, and ran.

~~~

The flight to Orlando was packed. Twilly Spree felt lucky to score an aisle seat. The man and woman sharing the row told him they were going to Disney World for their honeymoon. At first Twilly thought they were joking, the Magic Kingdom being as romantic as a food court. But it turned out the young couple wasn't kidding. Twilly felt bound to warn them that they were doomed to return to Disney every time their family expanded, the woman seeming to absorb this forecast with less cheer than her husband. They were a gregarious duo, however, with numerous questions about Florida in general. Was it safe? What about the alligators? When's the next space launch? Where's the best place to swim with a manatee?

His patience soon sapped, Twilly faked an asthmatic episode and turned away to drag on a realistic-looking inhaler. It was a prop he carried at all times in public. Across the aisle sat an attractive woman in her early forties, auburn hair pinned up. She was wearing tortoiseshell glasses and reading a *New Yorker* magazine, which made Twilly self-conscious about the *USA Today* on his lap. Seeing no wedding band on the woman's ring finger, he uncharacteristically made a stab at conversation.
~~~

"Do you live in Orlando?" he asked, pocketing the mock inhaler.

"Hush," she said firmly but gently, as if speaking to a child in church. She didn't look up from the article she was reading.

Twilly wondered if she'd purchased the magazine on the trip or brought it from home. In any case, her surgical concentration on the contents was alluring.

He folded his newspaper into the seat pocket and opened a book on his iPad. It was a biography of a poet he'd never heard of, a supposedly volcanic talent who remained obscure and unappreciated until his tragic death at age thirty-two. Twilly assumed that the misunderstood soul had taken his own life, but it turned out that he'd perished in an electric skateboard accident after partying all night with Lululemon models. Death by suicide would have been a cliché, his biographer wrote solemnly in the foreword, and the rebellious young poet was a sworn enemy of clichés. Evidently, skating into the path of a Coors truck on the Pacific Coast Highway had certified the stature of his untamed genius. Twilly deleted the remainder of the book, having no idea how it had gotten downloaded in the first place. Perhaps the prankster had been Janine, back in happier times.

The flight got bumpy, and the honeymooners clutched each other's hands. Twilly waited for the auburn-haired woman across the aisle to put down the magazine, which the plane's bouncing would have made impossible to read. After a time she gave up trying, took off her glasses, and closed her eyes.

"You okay?" Twilly asked.

"What?"

"I've got a Valium if you need it."

"Behave," the woman said, still with her eyes shut.

The pilots were weaving around one of those towering mid-Florida thunderstorms. Twilly could see deep purple clouds through the aircraft's windows on one side, bright and deceiving sunshine through the other.

"I think we're in a holding pattern," he said to the woman.

"The plane, you mean."

"Yes. Of course."

A few minutes later, the woman said, "So, I actually have your book."

"Wow, which one?"

"*How to Let Happiness Find You.*"

"And?"

"Did nothing for me," the woman said. "Completely useless."

"I'm sorry to hear that."

"Are you working on a new one?"

"No, I'm not."

"Good," the woman said, putting her glasses back on.

Twilly had never written a book, and had never heard of the one she was complaining about. Still, he was intrigued that she thought she recognized him from a photograph on a jacket flap—and without seeming to even glance in his direction.

"I'm not qualified to do a self-help guide," he said.

"No kidding."

"Do you want your money back?"

The woman sighed and said no. He liked her attitude. She wasn't going to smile, no matter what.

"Was that albuterol?" she asked.

"Sorry, what?"

"Your inhaler."

"Oh. Right," Twilly said, patting his pocket. "For my asthma."

"I had a husband who used that stuff. Kept him up all night."

"That's when I do my best writing."

"Maybe switch to cocaine," the woman said.

The plane found smooth air again, on final approach, and the young newlyweds sitting beside Twilly began reciting one of the lesser-known Psalms. He was impressed by the couple's courage to pray out loud in front of Florida-bound strangers. After the landing, he allowed the devout duo to file out ahead of him and—not wishing to further annoy the cool, pretty woman across the aisle—remained in his seat until all the passengers had debarked.

Right away Twilly noticed that the woman had left her *New Yorker* behind, so he put it in his backpack before leaving the plane. On the Uber ride from the airport he took out the magazine and smiled when he saw an address label on a bottom corner of the cover; she wasn't just a casual reader, she was a *subscriber.*

The name printed on the mail sticker: V. Morales.

And her address was an apartment in Tangelo Shores, another pleasant surprise.

Twilly had assumed that she was visiting the state on business or a vacation, but she was actually coming home.

It was encouraging. Twilly felt that way whenever he crossed paths with a potentially intelligent person. Perhaps she was even registered to vote.

~~~

Viva walked in and found Dale Figgo seated at the kitchen table filling sandwich baggies with flyers and what appeared to be novelty key chains. They looked like ping-pong balls stamped with crooked swastikas and a website address. Figgo wore a Velcro-strapped brace on his right wrist and hand. A bucket half filled with beach sand was positioned on the linoleum floor between his bare hairy feet.

"Yo, how do you spell 'Fauci'?" he asked, waggling a red Sharpie.

"Nope," Viva said.

"Aw, come on."

She was renting a room in Figgo's townhouse. The kitchen had been designated a neutral zone. In return, Viva had agreed to remain out of sight during the meetings that Figgo occasionally held. Recently he'd formed his own white nationalist group, the Strokers for Liberty, and Viva's scalding derision had already run off several prospective members.

"The deal," she said to Figgo, "was that you keep your crazy bullshit out of the common area."

He bristled and scowled. "We're at war against the enemy within! What's crazy about that? This comes down from the president himself."

"Sure. The enemy within. They're everywhere."

"Open your eyes, missy."
~~~

"All I see is a messy kitchen," Viva said. "Kindly clean off the damn counter."

At first she'd regarded her landlord as repugnant but harmless—an empty pointed hood, as it were. He had no leadership skills and a pliant philosophy. When she'd asked him why a white supremacist would rent space to her, a progressive Hispanic woman, he looked puzzled.

"Why the hell wouldn't I? You pay on time," he'd said. "Also, two of my best bros in the Proud Boys were Cuban dudes from Miami."

"So basically you draw the line at Blacks and Jews."

"And illegals, by God."

"Thanks for clarifying, Dale."

It was nothing Viva hadn't heard before. One of her ex-husband's uncles was a slobbering white zealot who had ruined every family gathering until a coral snake bit his ankle while he was on migrant patrol with his homegrown militia in an Arizona desert. The man didn't die, but he claimed to experience apocalyptic visions. Soon after being discharged from the hospital, he joined a doomsday cult and disappeared off the grid. Dale Figgo seemed destined for a similar obscurity, though his growing collection of semiautomatic weapons had caused Viva to reassess the threat level that he posed.

As Figgo transferred his flyer-stuffing operation to the living room couch, Viva asked what topic he had chosen for this week's screed.

"The rise of the international Zionist cowbell," he said.

"You mean 'cabal.' "

Figgo sneered. "I ain't fallin' for that."

"Are you bozos still throwing Ziplocs in people's yards?"

"Hey, it works."

"You know, there's this thing called the internet."

"People can block your emails," Figgo said. "They can't block a bag full of truth from landing on their driveway."

He handed her one of the leaflets, which was titled "EVERY SINGLE ASPECT OF THE EVIL COVID AGENDA IS JEWISH."

Viva yawned and said, "Again with the Jews?"

"Them and the Chinese got a new germ in the hopper. Just wait."

"Dale, you told me you got vaccinated last time."

"Only to spare someone innocent that might not be as tough as me."

"But then you had your boosters, too."

"Shut up," Figgo snapped. "I got one a them high-risk conditions."

"Which is . . . ?"

"I'm a type 2 diabolic."

"Oh dear," Viva said.

Figgo grabbed the flyer away and glowered as Viva made a show of scrubbing her hands at the kitchen sink. She asked why there was a blue hurricane tarp over his truck.

"To keep the crows from shittin' on it," he lied.

"That won't fool 'em."

"Who? The damn birds?"

"The repo guys, Dale."

"No, no, I got all that nonsense straightened out."

"Liar," Viva said, and started up the stairs with her carry-on.

"By the way, you owe me forty-nine bucks," Figgo snarled after her.

She stopped on the landing and turned around. "Do tell, Dale."

"For the can of grizzly mace you wasted on that puny little roach."

"I wouldn't call it a waste," Viva said.

"Add it to your next rent check."

"Fine, Dale. When are you going to fix the drain in my tub?"

"I'm still waitin' on a part."

"You truly suck," Viva said.

This was her eighty-ninth day in rental purgatory, with nine months left on an ironclad lease. She'd found the room on Craigslist; it was the only place she could afford, having been not only dumped but also cleaned out by her husband of four years. *Four fucking years!* An embarrassingly long time to have overlooked so many red flags—the day drinking, the aversion to salaried employment, the multiple cellphones, the mysterious "hot springs meditation retreats" to which she was never invited. Her humiliation was compounded because her professional background was human resources, and still he'd snowed her completely.

His name was Malcolm, and he was younger than Viva. How he'd hacked into her private money market account she had no clue; he'd already moved out by the time the bank notified her. The thieving jerk also racked up eleven thousand dollars on one of her credit cards before he got busted, driving a newly leased G-Wagen due west across South Dakota. He was returned to the Twin Cities in handcuffs.

Viva had flown back to sign the divorce papers and reclaim her laptop, a charm bracelet that had belonged to her grandmother, a red sports bra, and other items that Malcolm had taken when he moved out. The bra had been hanging from the rearview mirror of the G-Wagen when he was pulled over by the cops. Viva stuffed it into a trash basket at the police station in Minneapolis. Detectives placed the odds of recovering her life savings at approximately nil, Malcolm having wired the modest balance overseas.

For a fresh start, Viva had chosen Florida because her sister had once lived there and raved about it. So far, the enchanting aspects of the state had eluded her. Dead broke and deep in debt, she'd found a job that paid just well enough to begin reviving her credit rating. Her title was "wealth director" for a nonprofit called the Mink Foundation, which gave away millions of dollars with the goal of getting as many buildings as possible named after Claude and Electra Mink. The couple, not yet deceased, made a souring appearance in the office almost every day.

And every evening Viva would go home and deal with Dale Figgo—bigot, slob, conspiracy nut, and hatemonger. She had known none of this when she'd rented the room at his townhouse. On the plus side, she had the washer-dryer all to herself, Figgo believing the machine was equipped with software that could read and report the seditious slogans on his tank tops.

Viva got in the shower and stayed there until the backed-up

water rose to her ankles. Afterward she put on granny pants and a pullover, and went downstairs for a sandwich. So far, only one of Figgo's fellow white supremacists had arrived for the meeting, a rat-eyed brute named Jonas Onus. He was tall but bottom-heavy, with chipped brown teeth and a long wild beard dyed red, white, and blue. Although Viva had met him twice before, he reintroduced himself before joining Figgo at the baggie prep station. The men were seated shoulder to shoulder, whispering in serious tones, when Viva headed back to her room with a flat Sprite and a tuna salad on rye.

Later she picked through an unpacked box of books and found *How to Let Happiness Find You*, another unforgivable gift from her sister. Viva had made it only midway through the third chapter ("How to Let Yourself Let Yourself Go") before tossing the book aside. Now she studied the author's photo on the jacket flap and saw that he wasn't the man on the airplane, who'd had a dent on the bridge of his nose and a leaner, more weathered face. She felt foolish, and hoped the stranger on the flight had played along because he was polite, not predatory.

Downstairs, the meeting had started and the music was cranked up loud—heavy metal, as always. The bass lines pounded through the floor; Figgo believed that blasting Iron Maiden or Korn at painful decibels would thwart any eavesdropping devices the government might have installed. However, he kept the volume level so high that the Strokers for Liberty were unable to converse normally; they communicated mostly using Sharpie-scrawled notes, which Figgo would later rip into pieces and flush down the toilet. It was a practice that exacerbated the myriad plumbing problems in the townhouse. Viva had suggested that the men take their team building to an outdoor venue—a firing range, for example—but Figgo feared drone surveillance.

The notion that federal agents were spying on the Strokers struck Viva as far-fetched; from what she'd seen of the members, they were too disorganized to be taken seriously. That they all carried firearms prompted Viva to be watchful, but she wasn't afraid, having grown up in Texas where everyone's packing. Occasionally she used Figgo's paranoia to her own benefit, on one occasion scoring high-end Levolor shades for her bedroom after convincing him that trench-coated prowlers were aiming laser pointers at her window late at night.

As Figgo's playlist blared from the first floor, Viva lowered the shades, put on her noise-canceling headphones, and fell asleep. Some time later she was awakened by a talking-coyote dream, not her first. It wasn't a humorous cartoon coyote, unfortunately, but a smaller and more cynical one.

The townhouse was quiet, so she took off the headphones and slipped down to the kitchen for a glass of ice water. She saw that the living room lights were still on and the front door was ajar. A tow truck was backed up to the driveway, where Figgo and Onus stood supervising the treatment of Figgo's prized Ram 1500, still tarped. The two seemed unusually calm and cooperative, leaving Viva to conclude that both men were familiar with the icy protocol of vehicle repossession.

She was still in the kitchen, eating seedless grapes out of a bowl in the refrigerator, when Figgo reentered the apartment alone.

"What're you doin' up?" he said irritably. "Don't be creepin' round my personal shit."

"Did Avatar Sasquatch go home?"

"Shut up," Figgo said. "Dude's got a master's from Valdosta State."

Viva closed the refrigerator door. "So, which of you is the boss?"

Figgo looked peeved. "Just wait. We're gonna make some big moves, and then you won't be laughin'."

"Good night, Dale."

"Hang on. I wanted to ask could I use your car for a little while tomorrow after work."

"That would be a hard no," Viva said.

"My truck's gonna be in the shop. Torque converter locked up."

"You definitely cannot borrow my car."

"I'll top off the tank when I'm done."

"Under no circumstances, Dale."

"Why you gotta be such a c-word?"

Viva thumped him between the legs and said, "I'm telling your mother."

Figgo stumbled back, clutching himself. "Leave Mom out of it!" he said. "Don't get her all jacked up again."

"Then let's hear an apology."

"I'm sorry, 'kay? Jesus Christ."

"And fix the drain in my bathtub."

"Yeah, yeah."

"I'm not kidding. I'll call her first thing in the morning," Viva said. "Swear to God."

Figgo retreated to his room, thinking he could hardly wait for the day when Viva and especially his mother saw him differently, the day when the Strokers for Liberty stormed into history.

CHAPTER 2

Twilly still lived alone a year after his best dog died, two years after he sank a city councilman's party barge, and three years after his divorce from Janine. Gone, finally, was the electronic ankle bracelet that had been an awkward impediment to new relationships. His court sentence had been more lenient than expected, considering his record. It had played out in his favor that no one was aboard the pontoon boat on the night of the sinking, that the vessel had been purchased with bribery proceeds, and that the crooked councilman who owned it fled the country in advance of a federal RICO indictment. Twilly was now permanently banned from the city of Bonita Springs, but other than that he was free to roam.

He kept small first-floor apartments all over Florida, seldom spending more than a few nights in one place. The inheritance from his land-raping grandfather evidently would never run out, as Twilly continued receiving sizable interest payouts from bond funds into which he'd blindly dumped the money decades ago. He didn't know how much he was worth because he never looked at the quarterly statements. He communicated with his tax accountant only once a year, on the 14th of April.

Twilly had no children of his own due to a precocious realization that he was unfit for parenthood. On his twenty-second birthday he'd flown to Denver for a vasectomy after telling his parents he was at a dude ranch, learning to ride Western.

As usual, a key part of his latest plea deal was anger management counseling. At Twilly's request, the judge had allowed him to attend a rehab-slash-retreat center near the Boundary Waters in upstate Minnesota. The spacious cedar lodge was comfortable, the lake was full of walleyes, and his eleven fellow "pathway seekers" steered clear of him between sessions, apparently having been forewarned. Once again Twilly proved resistant to the trendy mindfulness therapy that was supposed to quell reckless impulses and tame tempers. He had no desire to peel back his own emotional layers, or anyone else's. He was mercilessly self-aware, and his understanding of why he did the things that he did was crystal clear.

Still, thirty days at Placid Valley wasn't a total waste of time; Twilly caught lots of fish, reread Ed Abbey, and heard enough stories at the group meetings to verify that he wasn't the most fucked-up person in the program. He'd flown back to Florida in relatively solid shape, a trip highlighted by his encounter with V. Morales. Once he had her name and address, finding the phone number wasn't difficult.

"Hi, I'm the asthma guy from the plane," he said when she answered. "I owe you an apology."

"You *definitely* owe me an apology—for calling."

"That, too. You left your magazine on the plane. I got your information off the mailing label."

"And my cell number?"

"Found it online. One of those reverse directories."

"That's not creepy at all. And your name is . . . ?"

"Twilly Spree. What does your *V* stand for?"

"Viva," she said. "Mr. Spree, where shall I direct the police to pick you up?"

"I didn't really write that book you mentioned on the flight. I should've told you the truth."

"That one was on me," she said. "Actually, you don't look much like the author. He's way younger around the eyes."

"Nonetheless, I apologize for letting you think I was him."

"And that's the only reason you called?"

"Also, I don't actually have asthma," Twilly said. "It's just a phony excuse for not engaging with strangers."

"Except women who read."

"A weakness of mine. It's been nice talking with you, Viva. Thanks for not hanging up on me."

"Wait a second," she said. "After all this, you're not even going to ask me out?"

"God, no. That would be stalker-y."

"It would be more stalker-y if you didn't."

"You might be right," Twilly said. "Let me sleep on it."

⁓⁓

Dale Figgo watched the early-morning news on TV, anxiously flipping between stations. There were no media reports about a hit-and-run at Sanctuary Falls. Ditto for the county sheriff's Facebook page.

Maybe that skinny old dork wasn't hurt too bad, Figgo thought.

Viva agreed to give him a lift to work. On the way she asked again if his pickup truck had been repossessed and not towed off for repairs. That pissed Figgo off, though he held his tongue. The last thing he needed was another blunt lecture from his mother, and Viva wouldn't hesitate to contact her. She'd done it once before, when the issue was galloping bedbugs.

Figgo worked in a large unmarked warehouse owned by a company called Bottom Drawer Novelties. His job was packaging soft polymer sex toys that were manufactured in China and sent in bulk on container ships to the port of Tampa. The top-selling item was a "wheat-hued" female trunk that was graphically lifelike and supposedly cast from the body of a popular porn actress. It was called Darcy's Dream Booty and weighed thirteen pounds. On an average day Figgo boxed four dozen units, each having to be manually unstuck from a shipping pallet, wiped clean, and inspected for defects such as extra orifices. Every Dream Booty fit into a cardboard box measuring 15 × 15 × 10 inches. The retail price was $89.95, and occasionally Figgo would steal one and gift it as a recruiting enticement to a prospective Stroker for Liberty.

He'd landed the warehouse gig late in the pandemic. The pay was eighteen bucks an hour and he didn't mind the hard work, though the repetitive packing motion aggravated the carpal tunnel pain in his right hand. Initially the condition was caused by a brutish masturbation regimen that Figgo had commenced on the day he was expelled from the militantly anti-wanking Proud Boys. Figgo had then applied to join the Oath Keepers, who took no stance on self-pleasuring, but he was flatly rejected. Other high-profile hate groups shunned him, as well.

This rare blackballing by the white-supremacist establishment followed a humiliating blunder that occurred during the January 6th siege in Washington, when Figgo had posted a video of himself flamboyantly smearing feces on the statue of James Zachariah George of Mississippi. A Confederate war veteran, state supreme court justice, and rabid secessionist, James George had been a lifelong crusader against equal rights for Blacks. He'd also happened to have a beard, causing Figgo in the fog of zeal to mistake the head on George's statue inside the Capitol for that of Ulysses Grant, whose memorial famously stands outside the building, at the reflecting pool.

Later Figgo explained to fellow insurrectionists that it was an honest mix-up, and that the fecal matter wasn't his but rather canine in origin, scooped from a sidewalk during the rowdy march down Pennsylvania Avenue after the president's inspirational rally. Yet, as soon as the James George defacement video went viral in the Deep South, the Proud Boys disowned Figgo. He'd hoped to regain their favor by getting indicted and making a defiant anti-government speech at trial, but the fucking feds never charged him. Not for the poop, not even for trespassing! Meanwhile the Oath Keepers accused him of being an infiltrator sent by the FBI, and blocked him from their chatter on the dark web.

The following election had required no uprising, which was just as well because Figgo hadn't been ready. A stretch of personal turmoil—mostly spent running from bad checks—had delayed his plan to fund and organize his own white nationalist group. Now, with the government in safe hands, enthusiasm for the movement seemed to be waning. Still, Figgo refused to give up on his dream.

Recently he and Onus connected in a chat room for fuming white people who believed their ambitions had been steamrolled by affirmative action. Onus's story was that he'd been passed over for a promotion at the Houston fire department because a firefighter of mixed race had applied for the same job. Figgo, meanwhile, claimed that his dream of a college education had been dashed when the University of Miami had rejected his application, undoubtedly to make room for a Jew or a Black. He didn't mention the manifest deficiencies in his high-school transcript, which in his mind had nothing to do with him being passed over by the college.

Eventually he and Onus met up in person, at a Denny's, to share prejudices and complain about their respective plights. In Figgo's view, Onus was not only a brother warrior but a potential friend. He verbally committed to the Strokers for Liberty on the same morning that Figgo presented him with one of Darcy's Dream Booties.

The men didn't hang out as much as Figgo wanted due to Onus's complicated domestic situation. Still, Onus usually found time to answer the call of duty, even on short notice. He was waiting at the townhouse when Figgo returned from work.

"Hop in the back of the truck," Onus told him.

"Why?"

"It's easier to throw the baggies from there. Also, Himmler's up front with me."

Onus drove an older white Tundra pickup with a single bench seat. Himmler was his dog, a pit-mastiff mix that weighed a buck twenty and refused to be muzzled. Figgo was sensibly terrified of the animal. He also wasn't thrilled about riding in the open bed of a truck, but he was grateful to Onus for agreeing to be the wheelman. Unlike Figgo, Onus had no job responsibilities to interfere with clandestine activities. A spurious disability claim had enabled him to retire at age forty-one from the fire department, despite the fact that none of his fellow firefighters recalled seeing a smoldering beam strike his head on the night the Sleepy Angel baby mattress factory burned down. A lifetime income assured, Onus immediately moved to Florida and gained forty pounds.

"What's the target?" he asked as Figgo climbed over the tailgate.

"Blue Mallard Run. It's a gated deal, but I got the code from a guy I know sprays for lawn fungus out there."

"Mallards aren't blue."

"Who cares," Figgo said.

"And they don't run. They fly."

"All of a sudden you're the fucking Discovery Channel."

"I heard some PGA pros live out there," Onus said. "Ballers, too."

"Doesn't mean they're all sold on the Holocaust."

"The golfers I'm not worried about. It's them brothers from the NBA can cover some ground when they want."

"That's why God created V8s," said Figgo.

He informed Onus that the tracts to be dispersed on today's mission focused on the unholy influence of Jews, not Blacks. (Figgo had recently finished writing a leaflet called "The Demonic Disgrace of Critical Race," but a Haitian clerk at Kinko's had pulled the plug on the printer after peeking at the first draft.)

When the men arrived at the main gate of Blue Mallard Run, Figgo hopped down from the truck bed and tapped in the entry code he'd been given. Four times he tried the sequence, and four times it failed. Onus squeezed his shaggy gourd of a head out the truck's window and advised Figgo to start with the asterisk key, but Figgo couldn't find one on the keypad.

"Then fuck it. Let's bounce," Onus said.

"No way. Not yet."

Himmler spotted an elderly woman walking a cocker spaniel and began barking dementedly, flinging drool all over the interior windshield.

"We gone," Jonas Onus called out to Figgo.

"Just wait, goddammit!"

Figgo hastily snatched up the Ziplocs—a total of three dozen—

and began lobbing them one by one over the closed gate. It was a slow process due to the brace on his dominant hand. Not wishing to be memorialized on security video, Onus sped away in reverse. Figgo was so focused that he didn't notice he'd been abandoned. As he launched the last bag, the gate beeped twice and began to slide open. Looming on the other side was a county garbage truck, its driver and crew waiting to exit Blue Mallard Run.

Figgo hid behind a tree and morosely listened to the sound of twenty-five tons crushing thirty-six plastic balls, the key-chain tokens popping like cheap firecrackers inside the baggies.

Afterward he went searching unsuccessfully for Jonas Onus. Eventually he took a taxi back to the townhouse, where a note had been taped to the front door. An investigator from the Florida Highway Patrol wanted to question him about a "serious incident" that had occurred the previous day in the community of Sanctuary Falls.

Figgo groaned and said, "Well, fuck me with a fence post."

He hurried inside, shredded the note, and flushed it down the toilet in his bathroom. Then he sat down to clean his newest AR-15, following a simple instructional video on YouTube.

~~~

It was a table for four—Claude and Electra, Viva Morales, and a mystery guest who was running late. The Minks were already half bombed.

"Have some wine, dear," Electra kept saying to Viva.

"Or don't," her husband would say. "It's ninety-six bloody dollars a bottle."

Viva ordered a Pellegrino. They were seated in a private dining room at a French restaurant that had received slavering reviews on Yelp. Claude and Electra practically commanded Viva to order the peacock terrine, but she declined. Her stomach was a mess—all day coping with the Minks, and now dinner, too. The ancient couple was diminutive and pinch-faced, with matching complexions that suggested a two-for-one exfoliation coupon.
~~~

"I'm done waiting for him," Claude Mink grumbled.

"He's a busy, busy man," his wife said. "And, most important, one of us."

Yikes, Viva thought.

She excused herself to go to the restroom. When she returned, the tardy guest had arrived. He was tall and long-necked, with wide-set eyes, a sharp chin, a high-cliffed brow, and jet-black hair spiked sharply in the front. The effect was that of an anime woodpecker in a pinstriped suit. The man took Viva's hand and introduced himself as Clure Boyette.

"The congressman, of course," Electra Mink cut in.

"Viva knows who he is," said her husband. "She damn well better."

"Of course I do," Viva said, though she didn't.

"And what's your name?" Boyette asked her.

"Viva Morales."

"Love it."

Clure Boyette was wearing an American flag pin on one lapel, a state of Florida flag pin on the other, and a red necktie featuring the entire text of the Second Amendment. He made no apology for being late, and told the Minks that he didn't have much time.

"Can we get down to business?" he said, taking a chair at the table.

Viva was distracted by his teeth, which looked like dentures for a Clydesdale.

"I came to ask for a donation," he began. "And don't worry—it's not for my re-election committee."

"Good, because we've already got that covered," Claude Mink cut in.

"This money is for a charitable foundation I'm starting," the congressman continued. "It's called the the Wee Hammers. We're a 501(c)(3), so it's—"

"Tax exempt," Electra said. "We get how that works."

Boyette smiled greasily at the Minks. "I just wanted you both to know that this cause is dear to my own personal heart."

"I'd love to hear more," Viva said.

"And I love that you speak so well—and no trace of an accent."

"My family's been in this country for four generations, Mr. Boyette."

"Now, that's the kind of narrative I like to hear," the congressman said. "Hard work, assimilation, then citizenship."

"Oh, we're a proud folk," Viva said.

"Cuban, I assume?"

Electra interrupted, telling Boyette to finish his pitch.

"So, my foundation is modeled on Habitat for Humanity," he said, "except all our houses will be built by kids, not grownups."

"Normal-sized houses?" asked Claude Mink.

"Seventeen hundred square feet, give or take." Boyette smiled. "Of course we'll have licensed subs overseeing the work. Each construction site will be like a Bob the Builder fantasy camp for boys and girls!"

A server brought a double vodka tonic for the congressman and another bottle of Merlot for the Minks. Viva requested a gin martini.

"This is such an admirable idea," Electra told Boyette, "keeping at-risk youths off the streets. Even better, they'll be learning a trade."

"And of course we'll provide hard hats in junior sizes," the congressman said.

"Wait—you're serious?" Viva asked. "What about the child labor laws?"

Boyette smiled patiently. "The Wee Hammers aren't getting *paid*, dear. They're volunteers. And it goes without saying that safety comes first. For instance, no youngster under thirteen will be allowed to run electrical wiring."

Viva, dumbstruck, said, "You're pulling them out of school?"

"Only Thursdays and Fridays."

Claude Mink had another question. "What happens to the houses when they're finished?"

"We give them away to deserving families that enter a lottery.

They'll have to pay for their own window fixtures, sod, hurricane insurance, et cetera. I mean, there's only so much we can do as an organization."

Electra nodded in approval. "It's still a cutting-edge concept, Clure. Throw us a number to chew on."

"I was thinking three million to start."

"Think again," Claude Mink said. "We'll do two."

"Done." Boyette raised his glass. "Thank you both very much. Here's a toast to the future Wee Hammers!"

"Well, wow," Viva said.

The congressman rose, pecked Electra on both cheeks, and turned to do the same to Viva. She ducked under the table, pretending to retrieve a napkin.

Later, after Boyette was gone and Viva had finished her martini, she asked the Minks if she could speak frankly.

"What a question!" Electra said. "Your input always has value, dear."

"Funding the Wee Hammers is a truly terrible idea."

Claude Mink shrugged. "How so?"

"First-graders shooting nail guns?" Viva said.

The Minks assured her that Clure Boyette would never put a child in harm's way, and said she should process his grant request as soon as possible. "The application will be arriving by email tomorrow morning," Electra added. "Check your inbox, first thing."

She and her husband alternated trying to stand up. Eventually they locked chicken-wing arms and teetered toward the door. Viva waited beside them in front of the restaurant until their ride pulled up. Carefully she helped the driver tilt the drunken millionaires into the back seat of their pearl-colored Maybach.

Afterward she drove home mumbling to herself. Dale Figgo didn't hear the door open. He was snoring at the kitchen table surrounded by the disassembled parts of his AR-15. Viva took the trigger and walked up the stairs to her room.

∿∿∿

The hotel kept a junior suite reserved for Clure Boyette, booked under the name "Dylan Cash." It was an ideal location—five hundred and five miles from his home in Carpville and the conservative Panhandle district that continued re-electing him to Congress. There were no young women like Galaxy in Carpville.

"Sugar, we gonna do it or not?" she asked.

"Hang tight. This is important," Boyette said.

"So am I."

"Sweetheart, please."

Standing hunched over his iPad, the congressman was nude except for an ermine collar attached to a rhinestone leash, a Doberman muzzle, and snowshoes. The email he was studying had been captioned "Talking Points for Tomorrow."

Galaxy sat up in bed, turned on the television, and placed the remote between two empty champagne bottles on the room service trolley.

"You play pool?" the congressman asked.

"I could kick your ass any night, Spanky."

"Well, listen to this. The woke police are trying to get all the eight balls changed from black to rainbow-colored!"

Galaxy rolled her eyes. "Who said that?"

"Fox."

"Who on Fox?"

"Judge Jeanine," said Boyette.

Galaxy let out a hoot. "I'm going to pretend you know that's total bullshit."

"No, it's not. She says they've got Washington lobbyists putting pressure on all the billiard companies."

Galaxy said, "You find more dumb ways to kill a vibe than any guy I've ever been with."

She grabbed Boyette's leash and jerked him into the sheets. Clinging to his iPad, he said, "Wait! I gotta tweet about this right now. Before any of the others."

By the time he finished posting the woke eight-ball bombshell (including his disdainful commentary) on social media, Galaxy was putting on her clothes in the bathroom. The congressman knocked and said he was ready to play Good Dog, Bad Dog. She told him she was no longer in the mood.

"Don't be such a child," Boyette said through the door.

"But isn't that why you picked me?"

"Not so loud, G."

When she emerged—Gator hoodie, cutoff jeans, sandals—he tried to hug her.

Deftly she ducked past, saying, "You missed the launch window, Spanky."

Reminding Boyette that her father worked for SpaceX at the Cape. An actual rocket scientist, of all things.

"Don't go yet," he implored, but she did.

He unclipped the leash, shed the muzzle, kicked off the snowshoes, and opened the Venmo app on his phone. Five hundred dollars was Galaxy's regular fee, which he always listed as "pastry." Now, in a sulk, he sent only two-fifty.

Boyette had been looking forward to a celebratory romp. The Wee Hammers scam finally was in motion; a cheap fake house would be built while the rest of the Minks' "donation" got diverted to jump-start the forces that would ensure Boyette's re-election—and perhaps a legacy beyond. The old couple had not only kept their promise, but had also played along convincingly in front of their unsuspecting new director of wealth, Ms. Viva Morales.

Whom the congressman would definitely have hit on, had Claude and Electra not been present.

He phoned his father, who, though not a rocket scientist, was very smart in other ways. Clay Boyette was the only reason that Clure Boyette had a law degree, a sanitized rap sheet, and a seat in the U.S. House of Representatives.

"Don't you ever check your voicemail?" he asked his son.

"Sorry, Dad. I've been in a meeting."

"You mean Dipshits Anonymous? I left three goddamn messages."

"What's wrong? Is it Nicki?"

"She went to see Fistman today."

29

Oh fuckeroo, thought Clure Boyette.

Harold Fistman, the most ruthless divorce lawyer in northwest Florida, was also the most expensive.

"This could be a disaster for your campaign," Boyette's father said.

"Why? What's she got?"

"You tell me, boy. Texts? Video? Amex receipts? Last time it was those dick pics you sent to that married weather gal in Panama City."

"Dad, I'm not an idiot. I don't do that stuff anymore."

"First off, you *are* an idiot. Second, get your ass home and make this right."

"How?"

"I don't know, Clure, she's *your* wife. Go buy her something huge."

"Like a new car?"

"Like a dealership," Boyette's father said. "Whatever the fuck it takes."

The line went dead. Clure Boyette rolled into bed, found a pay porn channel, and fell asleep with his mole-faced cock in his right hand. When he awoke early the next morning, he felt rough and foggy. He stood with his crusty eyelids closed under a steaming shower for ten minutes before realizing that the ermine collar was still around his neck.

CHAPTER 3

The hitchhiker who resembled Danny DeVito waited until he made it across the Georgia border before calling the Florida Highway Patrol. He was put on hold and then transferred to the investigator assigned to the hit-and-run at Sanctuary Falls. The investigator informed the hitchhiker that the victim was expected to recover, though a head injury had muddled his memory. The hitchhiker told the investigator that the vehicle involved was a black, late-model Ram 1500 pickup with a lift package.

"Yes, we got it on video," the investigator said. "What can you tell me about the driver?"

"White guy, mid-thirties, lumpy face."

"Beard?"

"He was trying," the hitchhiker said. "Looked like ginger pubes."

"Big dude?"

"Not small. Super-hairy arms. He had on a tank top that said 'White Lives Madder,' but spelled like 'M-A-D' mad."

"Where were you when the victim was struck by the truck?"

"Sitting next to the asshole that was driving," the hitchhiker said.

"Do you know his name?"

"Didn't ask. He had a gun and a can of bear spray on the back seat."

"A firearm?"

"Yup, an AR."

"Was it loaded?" the investigator asked.

"Didn't ask about that, either. There was a bunch of plastic bags he made me throw in people's driveways. He weighted 'em down with sand."

"Yes, the neighbors turned in a few."

"One other weird thing," the hitchhiker said, "the dude had a life-size rubber ass in the truck."

"A what?"

"It was tan-colored and looked like the real deal."

"You mean a sex doll," said the investigator, who was a woman.

"Not a whole doll, no. Just the butt cheeks, with the lady parts in the front."

"I see."

"You know. Where they're supposed to be," the hitchhiker said.

"Got it."

"Hell, all I wanted was a ride to the interstate."

"Can you come to our office for an interview?"

"Too late, ma'am. I'm long gone from your jurisdiction."

"Then at least let me get your name," the investigator said.

"I'll pass on that, too." The hitchhiker didn't want to end up in a courtroom testifying against the psycho pickup driver. "No offense, but I won't be back in Florida anytime soon," he added.

The investigator delivered her pat lecture about leaving the scene of an accident with injuries, a serious crime.

"Runnin' for your life is against the law now?" the hitchhiker said. "The truck fled the scene, so I fled the truck."

"Sir, this process doesn't have to be hard. Now that we've got your cell number, it would be easy to track you down if we wanted."

"You've got *a* cell number, that's true. The preacher here at the Bible camp where I'm stayin' is lettin' me use his phone to call long distance. He said Jesus Christ would have done the same thing, no matter what plan he was on."

The investigator sensed that the interview had stalled.

"Is there anything else you recall about the hit-and-run driver?" she asked. "Any detail that sticks with you?"

"Yeah," said the hitchhiker. "The dumb shit can't even spell 'Holocaust.' "

⌄⌄⌄⌄

Dale Figgo was on his hands and knees searching for the trigger of his AR-15 when Viva Morales left for work. She dropped the crucial gun part into a dumpster behind the bank building where the Mink Foundation leased its office. In her view, the theft was a public service because Figgo was the opposite of a responsible firearm owner.

Waiting among Viva's incoming emails was Clure Boyette's application for the Wee Hammers grant. Electra called in to make sure that the two million dollars would be wired before noon. Viva reiterated her doubts about the congressman's project, diplomatically choosing the term "high risk" instead of "fucking batshit." Electra told her to stop with the worrying.

After completing the paperwork and transferring the money, Viva phoned Twilly Spree to ask if he'd reached a decision about asking her out. He offered to meet for lunch at a seafood restaurant on the beach. They both arrived ten minutes early and shared a laugh about it. Viva commented on Twilly's attire—old jeans, flip-flops, and a faded gray tee shirt with a dime-size hole in one armpit.

"You're making quite a statement," she said.

"The grilled mahi is good. That's my statement."

"Relax. This doesn't count as a date."

"Another winner is the fried hogfish," Twilly said, pretending to study the menu.

"You seem cautious, so I'll go first. How far back?"

"Five years?"

"All right. That's easy," Viva said, and told him the story of Malcolm, the larcenous heartbreaker, and how she'd ended up in Florida.

Twilly used his turn to recap his relatively bloodless divorce from

Janine, the party barge sinking, the chafing caused by the court-ordered ankle bracelet, and the loss of his old dog Keith. It didn't cover a full five years, but there was plenty for Viva to consider.

She whistled and said, "All that, and you read *The New Yorker,* too."

"Only the cartoons."

"Tell me again why you tracked me down."

"I couldn't live with the idea of you thinking I was a writer."

"That's not the reason. That's the excuse."

"Okay, busted," Twilly said. "I'm actually searching for a life partner."

"Me, too! I'm desperate to get married, lied to for years, and lose my life's savings again."

Viva ordered the mahi with a spring salad. Twilly selected the hogfish and a bottle of Stella. Before the food arrived, they watched a lineup of surfers in the water and discussed the reason for the big waves, a late-season storm that had nicked the Bahamas. Hurricane Kayden.

"Who's going to take that name seriously?" Viva said. " 'Kayden' is the guy who shows up early for Sunday Pilates, humming to himself."

"A sensitive young fellow," Twilly agreed, "and misunderstood."

"I need to ask what you do. When you're not sinking politicians' boats, I mean."

"My rich grandfather foolishly prioritized me in his will," Twilly said, "leaving me with no adult responsibilities. How about you?"

When Viva told him about her position with the Mink Foundation, he chuckled and leaned back. "Would that be Mr. Claude Needham Mink?"

"And his wife, yes."

"Have they mentioned where all their wealth comes from?"

Viva hung her head. "This is going to ruin my appetite, isn't it?"

"After lunch we'll take a ride."

Twilly drove a mud-crusted Suburban, the satellite radio tuned to Underground Garage. He put on aviator sunglasses and a faded Florida Marlins cap. Viva half expected him to top off the stereotype by lighting a Camel, though the SUV smelled like coffee, not cigarettes. In the back was some sort of empty metal cage.

"I'm still not sure about you," she said as he headed west, beyond the interstate. "You could be wanted for murder in Alaska."

"As could you."

"Where are we going?"

"Wait till you see this place," Twilly said.

It was halfway to Yeehaw Junction—two thousand acres bulldozed to a moonscape. Twilly parked in front of a padlocked double gate.

"What used to be here?" Viva asked.

"Oranges and grapefruits. What the Minks do, they buy groves from old citrus farmers, rip out the trees, then resell the land to developers. Correction: They buy groves from the bored young heirs of old citrus farmers. What you see now is the product of a well-greased zoning board—the future site of forty-five hundred houses, a couple of golf courses, ten pickleball courts, a strip mall, who knows what the fuck else."

"Pretty much the story of Florida, right?"

"Which makes it no less nauseating," Twilly said.

"Shall I quit my job on principle?"

"I'm unfamiliar with the philanthropic habits of the Mink family, but I do know something about tax write-offs. My soulless grandfather had a foundation, too. It's a shame he never hired someone like you to run it."

"Speaking of which," Viva said, "I should get back to the office."

"Of course. Largesse awaits distribution."

"Tainted largesse, according to you."

"If they're actually helping the poor and hungry, then hooray for them."

"Medical wings," she said. "That's mainly what they fund."

"Neonatal? Oncology?"

"You name it."

"Then no, don't quit your job," Twilly said.

On the ride back to town, she asked about the cage-like contraption in the back of the Suburban.

He said, "It's a live-catch trap. I bait the tray with sardines."

"What kind of critters are you trapping?"

"Feral cats. They eat too many songbirds."

Viva wasn't a cat person, but, fearing the worst, she had to ask: "What do you do with the ones you catch?"

"The cats?"

"Yes, Twilly."

"I put collars on 'em, then I let 'em go. Collars with little bells."

"So the birds can hear them coming and fly away."

"That's the idea," Twilly said. "You look relieved."

Viva smiled. She rolled down her window and tried to imagine the scent of orange blossoms.

⩘⩘⩘

The man that Dale Figgo struck with his truck wasn't Jewish. He was a Scandinavian agnostic named Noel Vale Kristiansen. From his living room he'd witnessed trash being hurled from a truck onto his property, and had stalked outside in the rain to confront the culprits. What Kristiansen had first thought was an instance of annoying but casual littering turned enraging when he emptied the sandy contents of the Ziploc. Even inaccurately drawn, the swastika set him off.

But now his memory was in puzzle pieces. The doctors told him he had a concussion, two broken ribs, and a bruised tailbone, all of which he could have figured out for himself from the pain. A female police officer showed up at the hospital to question him about the incident. Kristiansen remembered that the color of the pickup truck was black but didn't remember the make or model. The driver was a white man, but his face was a smudge. Same for the passenger, the baggie thrower.

Kristiansen had no recollection of his own skull smacking the vehicle's windshield, but he recalled being flat on his back on the wet ground, craning his neck in hopes of seeing the fleeing cowards' license plate. But then the sky had turned dark and settled on him like a shroud.

The investigator said, "We already got the make of the vehicle and tag number from a street cam."

"So, go arrest those goons!"

"First we're interviewing witnesses."

"I'm more than a witness. I'm the damn victim."

"You're lucky you weren't killed."

"Can you tell me the license plate?" Kristiansen asked.

"That's not how this works," the investigator said.

The second person to visit Kristiansen at the hospital was a breathtaking Black woman he recognized as his wife, though her name eluded him. She was accompanied by a small, sharply dressed white man with rodentine twitches and an improbable ostrich briefcase. Evidently he was a neighbor of theirs at Sanctuary Falls, a lawyer who happened to specialize in traffic-related injuries. Kristiansen's wife introduced him as Fred Something Jr., and right away the man began chattering about how he intended to structure the settlement. Kristiansen shut his eyes and squeezed the morphine pump.

His wife was alone at his bedside later, when he peeked. Her name was Mary, right? She confirmed it. They'd been married thirty-four years. Two grown daughters—one a senior flight attendant for JetBlue, the other a Chicago bond trader.

"What about me?" Noel Kristiansen asked hoarsely. "What do *I* do?"

"You're retired, sweetie. From the pharmaceutical sector."

"Pfizer?"

"No, Moderna."

"Was there a stock plan?"

"We're doing just fine," Mary Kristiansen said.

Noel had left the company when he turned sixty-five, in the midst of the pandemic. He was a senior vice president in the marketing division, yet had stoically volunteered for the first vaccine while it was in early trials. Mary had waited for her shot until they relocated from Massachusetts to Florida, where the emergency rooms were overflowing with gasping deniers.

"The girls are flying in to see you tomorrow," she said to her husband.

"I'm sorry, tell me their names again."

"Julia and Jill."

"So they're twins?"

"No, sweetie. Julia is four years older."

"Can you please write all this down?" Kristiansen asked.

"Get some rest and you'll feel much better," his wife said. "Fred has generously agreed to represent us. Tomorrow a few more doctors will be coming to see you. Doctors that Fred works with regularly."

"Who the hell are we suing? Those clowns that ran me down probably don't have insurance."

"We're suing the HOA, Noel. Our homeowners association. There was a dire security lapse, obviously."

"Don't they have cameras on our street?"

"They do. Fred's already demanded copies of the videos."

"Good. That's all I care about," Kristiansen murmured woozily.

"Speak up, Noel. I can barely hear you."

"I don't give a damn about suing anybody," he said. "All I want to do is find the shitbirds that tried to kill me."

Mary bent down and kissed his forehead, simultaneously creeping one hand across the bedsheets toward the morphine pump.

"You need your sleep," she said.

"To hell with the HOA," Noel Kristiansen sighed, floating off again.

Jonas Onus had three children, all boys, with three different women. The kids had been born within a week of each other and Onus was the confirmed father, though he no longer bragged to strangers about his stallion-like fertility. The firefighter pension checks that once made him feel flush now seemed stingy and late-arriving. Having devoted his days of unearned retirement to the cause of white supremacy, he felt increasingly constrained by the demands of parenthood. He remained bitter about missing the January 6th insurrection—one of his brats had swallowed a baby turtle out of the terrarium and required emergency transport. The mother was on a girls' trip to Universal, the cold bitch posting selfies from fucking Hogwarts while Onus stewed in front of the television in the ER waiting room, watching his brethren beat on the Capitol Police. That most of the rioters wound up indicted, jobless, and dead broke from legal bills did not diminish Onus's remorse. He should have been up in Washington fighting side by side with the others! In fact, his bag had been packed and he was halfway to the door when the sitter had come flying down the stairs yelling that Jonas Jr. had inhaled that little river cooter like it was a goddamn Jolly Rancher.

Four years later Onus was speeding up I-95, halfway to Philadelphia for a freelance siege of an election supervisor's office, when he learned on Rumble Red Radio that no mob action would be necessary this time around. The libtards had been stomped! Onus feigned relief, but privately he was bummed that history had failed to repeat itself and given him a chance to participate.

Since that day, he had hewn to a domestic routine that mimicked laziness but was actually him conserving energy for the next patriotic storming, which was bound to come. Mornings began with a pop-in at each of his three chaotic households, followed by a period of contemplative isolation. There was a tall shady oak on Elm Street under which he would sit in his Tundra for hours, listening to dark-state conspiracy news on talk shows and podcasts.

His favorite host was the viciously persecuted Alex Jones, who'd made a triumphant return to the airwaves. Although Onus wasn't a prepper, he made sure all his young children were being raised on deliquesced servings of the tasty doomsday rations that Jones hawked on his show. There were other useful products, too, and Onus loyally stocked up. He didn't consider himself a gullible boob, and he yelled at the ICU nurse who called him that. However, after his fourth serious bout with COVID, Onus quit drinking the two-hundred-dollar "silverized" elixir that Jones swore would fend off the virus. Believing it was his own weakened metabolism that prevented the potion from working, Onus did not seek a refund.

In what now seemed like the distant past—during a spell when the fire-breathing Jones was on trial and away from his talk show—a substitute host had delivered a harrowing monologue about the supposed side effects of Chinese-made condoms, which in addition to impotence included a florid edition of genital eczema for which there was no discreet treatment. Onus had gotten so freaked that he threw away all his Durexes and switched inexpertly to the pullout method of contraception, resulting in the simultaneous trio of pregnancies that had altered his life. Still he never blamed Jones, who later informed his listeners that the substitute host had turned out to be a ringer, a Soros-backed prankster who had duped the program's producers.

On some afternoons, glued to the bellowing pundits, Jonas Onus became so infuriated by the libs' relentless assault on decency that for self-soothing he turned to his Darcy's Dream Booty, the jacked-up Tundra jouncing on its custom struts. The vehicle's tinted windows created a deep blue pod of privacy, while curious pedestrians were frightened off by the sight of Himmler, chained somewhat loosely in the bed of the truck. During such reveries, Onus would turn up the volume so all he heard was the clarion voice of Jones, Hannity, or whoever, and not the weird rabbit squeak of flesh against sculpted polymer. Onus went at the Dream Booty purely by instinct, Dale Figgo having assured him that no instructions were necessary.

Naturally Onus was curious about Figgo's job packing such porny merchandise, but Figgo didn't seem keen to talk about it. The default topic of discussion was Figgo's unfair banishment by the Proud Boys and Oath Keepers following the mistaken defilement of the segregationist's statue at the Capitol riot. Onus surmised that if he'd been with the freedom mob in Washington—not eight hundred miles away, stuck at a hospital with an omnivorous brat—he might have prevented Figgo from committing such a mistake. Then again, Figgo was a certifiable blockhead, and it would have been a pain in the ass to babysit him for the duration of the uprising.

Onus himself hadn't been born spring-loaded with hatred, though his old man was a rager who used family dinners as a soapbox for his xenophobic grievances, master-race theories, and white-man-as-victim monologues. No minorities escaped blame for the elder Onus's recurring business failures. And while Jonas himself had never formally joined any of the established white nationalist groups, he'd accompanied his dad to a few rallies and enjoyed the barbecue food-truck fare.

Initially he was skeptical about throwing in with a start-up like the Strokers for Liberty, but Figgo kept alluding to a pending windfall that would fund a nationwide groundswell and future tactical operations—presumably something more ambitious than lobbing Ziplocs crammed with handmade leaflets and cheapo key chains.

Onus was under the familiar shady oak, scrubbing the Tundra's upholstery with sanitary wipes, when Figgo called.

"Is your fat ass sittin' down?" Figgo asked with a cackle.

"Whassup?" Onus said, turning down the radio.

"Good news. I got that payload we been waitin' on!"

"Sweet."

"I'm talkin' about the money, dude."

"Yeah, I know," Onus said. "How much?"

"It was the man himself that called."

"What man?"

"The *congress*man, dude."

"Okay." Onus assumed that "congressman" was the code name for somebody rich and highly placed. "How much?" he asked Figgo again.

"How does two mil sound?"

"Like you're baked outta your goddamn mind."

"I'm serious as a dick wart. Two million bucks."

"Jesus Jackson Christ." Onus tossed the box of wipes behind the front seat, next to his damp Dream Booty. He heaved himself behind the wheel and said, "If this is a joke, I'm gonna boil your balls and feed 'em to my dog."

"Ain't no joke, man. The Strokers, we be strokin'."

"I'll meet you at the townhouse," Jonas Onus said. "One hour."

Figgo laughed on the other end. "Bring your imagination, brother."

CHAPTER 4

The walls of Viva's modest office at the Mink Foundation were decorated with photographic tributes to the couple's philanthropy: the Claude and Electra Mink Small Organ Transplant Center (Palm Beach Gardens), the Claude and Electra Mink Pediatric Sports Medicine Complex (Boca Raton), the Claude and Electra Mink Radiology and Imaging Annex (Sarasota), the Claude and Electra Mink Shingles Research Park (Ocala), the Claude and Electra Mink Lateral Stenosis Pavilion (Jacksonville), and the Claude and Electra Mink Squamous Cell Plaza (Daytona Beach).

On every building the words "CLAUDE AND ELECTRA MINK" were as tall and bright as a Times Square marquee, so as to be visible from the nearest interstate highway. Viva regarded the Minks' ostentation as forgivable considering their generosity. That the couple's donations also brought whopping tax benefits didn't trouble Viva either, despite Twilly Spree's cynical digs; without such incentives, the essential business of charity would shrivel.

What nagged at Viva was the bizarre Wee Hammers project. She knew Florida's reputation for rats-in-the-sewer politics, but Clure Boyette reeked of something even worse. The normally circumspect Minks seemed to trust the congressman blindly, though Viva's deep dive on the internet turned up no evidence that Boyette gave a shit about at-risk youths or any other community causes. He was invisible in his hometown, except during election campaigns, when he'd hand out sloppy joes at a local food bank. His political foes invariably painted him as the lazy horndog spawn of a rich crafty fixer. Boyette seldom bothered to respond to those insults, because there was no need; his father's tentacles were far-reaching, and his district was the deepest of red.

Viva's opinion of the congressman did not improve with the delivery of three dozen white roses, accompanied by a card that read: "Viva, thanks for helping to make the tall dreams of my Wee Hammers come true. We should get together for dinner one night soon. I do an epic gumbo."

Says an epic douche, Viva thought as she carried the flowers outside to the dumpster.

The Maybach pulled up just in time for Electra Mink to witness the tossing of the vase. She rolled down her window and said, "What on earth are you doing?"

"They were crawling with bugs," Viva said.

"Those exquisite roses?"

"Aphids, I believe. Or possibly spider mites. Anyway, I didn't want the office to get infested."

"Who sent the flowers, dear?" Electra asked.

"Congressman Boyette."

"How thoughtful! Did you save the card?"

"I'm afraid not." Viva manufactured a wince and nodded toward the dumpster. "Aphid droppings," she whispered.

"Still, I should call and thank Clure for thinking of Claude and me."

"I'll take care of it, Mrs. Mink."

Viva left the office at five on the dot. When she arrived at the townhouse, Dale Figgo's black Ram pickup was back in the driveway. Obviously it hadn't been repossessed. A stocky uniformed cop was using her cellphone to take pictures of the truck. She waved

Viva over and introduced herself as Corporal Dominguez, an accident investigator for the Florida Highway Patrol.

"Do you know where the owner of the vehicle is?"

"I thought he was home," Viva said.

"Nobody answered the door. Are you his wife?"

"God, no! I'm just a tenant. You thought I was his wife?"

"Mr. Figgo's truck was involved in a hit-and-run a couple days ago. Did you notice any recent damage to the front end? Because it looks like the hood and windshield are new."

Viva told Dominquez that Figgo had spread a tarp over the quad cab and got it towed off, supposedly for repairs. "He said it was the torque converter," she added, "whatever that might be."

The corporal shook her head. She stepped to the rear of the pickup and snapped a photo of the license plate.

"Can you tell me what happened? Was somebody killed?" Viva asked.

"A pedestrian was seriously injured. He's in the hospital."

"And Dale didn't stop to help after the accident?"

"We've got reason to believe it wasn't an accident."

"Seriously?" Viva said, thinking: *I need a new landlord.*

"Has Mr. Figgo mentioned anything about this?" Dominguez asked.

"Not a word."

The investigator showed Viva one of Figgo's printed rants about the imaginary COVID conspiracy.

"Yeah, I've seen that one," Viva said. "Honestly, I thought he was too dumb to be dangerous."

"So you're not involved with his group?"

"Don't tell me he ran over a Jew."

"No, ma'am."

"A Black person?"

"The victim is a Caucasian male with no religious preference," Dominguez said. "There was some sort of altercation on the street. A hitchhiker was riding with Mr. Figgo at the time, but he won't come back to Florida and give us a statement."

"How can I help?"

"Just let Mr. Figgo know I need to speak with him."

"Of course," Viva said, "but be aware that he's not the brightest bulb."

She watched the trooper drive away before she entered the townhouse. Dale Figgo was hiding under his bed, clutching a combat knife and some sort of short-barreled machine gun. He crawled out, proclaiming that he didn't run over the dude on purpose, it was an accident.

"But you left the scene, Dale."

"And they're gonna hang me for *that*? It was raining, for fuck's sake. Plus the asshole hit me in the face with one of my baggies. Then he tried to spit on the truck!"

"Truly I don't know where to begin. Put down the gun and the knife."

"When it's safe."

"Go to the cops and tell them what happened."

"No chance," Figgo said.

"Then I'll be packing up and moving out tomorrow."

"You can't break the lease!"

"Oh, just watch me."

"Keep your mouth shut about this, and next month's rent is free. Utilities, too."

"You're a slick one," Viva said. "It's a deal."

Then she went to her bedroom, shut the door, and called Dale Figgo's mother.

~~~

Twilly Spree knew a police officer in Fort Lauderdale who drove his K-9 partner to a landfill every Friday night. The cop would leave the patrol car's high beams on and open a beach chair while the leashed German shepherd would be made to lie motionless at his feet. It was a training test for the K-9, whose name was Ripple.

The landfill abounded with rats and stray cats, but the police dog wasn't allowed to chase them. He knew he'd be punished if he so much as growled without the officer's permission. The rats and
~~~

cats had grown accustomed to these visits, tauntingly strolling in and out of the headlights. After precisely one hour of this ordeal, the police officer would rise, fold the beach chair, unclip the miserable shepherd's leash, and quietly say the word: "Now."

Ripple was then free to maul whatever he could catch, which was usually nothing, because, of course, the rats and cats had learned the drill. Twilly empathized with the K-9, because a day rarely passed that he himself didn't witness something that made him burn to engage. Usually he held back, knowing a confrontation could lead to jail or a lawsuit. Sometimes, though, he slipped.

Put yourself in my position, he would later say to Viva. Minding your own business, sitting in a drizzly rain on an empty stretch of beach, watching the snook bust minnows in the surf.

And along comes this individual, walking alone along the tide line. Doesn't really matter what he looks like, but let's say he's as pale as cauliflower and extremely overfed, and would do the whole sighted world a favor if he put on a goddamn shirt.

And so what does he do, this rude-ass touron, right in front of you, with public restrooms in plain sight not fifty yards away? He removes his baggy board shorts and wades into the ocean up to his vast round belly, eases into a crouch, and proceeds to unload a Boone-and-Crockett-size bowel movement.

You can't believe your fucking eyes. You, who have seen all extremes of bad behavior.

Now the albino walrus is paddling on his back, violently kicking away from his own floating turds.

And you have a decision to make, do you not?

So you take a deep breath and tell yourself to calm the fuck down.

It's possible the man's got a medical problem, an uncontrollable intestinal disorder. Or maybe he comes from a remote culture in which dropping a massive public deuce is accepted custom . . .

Then the following happens: A sea turtle appears between the waves—a young loggerhead, popping up for air an arm's length from the naked defecator.

Who howls like a baboon on fire and punches violently at the confused turtle's small brown head, which he has mistaken for one of his own foul chunks.

And, well, you've seen enough.

Still you are a portrait of mindfulness as you walk—not run—to the ocean's edge. By the time you get there, the frightened loggerhead is halfway to Bimini and the outlaw shit maker is frantically sloshing back toward the beach.

"Hey, those are my shorts!" he yells at you.

"I know," you say.

"What the hell are you doin', dude?"

You enter the water up to your knees, blocking the man's exit. Then you explain what's about to transpire, and give him a credible reason to believe he has no choice. The nearest lifeguard station is a long run down the beach.

Angrily the man tries to shove you out of the way, loses his balance, and tips over. He comes up spluttering and rubbing the salt sting from his eyes.

"Get after it," you say.

"I'm calling the cops!"

You shake the phone from his board shorts and skim it into the surf.

"Better hurry," you say to the stunned befouler, and point to what he left behind.

The roundup doesn't take long. Arms extended, cupped hands brimming, the man lugubriously trudges out of the water. He follows you to a waste receptacle at the dune line, where free dog poop bags are available. He fills three of them, drops them into the wooden garbage basket, and feverishly begins scrubbing his palms using sea grape leaves under the faucet.

You notice a young family coming down the beach, laughing in the rain—Mom, Dad, three kids, the obligatory black Lab puppy. You wave them off and toss the board shorts to the defecator.

"Where you from?" you ask.

"Phoenix."

"And what you did here today is acceptable behavior in Maricopa County, Arizona?"

“It’s a free goddamn ocean.”

“Where’d you get such an idea?”

“Ever heard of the U.S. Constitution?” the defecator says.

“Ever heard of Portuguese man-o’-wars?”

“What?”

“Those little blue balloons you see on the beach—poisonous jellyfish that’ll burn your junk like a butane torch. But what a story to tell your friends back home!”

The Arizonan fumbles to put on his board shorts, his white knees shaking. You take another deep breath and tell yourself, again, to calm the fuck down.

“Mister, you owe me a thousand-dollar phone,” the man says.

“Get out of my sight,” you advise, and he does.

Later, at dinner, Viva would comment on your lousy mood. When she heard what happened, she would say, “Good thing you didn’t hurt that fool. I’d call it progress.”

“But is it really?”

“If they were selling tickets, I would’ve bought one.”

“I’d like another drink,” you say. “How about you?”

“First, I need to ask a favor.”

And, because she looks so serious and lovely, you say, “Sure.”

Dale Figgo and Jonas Onus celebrated the two-million-dollar windfall with a handle of Jim Beam on Figgo’s cousin’s airboat. They came back mewling drunk and turned the townhouse upside down looking for the lost trigger of Figgo’s AR-15. The men searched everywhere except Viva’s room, which Figgo suspected was mined with hidden cameras and microphones. Unable to find the gun part, they poured more drinks and sprawled on the black pleather sectional in the living room. Onus had been pressing to learn more about the money from the slippery “congressman,” but presently he was in no condition to retain information. Figgo said he wasn’t sure if the Strokers for Liberty would have direct control of the Wee Hammers funds, but he felt confident that any amount needed could be obtained swiftly with a phone call.

"I should maybe open a bank account," he said.

Onus nodded, letting his eyes close. "Put my name on it, too."

"No way. I'm the founder and commander. You're just a soldier."

"Fuck you, Dale. I'm head of tactical."

The question, Figgo said, is what to do with all that dough.

"I'm thinkin' January 6th, only bigger," he said. "By bigger I mean something that actually sticks."

Onus opened one eye. "Civil war?"

Figgo shook his head so hard that he made himself fart. It sounded like a dying bullfrog.

He said, "The congressman, he says a civil war would kill tourism."

"Well, yeah. Duh."

"It's the economic lifeboat of Florida."

"You mean 'lifeblood,'" Onus said.

"Nobody's bringin' their kids down here to see Mickey Mouse if the streets of America are on fire. Nobody's packin' for a week at the Magic Kingdom."

"Who's this 'congressman' dude? What's his deal?"

"He's for real, I checked him out," Figgo said. "If you go online, there's a picture of him and Trump on the golf course."

"Aw, bullshit."

"The man believes in what the Strokers stand for, our value system and so forth. That's why he went and scored us all that money."

"Tell me his real name," Onus said.

"For now he wants to stay in the shadows, away from the radar. But time comes, he'll stand arm in arm with us, proud and loud. That's a promise."

Onus remained doubtful. "How'd someone like you meet a actual congressman, Dale?"

"That ain't rev'lant."

"What?"

"Important. It ain't important."

Figgo had first encountered Clure Boyette at a faux Asian massage parlor, where they were awaiting separate appointments with a woman who was neither Asian nor a licensed masseuse. This was in St. Petersburg Beach, a week or so after the failed rampage at the Capitol. Boyette had been one of the few House members who missed the hair-raising siege; instead the congressman spent most of January 6th in a junior suite at a Kimpton near Embassy Row, sleeping off the ketamine-infused oysters he'd inhaled at an all-night party thrown by lobbyists for a Finnish distributor of gray-market fracking equipment. Lying in bed beside Boyette was a young professional escort whose full name was unknown to him, but who'd gamely accompanied him to Washington on a private jet owned by his father.

It was a furious phone call from the old man that had roused Boyette at the Kimpton. He made it back to the House floor just in time to vote against certifying the presidential election, and falsely told his caucus that he'd been hiding under his desk during the hours of occupation, shielding a terrified young intern from Liberty University. To get caught up on the failed insurrection, Boyette gorged himself on the cable news coverage and videos posted by the rioters, which was how he came to recognize the burly patron at the massage parlor as the same man who'd smeared feces on the statue of a Confederate hero.

Dale Figgo had been up front about it, and genuinely chagrined by his mistake. Clure Boyette expressed sympathy. Also: support for the cause!

He didn't reveal himself as a congressman until later that evening, after their respective sessions with "Tam Lin," when the two men met up for beers at a Ruby Tuesday. Figgo complained to Boyette—as he did to everyone—about his post-riot snubbing by the Proud Boys and Oath Keepers.

Screw those losers, Boyette had said. Both groups were radioactive now, riddled with snitches. He'd encouraged Figgo to start his own outfit, and promised to provide the seed money.

"Since when do politicians make that kinda dough?" Onus asked Figgo.

"Hell, it ain't *his* two million bucks. He's got mega-rich friends behind the scenes. 'Angel patriots,' he calls 'em. They could bankroll a whole white Christian army, they wanted."

"Well, God bless America."

"Duh," said Figgo.

The men grew quiet. There was a baseball game on television, the Rays and the Yankees heading for extra innings. Figgo yawned and kicked off his boots. Onus was on his phone scrolling through remonstrative texts from the mothers of his children.

Somebody knocked sharply on the door. Figgo grabbed a loaded Glock from beneath a sectional cushion.

"Maybe your cunty roommate forgot her key," Onus said.

Figgo got up unsteadily. The knocks turned into pounding.

"Get lost, asswipe!" Figgo yelled, thinking it was probably someone from the Dodge dealer's collection agency.

"WHAT DID YOU CALL ME?" said the voice on the other side of the door.

"Oh shit." Figgo tossed the handgun to Onus and told him to hide it, along with the flyers and Ziplocs.

"Dale, open up right this minute!"

"I'm comin', Mom."

She entered in a fighter's pose, nailing Figgo with a sweeping right hook to the ribs. He went slack instantly, like a blown tire.

Onus stood up and said, "Chill, Mrs. Figgo."

"Hit the bricks, Jonas. Go tend to your whores and bastard snot mongrels."

Onus sneered and walked extra slowly out the door. Dale Figgo crawled moaning to the pleather sofa. His mother sat down beside him. She had been a collegiate boxer and never lost her timing. As a boy, Dale would sit in his room and listen to her hammer a heavy Everlast that she'd hung in the garage. His cheating father had a mouthful of new teeth by the time Donna Figgo filed for divorce. Now she was a sixty-one-year-old gym rat living with a blockchain tycoon half her age.

"Was it Viva that called you?" Figgo asked bitterly.

"She says you're bein' rude. Swearin' all the time. You know my feelings about that."

"I'm under a shit-ton of stress at work."

"Dale, did I raise you to be a whiny little puss-boy?"

Figgo's mother was unaware that his job was packaging latex sex torsos. He'd told her he worked at a semiconductor factory. She did know that he'd gone to the January 6th demonstration in Washington, but not that he'd entered the Capitol and defaced random statuary. He had divulged not a word about the fledgling Strokers for Liberty, and hoped that Viva hadn't spilled the beans. He wanted his mother to keep thinking he was all talk.

"So, I suppose you're too stressed to fix the drain in your tenant's shower?" she said. "The cute tenant who keeps to herself and pays the rent promptly the first of every month."

"I'm on it, Mom."

Donna Figgo stood five feet eight but, except for those arms, was as skinny as a flamingo.

"And what did I tell you about keepin' guns in the house?" she said, scanning the living room.

"I don't keep 'em in the house. I just *clean* 'em in the house."

"I see your pickup got fixed."

"Did Viva tell you that, too?" Figgo growled.

"Breck drove by the other day on his way home from golf and saw a blue tarp on the Ram, like the windshield was broken. Now I see it's good as new."

"Nothing happened to the truck. I use the tarp 'cause of all the crow shit."

Figgo was pissed. Breck, his mother's boyfriend, had no reason to be in the neighborhood except to spy on Figgo. The millionaire snowflake in his Volvo hybrid. Well, fuck him.

"Dale, what's going on with the Highway Patrol?"

"I don't know what you're talkin' about."

"How dare you lie to the woman who brought you into this world."

"*Viva!* I knew it."

"No, son." She reached over and swatted the side of his head. "The officer called me up and said your truck did a hit-and-run. A man was hurt bad and he thinks you did it on purpose."

"No, no, no, no—"

"They've got your vehicle on video, Dale."

Figgo wilted. "So what do I do? What do you *want* me to do?"

"First, fix the drain in your tenant's shower."

"Okay."

"Second, I'll text you the name of a good lawyer," his mother said. "Tomorrow Breck and I are flying to St. Kitts for our annual infusions. Cuttlefish stem cells—it's the only place they're street legal. I'll call you from down island."

"Saint *who*?" said Figgo, as she walked out the door.

~~~

Noel Vale Kristiansen awoke in the middle of the night. He didn't squeeze the morphine pump and he didn't ring for a nurse. His head throbbed, but his memory was improving. His wife's middle name was Suzette. His daughters, Jill and Julia, were coming to visit tomorrow, after he got home from the hospital. His address in the Sanctuary Falls subdivision was 2345 Curlew Lane. On the day he'd retired from Moderna, the stock closed at $341.28 per share.

His wife was allergic to bananas and cats. One of his brothers, Dirk, was married to a retired opera singer. His other brother managed a chain of cheese-themed airport kiosks in Southern California. Daughter Julia had a titanium pin in one knee—her left knee?—from a snow skiing accident at age thirteen. And Jill, she owned a shar-pei named after Liz Cheney. Earlier there was baseball on television, the Yankees beating the Rays 6–5. The combination to the safe in his bedroom closet was 4-10-29-63. The truck that nearly killed him was a black pickup with a white man at the wheel and another in the passenger seat. Dominguez was the name of the Highway Patrol officer investigating the case. A corporal. Either Danielle or Dorothy Dominguez.

And StrokersforLiberty.org was the alt-right website promoted
~~~

on the flyer folded inside the plastic bag that those assholes threw on his driveway.

Noel Kristiansen remained in a state of suppressed wrath. What kind of idiot thinks he's winning converts by throwing Nazi-inspired leaflets in random neighborhoods? Whose playbook did that repugnant idea come from? You might as well hire a banner plane to fly a huge swastika up and down the beach, the same way they sell Bud Light during spring break.

One thing Kristiansen knew for certain: If those creeps despise Jews so much, they undoubtedly despise Black people like Mary, too.

Still she'd urged him to let it go, and concentrate on getting well. He couldn't let it go, though. Not even premier painkillers dulled his fury.

Back off so the police can do their job, Mary had implored. *And Fred, too.*

The lawyer, their neighbor. Fred Something Jr.

Brillstein, that's it. Fred Brillstein Jr.!

Who can't wait to sue the neighborhood HOA.

Who told Mary that it wasn't worth hauling white supremacists to court, because usually they had no assets. Losers that couldn't even afford a spell-check app. "Holocaust" with a *k*? The Dodge Ram was surely the most valuable thing they had, Brillstein said to Mary, and a bank probably owned the damn thing.

When Noel Kristiansen said that he didn't care about getting any money, that this was a battle of good versus evil, right versus wrong, darkness versus light, Fred Brillstein Jr. gave him a pitiful look, like Noel was a grown man who still believed in Santa Claus and flood insurance.

Fred who, being Jewish, should be way more pissed than Noel, a Lutheran whose family tree was untrimmed by genocide.

Make that a churchgoing Lutheran. And conservative, as well, sometimes to Mary's dismay. A registered, rock-ribbed Republican, for God's sake.

They'd never see him coming, those dumbass Strokers.

The whitest white man they'd ever meet.

CHAPTER 5

Twilly said yes to Viva Morales because he liked her and had nothing else to do. He spent a week digging up information on Clure Boyette, none of it shocking. Three of the congressman's former staff members, all women, painted the same picture: Boyette was an unrelenting lech. Also: lazy, arrogant, entitled. Twilly poked around Carpville collecting anecdotes, busting out the fake asthma inhaler whenever he'd heard enough. Then he drove to Tallahassee, where Boyette had served two terms in the state legislature. A law enforcement contact told Twilly about some messy DUIs, but Boyette's wealthy father had arranged for the court records to disappear.

There was also an assault case from Boyette's time at the University of Florida, where the Sigma Alpha Epsilon fraternity had whimsically put him in charge of hazing. Boyette thought it would be clever to make the line of pledges bend over, insert strings of flashing Yule lights in their rectums, and sing carols on the house balcony. When one young man refused, Boyette performed a forcible installation while his frat house brethren crooned "Blue Christmas" in three-part harmony. The SAE pledge ended up in the emergency room and dropped out of school the following week. He refused to return to Gainesville and testify, so the cops dropped the charges against Boyette and redacted his name from the files. Eventually the future congressman graduated with a 2.1 GPA and a bachelor's degree in political science. He was given a no-show job with his father's lobbying firm to await the lingering death of eighty-six-year-old Norman "Noose" Anderson, a crusty Panhandle icon to whose seat in the statehouse Boyette would be appointed. Thus began a torpid career in the public sector that gained speed only after he was offhandedly singled out for praise by the then forty-fifth president, who mispronounced Boyette's last name so that it rhymed with "toilet." After that, his next stop was Washington, D.C.

Nobody Twilly interviewed about the congressman mentioned a charitable streak. His was the only name on the incorporation documents for the Wee Hammers, which had been registered to a post office box in Bonifay County. It was a one-off; there was no national organization, no phone number, no online portal for public donations.

"I need to tell the Minks," Viva said.

Twilly smiled. "They already know."

"That it's just a front?"

"I'm sure they're aware, Viva. Some people use bogus charities to move money."

"Where? What for?"

"The Minks would never say, but the congressman might. He's a fan of cocaine and Tito's, if you want to open that particular door."

"Would you help me?" Viva asked.

"You must think I'm one of those bored middle-aged guys desperate for excitement, but I keep a busy schedule."

"Doing what?"

"Working to be the best version of myself," Twilly said.

Viva faked sticking a finger down her throat.

They were sitting on a blanket in the sand by the dunes and sea oats, along the same beach where the tourist from Arizona had crapped in the water. Viva was on her lunch break. She wanted to pay Twilly for the time he had spent digging up the background information on the congressman, but he kept saying no and changing the subject.

"Is your lowlife landlord planning to turn himself in?" he asked.

"No, he's sticking to his story," Viva said. "The whole thing was the victim's fault, et cetera." She had told Twilly about the hit-and-run.

He said, "I see storm clouds in young Dale's future."

"And your wisdom on the subject would come from where?"

Her hair was breeze-blown and she looked terrific.

"A long-ago version of me blew up my uncle's bank," Twilly said. "I did it on a Sunday, to make sure nobody was inside. I was mad because he'd arranged a five-million-dollar loan to a rock-mining company that was digging borrow pits in the Everglades."

"So, wait—you bombed the actual bank building?"

"Just a branch office," he said. "It was a poor decision. I was young."

"And now you're a changed man."

"Much more careful."

"Fine. Then please recommend somebody else who can help me."

"Build you a bomb?"

"God, you're so annoying," Viva said.

Garlands of pungent brown seaweed lined the shore in both directions, repelling beach walkers. A steady wind blew from the southeast, and the sun was bright.

"Gary Snyder," Twilly said.

"I do *not* need a real bomb maker."

"He's the poet I'm reading now. *Turtle Island*. Give it a chance."

Viva looked away, wondering how he would handle the news.

"That two thousand acres you showed me near the interstate? Used to be orange groves?"

"What about it?" Twilly asked.

"When the Minks flipped the property, they kept a piece of the action. All the parcels they've been buying and reselling out there are being connected by roads and canals. It's going to be a massive 'planned community' called 'The Bunkers.' Eventually they'll incorporate."

"The shit never ends," Twilly said starkly. Citrus farms were harder on the land than native pine scrub, but anything was better than poured concrete.

"How'd you find out?" he asked Viva.

"I opened an email I wasn't supposed to see."

"And they're seriously naming it 'The Bunkers'?"

"There's a golf connotation and a military connotation," Viva explained, "so they can market for both recreation and personal security."

"Once they've got the rezoning, it's a done deal." Twilly felt a familiar hot itch deep inside his brainpan.

Viva said, "I need somebody to show me how this works."

"The payoffs and so forth."

"Sorry, I'm new to Florida."

"Hell, it goes on everywhere."

"But not like it does here. I'd love to know exactly how Boyette's involved, if the two million he got from the Minks is for bribes, or for something else."

"Suppose you find out. Then what?" Twilly asked.

"I'll quit. Go public. Testify. Move on."

"Following money isn't easy. It's more a job for somebody with a badge, subpoenas, or at least an accounting degree."

They walked down to the water, Viva carrying her shoes by the straps. A manic fleet of sandpipers skittered past, pecking goodies from the acrid sargassum. Twilly picked up a slimy water bottle that had floated in from somewhere.

Viva said, "The congressman sent me roses. White ones."

"Safer than red. Good move."

"I think I'm going to follow up."

"Definitely an opportunity," Twilly said. "Just be careful."

"Don't worry, I've got you on speed dial."

"I feel truly honored."

"As you damn well should," said Viva.

A day didn't pass in the life of Corporal Danielle Dominguez when someone didn't lie to her face. Florida was the hit-and-run capital of the hemisphere, and every guilty driver had an alibi. Dale Figgo's wasn't original:

"It wasn't me driving my truck. Somebody stole it from my house."

"Just for the afternoon?" Dominguez asked.

"I left the key fob on the console."

"And the thief returned the vehicle when he was done?"

"No, ma'am, he left it parked by a road. A friend of mine spotted it and called me."

"Which road, Mr. Figgo?"

"The one that goes to the place where you said the accident happened."

"Sanctuary Falls. And I didn't say it was an accident."

"Either way, I ain't never been there," Figgo stated.

"Why didn't you report the theft of your vehicle to the police?"

"I been super busy at work."

Dominguez pretended to be patient. Because she was a woman, lots of suspects didn't take her seriously at first. She said, "That's an expensive truck. What did you tell your insurance company about the damage?"

Figgo had hoped to win brownie points for voluntarily coming to the Florida Highway Patrol office, but he wasn't getting a positive vibe from the lady corporal. He should have brought a lawyer, like his mother suggested.

"It wasn't me that run that guy down," Figgo said to Dominguez. "What the hell was he doing, anyhow, walkin' in the rain like a retard?"

"Tell me about the hitchhiker."

"I don't pick up hitchhikers. That's a rule."

"We spoke to the man already," Dominguez said.

"Then he's a goddamn liar. Some scammer tryin' to set me up."

"Who are the Strokers for Liberty?"

"The what?" Figgo heard his voice crack.

Dominguez showed him one of the flyers saying COVID was a secret Jewish plot. She said she had street-cam video of his vehicle driving along Curlew Lane.

"A person on the passenger side was throwing bags containing this hate literature," she added.

Hate literature? Figgo fumed silently. *Try raw pure fact.*

"Can I look at the video?" he asked.

"That's not how this works, Mr. Figgo."

Dominguez didn't want Figgo to know that the security footage wasn't of prosecutorial quality. Bad weather on the day of the hit-and-run had affected the various neighborhood cameras, none of which had captured clear facial images of the driver or passenger inside the black quad cab.

Figgo handed the COVID flyer back to Dominguez. "This isn't mine," he said. "I got no issue with the Jews."

"Do you have a receipt from the body shop that fixed your truck?"

"Not on me, no."

"What was the name of the place?"

"I think it was a Midas," Figgo lied. One of the junior Strokers had done a backyard repair of the quad cab using parts of shady provenance.

"How about a copy of your insurance claim?" Dominguez asked.

"Not on me, like I said."

"We'll need to see those documents."

"Okay, if I can remember where I put 'em."

"Think hard," said Dominguez. "We'll be in touch."

Figgo raced back to the townhouse, dumped the standing bucket of beach sand in the backyard, and tore through the downstairs rooms gathering items that might be confiscated in a police search—his new AR-15, other guns, ammo clips, pistols, body armor, gas masks, throwing knives, Chinese stars, boxes of Ziploc bags, stacks of undistributed flyers, his pro-insurrection hoodies, his keepsake Trump-Pence boat flag, the Rolaids he'd swiped from Nancy Pelosi's desk during the Capitol takeover, and several boxed Darcy's Dream Booties. Everything went into the pickup truck, which Figgo drove off and unloaded at a storage unit rented under a false name.

Later he caught up with Jonas Onus, parked under the special oak on Elm. Figgo approached slowly to make sure he wasn't interrupting one of his friend's self-intimacy sessions. The windows of the Tundra were rolled down and *The Very Best of Rush Limbaugh* was blaring. Onus waved Figgo closer, but the passenger seat was occupied by an unchained Himmler. Figgo stayed back. Onus waited for a commercial break, turned off the radio, and stepped out of the truck.

To the dog he said: "Don't move, cocksucker."

He and Figgo sat down on the rear bumper with the trailer hitch between them.

"It ain't safe to use the townhouse as HQ right now," Figgo began in a low voice. "They're tryin' to nail me for hit-and-runnin' that dude. I expect a full-on raid any day."

"Who? The Feebs?"

"No, the Highway Patrol."

"They do raids? Since when?" Onus felt that Figgo was sometimes overdramatic.

"Jonas, we gotta pick somewhere else for the group to meet. Someplace where the bastards can't hide mics and mini-cameras in the light sockets."

"That actually happened to you?"

"Dude, open your eyes and smell the coffee," Figgo said. "I wouldn't be surprised if they bugged my fuckin' crapper."

"Let's not meet there."

"It's no joke."

"How about Fever Beach?" Onus suggested.

Figgo pondered for a moment, grinned, and said, "Love it."

The men bumped fists. Fever Beach was midway down a twelve-mile strip of seashore owned and protected, ironically, by the same federal government that the Strokers for Liberty distrusted. The location was relatively isolated; getting there required a sweaty hike that discouraged even the locals.

"I'll let the other men know," Figgo said. He communicated with the Strokers using an obscure social platform called KRANKK. The teenage skateboarder who'd charged forty bucks to hook him up was, by Figgo's reasoning, too young to be an FBI informant. He was, in fact, a low-functioning stoner.

"So we'll all meet there tomorrow night," Figgo said to Onus. "Nine sharp."

"And tell 'em no goddamn ATVs. They're too loud."

"Now we got all this money, me and you should rent a boat. A fast one."

"Oh sure," Onus said snidely. "Because there's no Coast Guard in Florida, right?"

"Then forget it. We'll just walk." Figgo stood up. "You could use the exercise, anyway."

Onus glared at him. "Dale, you know what I bet is good exercise? Runnin' from a jet-fast killer dog." He whistled for Himmler, and Figgo took off.

~~~

Clure Boyette's wife had dressed for yoga but was actually heading to the law office of the barbarous Harold Fistman. When Boyette intercepted her and presented her with the Aston Martin convertible, she tore the bow from the hood and hurled the key into the coral fountain in the driveway.

"Nicki, it's solar bronze! Your favorite color."

"Too late, douchebag."

"How many times do I have to say I'm sorry?"

"I don't know, Clure. How many times have you cheated on me?"

The question was rhetorical. They'd been married six years and Boyette had behaved like a rutting swine from day one. They were introduced to each other by his father, who'd unsuccessfully hit on Nicki first. At the time she was selling pre-owned BMWs and was active in her church. Clure Boyette proposed two months after their
~~~

first date, on the same night she'd agreed to switch her party registration from Democrat to Republican. It was no big deal; Nicki wasn't interested in politics and rarely voted.

Fleeting was the fairy-tale stage of their marriage. Boyette often disappeared on vaguely described political trips, and when he was home displayed off-putting traits that he'd suppressed while they were dating. She vetoed his request for a threesome and likewise experimental bondage with a dog-show motif. During sex he emitted noises like a sumo wrestler passing a kidney stone, making it impossible for Nicki to orgasm. When dining at home he chewed with his mouth open and occasionally cleaned his fingernails with an oyster fork, things he never did at public events.

Eventually, Nicki quit the car business, got a real estate license, and took up tennis at the country club. On their first anniversary, she learned that Boyette was having an affair with a skydiving instructor at the airport. He staged an emotional apology, bought Nicki a diamond-and-emerald bracelet, and promised never to stray again. The scenario had repeated itself so often that Nicki had numbed herself to the snarky town gossip while filling a closet safe with David Yurman pieces, the congressman's go-to act of contrition.

Now she was being avidly pursued by a retired Olympic pole vaulter with a Wheaties contract, and he was begging her to dump the congressman and move in with him. Nicki was familiar with the pole vaulter's spacious postmodern house because she'd shown it to several prospective buyers while it was on the market. The place needed only hardwood floors and an updated Sub-Zero.

So she was finished with Clure, finally.

He said, "Sweetheart, I'll do anything to make you stay. Please."

"You're the one that's moving out. I'm not going anywhere." Of course she planned to list the marital residence herself and snag the commission.

Her husband's most recent confirmed offense was age twenty, a drum majorette with the FSU Marching Chiefs. The student's mother and father had called Nicki to complain after their daughter accompanied the congressman on a private jet to Louisville for a Seminoles football game. Since the young woman was supposed to travel by bus with the rest of the band, resentments festered among her fellow majorettes, and team spirit waned. The jet belonged to M'Noor Mining Resources, a multinational fertilizer company that operated phosphate mines in Florida and contributed heavily to Boyette's PAC.

After extracting the tawdry travel timeline over the phone, Nicki had apologized to the young woman's parents and promised a significant donation to the university's marching program. Later that afternoon, she'd hired the viperous Fistman.

"Huge mistake," Clure Boyette said. "He'll end up with all our money."

"*Your* money. I'll do just fine."

The congressman fished the car fob from the fountain and trailed Nicki into the house. They squared off again in the kitchen, Boyette blocking her path to the wine fridge.

"Tell me what I can do to make this better," he said.

"I don't know. Go blind from an STD?"

Boyette, never a nimble counterpuncher, felt stumped. The Aston Martin was a sweetheart lease, the dealer being a crony of the congressman's father. Nicki had a thing for convertibles; it was incomprehensible that she wouldn't take the damn sports car and quiet down.

"How about a condo on Fernandina Beach?" Boyette said. "No mortgage. I'll even cover the windstorm premiums."

"Damn, Clure, your old man must be scared shitless."

"Of what?"

"Me telling a judge about all your whore-hopping. And the drugs."

The congressman grimaced. "Can we please just hit the pause button till November? After the election's over?"

The condominium offer had indeed been his dad's idea. The place had been purchased out of foreclosure, three bedrooms with a small balcony overlooking a stagnant duck pond.

Nicki said, "I'll talk to Fistman."

"Thank you, sweetheart."

"If you call me that again, I'm coming for the jet card."

"What? Sorry." Boyette was distracted by his phone, vibrating with an unexpected text from Viva Morales.

Thanks for the roses. Now I'm gumbo-curious

Yes! Boyette exulted, and cupped a hand over the display screen so his wife couldn't see it.

"Hey, Clure?"

"Uh?"

"Who's texting you?"

"Electra Mink. More paperwork for tomorrow."

"Right," Nicki said. "For your new charity. What's it called again? The Wee Willies?"

"The Wee *Hammers*."

"Could you please get out of my way?"

Boyette moved aside so his wife could access the wine. His phone trembled again, and he peeked at the new message. A rush of queasiness followed.

WTF? I checked my Venmo, u cheap shitsucker

It was Galaxy, obviously unhappy about the $250 adjustment in pay for her last visit.

I'm done with u, she texted, **and u are DONE, fuck-o**

Nicki watched her husband go pale and asked, "What is it now?"

"Nothing. Just spam."

He hurried to a bathroom down the hall and splashed his face with cold tap water. From there he could hear the pop of a cork, then Nicki talking on the phone.

The Minks were in a huff. They'd pledged five million dollars to upgrade an urban dialysis center in Miami, but were withholding the final installment because their portrait wasn't displayed in the waiting area. When it was explained to the couple that the portrait frame was too large for the only internal wall that didn't have windows, they demanded that a new solid wall be erected in the center of the facility. It was an impossible order, the care staff requiring a clear view of all patient beds and hemodialysis machines. Moreover, the clinic's insurance company threatened to cancel coverage if an obstructive barrier was built. Still, Claude and Electra remained adamant. To Viva fell the task of crafting a compromise.

The portrait itself was a horror, painted from an old retouched photo of the Minks on horseback—riding the same horse, actually. Wedged together on a Western saddle aboard what was plainly a distressed palomino, Claude and Electra were both turned to the left wearing waxen smiles and tweed-like riding coats with suede elbow patches. The setting appeared to be the Bluegrass region of Kentucky.

In the painting, the Minks looked several decades younger. Back then they'd been moderate Democrats, a period about which Viva had been warned never to inquire. The couple's swing to the political right had been abrupt and vengeful, spurred by an inferior table assignment at a Washington gala to which they'd donated two hundred thousand dollars. Instead of being seated up front with Walter Mondale, their party's presidential nominee, the Minks found themselves at a distant eight-top pinned between the Utah state comptroller and a Halliburton lobbyist with breath like a bull fart. Electra and Claude stalked out before the first course—a grilled-pear salad—was served. The next morning they flew back to Florida and switched their voter registrations to Republican.

"Here's one idea," Viva said to the couple during a meeting with the administrator of the dialysis facility. "Instead of placing a portrait inside the building, let's just make your names larger on the outside, above the entrance."

"What's the font?" Electra asked.

"Bookman Swash," the administrator said. "As big as you want."

Claude grumped, "I don't give a shit about the signage. I want our painting hung."

Viva was ready with sketches of another option. "See, it's not a wall. It's a clear acrylic panel that attaches to the interior ceiling. Very modern and dramatic."

"But it looks so plain," Electra said.

"We'd frame it with LEDs," Viva went on. "Amber, neon blue,

or velvet red. You can change up the colors for the holidays, too. Super cool."

"And our staff and patients would be able to see the full portrait image from both sides," the administrator added. "It's basically 3-D."

He didn't mention that the acrylic panel would remain folded flat against the ceiling and out of sight, except on the rare days when the Minks came to visit.

Viva felt confident stating: "No other dialysis clinic in the country has one of these."

"That's what I like to hear," Claude said.

Electra was on board, too. "The uniqueness factor," she agreed. "How soon can you get it done?"

The administrator estimated that the project could be completed in a month. Mollified, the Minks shuffled out of the room. Viva followed, carrying the sketches and a cup of coffee. The car ride back from Miami took three hours, the old couple dozing and coughing through most of it. Viva put in her buds and listened to a book of Gary Snyder's poetry on Audible. She was hoping to learn something reassuring about Twilly Spree, as she was considering a relationship and had never been with a man who'd blown up a bank.

Meanwhile, Clure Boyette had been messaging all afternoon, galvanized by Viva's gumbo text. She thought it might be him when the doorbell rang shortly after the Minks' Maybach dropped her off at the townhouse. Through the peephole she observed a tall figure waiting stiffly under the porch light. It wasn't the congressman, and it wasn't Twilly. The person had a starter beard and a Bass Pro cap. He had garbed himself in a wrinkle-free reproduction of a Confederate military tunic.

Viva was in no mood. She took the lipstick canister of Mace from her purse and cracked open the door.

"Hello, I'm looking for Dale Figgo," the man said.

"He's not here. I assume you're one of them."

"Uh—"

"Wankers for Freedom. Whatever."

"Well, yes, I checked out the website," the man said, "and I'm interested in talking with Mr. Figgo."

"About joining up?"

"That's right. I like what he has to say."

Viva opened the door a little wider. "I handle all the pre-interviews," she said. "What's your name?"

"Jerry Jeff Tupelo. Can I come in?"

"Not a chance." She flashed the Mace.

"Whoa, take it easy." The man took a step back.

"First question: How'd you hear about Mr. Figgo's organization?"

"On the internet, like I said."

"Second question: How do you stand on gay marriage?"

"It goes against the Bible."

"Interracial couples?"

"Ditto," the man said. "God's word is law."

"What about mandatory vaccinations?"

"A global Zionist plot. There's big money involved. Billions."

"Last question," Viva said. "What's your favorite shade of blue?"

The aspiring recruit was perplexed. "Um . . . indigo?"

"Get lost," Viva said.

"What?"

"Hit the bricks, Jasper. Indigo? What's wrong with you?"

"Navy. I meant *navy.*"

"The Strokers need fighters, not decorators."

"No, wait—!" the man pleaded as the door slammed in his face.

Viva took a beer from the refrigerator and scanned the downstairs area, which Figgo had purged of firearms, propaganda Ziplocs, and Strokers paraphernalia. There were no visible clues that a right-wing chowderhead lived there, leaving Viva to conclude that Figgo had tidied up to please his mother.

She went to her room and listened twice to a short Snyder poem about roadkill. It was good, though it didn't seem like something that would move Twilly Spree. After finishing the beer, she slid under the covers, thinking that the walls looked bare and dreary, and that maybe she should tack up some travel posters or inexpensive bird art. Audubon knockoffs didn't cost much.

The phone dinged—another text from Clure Boyette.

r u playing hard 2 get??

Loser, Viva thought.

She dialed the number and said, "Hello, Congressman."

"This is a nice surprise—an actual phone call. What're you doin', Viva?"

"Lying in the bathtub shaving my legs."

"Oh God. Really?"

"Deal with it."

"Send a picture," Boyette said.

"Not a chance."

"Please tell me you're free tomorrow night."

"So happens I am."

"That's the best news ever!"

"Yeah," Viva said, "You should be over the moon."

CHAPTER 6

It was a low-key gathering, with tiki torches but no bonfire or music. Dale Figgo called the roll and logged seventeen replies, the entire current membership of the Strokers for Liberty. Rumors about the windfall brought them all out—that and free food, although the calzones were no longer warm after the trek to Fever Beach. Figgo liked the remoteness and expanse of the venue—there wasn't any tree cover to serve as hiding places for federal agents, and nowhere for them to conceal thermal cameras or directional microphones. It was definitely an aesthetic upgrade from the townhouse and the brain-blasting music. On Fever Beach, no Sharpies and paper were necessary; the Strokers could freely speak and be heard.

They planted their torches in a circle and sat down in the sand, a northeast wind snapping the Stars and Bars carried by a member known as Das Regulator. Like several of the Strokers, he had quit the Proud Boys in protest of their onerous masturbation rules, which limited the act to once every thirty days. The titillating gift of a Darcy's Dream Booty had clinched Das Regulator's decision to join up with Figgo.

Jonas Onus, who had never seen the whole bunch assembled, thought that some of the attendees appeared unstable. He had agreed with Figgo's decision to ban alcohol from the gathering, but now he wished he'd brought Himmler along to enforce the peace.

One Stroker who'd arrived drunk was crawling around on his knees, ferociously digging holes. Two other members got into a fist-fight arguing about Kanye, specifically whether his slams on Jews were genuine or a punk-ass PR stunt. Yet another Stroker, high on crystal, plucked on a camo-skinned banjo while belting out a ditty called "Go Strangle Us a Migrant," to the tune of "Go Tell It on the Mountain."

Order was eventually established, Figgo leading the group in a modified version of the Pledge of Alliance ("one *white* nation, under God, with liberty and justice for all *the chosen*"). Next he presented a short refresher on how to log on to the KRANKK platform using three-factor authentication, and how to conceal the app on a cellphone. This lesson was followed by Figgo reading a statement reminding the Strokers that the leadership (specifically him) was not responsible for legal fees racked up by members engaging in nonpolitical activity such as bar fights, shoplifting, lobster poaching, and nonpayment of spousal support. A few of the men murmured discordantly, and Figgo quickly moved to the most significant item on his agenda: the money.

Over the sound of soft-breaking waves, he announced: "This week I got the big news we've all been waitin' for—two million dollars. That's no joke. Two million bucks! That means we can finally do what needs to be done, what the Lord has called on us to do, and we can do it right!"

Questions flew like hailstones, and Figgo raised both hands, saying, "I'm not allowed to tell you where it came from, so quit askin'. Lucky for us there's some rich-ass patriots out there who believe in our cause."

One of the younger Strokers wanted to know if Figgo was in personal possession of the funds. Figgo said he had ready access to it.

"Is it buried somewheres?" another Stroker asked.

"It's in a bank, brah, not my backyard."

"No strings attached?"

“No fuckin’ strings,” Figgo said impatiently.

A Stroker who’d traveled all the way from Hialeah asked if members could now seek reimbursement for gas and mileage. Figgo shook his head and reiterated that the money was strictly reserved for ground operations, which was word for word what Clure Boyette had told him to say. In truth, Figgo wasn’t sure how much spending leeway he’d been given; the congressman had been vague about that.

As the moon rose over the Atlantic, the surf turned silvery. Figgo cut off the questions and opened the sharing part of the program, which was modeled after the successful AA format, except that the Strokers were encouraged to use nicknames or aliases when introducing themselves. Skid Mark, Raw Dog, Bottle Rocket, Komodo, and so on—one by one they recounted personal experiences of discrimination and oppression for the benefit of Jews, Blacks, Muslims, Asians, gays, nonbinaries, transgenders, immigrants, and pederast liberals. Jonas Onus’s attention began to flag, the stories being delivered with the same shopworn tone of indignation. One man got up and said he joined the group after a Black coworker put glass shards in his ChapStick. Onus was doubtful; he’d come across the exact same testimonial on a Blood Tribe website, except the coworker was Mexican.

Soon a wordless altercation broke out, resulting in the drunken hole-digger being knocked unconscious by the meth-head banjoist. Onus’s thoughts shifted coldly from the Strokers for Liberty to the whopping fortune that Dale Figgo now controlled, and how easily this band of fuckwits could piss it all away.

Figgo’s phone began to ring. He hushed the group and motioned for members to tighten the circle. Together they scooted forward, trenching the sand with their butts. Figgo held up his phone and put the male caller on speaker.

“You don’t know me personally,” the man told the Strokers, “but I’m Mr. Figgo’s pipeline to your new financing. What I’m about to propose must never, ever be traced back to me. Someday you’ll understand why.”

Onus spotted the lights of a speedboat running offshore and signaled for the men to snuff their tiki torches. Fortunately, the boat kept going.

Figgo's mystery caller continued: "Things in our nation's capital aren't as rosy as we're being told. The dark state is alive and strong, scheming day and night to take over. I'm warning all of you to stay prepared and, above all, vigilant. Someday we'll need you to show up in Washington again—I promise!—but for now I've got a different mission in mind."

"You do?" Figgo said. He'd assumed that he would be the one doing the plotting.

Onus spoke up firmly. "Let's hear your plan, bro," he said to the voice on the other end of the line. He strongly suspected that it belonged to "the congressman."

"Precinct 53," the voice said.

"Where's that?" Figgo asked.

"It's in Carpville."

"Whatville?"

"Bonifay County, Florida," the man on the phone said.

Skid Mark called out, "What's the mission, sir?"

"Yeah, dog," Onus said. "Tell us the target."

"Details to come. Time for me to sign off, gentlemen. I'm meeting m'lady for dinner."

The line went dead. Figgo pocketed his phone. When the Strokers relighted their tiki torches, they saw the pale sweep of beach bristling with ghost crabs, poised to flee down their hidey-holes. On the horizon, a long freighter was motoring north in the Gulf Stream.

Figgo directed the distribution of Diet Cokes and truffle fries along with the boxed calzones. After the men finishing eating, he stood up and whistled for their attention.

"All of us will remember this night forever," he said emotionally. "The battle to re-clinch America begins right here, with us, on Fever Beach! Someday there'll be a damn plaque."

Das Regulator raised his hand. "I got a question."

"Fire away, brother."

"Where in the name of fuck is Bonifay County?"

"I'll get back to you on that," Figgo said.

Onus scratched his tricolored beard and looked away, across the moon-kissed sea.

Viva couldn't figure out the source of her talking-coyote dreams. Malcolm didn't resemble one, nor did her father. She didn't recognize the cement mixer voice, either. "Take me home, babe," it would say. "I'm hungry."

Or sometimes: "Steer clear of crypto. I just lost my ass."

The coyote in Viva's dreams was the size of a Yorkie, so she had to kneel to hear its voice. Once she'd tried to stroke its snout and the animal dissolved into a foul-smelling mist. The setting was always the same foggy garden, full of soft flowers and root vegetables. This was also inexplicable, for Viva during her entire life had never planted so much as a sunflower seed.

She didn't believe it when Twilly Spree told her that he never dreamed. Immediately she found an old *Atlantic* article online stating that everyone has dreams, though some people can't remember theirs. Twilly laughed and said the theory was conveniently impossible to disprove. In any case, he definitely wasn't conversing with canine scavengers in his sleep.

"Maybe I should see a therapist," Viva said.

"That's an expensive way to find out you're normal."

"I am *not*."

"I said normal, not ordinary." Twilly put a fifty-dollar bill on the bar. "It's still your turn," he said.

Viva told him about her mostly uneventful childhood in Texas, where her parents still lived. The college years at the University of Minnesota, where for no practical reason she majored in sociology. Her annoyingly competitive sister, Maya. Her first serious boyfriend, a breeder of black-market French bulldogs. Her second serious boyfriend, a twice-divorced soybean agronomist. Her previous job as vice president for human resources at a midsize mortgage company in St. Paul. And of course she again went on too long about thieving Malcolm, about how blindly, stupidly trusting she'd been.

"Once in a while I miss him," she admitted. "That's the fucked-up part."

Twilly said, "I'm a poor advertisement for psychotherapy. I've been burning through shrinks since high school. Do we have time for another drink?"

"One more," Viva said, and ordered bourbon shots for both of them. She was wearing her tallest heels and the only sleeveless black cocktail dress she owned. Her hair was blown out and styled down to her shoulders.

"How are you feeling about tonight?" Twilly asked.

"Jumpy. The Minks want a full report."

"I'm jumpy, too." He checked his watch. "Remind me why you're doing this."

"Because charity fraud is a crime for scumbags. Also, I've been bored out of my mind with this job, until now. And what else—oh, I want to know what it feels like to do something righteous and semi-brave. How's your arm, by the way?"

"Dandy," Twilly said.

"Is the sling too tight?"

"Not at all."

He'd told her that he twisted his left elbow playing basketball with a bunch of guys half his age, which wasn't true. He had pulled a tendon while forcibly detaching the door of a construction trailer on the future site of The Bunkers.

"Don't forget your Mace," he said to Viva.

"Are you my mother?"

"I'd better go now."

"You didn't touch your drink," Viva said.

The bar was filling up and getting louder. Twilly couldn't deal with crowds.

"Let me know when you get home tonight," he said.

"You're not an emoji person, are you?"

"Text me an actual sentence." He squeezed her hand, stood up, and walked out.

Charmer, she thought.

Clure Boyette showed up a few minutes later wearing pressed jeans, a blue blazer over a white Oxford shirt, and cologne that smelled like a gardenia bed sprinkled with kerosene. He was yapping on his phone as he took the barstool next to Viva.

"It's time for me to sign off, gentlemen," he was saying. "I'm meeting m'lady for dinner."

After he put down his phone, Viva said, "I'm not your lady."

The congressman pointed at the shot glass full of whiskey. "Yet you had a drink waiting for me, didn't you?"

She picked up the glass and drained it. "Nope," she said.

It had been her idea to pre-meet at a busy bar. After that, she'd told him, she would decide whether or not to go to his place for homemade gumbo, his place being an oceanfront condo to which he claimed to have unlimited access. It belonged to a campaign donor, he said, a rich widow on her last legs.

"Then where do you actually live?" Viva asked.

"Up in the Panhandle," Boyette said. "I flew here private today just to see you."

"What does your wife think about that?"

"We're separated, luv. Nicki does her own thing, I do mine."

Viva reined in a comment about the untanned stripe on Boyette's finger; the wedding ring was probably in his pocket. She asked how he knew the Minks.

"From politics. That's how I know practically everybody I know." The congressman flagged the bartender and presumptuously ordered Tito's martinis for both of them. "Claude and Electra, they're good people," he added.

"Oh, the best."

"Very generous and civic-minded."

"I'm still curious about the Wee Hammers," Viva said. "How many houses do you plan to build with the Minks' donation?"

"Good question. A lot depends on our workforce."

"The kids. Underage minors."

"Yeah, we can't just go throw a net over a playground. There'll be a strict selection process, and the ones we choose will get some training in basic construction skills. That'll take a few days, depending on their past experience with power tools."

"How are you even keeping a straight face right now?" Viva asked.

"What do you mean?"

"This bullshit story that the Wee Hammers is a real thing."

Boyette frowned. "Of course it's real. What are you saying? We've already poured the slab on our first lot."

"And where might that be?"

"Carpville, in my home district. I'm up for re-election, as you know."

The martinis arrived. Viva pushed hers to the side. Boyette asked what was wrong. She said it was difficult to warm up to someone who lied so easily. He moved his stool closer until his shoulder was pressing against hers.

"It's loud as hell in this place," he said. "You wanna come out to the car and do some blow?"

"What a sweet offer. The answer is no."

Looking at Boyette in profile, Viva observed that every angle of his face was exaggerated, like a Dick Tracy villain. Whatever product he used to sculpt his hair made it shine like roofing tar.

"Aren't you getting hungry?" he asked.

"Just the opposite."

"Don't be like this, Viva."

"Then tell me the truth about the money," she said.

"I can't."

Then: "Maybe later."

Finally: "What does it matter? It's not your two million bucks."

"But I'm the one who transferred it to the account you set up," she said.

The congressman stroked her arm.

"You didn't do anything illegal. Is that what you're worried about?" His hand spider-crawled up to her shoulder. She flicked it away.

"I'm outta here," she said.

"So, no gumbo?"

"Correct-o." She stood up to await Boyette's last plea.

He said, "I'd never do anything that would get you in trouble. Neither would Claude and Electra. They think you're fabulous."

"Me, too."

His phone started ringing. He frowned at it and said, "This won't take long. Please don't leave yet, Viva."

But her seat was empty by the time he got off the call, which lasted nine painful minutes. Afterward Boyette rushed out of the bar and drove straight to the condo.

Twilly didn't steal anything from the construction trailer, but he took pictures of the site plan and a marketing strategy file. The Bunkers would be every bit as vast and awful as Viva had warned, and the project appeared unstoppable. Twilly had charged down many paths like this that had ended in enervating defeat. The Bahamas were looking better and better; he'd located another small island for sale in the Exumas. He could build a house there and install solar panels. Spend the rest of his days catching snappers and diving for queen conch.

Viva texted to say she'd ditched the congressman, but Twilly didn't respond. He was boiling about one of the sales pitches he'd photographed:

> **The Bunkers is designed for the discerning, amenity-minded, security-conscious buyer. These will be newcomers who can afford to live anywhere, but are looking for an exclusively curated rendition of Florida. All entrances to The Bunkers will be gated, as will each separate subdivision within the community. Of course we'll have our own police force equipped with drones, a helicopter, and an animal control unit to ensure "gator-free" experiences on the golf courses . . .**

Twilly tossed the phone on the bed, unfastened the sling from his arm, and stepped outside. The night was mild, so he walked down to the boardwalk at the beach. There he sat on a bench listening to sea sounds and thinking about how, every couple of years, he recycled the Bahamas fantasy. Once he'd even put in an offer on a virgin ten-acre island, only to be outbid by a cruise line company that renamed it Tequila Key, dredged a deep ship channel through the bonefish flats, and built a floating casino. Same old shit.

He watched from a distance as a young couple undressed and dashed into the surf. It was a classic tourist move, splashing around after dark in shallows favored by bull sharks and blacktips. Briefly he considered letting nature play out the scene. Still, numbskulls or not, the swimmers were just kids, probably in their twenties, and screwing in the ocean was less disrespectful than taking a dump. They didn't deserve to be punished with a maiming.

So Twilly walked down to the shoreline and gave them a friendly heads-up about the shark situation. They failed to appreciate his concern. The young man called Twilly an a-hole and the young woman called him an old perv. They were treading water naked, the guy's untanned arms locked protectively around his date.

"Where you from?" Twilly asked from the beach.

"Go away!" the woman cried.

"Tennessee? Arkansas? I'm trying to place the accent."

The man said, "I'm about to come kick your ass."

"That's adorable."

"Dude, I am *not* fuckin' around!"

Twilly informed the couple that bull sharks, common in Florida, were the third most dangerous species in the world. Only great whites and tiger sharks attacked more humans. And even if a bull didn't devour you entirely, a single bite was so deep and wide that you could bleed to death in minutes.

Finally the young woman was paying attention. She told her boyfriend she wanted to get out of the water, which further aggravated him. A whispered argument began.

"Good luck, you silly lovebirds," called Twilly, and strolled back toward the boardwalk.

"Hey, asshole," the boyfriend bellowed after him. "Don't touch our fuckin' clothes!"

Put yourself in my position, Twilly would later say to Viva. You reach out to help your fellow humans, pass along some useful local knowledge, possibly save them from losing a limb or at least a liter of blood, and this is the thanks you get—insults and insinuations.

The thing is, it doesn't even occur to you to take the man's clothes until the ungrateful dipshit says what he says. It feels pretty good when you do it, let's be honest, but you don't go gonzo. You leave his brushed-calfskin man-purse lying in the sand, the cash and credits cards untouched. His iPhone, too, which you feel like stomping to pieces, but then your calmer, more evolved self says to take a deep breath and calm the fuck down.

Afterward it doesn't take long to locate the sleepy homeless fellow who lives in the holly trees behind the Winn-Dixie. Bubbo is his name. And when he steps into those white linen slacks, you can't believe your eyes because they fit *perfectly,* as if stitched by an English tailor. Bubbo is so excited that he's stammering thank you mister thank you thank you mister, which makes you feel even better about what went down with the rude naked swimmers. And when Bubbo puts on the guy's shirt—also linen but sea-mist green, long sleeves—his fried old eyes well up. He needs help with the buttons because his hands are shaky, but after that he starts dancing his scrawny butt off and you're clapping along to whatever rollicking tune is playing in his head.

And you don't walk home feeling like a saint or anything, but you sure as hell don't feel like a thief.

"I'm worried about you," Viva said after Twilly finished the story.

"No need."

"Is there a day that goes by in your life without some kind of confrontation?"

"This was more of a random interaction," he said.

She had unexpectedly dropped by his apartment after her aborted date with Clure Boyette. Twilly didn't recall giving her the address, but he was glad to see her.

He said, "Look, I lied to you about dreaming. I've had a nightmare about how they wrecked Marco Island."

"I haven't been there. Wrecked it how?"

"High-rises. Subdivisions. Mini-malls. Mobs of humans."

It had been a frightening dream in which Twilly was still a boy. A supernatural Gulf surge was pulverizing Marco's famed beach, trapping Twilly in a canyon of condos. The water that rose to his neck was as frigid as the North Atlantic.

"But in the end you survived," Viva said.

"Unclear. I woke up as the current swept me away."

"And it's the only dream you've ever had?"

"Maybe one or two others."

"Well, then you're a freak," Viva said. "I could go for a Coke."

Twilly's one-bedroom layout was small but tidy. Clearly he didn't require much space. There was no Coca-Cola in the refrigerator, but he found—left over from some past date—an artisan root beer. Viva drank it straight from the bottle. She saw his arm sling draped on a lampshade and asked why he wasn't wearing it.

His response: "You look good in that dress."

"What?"

"Sorry. That slipped out."

"I'm here strictly on business," Viva said.

"The people's business."

"Nobody likes a smartass, Twilly."

"How'd you find me?"

"Voting records," she said.

"Am I still registered? Wow. Which county?"

"The reason I stopped over was to tell you about my drink with the congressman. He didn't want to talk about the Wee Hammers money, but he more or less admitted it's going somewhere else."

"What if the Minks find out you've been asking? You'll get fired."

Viva shook her head. "Boyette won't say one word to them. The dude still thinks he's got a shot at getting laid."

"Even after you walked out on your big date?"

"Oh yeah."

"They call that tragic optimism," Twilly said.

"He took a private jet down here just to see me."

"And you think he paid for that out of his own pocket?"

"Doesn't matter," Viva said. "He's not giving up on me yet."

"Because you're so enthralling."

"If the shoe fits, yeah."

She asked Twilly why there was a map of the Bahamas on the wall. He told her he was thinking about moving there.

"Not before we take down the Minks and Boyette," she said.

"Well, listen to you, all on a mission."

"Don't bail on me, buddy boy. Not yet."

"I've got a highly motivated real estate agent in Nassau," Twilly said.

"How about dinner tomorrow night?" Viva asked.

"Sure. Your place?"

"That's not even funny," she said.

~~~~

Galaxy's real name was Janice Eileen Smith, and her Instagram handle was Teenderoni. The name on her Venmo account was Galax$y, and she resented being shortchanged by rich johns. She didn't have a pimp, but she had a wicked temper. And the stupid congressman, whom she'd known for more than a year, had stupidly given her a key to the condominium.

First she stopped at Costco, where she purchased fifty pounds of king salmon, four gallons of rice vinegar, nineteen wheels of Camembert cheese, and—in the outdoor section—a half dozen spray bottles of whitetail doe urine.

By the time she was finished with the condo, it was a stinking hellhole. Yet, even after seeing the expression on Clure Boyette's face, she felt unsatisfied. He acted more angry than gut-punched. Apparently a neighbor had phoned him to report that a crazy woman was trashing the place.

For the siege, Galaxy had put on an old two-piece swimsuit that she could throw away afterward. Exhausted from the vandalizing, she didn't smell so angelic herself. It was hard to make out what the
~~~~

irate congressman was saying, because he had covered his nose and mouth with the gold pocket square from his blazer. When he got up in her grill, she shoved him away and snatched a blade from her handbag. She was tickled to see how fast he settled down.

They went outside to escape the stench. Boyette put away the pocket square, and Galaxy put away the knife. They walked three flights down to the parking lot.

"Check your damn Venmo," he huffed. "I sent the rest of your fee."

"Another two-fifty. Whoopeee."

"Now we're even, so get out of here before I call the cops."

Galaxy wondered if Boyette was truly that dense, or just naturally condescending to women. "You actually think we're even?" she said.

"Not really. It'll cost me a fucking fortune to clean up the apartment."

"Anyone calls the police," she said, "it'll be *moi*."

"Because . . . ?"

"I'm a minor, and you solicited me to have sex in exchange for money. At least eleven times, by my count."

"It was consensual!"

"Still a crime, Spanky. And my Venmo, she don't lie."

Thundercunt! Boyette thought.

He'd been blackmailed before, but the timing of Galaxy's threat couldn't have been worse. He was dealing with a re-election campaign, Nicki's hiring of a savage divorce lawyer, and the launch of the Wee Hammers scam. Usually it was Boyette's father who slithered in to mop up his messes; this one would be challenging and expensive. And Clay Boyette would be livid because his son had allowed a paid escort to take videos and pictures of him prancing on a rhinestone leash. The fur collar, the snowshoes, the whole drunken dick-twirling scene. The congressman's constituents back in Carpville were churchgoers who would ardently want to believe that a prostitution scandal was fake news, but that kinky slide show would be a problem.

"You also had me buy coke for you a bunch of times," Galaxy reminded him brightly. "Remember how you snorted it from between my toes?"

Boyette wished she was wearing something less distracting than a bikini. "You're not playing fair," he said.

"This isn't a game, bro."

"I'm going back to Washington in the morning. What do you want from me, G?"

"I'll make a list," she said.

"Do you like convertibles?" Boyette was pleased with himself for thinking fast on his feet. Nicki didn't want the car, but Galaxy would love it.

"What if you woke up tomorrow," he went on, "and there was a brand-new Aston Martin in your parking spot?"

"This isn't your first rodeo, is it?"

"Happy almost-birthday, babe," said the congressman.

"Aw, Spanky, you remembered." Galaxy smiled and sweetly touched his cheek. "What color is the interior?"

CHAPTER 7

Before he was hired at the sex toy shipping facility, Dale Figgo had worked for Amazon, UPS, the U.S. Postal Service, and FedEx Ground. Although he was an excellent truck driver, none of the jobs worked out because all his supervisors were prejudiced against white men. That's what Figgo told his mother. Every time he got fired, he called her to complain that he'd been falsely accused of stealing packages. In fact, though, the townhouse was almost entirely furnished by the spoils of larceny. Donna Figgo knew her son was lying long before he brought her coffee in a Le Creuset mug.

He was the youngest of four brothers, and the only one to drop out of high school. The principal had been a Black man, which was the only excuse Figgo needed. The roots of his full-spectrum prejudice remained a puzzle to his mother; his now-estranged father had regularly donated money to the ACLU and even marched with the counterprotesters at Charlottesville. Equally vexing was Dale's stubby intellect, since all his brothers were sharp, articulate, and prosperous in business.

What happened to my baby boy? Donna wondered on occasion.

Dale hadn't finished a book since ninth grade, his grammar

sucked, and he couldn't spell for shit. Somehow he'd grown up to be the dictionary definition of a dolt. Donna blamed it on a troop of dull-eyed teenage peckerwoods who had recruited Dale as a friend only because he had a car. Two of the geniuses eventually vaporized themselves trying to bomb a synagogue, and the others were in state prison proudly climbing the ranks of the Aryan Brotherhood.

Despite her boxing skills, Donna Figgo had been gentle with her boys when they were young. In fact, she'd never laid an angry hand on Dale until he was thirty-one, when he said something crude about a man she was dating. Donna then decked Dale with a right cross so spontaneous and crisp that it surprised both of them. She'd simply had her fill of his meanness, moping, racist diatribes, and fuck-doodle conspiracy theories. From that day on, Figgo knew what was coming if he mouthed off to his mother.

She had called from her extended trip to the Caribbean to make sure he connected with the defense lawyer she'd recommended.

"I'm in his waiting room now," Figgo reported sullenly.

"Do what he tells you, and there's a chance you'll slide free of this mess."

"Have a nice trip, Mom. Say hi to Brickhead for me."

"It's Breck. And, guess what, he never speaks ill of you."

The lawyer's name was Pete Webster. He'd spent many years in the Public Defender's Office and consequently was unfazed by anything that crossed his desk in private practice. His hair was long and prematurely silver, and the basset hound pouches under his eyes made him look older than he was.

When Figgo introduced himself, the lawyer said, "I know who you are. You're one of the Capitol shitters from January 6th."

"That's not why I'm here."

"Go on," Webster said.

Figgo stuck to the lie that he was being framed for a hit-and-run he didn't do. Although he didn't mention the pro-Nazi flyers he was distributing, Webster knew about them from the police reports.

He said, "Wild guess, Mr. Figgo. Somebody jacked your pickup truck the day before the accident."

"Right! How'd you know?"

Webster made some notes on a legal pad. "Any priors?"

"I had a few scrapes but nothin' heavy."

"And you haven't been officially charged in this case yet?"

"Oh, it's gonna happen," Figgo said. "There's a Latino state trooper, she's got a hard-on for me."

"Why's that?"

" 'Cause I'm white. Duh."

Webster capped his pen. "I'll talk with the prosecutor's office and see if they'll cut a deal."

"You don't think a jury would believe me?"

"Not for a second," Webster said.

"Does that mean *you* don't believe me?"

"My retainer is ten thousand dollars, Mr. Figgo. I can probably keep you out of jail, but you might lose your driver's license."

"No way. For ten grand, I want the whole damn trial. Judge and jury!"

"Ten gets you as far as the courthouse steps," Webster said. "After that, we're talking serious money."

Figgo didn't have even ten thousand dollars. He knew better than to ask his mother for a loan, but there were other sources. "Do your thing," he said to Webster.

"My assistant will prepare the retainer agreement."

"I got one more question. You don't look super Jewish."

"What's the point, Mr. Figgo?"

"Everybody knows Jews make the best lawyers."

"I'm pretty good," Webster said with an arctic smile, "for an Episcopalian."

"We'll find out, right?"

By patrolling a few leftist chat rooms, Figgo had learned that, despite their performative Christian fervor, many of the January 6th defendants had quietly hired Jewish defense attorneys. In Figgo's case it would have been a rough fit, his alleged crime having occurred while dispensing anti-Semitic screeds.

Pete Webster informed him that the retainer was due in five business days. Figgo said no problem. Driving home, he left a message on the congressman's voicemail: "Ring me back, dude. I need a solid."

As he pulled into the driveway of the townhouse, he was approached by a tall white man wearing a Bass Pro cap and a Civil War jacket.

"Back off, it was a honest mistake!" Figgo barked, and exited the Ram pickup waving a Glock.

Slowly the man raised his hands. "I don't know what you're talking about."

"Judge James Zachariah George."

"Who?"

"I'm the one that put shit on his statue," Figgo said. "But, see, nobody told me it was him."

"Honest mistake. I believe you."

"Good. Now get your ass off my property."

"Hold on, Mr. Figgo," the stranger said. "I don't know anything about James George, and I don't give a damn whether you peed, shat, or puked on him."

"But you're dressed like a Johnny Reb."

"It was a big army. Lots of heroes to choose from."

"True dat." Figgo had never heard of Judge George either, until January 6th.

The stranger said, "I came here to talk with you about the Strokers for Liberty. I think I can be a help. I want to join."

Figgo lowered his gun. "No shit?"

"My name's Jerry Jeff Tupelo. I stopped by the other day, but the woman at the door said I failed the pre-interview. Now I'm here to ask for a second chance."

That bitch Viva, Figgo thought.

"I'm the one does all the interviews, not her," he said to the man. "Come on in and have a beer."

"Thank you, sir."

"But first strip off that outfit. I need to frisk you for wires."

"I understand totally. These days you can't be too careful."

"Fuckin' A," Figgo said. "What'd you say your name was?"

Mary and Noel Kristiansen first met at a pharmaceutical convention in Santa Barbara. He was then a young sales rep for Pfizer and she had a mid-level corporate job with Walgreens. Their first official date was a Prince concert. Their second date was Milli Vanilli. They went together for six months before renting an apartment together, and six months later they got married. For the honeymoon they went to Hawaii, where they were the only interracial couple at the welcome luau put on by the hotel. By then they were getting used to it. From the start, their relationship was solid, bulwarked with the understanding that Mary was the more pragmatic partner.

She was home alone when Corporal Dominguez stopped by with an update on the hit-and-run investigation. Mary told the officer that Noel was out, and invited her to wait inside. Dominguez said she wanted the Kristiansens to know why the suspected driver of the Ram pickup hadn't been arrested yet—there was a problem trying to conclusively establish that he was the person behind the wheel. Rainy weather on the day of the crime had "impaired the clarity" of the neighborhood street videos.

"But we're a long way from giving up," Dominguez said.

"That's not even an option, is it?" Mary drilled her with a hard look.

"No, Mrs. Kristiansen. Of course not."

"Noel says there were two of them, but he still can't remember their faces."

"The passenger was a hitchhiker. We believe he had no part in the assault on your husband."

"Then tell me about the driver," Mary said. "What's his name?"

"I can't give out that information yet."

"The group he belongs to goes after Jews. I've seen the flyers. Noel went on their website. They hate Blacks, too."

"Yes, that's my understanding," Dominguez said.

"Strokers for Liberty, my ass."

"How is Mr. Kristiansen doing?"

"Physically? Better every day," Mary said. "But he's still messed up emotionally by what happened."

"Wouldn't be normal if he wasn't."

"We hired a lawyer who's suing the homeowners association. Noel doesn't seem to care, but I do. The neighbors, too. You might be called on to give a deposition."

Oh joy, thought Dominguez.

Mary walked the trooper to the door and asked her to stay in touch. Not long afterward, Noel Kristiansen arrived home looking tired and flushed. His polo shirt was damp with sweat.

"How was the mall?" Mary asked.

"The usual."

"Did you do a walk like the doctor told you?"

"Eight-tenths of a mile," Noel said, pointing at his wristwatch. "My ribs still hurt. My butt bone, too."

"But no dizziness?"

"Did the girls get home okay? It was nice of them to come visit."

"How are the headaches?"

"I'm fine, Mary."

Later they went to dinner at the country club. Mary told Noel about Corporal Dominguez's visit, and said she was exasperated by the investigator's refusal to divulge the name of the prime suspect.

Noel said, "Fred Brillstein can get the bad guy's name, but it's not a priority for him. That's not who he's suing."

"But still," Mary said pensively.

"Yes, exactly. Though you were the one that told me to let it go."

"Because I assumed the driver would be locked up by now."

"Not me," said her husband.

The country club had a first-rate chef. Noel was working on a ribeye and mashed potatoes. Mary had grilled pompano, the catch of the day. They were sharing a bottle of Tempranillo.

Mary said, "Brillstein wants us to let the police handle it. If we go after the man who ran you down—"

"The *shithead* that ran me down," Noel interjected.

"—if we go after the shithead, it could complicate our case against the HOA. And by go after I mean taking extralegal measures."

"I'm surprised you'd even consider it."

"No, I'm just venting," Mary said. "That's all."

Her husband wasn't sure that was true. He knew how relentless she could be on such matters. One time, after overhearing a white clerk at Walmart refer to her as an "Aunt Jemima," Mary not only got the man fired, she also posted his photo on Facebook and Reddit along with a detailed account of the incident. Other customers and even the clerk's coworkers joined the online convo to share anecdotes about his offensive attitude. The backlash prompted him to shave his head, dye his mustache, drive forty-seven hours nonstop across the country, and sign up for a logging job in Springfield, Oregon.

That young man, however, was a simple, garden-variety bigot—not the leader of an armed band. Noel Kristiansen didn't want his wife venturing anywhere near the Strokers for Liberty.

He didn't know it, but she already had the name of the man who was driving the pickup truck that hit him.

And so did he.

⁓

Nicki Boyette said no to the condo in Fernandina Beach. Her husband received the rejection in a prickly email from Harold "the Colonoscope" Fistman, Nicki's divorce attorney. He informed the congressman that Nicki would no longer be communicating directly, and that he should hire his own counsel as soon as possible.

In a glum reflex Clure Boyette forwarded the email to his father. Then he returned Dale Figgo's call to find out what type of favor he wanted.

"I need ten grand," Figgo said.

"What the hell for?"

"To hire a lawyer. He wants a reclaimer."

"Retainer, you mean."

"Money up front."

"The fund is designated for Strokers operations, not your personal fuckups. How come you need a lawyer?"

Figgo explained that he might soon be arrested for allegedly striking a man with his truck in a gated community. He said he was being framed by rival white nationalists, and that his attorney was charging ten thousand dollars to take care of the case.

"Well, shit," the congressman said. A plea bargain was the only way out. Figgo would make a disastrous witness, especially if he veered off his lawyer's script. Criminal trials were televised in Florida, too. The prospect was sobering.

"Did the guy die?" Boyette asked.

"No . . . not even close."

"Why are you breathing so hard?"

Figgo said, "I just got back . . . from a run."

Even the congressman would have been creeped out to know that, on the other end of the line, Figgo was strenuously practicing a left-handed style of masturbation. The carpal tunnel symptoms that hobbled his dominant right wrist had not abated.

"Where'd you find this shyster?" Boyette asked.

"My . . . mom."

"So she knows about what happened. Who else have you told?"

"Nobody."

"What's the lawyer's name? I want to call him."

"Something Webster, I think . . . it's in my phone."

"Text it to me," the congressman said. He was standing in a crowded hallway, so he lowered his voice. "Dale, do you understand the concept of keeping a low profile?"

"Sure . . . it's like . . . stay out of trouble," Figgo panted.

"You should've told me about the goddamn accident right away."

"I got my truck fixed . . . back to normal . . . so I figured everything was . . . cool."

"So you *did* hit this guy?"

"Yeah . . . but it wasn't like they said . . ."

From the day they'd met, the congressman knew that Figgo was borderline pea-brained. Fortunately, Boyette didn't need a gang of smart people; he needed people who'd believe whatever they were told, and do whatever they were instructed.

"Who do you think set you up?" he asked Figgo.

"Goddamn Proud Boys . . . They're just jealous 'cause . . . I went independent . . . and now I can do whatever, whenever . . . I want."

"And you're sure they'd go to all this trouble?"

"Or maybe . . . it was the . . . fuckin' Oath Keepers."

No way, Boyette thought. "The man you ran over—"

"He wasn't run over like a frog or somethin' . . . He just kinda flew up and . . . cracked the windshield."

"With what? His head?"

"Pretty much."

"Great. What's his name?"

"I dunno," Figgo wheezed. "Want me to find out?"

"No, Dale, I want you to lie low and shut up. Let's keep this between us. I'll wire you the money, reach out to the prosecutor, and circle back in a few."

After hanging up, the congressman got online and transferred $9,999 from the Wee Hammers Fund to the special bank account that Figgo had recently opened. Then he hurried back to the floor of the House of Representatives and gave a speech promoting his bill to ban any color but black on all regulation-size eight balls manufactured in the United States.

∿∿∿

The person who first held Viva's position at the Mink Foundation was a woman named Rachel Cohen, who'd had a long solid career in fundraising for charitable organizations. One Monday, Rachel didn't show up for work, which was unusual. A week passed before the Minks called Rachel's relatives in Milwaukee, and nobody had heard from her. Authorities in Florida put out a Silver Alert, about which Rachel would have been mortified, being only fifty-three and with hardly a gray hair on her head. Her paid-off Hyundai Accent was found in a parking lot at the Hard Rock Stadium on the morning after a Foo Fighters concert—a worrisome development, as Rachel Cohen was known not to be a fan of grunge rock.

Family members flew down to prod the police to investigate her disappearance as a crime. A detective interviewed the Minks, who said that Rachel had been behaving strangely at the office and they suspected an early onset of Alzheimer's. The detective assumed she'd become disoriented and wandered off, like many aging Floridians do, and her missing-person case ended up in the pile.

But the Minks had been lying. Nothing was wrong with Rachel Cohen.

Still sharp as a tack, her sister-in-law Shirlee recalled. So sharp, in fact, that Rachel had caught a small but significant inconsistency in a grant application and brought it to Electra Mink's attention. The chairman of a fledgling nonprofit called Cops in Recovery had spelled (and signed) his own name two different ways on the paperwork—Dick Richards on the first page, Dick Richardson on the last. Electra Mink had laughed off the discrepancy and blamed it on the man's dyslexia. She told Rachel to expedite a transfer of three hundred thousand dollars from the Mink Foundation to the group, which was supposedly based in Richmond, Virginia.

It was later, a few weeks after the January 6th insurrection, when Rachel Cohen read on *The Washington Post*'s website that the FBI had identified Cops in Recovery as one of the militant right-wing organizations that had stormed the Capitol; most of the group's members had never served in law enforcement or sought help for substance abuse. Rachel immediately printed out the story and brought it to the Minks, who berated her for believing anything published by such a liberal rag.

"But this group doesn't do anything to help addicted police officers," Rachel protested. "Your money bankrolled a bunch of thugs and traitors!"

"That's enough lip from you," snapped Claude Mink.

That afternoon, Rachel went home and composed her resignation—an email that was never sent. Shirlee Cohen showed the printout to Twilly Spree on a Zoom call.

"I found this on her laptop," Shirlee said. "The night she wrote it was the last time anyone saw her."

"Where?"

"At a Taco Bell in Rockledge. We got the video from the restaurant. Rachel's phone stopped pinging half an hour later. Do you think she was carjacked?"

Twilly said, "I think if it ever came out that the Minks tried to bankroll a coup, their name would disappear from a lot of buildings. Rachel might have been killed to make sure that didn't happen."

Shirlee began to cry, and Twilly felt awful. He asked if her sister-in-law had mentioned any other problems with the Minks.

"They didn't pay very well," Shirlee said. "When Rachel asked for a raise, they told her to try again in five years. She said they weren't joking."

Twilly had gotten Rachel Cohen's name from Viva Morales after asking her to look up her predecessors at the foundation. Rachel had worked there the longest, almost eighteen months. Twilly found Shirlee on Facebook.

"At first we thought she just got scared and went into hiding," Shirlee said. "But nobody's heard anything from her in all this time."

Twilly promised to make some calls, and he did. A friend with FDLE connections obtained a statewide list of unidentified human remains. Only one case was a white female in her fifties. In the spring of 2021 a bass fisherman had come across the decomposed body in a lake not far from the town of Carpville, in Bonifay County. The local medical examiner said it was impossible to determine the cause of the woman's death, the gators and snapping turtles having gone Cracker Barrel on the corpse.

Twilly texted the coroner's phone number to Shirlee Cohen and said he hoped the dead person was someone other than her sister-in-law. He had a feeling the news would be bad. His attention now turned to Viva's future safety during her employment by the Mink Foundation. It would be the number one topic of conversation during their dinner date tonight.

With an hour to kill, Twilly went cyber-scouting for Bahamas real estate. The gem of an island that had been for sale in the northern Exumas was now off the market, purchased "sight unseen by a privacy-starved Hollywood A-lister," according to an item in *The Nassau Guardian.*

However, another nearby island was available—seven acres, about half of which was bare limestone rock. Twilly was able to locate it on Google Earth, the only structure visible from the satellite being a shack with a corrugated aluminum roof. The island's previous name was Porker Cay, owing to a herd of feral hogs that swam around shitting in the water and begging food from day boaters. For marketing purposes, the island recently had been rechristened Starfish Point and fitted with a whimsical price tag of $3.2 million. Twilly called one of his bankers and asked if he could afford to buy it.

"Easily," the man said. "But why would you?"

"Maybe I'm ready to settle down."

"We've had this conversation many times before."

"Maybe I'm done daydreaming," Twilly said. "Maybe I'm ready to take the big step."

"Wouldn't you like to know the balance in your accounts?"

"Not particularly."

The banker put down the phone assuming that Twilly's latest fantasy would fade like the others, though it was impossible for a responsible wealth manager to relax when a client cared so little about his wealth.

Dale Figgo's phone chirped—an automated message from his bank, confirming the not-quite-ten-thousand-dollar deposit from the Wee Hammers and saying he now qualified for free checking. He suspected that the last part was a government trick.

"Why can't you tell me the congressman's name?" Jonas Onus asked.

" 'Cause I'm the only one needs to know."

Onus was sore about the money. He wasn't convinced that Figgo would really spend it on a defense attorney.

"What if *I* need a lawyer?" Onus said. "Will the congressman pay for that, too? What if all the Strokers end up needing fuckin' lawyers?"

"Ain't gone happen, bro."

The two hatemongers were back at the townhouse stuffing Ziplocs. Figgo added the sand while Onus was tasked with folding the flyers. Figgo had printed them on a new Canon color laser that he'd stolen from a BrandsMart truck. Now that he had a big-shot attorney on the payroll, Figgo wasn't so worried about a government raid.

Onus skimmed one of the tracts and said, "What the hell is the Great Repavement Theory?"

"You don't know? It's how pure white folks everywhere are gettin' paved over by people of color—Muslims and Negroes and immigrants of all shades. The Jews came up with the whole plan! They're in charge."

Onus was confused. "The Muslims and Jews are in on this together? I thought they hate each other's guts."

Figgo cackled. "Dude, that's what they *want* us to think." He put a scoop of sand into another baggie.

"This is a waste of fuckin' time," Onus said. "We should be field training for the Carpville op."

"Oh, we will. It won't be long." Figgo was secretly planning an earlier operation, a high-profile action that was certain to impress the congressman and his rich benefactors. Fearing a leak, Figgo had decided not to brief Onus and the other Strokers until shortly before the strike.

Meanwhile Onus continued bitching about the Ziplocs. "I never heard of a legit militia drivin' around throwin' baggies in people's yards."

"It's called community fuckin' outreach," Figgo shot back. "First you gotta enlight the citizenry. Then, when the shit goes down, they'll line up on our side."

"Personally, I'd be pissed if some douche was tossin' garbage on my front yard."

The two men bickered until Viva came into the room. She held up a mangled magazine and said, "Dale, why was this in the downstairs bathroom?"

"It came in the mail," he replied.

"All ripped up like this?"

"Naw. I was readin' it."

"Oh? Which article?"

"Hell, I don't remember. Somethin' about New York."

"Yeah, well, it's *The New Yorker,*" Viva said. "Give me the truth."

"I ran out of TP. Big deal."

Viva looked at Onus and said: "May I speak with Dale alone?"

Onus was glad to get out of bag-prepping duty. Figgo's tenant was pretty to look at, but Onus didn't trust her. It seemed like she didn't take the Strokers seriously.

"I'm the one needs to talk to *you*!" Figgo shouted at Viva as soon as his friend was gone. She was wearing her tortoiseshell glasses, which intimidated him. "You tried to scare off my man Tupelo, but guess what? He came back to see me and now he's all fired up!"

"To do what?" Viva asked.

"Save our God-blessed country."

"Mr. Tupelo didn't strike me as a fellow who defecates on statuary." She plucked a flyer from Figgo's hand and smiled. "Aw, Dale. The Great *Repavement*?"

"Read it and maybe you'll learn somethin'," he snapped.

"I think you mean the Great *Replacement*. That nutty Frenchman's idea."

"You don't know what you're jabberin' about. I don't talk French and neither do you."

"Sit down, Dale," Viva said, and began questioning him about the status of the hit-and-run case. He told her that he'd hired a lawyer, who was trying to cut a deal.

"What about the man that got hurt?" she asked.

"The lawyer said he's gonna be okay."

"Still you could end up in jail."

"You wish," Figgo said. "Also, what I said about next month's rent bein' free? That's off now. My mother already found out about the accident."

Viva told him to hide the plastic bags and hate flyers. "I've got a date picking me up soon, and I don't want him to see this crap."

"Ha! You're just scared he might wanna sign up."

"I'm more afraid he might beat the snot out of you," Viva said. "Where'd you get the printer, Dale?"

"There was a sale online."

"What if someone asked to see the receipt?"

"What if someone wasn't no longer allowed to use my washer-dryer and had to haul their dirty panties to the laundry-mat every week?"

"Please clean up this place, and don't ever touch my magazines again," Viva said, and went upstairs to get ready.

Figgo moved the baggies and literature under the sofa. He was heating a frozen dinner when Viva's date knocked on the door. Warily Figgo invited him inside; the man was in good shape except for a sling on one shoulder, and his face looked like it had seen a fight or two. Maybe Viva wasn't bluffing. The guy introduced himself as Twilly Spree, and he had a bone-cracking handshake. Figgo asked what had happened to his arm.

"I'm a toreador," he replied. "Freelance."

Figgo didn't know what that meant, but it sounded hardcore. He took two beers from the refrigerator and tossed one to Viva's date, who deftly caught it in the web of his sling.

"What's in the bucket?" he asked.

The one thing Figgo had forgotten to hide. "Sand," he said. "From the beach."

"What's it for?"

"You really want to know? I'll show you."

"Why not," the man said agreeably.

A short while later Viva came down the stairs and found Figgo stuffing Ziplocs again while explaining the Great Repavement Theory to Twilly.

"The hell's going on?" she asked.

"Nuthin'," Figgo said, sand glittering on his fingertips. "Your boyfriend asks lots of smart questions."

"About *what*?"

"Big Brother. Freedom. The natural order," Figgo said. "I like this dude. He's solid."

Viva glared at Twilly, who smiled back with an oddly shaded expression.

"Just guy talk," he said to Viva. "You look great, by the way."

CHAPTER 8

Clure Boyette caught a late JetBlue flight back from Washington because his father wouldn't let him fly private. It was punishment for Galaxy trashing the condo, which would have to be gutted. She displayed zero remorse.

"Wanna ride in my smokin' new car?" she said when the congressman arrived at her apartment.

"So you like it?"

"*Love* it, honey. I could cruise around all day long with the top down. That would be my dream life."

A dope ride, the Aston Martin, though a high price to pay for Galaxy's silence. Boyette hadn't yet worked up the nerve to tell his father.

"Let's go somewhere bad and have a drink," Galaxy suggested. She'd already named the car "Marty" and shown it to her high-school peeps.

"First can I take it for a spin?" Boyette asked.

"No way, Jose. Not unless you pass a pee test."

The congressman had assumed that his gift of a luxury import meant that Galaxy would no longer charge him for sex. She hooted when he raised the subject.

"Next time you Venmo me," she added, "put it down as 'Marty's insurance.'"

"But I shouldn't have to pay for anything. You know how much this fucking car cost?"

"Oh, I'm sorry. I thought you wanted to be governor someday."

"Funny," Boyette said through clenched jaws.

"Don't worry, Spanky. All those triple-X pics of us, they're locked away up in the Cloud. Nobody but me can ever find 'em."

"I appreciate that, G."

"Dude, I ain't no blackmailer," she said.

"Of course not. The thought would never cross your mind."

They went to a noisy country bar, where they ended up drinking more than talking, because they couldn't carry on a conversation over the din. Hundreds of miles from home, the congressman wasn't worried about being recognized. He noticed a few men waving to Galaxy, all of them big enough to kick his ass. When he asked her to dance, she looked at him like he'd lost his mind. Instead they held hands under the table. At two a.m. he pointed at his watch, and she followed him out the door. The air was cool, and a light fog was settling in. Boyette suggested calling an Uber, but Galaxy didn't want to leave precious Marty in the parking lot overnight. She got in on the driver's side, put the top down, and, after some fumbling, strapped herself in. Boyette was too hammered to figure out the mechanics of the seat belt, so he rested his head against the window.

Soon thereafter Galaxy fell asleep at the wheel, causing the Aston Martin to drift off the road and crash into a strip-mall surgical clinic that specialized in "pneumatic Brazil-inspired butt lifts." The speed of the sports car at impact was only twenty-nine miles per hour, but that was enough to set off multiple airbags, leaving Galaxy with singed cheeks and puffy lips, her lap covered with broken glass.

That's how the first responders found her—weeping, cursing, alone in the crimped convertible.

"I fucking killed my Marty," she warbled.

"Who's Marty?" a paramedic asked.

"You know. *Marty*. Goddamn it." She beat her small fists on the dashboard.

"Try to hold still, ma'am."

"Wait, where's the asshole congressman?"

"Which asshole congressman?"

"Spanky. Did I kill him, too?" Galaxy cried, looking around. "Oh shit!"

"Calm down, honey," another paramedic said. "Nobody's dead here."

Clure Boyette was gone, running the other way. His form was stork-like, but his long legs could cover some ground. He'd departed the scene with a throbbing knot on one side of his head and bruised kneecaps, which slowed his pace. Whenever he saw headlights approaching, he veered off the foggy pavement and crouched behind whatever foliage was available. He was worn out and dripping wet by the time he paused to throw up under the blazing-bright sign of a convenience store. The phone call he then placed woke up Clay Boyette, who didn't wait to hear the entire pathetic story before saying, "Son, you have turned me into a turd juggler."

"Nicki didn't want the car, so I loaned it to this girl I know—"

"The brand-new Aston?"

"She was the one driving when we hit the building. Not me, Dad."

"Is she dead? This girl. Was she hurt?"

"I'm not sure. I took off."

"Are we talking about the same batshit tramp that destroyed the condo?"

"Yeah, but I can explain."

"Me, too. You're a goddamn moron. That's the explanation," Clay Boyette said. "Spell her name for me."

"G-A-L-A-X-Y."

"Not her stripper name, son. Her given name."

"I don't know it," Clure Boyette admitted.

"Yet you 'loaned' her a three-hundred-thousand-dollar car."

"She's got some crazy party pictures of us. Since the election's coming up, I was just trying to keep her happy."

The dumbest of my kids by a country mile, Clay Boyette mused bitterly, *yet he's the one in Congress.*

"How old is she, son?"

"Dad, my head hurts and everything's spinning," Clure Boyette said. "Maybe I got a brain bleed."

"Nobody will notice, trust me," said his father. "Get your sorry ass to the nearest airport."

~~~

Driving to dinner, Twilly remained quiet while Viva talked through everything she knew about her dull-witted landlord and his band of white supremacists. When she was done, Twilly said that stupid people can also be dangerous people, and he advised her to move out of the townhouse right away. She explained that breaking the lease would cost her three thousand dollars, which was one month's rent and the security deposit.

"I'll give you the money," Twilly said. He felt the heat of her frown and quickly added, "I mean *loan* you the money."

"That's the only thing missing from life. Being in debt to a lunatic who sinks boats and blows up banks."

"A solvent lunatic, however."

"I'm not in a stellar mood," Viva said. "Don't make it worse."

Earlier Twilly had told her about the unidentified woman whose remains were inside a body locker in Bonifay County. The coroner there was seeking DNA samples from Rachel Cohen's family.

"You think the Minks had her murdered?" Viva had asked incredulously. "The old, stooped, gassy Minks?"

"They could've got it done with a phone call."

"Because she was asking too many questions?"

"Just like you," Twilly had said.

"I told Claude and Electra that I ditched Boyette at the bar last night because I didn't feel well. He texted, like, five times today asking for another date. Oh, and the fool sent more roses, which I mulched in the shredder before the Minks got there. Now the whole office smells like a hothouse."

The only excitement of Viva's workday had come during lunch,
~~~

when Claude Mink slurped a whole olive from his martini and started to choke, his face turning the color of rhubarb. Viva committed to a Heimlich but she wasn't strong enough to lift the old man out of his chair. Meanwhile Electra sat there watching, a peeled shrimp in one hand and a cranberry cosmo in the other.

"Sit down and relax," she'd said to Viva. "He does this all the time."

A muscular young server had then run to the table, jerked Claude Mink to his feet, and bear-hugged the gasping senior until the olive uncorked from his throat, shooting like a tracer round across the oak-paneled dining room. After resettling in his chair, Claude had downed the rest of his drink as if nothing had happened. When lunch was done, he'd left his customary tip of ten percent.

"I've been rethinking my move to Florida," Viva said to Twilly on the ride to the restaurant.

"You've got every right to be discouraged—employers who might be murderers, a married suitor who's also a crooked politician, and a Hitler-worshipping landlord with his own armed mob of mental defectives."

"What a ray of sunshine you are."

"But now you've met that special someone," Twilly said. "Me."

"Up until now, you had a sixty-forty chance of getting laid tonight."

"I know it's serious shit, but can you at least fake a smile? This is as lighthearted as I get."

"Should I go back to Minnesota? Texas, for God's sake? Some place new? Or do I stick it out here until it's over. Get the job done, in other words. Shut down the Minks and the congressman."

"And risk your life," Twilly said. "They're not worth it."

"I know how to handle Claude and Electra. I'm a good actress."

"With no plan whatsoever."

"Not true. My plan is to discreetly gather evidence and take it to the . . . whatever."

"Proper authorities."

"Yes. You'll assist with that part of it," Viva said.

"The smart thing would be to quit your job and move away."

"Except that's not what you'd do in my situation. You *live* for these situations."

"Because I have an aberrant personality," Twilly said. "Are you up for Italian?"

"Always."

Viva was thinking how Twilly couldn't have been more different from Mendacious Malcolm, who'd tested her for years. Malcolm would spend more time in front of the mirror than Viva. He always wore a Fitbit during sex so he could later brag about his nonresting heart rate. In social situations he would present himself in a polished, cocksure manner that belied his chronic slacker status. Twilly, by contrast, had no interest in impressing anybody. There was gray-flecked stubble on a side slope of chin that he'd neglected to shave, and he was driving with not one but two toothpicks sticking out of his mouth.

He said, "Let's say you decide to stay. What's the next move?"

"Try to make it through another date with Boyette. I still believe I can get him to talk."

"If you can't," Twilly said, "then it's my turn."

"As for Figgo, my landlord, he's odious but manageable."

"Oh, he'll want that on his tombstone."

"Plus, his mother really likes me," Viva said.

"His mommy. How marvelous." Twilly sighed, rolling the toothpicks.

They ate at a place called Tuppino's, cozy and quiet, where Viva drank a little too much wine and heard herself asking for more details about Twilly's failed marriage. He declined in a polite way, but nonetheless she was self-mortified.

"Can we go to your apartment?" she blurted, and immediately covered her face. "What I mean," she mumbled through her fingers, "is that your odds have improved due to the Barolo."

"No pressure."

"Don't say that, Twilly. They all say that."

"I was telling it to myself."

"The truth? I haven't been with anybody since Malcolm."

"So the bar is low," Twilly said. "That usually works in my favor."

It wasn't far to his place, a mellow ride until some d-bag in a two-tone Range Rover threw a lit cigarette into the grass median. Of course Twilly had to stop and pick it up. Then he was compelled to speed like a maniac to catch up with the smoker, whom he tailed to some skeevy nightclub in a warehouse district. Twilly parked a couple blocks away, shook off his arm sling, and told Viva to wait.

"Just let it go," she pleaded, but he didn't.

She watched him relight the recovered Marlboro before he got out of the car. Minutes later, he trotted out of the club rubbing his jaw.

"What did you do now?" she asked.

"Got sideways with the bouncer."

Later, when they went for a walk on the beach, he admitted that he'd been removed from the establishment after extinguishing the discarded cigarette in the right ear canal of the Range Rover driver.

"Litterbugs set me off," he said. "One of the triggers I wrestle with."

"I think you like to be triggered. I think you feed off it."

"It's a theory I've heard before."

"The truth is I'm not sure you're steady boyfriend material."

"God, no," Twilly said.

Viva went to bed with him anyway. He was strong and fun, and he didn't snore. On his dresser was a volume of Jim Harrison's poetry that didn't appear to be a prop; several pages were dog-eared. Viva wanted to peek at the poems Twilly had marked, but he'd fallen asleep with his arms around her waist. She couldn't move without waking him. In the morning, when he got up early to make coffee, Viva remained in bed.

"I wouldn't feel right borrowing money from you," she said. "I've decided to keep staying at the White Power B-and-B until I save up enough to move."

"That means we'll be seeing lots more of each other."

"I knew it." She burrowed her face in the sheets. "Don't do this, Twilly."

"Join the Strokers?" he said. "How could I not?"

Needing a break from his three families, Jonas Onus took a solo scouting trip to Bonifay County. The long drive was made easier by the feverish orations of Alex Jones, Laura Ingraham, and Dan Bongino. On some days Onus missed listening to the programs of other anti-vax radio hosts that he liked. All had died after short bouts with an especially potent variant of the coronavirus, which the CDC had secretly cultured for that purpose. It was frustrating to Onus that the leftist mainstream media had buried the story.

The Tundra blew a rear tire on the turnpike south of Wildwood. Before Onus put on the spare, he let Himmler loose to take a dump. Minutes later, the dog trotted back to the truck carrying a dead turkey vulture that smelled worse than a skunk. Himmler snarled murderously when Onus tried to pry the vile carcass from his jaws. Both the dog and its prize were hoisted into the bed of the pickup, and Onus drove on. Switching to AM, he came across a local talk station featuring a QAnon enthusiast who called himself Andy Rand. Some of what Rand was saying added up, though the stuff about alien lizard people infiltrating global governments didn't jibe with what Onus knew about reptiles, based on observable terrarium behavior. The lizards in Jonas Jr.'s tank showed no interest in anything except mealworms.

After a while Onus flipped stations to Outlaw Country. He kept one eye on the rearview, watching Himmler rip mouthfuls of fetid feathers from the limp vulture. When Onus arrived in Carpville, he stopped at a Wawa for a bag of fried pork rinds and a Mountain Dew. In the snack aisle he approached the only other customer, a young Asian-looking woman, and asked for directions to Precinct 53. She said she didn't know where that was. Onus found it spellbinding that her English was perfect. She said she was born in Apalachicola, and he said no way. Her parents had moved there a long time ago, she said, after Saigon fell to the North Vietnamese.

They'd escaped on one of the last American helicopters out. After resettling in northern Florida, her father and grandfather fixed up a scuttled fishing boat and began harvesting oysters. Sadly, the bay water changed over the years, and then a long drought wiped out many of the oyster beds. Now her family was in the RV business, she said, which she didn't find stimulating.

"Why'd you move here?" Onus asked.

"To be with my boyfriend."

"Oh. You guys still together?"

"Yup. He's a cop."

"Cool," said Onus, backing toward the door. "See ya."

His next stop was a small brick post office on Main Street. None of the postal clerks knew where Precinct 53 was. "Is it a new club?" one of them asked. "A restaurant? This town could use a good restaurant."

"Thanks for nothing," Onus said, and continued walking.

He came to a storefront where a large banner filled the window: "RE-ELECT CLURE BOYETTE TO CONGRESS." Inside, a pair of pallid, razor-cut twins greeted Onus like he'd won the Powerball. They fawned over his patriotically dyed beard, and took multiple selfies with him. Then they loaded his arms with Boyette campaign swag—bumper stickers, tee shirts, lapel pins, a trucker's cap, beach towels, pennants, a yard sign, and even a Boyette bobblehead.

Onus said he was looking for a place called Precinct 53.

"Is that where you'll be voting?" asked one of the twins.

"I'm just checking it out for now." Onus saw no reason to admit that he wasn't registered anywhere, and had never voted once in his life.

"The polling site is at the corner of Beet Boulevard and 17th," the second twin said, and showed Onus the location on a wall map of Bonifay County. "If you give us your email, we'll shoot you a reminder before Election Day."

"Is the congressman in town right now?" Onus asked. "Does he ever swing by here to see how it's goin'?"

"He's in and out," replied one of the twins.

"Always a fun surprise," said the other.

Onus returned to his pickup truck, where he dumped the swag in the cab and poured a bowl of water for Himmler in the back. All that remained of the dead vulture was its filthy yellow talons. Onus phoned Dale Figgo and said, "Hey, jackoff, I got one word for you: Boyette."

"Who told you?" Figgo demanded.

"You did. Just now."

"That ain't funny. Where the hell are you?"

"On recon, bro. Home tomorrow."

Grinning, Onus hung up and drove to Beet and 17th. The four corners were occupied, respectively, by a used-tractor lot, a Dollar Tree store, a Sonic, and a two-story, lushly landscaped compound called "Serene Transitions." Onus took a parking spot reserved for staff and lumbered in the front door.

The place had the look of a bright, airy hotel lobby. At the check-in desk stood a middle-aged Black man wearing sleek blue-rimmed glasses and a sharp gray suit.

"The Harley repair shop is three blocks on the right," he said.

Onus reddened. "I don't ride, dude."

This had long been a touchy subject. Because of his bearish girth, elaborate beard, and neglected teeth, Onus was often assumed to be a member of an outlaw biker gang. In truth, he'd been on a motorcycle only once in his life, a small dirt bike. He ended up half-skinned and scared shitless under a pig-hauling rig near Idaho Springs. The truck had dragged him half a mile down a fucking mountain.

"I'm lookin' for Precinct 53," Onus said to the Black man.

"You found it. We're the polling location for the precinct."

"You're messin' with me, right?" Onus saw a bunch of elderly people in wheelchairs—some cruising, some dozing. More residents were moving here and there on custom canes and walkers. Meanwhile a young orderly in blue hospital scrubs was fiddling with the TV remote, trying to find Fox News.

"This is where you come to vote in November," the Black man said.

"So it's like a pop-up deal?"

"Just on election days. We're a certified ALF, sir."

"What the hell's that?"

"ALF means 'assisted living facility.'"

"And you're sure this is 53?"

"That's right. Precinct 54 is the fire station past the old railroad tracks."

Onus tried to imagine what sort of lame operation the congressman planned for the Strokers. Was the mission to surround and seize an old folks' home?

On his way out of town he spotted a small gathering in front of Clure Boyette's campaign office. He parked the Tundra, squeezed into a "CLURE FOR SURE!" tee shirt, and hurried across the street to check out the scene. The congressman himself was there, posing for photos with volunteers and fans. He wore dark slacks, pointy-toed black shoes, and a gray checked blazer. His hair had been lubed into a sharp, unnatural crest that bothered Onus and colored his first impression of the man.

The pale buzz-cut twins spotted Onus and motioned him forward. Predictably, his beard was also a big hit with Boyette, who threw an arm around his shoulder and ordered one of the twins to take a picture for the website.

"Thanks for your support, brother," he said to Onus, in a voice loud enough for everyone to hear.

Onus said, "I'm not a political man. I work with Dale Figgo."

The smile didn't vanish from the congressman's face, but the look in his eyes changed quickly. Onus noticed a lump on the side of his head to which game-show makeup had been unevenly applied.

"What can I do for you?" Clure Boyette asked very quietly.

"It's about the op," Onus whispered.

"Meet me in fifteen minutes at the truck stop."

"Make it ten. I got a long fuckin' drive home."

The truck stop featured a high-energy diner. Onus grabbed a booth and ordered two stacks of crabmeat pancakes. Boyette arrived walking gingerly. He wore a denim bucket hat and inane, oversize sunglasses. Instead of sitting down he led Onus to the men's room and locked the two of them in a stall that smelled like Lysol and rotting Depends. Onus didn't waste any time; his pancakes were getting cold.

"Precinct 53 is a fucking rest home for geezers," he said. "Why do you need the Strokers to be there?"

The congressman told him what had happened during the previous general election: "Eight hundred and thirty-one people voted in that precinct, but only three hundred and seventy-seven of them went for me. Obviously there was fraud on a massive, massive scale."

"How do you know?" Onus asked.

"Carpville's my hometown. People here, they fucking love me. They put up a statue of my dad in the park!"

The old man had donated twenty grand for the bird fountain, and the statue more closely resembled the actor John Malkovich than Clay Boyette, but tribute was tribute.

"Listen to me," the congressman went on. "I won the last election, yeah, but I lost Precinct 53 by eight goddamn percentage points. That's impossible, and also a fucking embarrassment. It can't happen again, Mr. Onus."

"How'd you know my name?"

"I just called your pal Figgo. He gave me the scoop." Clure Boyette lowered the toilet seat and sat down. Now at eye level with Onus's crotch, he nonchalantly continued talking. "Figgo said you got a master's from Valdosta State. I dated a girl who went there. She was super hot. Played third trombone in the band, so you can just imagine."

"That's a good school," Onus said. He didn't have a master's degree; in fact, he'd dropped out in the first semester of his sophomore year.

"What was your major?" the congressman asked.

"Canada history." Perspiration was beading behind Onus's ears; he didn't mind lying, but he hated tight spaces. He felt trapped, forced to stare down at Boyette's weird plume of hair and inhale the vapor from whatever goop it was greased with. He also had a ripe view of the lump on the man's face.

"Somebody punch you out?" Onus asked.

"Fender bender. No biggie," the congressman said. "Let's talk about Election Day."

" 'Kay."

"I told Figgo I want at least eight or nine guys with ARs posted around the Serene Transitions campus. Masks, body armor, radio earbuds, all that paramilitary shit. Anybody asks, you're 'citizen poll watchers.' "

"What are we watchin' out for?"

"Those who don't qualify. Outsiders. Paid disrupters. Last time I ran, the county said Black voter turnout was sixty-three percent, but there's no way. They *had* to be bused in from out of state with fake registration cards."

Onus didn't know what a Florida voter's card looked like, and there was little chance he'd be able to spot the difference between a counterfeit and a real one.

"How about the Jews?" he asked the congressman. "Do we stop them, too?"

"Naw, they're always undercover. You can't even tell who's what—except for the Orthodoxers, and they're too straight to live around here."

"Latinos then?"

"Migrants only," Boyette said.

Onus thought of the woman he'd met at the Wawa whose family had come from Vietnam, the pleasant woman with the cop boyfriend.

"Okay, then what about Asians?" he asked Boyette.

"Definitely the Asians. Make 'em show a photo ID."

Onus suddenly felt unsteady, as if he might pass out from claustrophobia. Fortunately, the toilet stall was so cramped that there was no room to fall. Laboriously he twisted himself clockwise, so the congressman was now speaking to his right hip bone.

"Look, bro, the mission is simple as pie," Boyette said. "Stop these fuckin' people from stealin' Precinct 53 again."

"It'll be good practice, I guess."

"Exactly. Like a preseason game," the congressman said. "But if this shit ever leads back to me, I'll deny everything. I never met Figgo, never met you, never heard of the Strokers for Liberty. And if some asshole tries to throw me under the bus, I'll drive the damn thing over his head."

"Copy that."

"Now get outta here so I can do my business."

Onus had one more question:

"Where'd the two million bucks for the Strokers come from? Dale won't say."

"That's because Dale doesn't know," Boyette said. "Every important patriotic movement has patrons who prefer to stay anonymous. Angels, if you will."

"Patriot angels."

"Exactly. And special they are."

"No offense," Onus said, "but it's fucked up that Dale's the one in charge of all that money. Dude can't barely count to ten."

Boyette looked up narrowly. "Who says *he* controls the fund? That's bull."

"So it's you then."

"This convo is over." The congressman dropped his pants and grunted sonorously to initiate the moving of his bowels. Onus clawed open the latch and reeled out of the stall.

"Who are these 'angels'?" he called to Boyette over the door. "I won't tell nobody!"

Claude and Electra Mink deeply believed that, despite a political shift to the right, America continued spiraling downward and hellbound. They sensed a dangerous post-election complacency while core white values remained in dire peril; woke enemies abounded, lurking and plotting. Tucker Carlson's celebratory cackling had worn thin on the couple, who'd seen scant evidence that the country was back on track. One obvious example: Gay Pride parades were bigger than ever.

Also, the government fucknut in charge of mass deportation was botching the job. Among those snatched up by ICE was Papito, the Minks' longtime Mexican landscaper. Claude was so fearful of retribution by Papito's many American-born cousins that he struggled to drink himself to sleep at night. Often he lay in bed vibrating with his eyes wide open, velour slippers on his feet, and a loaded Beretta under the comforter. Electra unsympathetically relocated him to one of the downstairs bedrooms, and a bank of video monitors was installed so that he could watch the feeds from the expensive array of security cameras on the property.

He drove the police department nuts. One time he phoned to report a "rampaging mob of border jumpers" that turned out to be a family of agile raccoons. Another night the bomb squad was summoned to defuse a sleeping armadillo that Claude had mistaken for an IED. Still another call resulted in the choke-holding and Tasing of a bewildered driver from the Minks' favorite twenty-four-hour pharmacy, a Jamaican man who was merely delivering chamomile wrinkle cream for Electra. The effect of these recurrent false alerts was to elongate the response time of the cops, who'd come to view Claude as a semi-senile paranoid.

And so it played out that when a masked human intruder actually scaled the east wall of the Minks' compound and Claude dialed 911, the call was not treated as a top priority. Twenty-one minutes elapsed before the first patrol unit rolled up, and by then the intruder was gone. The officers who sat down with Claude to review the security video were genuinely surprised to discover that the rich old fruitcake had not dreamed up the nocturnal creeper.

Wearing a Marlins baseball cap, camo sun mask, gloves, and dark glasses, the man had walked unhurriedly from camera to camera while jotting on a small spiral pad. He'd made no attempt to enter the Mink residence and committed no vandalism. In the backyard he had even stopped to help a frog out of the swimming pool. Then he waved good-bye at the fish-eye lens on the underside of the diving board and exited over the west wall.

The cops got back in their cars and made several passes through the neighborhood. They found nobody on the streets.

Claude remained awake at his post, haggardly studying the bank of screens. His eyes felt like scalded walnuts, and his ribs ached miserably from the Heimlich episode at lunch. He considered rousing Electra but feared injury, as she often sat up punching at phantoms produced by the Lunesta and zoological-grade sedatives that she gobbled before bedtime.

The sleep disorders that bedeviled both Claude and Electra had begun after the January 6th fiasco, during which the spuriously minted Cops in Recovery had dissolved in hapless confusion along with the Minks' three hundred thousand dollar investment in coup building. Watching the Capitol siege on television, the couple was sickened to observe their recruits fleeing in a long wobbly line, like spooked penguins. Weeks later, when the Mink Foundation's wealth director, Rachel Cohen, found out that the group was a front, Claude contacted an associate of an associate who quickly removed Rachel as a threat. It was a difficult decision because Claude liked Rachel personally. She was a total professional, and her espresso was to die for.

Unfortunately, extreme measures were sometimes necessary when the future of the republic was hanging by a pube. On this Claude and Electra agreed.

It was three thirty in the morning when the trespasser unexpectedly reappeared on one of the security screens. Claude hunched closer, unnerved. The mask and gloves made it impossible to determine the color of the man's skin, but Claude felt certain he was either a Black gangbanger or an illegal alien. The prick was writing something in a notebook while positioned squarely in front of the camera mounted on the Minks' antique birdbath, a half-ton anniversary gift from Prince Andrew. Claude cursed at the nonchalant figure on the monitor and angrily reached for his cellphone.

The trespasser tore a page from his notepad and held it up to the lens:

PLEASE, SIR, CAN I BE A WEE HAMMER?

Claude Mink let out a yeep. The man on the screen saluted, turned, and strode away from the birdbath. Oddly, none of the other cameras picked up his presence on the property, as if he'd devised a hidden pathway out.

This time Claude didn't call the cops. He called Clure Boyette.

CHAPTER 9

Dale Figgo's supervisor at Bottom Drawer Novelties was a rangy, acne-scarred Russian who oddly demanded to be addressed as Pierre. Figgo didn't know if the guy was in the country legally or not. There was no upside to asking.

Pierre had a small stale office with a wall-unit air conditioner blowing warm at full blast. That was the first thing Figgo noticed when he sat down. The second thing that grabbed his attention was an unwrapped Darcy's Dream Booty on Pierre's desk. The polymer ass wasn't honey-colored like the one Figgo packed in shipping boxes all day; it was larger, riper, and creamy white.

"Is that a new model?" Figgo asked.

"Shut fuck up," said Pierre.

He had summoned Figgo because of an inventory discrepancy, and he suspected an inside job. Workplace pilfering was common in the sex toy industry.

Pierre said, "Last quarter we are thirteen asses short. All on your shift."

Figgo denied any involvement. "Somebody counted wrong."

"I think maybe you steal product for side hustle."

"No way, Pierre."

"Or maybe you just take home for self jacking. Sick fuck."

"No way!" Figgo exclaimed. He hadn't added up how many Dream Booties he'd boosted for gifts to future Strokers, but thirteen seemed like a high number. It was possible that some other worker on the line was stealing, too.

Pierre eyed the soft brace on Figgo's right hand and wrist. "Fuck happened?"

"It's for the carpy tuna syndrome."

"Because of job?"

"I guess. Yeah, absolutely." Figgo wasn't about to disclose the true cause, not with a sleazy theft accusation hanging over his head.

"So, you file claim?" Pierre asked warily.

"Oh. I haven't decided."

Pierre hated the American workers' comp system. So much stupid fucking paperwork. Only Pierre's bosses in New Jersey hated workers' comp more than Pierre did.

"Here's deal," he said to Figgo. "You don't file comp claim, I forget about product you steal from company. You file claim, I call cops and you go jail."

"I didn't swipe anything, but sure. That's cool." It had never occurred to Figgo to apply for workers' compensation. He hadn't missed a single day on the job, because he couldn't afford to.

"Also, one thing more," Pierre said. "If shipping count is short again, even by one fucking ass, I come for you with rebar."

"'Kay, but are you sure it was thirteen units off? That's a lot."

Pierre sighed. "Now Pierre is liar?"

"Dude, that's not what I meant."

"In my country, man who says Pierre is liar would get carpy tuna both hands, both legs, cock, balls, asshole. No more work for company. No more anything."

Touchy bastard, Figgo thought.

He pointed at the pearly white torso on Pierre's desk and said, "FYI, that's the hottest one yet."

"Is model SX-23."

"What kind do we pack on my line?"

"SX-19. How you not know this? Is stamped on every box," Pierre said. "Get fuck out."

Rising from the chair, Figgo asked how much the big white Booty cost.

"One twenty-six ninety-five," Pierre said.

"Damn. That's retail?"

"Yes, shithead. Retail."

"But, yo," Figgo said, "we get an employee discount, right?"

In a fury the Russian lunged across the desk. Figgo wrenched free and shot out the door. Back on the packing line, he worked faster than usual in order to reach his quota by day's end. He was not too dim to appreciate the fact that he wasn't being prosecuted, or at least fired for stealing. For now, he sorely needed his Bottom Drawer paycheck. He had grossly miscalculated the true cost of the Ram quad cab, and with every passing month he fell further behind. In the console of his pickup was a handful of nonpayment warnings from Dodge, and soon the repo squad would be on his trail.

Although he'd never served in the military, Figgo put a shoplifted U.S. Marine Corps decal on the truck's back window hoping the finance company might be more lenient with a service vet. More recently, as an added precaution, he'd asked Jonas Onus for permission to park the pickup at Onus's place during the night.

Knowing his job on the sex toy line would never pay enough, Figgo's plan was to convince the congressman to give him a salaried position on the Wee Hammers payroll. It seemed only fair, since supervising the Strokers for Liberty was practically a full-time duty. Meanwhile, for cash-flow purposes, Figgo grudgingly acknowledged that he was lucky to have a tenant who paid the rent on time, and whose checks never bounced. Viva Morales might be a woke-ass bitch, but she was a reliable woke-ass bitch.

With a boyfriend who had his head screwed on right.

The interview was set at Applebee's. Figgo drove there from work and snagged a booth. Twilly Spree walked in a few minutes later. They ordered beers and bone-in chicken wings.

"How'd you meet Viva?" Figgo asked.

"On a plane," Twilly said.

"Don't seem like you two got much in common."

"Yeah, it probably won't work out."

"So, I talked to the membership committee 'bout you," Figgo said.

"There's a committee?"

There wasn't, but Figgo said, "Absolutely. The vote was unanimal."

"I assume that's good."

"Hell, yes! You're in, bro, but here's the thing: You can't tell Viva *anything* the group is doin'. There's a code."

"Understood," said Twilly.

"You can go on bangin' her cross-eyed and so forth, but the Strokers are off-limits for the pillow-talk part. And she's gonna be askin' lotsa questions, I guarantee."

"She'll get nothing from me but a smile."

"That's my man. You got any guns?"

"The official answer is no," Twilly said.

"But you can shoot, right?"

"What do you think?"

Figgo laughed. "Sorry. Had to ask."

"As I'm sure you know, I can't legally own a firearm because I've got a rap sheet."

"Yeah, I seen it," Figgo lied. He had no law enforcement connections to help him screen applicants. In any case, he didn't consider a criminal past to be disqualifying; the recruitment pool for competing white nationalist groups varied in depth. Figgo asked Twilly if this would be his first time on the front lines.

"Depends what you mean," he said.

"The Strokers, we ain't like the Proud Boys. You can jerk off all you want at home."

"Good to know," Twilly said.

"That's the first thing most guys ask."

"It's all about freedom, right?"

"You bet your Christian ass," said Figgo.

After the men finished eating, they ordered another round of beers. Without mentioning the congressman, Figgo laid out the bare plan for Precinct 53. He called it the "Battle of Carpville." Twilly said he was familiar with the town; he didn't mention that he'd gone there to look up dirt on Clure Boyette.

"And there's another op before Carpville, but I can't tell you about it," Figgo added. "Not yet."

"When's it going down?"

"Soon. You do social media?"

"Totally addicted," Twilly said.

Figgo told him about the KRANKK platform and explained how to access it. "For security, we use three-factor authentorization."

"Smart," said Twilly without breaking character.

Figgo raised his glass and whispered, "Welcome to the second American Revolution. God bless the Strokers for Liberty."

"Amen." Twilly hoisted his beer.

"Any questions, brother?"

"Yeah. Is there any cool swag?"

"What?"

"You know—hats, tee shirts, koozies?"

Figgo frowned. "That's Proud Boy shit, man. Strictly for losers."

"I guess," Twilly said.

"But I got a special welcome gift in the truck. You'll like it, dude."

~~~

The coroner in Bonifay County confirmed the identity of the remains found years ago by the bass fisherman as those of Rachel Cohen. Viva got the news in a brief text from Twilly. She said nothing to the Minks, whom she viewed as prime suspects, and tried to go on with her work as if nothing was wrong. The couple seemed preoccupied, and was less meddlesome than usual. Viva overheard Electra on a call with Clure Boyette discussing a nighttime intruder who seemed to know about the Wee Hammers. Next Claude got on the phone—which was rare, because of tuning issues with his hearing aids—and loudly arranged for armed security 24/7 on the estate. Neither Mink would tell Viva what had happened, but she
~~~

planned to coax the details from Boyette on their date. Electra said she was glad that Viva was giving a second chance to such a promising young man.

"But be discreet, dear," she added. "He's not divorced yet, and there's an election coming up."

"I'll try to control myself," Viva said.

When she got home from work, she saw a big flatbed truck parked on the street in front of the townhouse. Two rough-looking characters covered with tats clambered from the cab and intercepted her before she reached the front door.

"Where's your old man?" one of them grunted.

"He's not my old man. He's my landlord."

"Where's the fuckin' Ram?" asked the other guy.

"Once you locate the elusive Mr. Figgo," Viva said, "ye shall find the vehicle ye seek."

"Maybe we'll just sit out here all goddamn night and wait."

"Suit yourselves, gentlemen."

Viva went inside, took a quick shower, and changed into black jeans and a loose beige blouse with coral buttons. After putting on her makeup, she brought two go-cups of lemonade and a jar of Costco cashews to the repo men, who seemed thrown off-balance by the gesture. Viva said she didn't know where Dale Figgo was, or when he would return.

"Where does he hang when he ain't here?" one of them asked.

"Usually with a friend."

"How about a name, hon?"

"Jonas Onus," Viva said. "That's O-N-U-S. I've no idea where he lives."

She was sincerely trying to be helpful. The repossession of Figgo's pickup truck would be a positive thing, hampering the distribution of his toxic flyers and possibly saving more innocent pedestrians from being run over. The only drawback was that Viva might find herself driving Figgo to work, but it seemed a minor price to pay.

"These are good nuts," one of the repo men commented while crunching a mouthful.

"I don't suppose you have a business card," Viva said.

"What the hell for?"

"Well, good luck on your quest."

"Don't tell him we was here."

"Wouldn't dream of it, fellas."

Clure Boyette was waiting in the bar when Viva arrived at the restaurant, a Greek joint owned by a Peruvian couple and operated by Serbian brothers. The congressman was wearing a dark pin-striped suit and stood out like an undertaker at a carnival. One side of his face looked puffy and over-powdered with makeup. When Viva asked what had happened, he told her he'd been hit with an errant golf ball at a country club owned by one of his dear friends, a wealthy sugar baron in Manalapan.

A hostess led them to a secluded corner table, where Boyette chirped on at length about his many political achievements and overall importance on the national stage. Then he went to the restroom and snorted two lines of coke, a fact later brought to light by his jibbering cross-examination of the server regarding the preparation of the pork chops.

Toward the end of dinner the congressman put a hand on Viva's knee and, although she was tempted to spear it with a salad fork, she let it linger.

"What's the latest on the Wee Hammers?" she asked.

"Glad you asked, luv," he said. "I know you're a skeptic, but look at this."

Proudly he opened a picture on his phone: a line of children holding gold-painted shovels, poised to dig. The kids—ages six to twelve, Viva guessed—wore shiny orange hard hats that covered everything but their little noses and smiles. They were standing in a cleared lot beside a big yellow backhoe. A bright banner attached to the claw of the machine identified the gathering as the groundbreaking for the first Wee Hammers house.

"But you told me the slab was already poured," Viva said.

"No, I don't believe I did. The pour is scheduled for this week. The kids are totally stoked."

"Which one gets to drive the mixer?"

"Very funny," the congressman said, obnoxiously squeezing her knee. He dove into a rant about the obscene price of concrete, which he blamed on the Chinese, the Democrats, and the CDC. He was so full of steaming shit that it was excruciating for Viva not to say so.

Instead she asked, "What happened at Claude and Electra's house last night? They were still pretty freaked this morning."

"Some rando jumped the wall. Won't happen again."

"Did he try to break in?"

"Naw, it was just some lame prank," Boyette said. "He went up to one of the outdoor cameras and held up a sign asking to join the Wee Hammers. A real fucking comedian."

"That doesn't sound random. How would he know about your foundation?"

"Electra talks too damn much at the country club. Or maybe it was you."

"Sure, because all my friends are so fascinated with the Minks. They're basically the new Kardashians."

Boyette shrugged. "The wall jumper covered his face so the cops couldn't ID him, but I've got a guy in the FBI analyzing the videos. I'm not too worried. The dude didn't steal anything and he didn't hurt anybody."

"It's still weird, Clure."

"The world we live in, darling."

"Apparently," said Viva. There was little chance that Boyette had a serious contact within the FBI, or that the agency would waste one minute reviewing the Minks' security images to help identify a prowler.

"Would you like a glass of port?" Boyette asked.

Viva said she'd rather have a nightcap at the rich widow's condo. The congressman was caught off guard.

"The condo, uh—it's being remodeled," he said. "But I've got a hotel room."

"I suppose that'll do."

"Is something hot about to happen?"

"Like what?" Viva said coyly. "You're still a married man."

She placed her hand over his hand on her knee, and lightly ran her fingernails across his skin. With a snicker of delight, he thrust his spade-edged face forward and said, "Hold that thought, luv."

Viva's strategy for the evening was contingent on Clure Boyette being drunk or otherwise impaired. The ideal condition: tipsy but not incoherent. It was a balancing act that Viva had perfected in her single days, before Malcolm came along, whenever she didn't want to sleep with a date, which was most of the time. She was betting the same system would work on Boyette; surely the congressman had consumed more than enough booze and blow.

They took an Uber to the Hilton, where Boyette had a junior suite on the top floor. Again he beelined for the bathroom, yanking off his necktie as he shut the door. On the coffee table stood a bucket of ice and an unopened handle of Jack Daniel's, courtesy of the hotel manager. Viva sat in a chair by the window and took off her heels and crossed her legs. The room had an outstanding view of the Marriott next door.

Boyette came out wearing wine-colored briefs, black socklets, and a furry collar around his neck. In one hand he twirled a red leash studded with cheap-looking stones.

"Aren't you just full of surprises," Viva said.

"Don't tell me you've never done this before!" Boyette spoke through a loose-fitting leather muzzle. He stroked the furry collar and said, "Alaskan ermine."

"A member of the weasel family, fittingly."

"Feel how soft," the congressman said.

"I'm good, Clure."

"Hell, I forgot my damn snowshoes."

"I knew something was missing," Viva said.

"Strip down to your panties right now. Come on."

"Not tonight," she told him. "You're too trashed to get the job done, erection-wise."

"What?" Boyette was stunned. "Wanna bet?"

"You've got coke dick, dude. It happens. Don't worry, you'll live to rise another day."

He peered down at himself and murmured, "I'm fine."

Boom, Viva thought. *Works every time.*

The congressman dropped the leash, turned his back to her, lowered his briefs, and began slapping distraughtly at his listless cock.

"Clure, don't do that," Viva said softly, sealing the deal. "You'll break a blood vessel."

"What?"

"I'm serious. It's a scary thing to see."

"STOP TALKING LIKE THAT!"

"Put the poor little guy away," she said, reaching for the bourbon bottle. "How about a drink?"

Morosely he downed three in a row, tilting sideways against Viva on the edge of the bed. She loosened his fur collar and—to take his mind off his masculinity crisis—began asking questions about politics. Boyette composed himself well enough to deliver a slurred list of imminent threats—the dismantling of the Constitution by leftist child molesters, the cyber-hijacking of laser satellites by Zionist astrophysicists, the transgender conspiracy to infiltrate women's volleyball, and so on. It was a day-to-day struggle, he said, almost impossible to bear.

"And I'm sure you've heard about the woke mob," he added, "trying to ban eight balls."

"Wait—is cocaine *not* against the law?"

"I'm talking about *real* eight balls, Viva. The ones on pool tables."

"And this 'woke mob' is who exactly?"

"Take a wild guess," Boyette said. "Your gays. Your Jews. Your people of color. The elite radical left, if we're being polite."

"Why start now."

"Rainbow-colored eight balls. That's the future, if we stand silent."

"God help us," Viva said.

She was surprised at the rabidity of Boyette's views, which were not so flagrantly displayed on his Facebook page. She wondered whether his prejudices were genuine, or had been tailored to lock down a small vicious base populated with Dale Figgos.

"My beliefs cost me my marriage," the congressman went on, dabbing at dry eyes. "But in the end, all these sacrifices will be worth it. As long as we stay vigilant, white Christian values will prevail."

"So you brought me here to pray?" Viva asked.

"Jesus preached love and togetherness."

"Did he also keep a suite under an assumed name?"

"You're a little pistol," Boyette said. His voice sounded ragged and his boozy breathing was shallow.

"Vigilance sometimes requires a low profile."

"But not sobriety, evidently."

"Something super-major is in the works, luv."

"Tell me."

Boyette touched a finger to his lips. "Not yet. Top secret."

Viva whispered, "Whose idea was the Wee Hammers Fund? It's a brilliant front."

The congressman grinned crookedly. "All mine," he said.

"What about the Minks?"

"They're just the bank. I'm the brains."

The prominence of Boyette's equine dentition was distracting; Viva could almost picture herself feeding him a carrot through the rails of a corral.

"So you've got people working on this?" she asked. "The rescuing of America part?"

"Serious fuckin' people. My job is to give them cover and stay invisible."

"Like I said—brilliant."

"Right?"

"Meanwhile you're building actual houses to make the foundation look legit."

"Just one," the congressman said thickly. "One little house."

"Ah."

"A two-two with a screened porch."

"Sweet," Viva said.

In slow motion Boyette keeled backward on the bed, trying to pull her down with him. With ease she shed his grip. He closed his eyes and said he didn't feel so great.

"I been overserved," he mumbled.

"Are your people local? The serious ones fighting the space lasers. Or do you bring them in from somewhere else?"

"Homegrown, luv. This is fuckin' free Florida. They post up here."

Viva reached over to jostle his shoulders. "Don't go to sleep, Clure, it's still early. Tell me about the big things you've got planned. Please?"

"Hodey ho ho."

"Want some coffee?"

"No, goddammit, I wanna crash."

And that's what he did.

He didn't hear Viva walk into the bathroom and empty the pockets of his pinstriped suit, and he didn't hear the door to the suite close when she left.

The county commission also served as the zoning board, and Lewin Baltry often was the swing vote, the one who changed his mind at the last minute. That meant he was the most prosperous of the seven commissioners, owing to a heavier stream of unreported gifts and favors from developers.

In order for the huge Bunkers project to move forward, the plowed citrus groves had to be rezoned from agricultural to mixed-use residential—traditionally a juicy opportunity for quick-fingered Florida politicians. The price of Lewin Baltry's vote on The Bunkers was $75,000 and a golf cart with Rolls-Royce grill-work. Electra and Claude Mink split the cost of the bribe fifty-fifty with their partners on the construction side. The money was pre-paid and sinuously routed to Baltry's Bermuda bank account, while the custom golf cart traveled on a luxe Harley trailer cross-country from Rancho Mirage, California, to Tangelo Shores.

On the night of what was supposed to be the final zoning board hearing for The Bunkers, Lewin Baltry called in sick and the development stalled on a 3–3 vote. The Minks and their partners were incensed, believing that Baltry was reneging. While it was true that the commissioner was lying about having the flu, the problem was more serious than a common case of greed. Baltry had been found out, and he was scared. He locked himself in his house and despondently watched the zoning vote unfold on the public access channel.

No sleep came as he thrashed in bed wondering if he'd been betrayed by political rivals, or had carelessly left clues to his past corrupt acts. In retrospect, buying a thirty-one-foot speedboat so soon after the outlet mall rezoning had been unwise. Ditto for the Rolex Daytona, which Baltry started wearing the day after he cast the deciding vote to approve a bullet factory across the street from a Chuck E. Cheese.

Now the pliant commissioner was being targeted by government agents. The man who'd warned him was a complete stranger who had jumped into his car in the drive-through line at a Wendy's, where Baltry had stopped on his way to County Hall for the Bunkers vote. At first he'd assumed that the stranger was a robber, and he offered up his expensive watch.

"Already got one," the man had said. "I wear it to funerals."

"Just don't hurt me! Here, take my wallet."

"Why? I'm richer than you are."

"Then what is it you want?" Baltry had cried.

"Listen to what I'm about to say. That's all."

"Okay, okay."

"The feds are looking at you. Hard."

"Why me?"

In response the man had grabbed Baltry by his comb-over and shaken him like a dirty Swiffer, saying: "Lewin, you know damn well what you've done. Bribery, money laundering, tax evasion."

"Let go! Who are you? Why do you care what happens to *me*?"

"I don't give a shit where you end up down the line," the man had said, "but at this particular moment you're more useful if you're not under indictment. So watch your ass, because they're tracking every move you make. By 'they' I mean the FBI and the IRS."

"How do you know that, mister?"

"You don't believe me, just stay greedy and keep at it. When you're in prison, I'll send you a gallon of lube for Christmas."

"What about the Bunkers vote?"

"Abstain, you dumb shit."

"But, see, I've already been . . . compensated."

"Then give it back," the man had said.

"The golf cart, too?"

"Be quiet, Lewin."

Baltry's car had rolled up alongside the drive-through window. He'd paid with his re-election committee's Discover card, and the teenager at the register handed out a sweaty bag of food. Baltry had offered a Baconator burger to the stranger, who chose a handful of fries instead.

"Drop me at the next corner," the man had said.

"Who do you work for?"

"I don't know. The youth of America?"

"What?"

At the stoplight, the stranger had gotten out of the car, walked around to Lewin Baltry's side, and said, "FYI, the Minks will be coming for you."

"Then what?" Baltry had peeped. "What the hell am I supposed to do?"

The man had handed him a scrap of yellow paper with a phone number written on it.

"If things get bad, make the call," he'd said. "Good-bye, Lewin."

"Wait, you never answered my question."

"Which question?"

"About the golf cart," Baltry had whispered. "Do I have to give it back?"

The stranger had stared back solemnly and said, "That's between you and God."

"Yes. Of course. You're right."

As far as Twilly Spree knew, there was no ongoing investigation of Lewin Baltry. However, it wouldn't be difficult to stitch one together, Twilly thought as he watched the crooked numbskull drive away. Baltry left a slime trail that was easy to follow. Developers with a major project pending before the county always retained among their corps of lobbyists a certain firm that happened to bundle campaign contributions for Baltry. In this way the commissioner's open-mindedness was assured. He was renowned for wavering or even pretending to support the project's opponents until the very last vote, typically at one or two in the morning after all the exhausted gadflies and environmentalists had gone home.

Twilly had been tipped off to Baltry's graft by a local news reporter Twilly had taken out for lunch. Later, reading through the minutes of several zoning hearings, he'd been struck by the lack of nuance in Baltry's flip-flops, and the haste with which the board would adjourn afterward. It was a far more unsophisticated charade than what went on regularly in larger, overdeveloped counties like Broward or Lee, where corruption was an ever-evolving art form.

After his chat with the corrupt commissioner, Twilly picked up a rotisserie chicken and returned to his apartment. He was studying satellite maps of the Bahamas when he got a DM that said "brass ballz," the brainless code phrase that Dale Figgo had chosen as a message alert for the Strokers for Liberty. Over and over Twilly tried logging on to KRANKK, with no luck. His attempts at three-factor authentication eventually locked him out of the web page, the third factor requiring users to sing the first two lines of a Kid Rock number into their laptop's microphone.

Breaking Strokers protocol, Twilly called Figgo directly to complain that KRANKK was a shitty, gummed-up platform. Figgo pretended not to know who Twilly was, and hung up. Half an hour later he sent a text that said only "fever." An hour later he sent the word "beach." At midnight he texted the numeral 8. An hour after that he sent "pm," and an hour after that the word "Thursday."

First thing the next morning, Figgo called Twilly from a blocked number to make sure he'd understood the message.

"I'm still trying to crack the code," Twilly said.

"Is that a joke?"

"I'll be there Thursday night."

Figgo said, "If you've got a tiki torch, bring it."

"Now you've lost me."

"It's not code. We need more damn tiki torches."

"I'll buy some," Twilly said. "Want me to scrape off the serial numbers?"

"How'd you like your membership present?"

"I haven't opened it yet."

"You're shittin' me."

"Sorry. I had a busy evening."

"Well, open the damn thing," Figgo said. "It was my last one, probably forever."

"Tonight. I promise."

"Bro, it's gonna rock your world."

"See ya at the beach," Twilly said.

CHAPTER 10

Viva slept poorly. In her first dream she was revisited by the dwarf coyote, who advised her to dump all of her Meta shares right away. It made no sense because Viva didn't own any stocks. When she tried to corner the misinformed critter, it bounded away, out of the garden.

The next dream featured her ex, Malcolm, who said that he'd nullified their divorce and wanted her to return to the Twin Cities and share a duplex. He was wearing loud country-club shorts and a purple Vikings jersey with a large number 0 on the back. Viva snatched a rake and chased him down a railroad leading to a copper mine, where he dove into the shaft. Viva didn't follow but she heard him calling out, pleading with her to leave his G-Wagen in the long-term lot at the airport.

She woke up unnerved, and decided to not close her eyes for the rest of the night. Keeping the lights off, she lay in bed with her laptop open on her tummy. After midnight she opened the *New York Times* app and tackled the daily Wordle puzzle, to which she'd become addicted. It took four tries to get the word of the day, which was **GNASH**.

Afterward she started researching places to move to after the shit hit the fan for the Minks and Clure Boyette. She really wanted to go to Manhattan and in fanciful moments felt like she already knew the place, from *The New Yorker.* But her sister said the city was hard on career women, and her parents said she could never afford to live there, and Malcolm once said he'd been robbed by a teenager flying a kite in Central Park, which, in retrospect, Viva would have paid good money to see.

The Boulder area looked interesting. Maybe San Diego, or even Honolulu on a lark. She bookmarked HR openings at a couple of resort hotels; the salary even for an administrator was so-so, but the health insurance packages were solid. The only negative about leaving Florida would be giving up the chance of a serious thing with Twilly Spree, who could afford to live anywhere but would never, ever move. Saying good-bye to him would be hard, though he'd handle it with class. Viva suspected that good women had been leaving him throughout his entire adult life.

Once the sun came up, she went downstairs for coffee. The kitchen counter was littered with crumpled paper napkins that had been marked on both sides with a black Sharpie—Dale Figgo, practicing his swastikas again. They still looked like stomped-on tarantulas. It was depressing to think of the effort that her loser landlord was devoting to such a task. He truly believed that he would rally a groundswell by scattering illiterate hate messages in neighborhoods where he imagined a Jewish family or two might live. Was his loathing real, or an acting job by a pathetic reject?

Viva put an ear to his door and heard snoring. She gathered up the swastika napkins and stuffed them into a neighbor's garbage can along with the FedEx packet containing a new trigger for Figgo's AR-15.

When she got to the office, she printed her screenshots of the contacts saved on Clure Boyette's phone, which she'd lifted from the inner pocket of his suit jacket the night before, after he'd passed out. The lame pass code, which she'd watched the congressman peck in during dinner, was 1-7-7-6.

Most of the names on the list were unfamiliar to Viva, though the Mink Foundation was listed. So were the private cell numbers of Claude and Electra. Boyette's wife, Nicki, was in there, too, with three different phone numbers. Viva was miffed to find herself saved only as "Viva," the informality of which implied an actual relationship. Numerous individuals were identified only by nicknames—Ballerina, Galaxy, Honey Drizzle, King Taint, Money $hot, Sapphire, Sir Turdley, and so on.

Viva had painstakingly photographed the whole list, A through Z, while hiding in a restroom in the hotel lobby while Boyette sprawled wasted upstairs. Afterward, she'd snuck outside and placed his phone on the floor of the parking garage, knowing he would try to track it after sobering up.

She wasn't sure how best to utilize the congressman's contact directory, but Twilly would know. She texted him **call me** and was still awaiting his response when the Minks entered the office in a palsied state of agitation, practically shouting over one another. Both were on their phones, connected with the same unknown person.

"Have you talked to Lewin?" Electra was asking. "Does that scumbag seriously want more money?"

"Fuck that, Barry. He gets nothing!" Claude cried.

"We pay you to keep these cockroaches under control—" Electra said.

"We also pay you to know what's going on inside their greedy little brains—" Claude piled on.

"—and to take our goddamn calls in the middle of the night!" Electra yelled.

The Minks were so upset that they barely noticed Viva at her desk. She kept her head down, listening to the uproar while fake-typing on her computer.

"Guess what, Barry," Electra went on. "I don't give a shit that you were in the middle of your niece's bat mitzvah. Neither does Claude."

"I don't care if it's your fucking *daughter*'s bat mitzvah!" Claude affirmed, practically strangling his phone.

"We've heard enough of your bullshit," Electra said to the person on the other end of the line. "Find out why Baltry skipped the vote. We want the answer today."

"Or it's your ass!" said Claude.

It took a while for the Minks to quiet down, and they remained in a pissy mood. Viva joined them in the meeting room to review the foundation's most recent grant requests, and the couple took turns nixing each one. Viva made a strong pitch for a group that sponsored mobile food banks in Ukraine, but Claude spit forth a "no."

"They're bankrolled by globalists," Electra remarked matter-of-factly.

"But they're not," Viva said.

"Don't be so naive, dear."

"They're only asking for twenty-five thousand."

"And I suppose you think that's just a drop in the bucket."

"It is, compared to what you gave the Wee Hammers."

Electra bristled. "Excuse me, young lady, but it's not your place to—"

"When's my urologist appointment?" Claude cut in.

"Fifteen minutes," Viva said.

Claude stood up noisily. "So, that's twice in twenty-four hours I get a thumb shoved up my ass. First that bastard Baltry, now the doctor."

"Call for the car," Electra snapped at Viva.

As soon as the Minks were gone, Viva went back to work on the congressman's phone contacts. There was no Lewin Baltry, but she did find a Barry—Barry D. Martino. When she called the number, a hyper-perky woman answered and said, "This is the Martino Group. How can I help you?"

Viva hung up and hopped on Google. The Martino Group was a heavyweight lobbying firm with strategic offices in Tallahassee, Orlando, and Washington, D.C. Barry Martino was the son of Alvin Martino, the founding partner, whose political brokering at the highest levels had been rewarded with an ambassadorship to the Bahamas.

And the name Lewin Baltry, it turned out, belonged to a local county commissioner. In his Wikipedia picture he wore the look of an orphaned marmot.

Viva was sure that Twilly could connect the dots. She texted him again, then got to thinking how she might make some progress on her own by *67ing through the nicknamed contacts. Her opening line: "Hello, I'm calling for Congressman Boyette. He was wondering if you'd be available to talk privately later today."

Predictably, "Ballerina" was a young woman.

"Talk about what?" she asked skeptically.

"The congressman didn't specify a topic."

"He knows I don't do the phone thing anymore," Ballerina said. "Tell him to text me the place he wants to meet up and what time."

"Yes, ma'am."

"And make sure he Venmos me before, *not* after."

"Of course," Viva said.

The next nickname she called was Sir Turdley, which Viva figured was either a pimp or a male prostitute, depending on the breadth of Boyette's appetites. She used the same opening line and got a much different reaction.

"Hell, yes!" the man said. "Me and the congressman got lots to talk about."

It was difficult for Viva to hear him over the clatter of machinery in the background.

"Shall I have him contact you at this number?" she asked.

"Talk louder, lady. I'm at work."

A nauseating tremor passed through Viva. That voice.

Holy shit, she thought. *Shit, shit, shit.*

"Yo, are you still there? Tell your boss to call me tonight, okay?"

"Certainly, Mr. Figgo," she said with an impromptu Australian accent so absurd that it wouldn't have fooled anyone but him.

~~~

Fred Brillstein Jr. went to speak with Noel and Mary Kristiansen at their home, a short walk from his own place in Sanctuary Falls. The lawyer brought two pieces of news, both positive.

First, the HOA wanted to settle even before Noel's hit-and-run
~~~

lawsuit was filed: seventy-five thousand dollars, plus all of Noel's medical bills.

"Too low," Mary said.

"Too high," said Noel. "It wasn't the HOA's fault. What about the shithead that ran me over? The Nazi scum."

"Neo-Nazi, technically. Or neofascist."

"Scum is scum, Mary."

Brillstein explained that, as he'd foreseen, the driver of the Ram 1500 was a total loser who had no money and wasn't worth suing. Mary knew this to be true because she had talked Brillstein's paralegal into providing Dale Figgo's name, and she'd spent a day online sorting through the many liens and small-claims judgments levied against the man during his thirty-seven sorry years on the planet. Figgo owned nothing of significant value. The townhouse in which he lived belonged to his mother, and the truck with which he'd struck Mary's husband was about to be repossessed. In fact, on paper it appeared that, since age twenty-one, Figgo had lost every vehicle, kitchen appliance, and king mattress he'd ever owned due to missed payments.

"We can't sue his car insurance company," Brillstein was saying, "because guess what? The schmuck doesn't have any insurance."

"Which is against the law," Mary noted.

Noel laughed harshly. "Like neo-scum would care."

"Well, somebody somewhere cares about keeping this guy out of court," Brillstein said, "because I received a second settlement offer, a weird one, from an attorney up in Bonifay County. He claims to represent a 'close friend' of the driver who wants to help wrap up this matter. Two hundred and fifty grand if you agree not to press criminal charges, sign a nondisclosure agreement, and make no effort to contact or publicly identify the client or his friend."

Noel said, "That's way beyond weird."

"It's also a decent amount of money."

Mary said, "I don't understand. The cops already know who he is."

Brillstein nodded. "But has he been charged with any crimes? No. I smell a plea deal in the works."

Noel was stunned. "Can they do that without me signing off on it?"

"Depends on the prosecutor and the judge. It's not an easy case, Mr. Kristiansen. You couldn't see the face of the driver. Nobody did, apparently, except the hitchhiker who skipped town. The guy who hit you's going to swear his truck got stolen the day before the accident, because that's what they all say."

Mary cut in: "Back to this settlement offer. I'd like to know who this lowlife's VIP friend is, and what he's trying to cover up."

"More Nazi shit, I bet," Noel said.

Just take the fucking money! Brillstein wanted to scream.

"The lawyer's legit. That's all I know," he said.

The Kristiansens seemed more interested in exposing and shaming the hit-and-run driver than banking a speedy cash settlement. It was irritating Brillstein, whose standard cut was thirty-three and one-third percent.

"The shithead in question is Dale F-I-G-G-O, white male, single," he said impatiently, "and, trust me, he has no reputation to ruin."

"Fred's right about that," Mary said to her husband. "I looked him up in the court files. Don't ask how I got his name."

"Doesn't matter," Noel said.

He should have known Mary would be doing her own detective work. Now, for her own safety, she had to shut it down. According to the website listed on the driveway leaflet, the Strokers for Liberty hated Blacks as much as they did Jews, Asians, and immigrants—and they loved, loved, *loved* guns.

Turning to Brillstein, Noel said, "Tell the HOA they're off the hook. Then call Mr. Figgo's friend's lawyer and counter with three hundred thousand plus all my medical bills and rehab. If they say yes, we'll sign the damn NDA."

"Noel, wait—"

"No, Mary. I appreciate what you did—and trying to keep me out of it, too—but we both need this to be over. Let's settle."

"Smart move," Brillstein practically chortled in relief. "Nothing's going to teach this creep a lesson. All that happens when people like him go to prison is they put on twenty pounds and get calluses on their knees. The man's never going to change, and there's nothing you can do to make him regret what he's done."

We'll see about that, thought Noel.

\~\~\~

Himmler's violent temperament was a credible excuse for Jonas Onus not moving in with any of the mothers of his kids. He'd purchased the animal with that in mind while the three women were pregnant; Himmler looked at children the way Snoop Dogg looks at gummies. Onus was content to be living alone in his own place.

He chased away the two repo goons by brandishing an AK-47 while Dale Figgo hid in the hallway closet. Neither of them could figure out how Figgo's Dodge truck had been tracked to Onus's personal residence. Afterward they shut Himmler in the bathroom and went to a gun range for target practice with a stash of empty Fanta cans. Figgo displayed surprisingly terrible aim. Onus offered some pointers, but his friend was stubborn and uncoordinated. It sickened Onus to see expensive ammo go to waste.

He waited until lunch at Popeyes before telling Figgo he needed money from the Wee Hammers Fund. "Ten grand, same as you," he said. "Fair's fair."

"Ten grand for what?" Figgo demanded. "Anyhow, my payout's for a damn defense lawyer."

"I got bills, too, startin' with rent on four fuckin' apartments."

"What about your pension and disabledy checks?"

"They don't stretch far," Onus said. "I got six hungry mouths to feed, not including me and the dog. I need for you to call your butthole-buddy congressman."

"No, the final word's up to me."

"Don't lie, Dale. He calls the shots."

"The Strokers' ops come first," Figgo insisted, "before personal rent and such."

"But there's two million bucks in that account!"

"Dude, the little Hammers are buildin' a for-real house. That ain't cheap. From the ground up!"

Jonas Onus scowled. "You don't believe that BS, do you? I thought we were brothers."

"Lemme sleep on it," said Figgo.

Onus had set his sights on significantly more than ten thousand dollars. He was testing the friendship, and also Figgo's backbone. The two men barely spoke during the ride back to Onus's apartment complex. There they discovered that Figgo's Dodge Ram had been confiscated, the paperwork cruelly positioned in plain sight under a rock on the asphalt.

"Motherfuckers!" Figgo cried, throwing both arms in the air and clomping in circles like a fuming toddler.

Onus said, "We should've left Himmler in the truck to maul those greasy pricks."

He figured that the repo goons must have staked out the place, waiting for him and Figgo to leave.

"How many payments you miss?" he asked.

"Six. Maybe seven, I dunno," Figgo said.

"That's not so bad."

"How can this shit happen to a free white man in America?"

"Bro, it's a fuckin' disgrace. This is why we rise up."

"I need a beer, dude. More than one."

"Come on in," Onus said.

They drank Bud Lights until Figgo fell asleep on the floor. Onus pawed through his billfold in search of banking information. It was a long shot that didn't pay off; there was no way that Clure Boyette would have given Figgo direct access to the Wee Hammers account. His faux-crocodile wallet contained thirteen one-dollar bills, an Exxon credit card, and three expired discount coupons from a Korean fusion café.

Figgo dozed only a few minutes. When he opened his eyes, Onus said, "Are you going to go talk with Boyette or not?"

"About payin' your rent? I can't do that."

"Then I'll call him myself."

"Don't piss the man off," Figgo said thickly as he sat up. "Yo, can I snag a ride? I gotta be somewheres."

"Take my bike."

"Come on, man. Be serious."

Onus uncoiled a woven steel cable attached to a studded collar. "It's Himmler's potty time," he said. "We be goin' for a walk."

~~~

Pete Webster happened to be staring out the window of his law office when the Capitol shitter pedaled into the parking lot on a rusty beach cruiser with a wobbly front wheel. It reminded Webster of client meetings back from his time as a public defender, except that he'd never represented any right-wing insurrectionists. Racists, certainly, but none of them had belonged to an organized group, much less founded one.

Dale Figgo walked in wearing loose jeans, dirty sneakers, and a sweat-soaked tee shirt that said, "GOD, GUNS, AND MORE GUNS!" He smelled like beer and Juicy Fruit.

Webster said, "Good news, Mr. Figgo. They're giving us a deal."

The prosecutor had reached out to Webster offering Figgo one year's probation for leaving the scene of an accident with injuries. Adjudication would be withheld if Figgo surrendered his driver's license for six months and covered all of Noel Kristiansen's medical bills, payable in monthly installments. The package was too sweet to be anything but an order from high up. Webster hadn't asked where it came from, but the prosecutor—with whom Webster regularly played tennis—confided that his boss had been contacted by somebody heavy on the federal side. That a fuckup like Figgo had such connections was perversely impressive to Webster.

"Noel who? Like the ark dude?" Figgo said testily.

"Kristiansen. The person you struck with your vehicle."

"They want me to pay that fucknut's hospital bills? He walked right in front of my truck! Then he spit on it!"

"This is the part where the client usually thanks me for keeping them out of jail."

Figgo grunted. "They yank my license, how'm I supposed to get to work?"

"Uber. Taxi. Bus. Thumb. Bicycle."

"That bike ain't mine!"
~~~

"Then ask a friend for a ride," Webster said. "My advice is to jump on this deal before they change their minds."

"And you pocket ten grand just for gettin' a phone call."

"There's more to it than that, Mr. Figgo."

"Bullshit. This is why people hate lawyers."

"There are many reasons," Webster said.

He'd dealt with unappreciative clients before, including repeat offenders who understood the system. Felons in general watched too much television, which skewed their expectations. None of the popular lawyer shows ever talked about fees.

Figgo said, "Gimme half of it back and we'll be square. Five grand."

"No refunds. You signed a retainer agreement."

"That's, like, total Jew talk. You might as well be one."

Webster rocked back in his chair, imagining how good it would feel to shove his brass letter opener up Dale Figgo's nose.

Instead the lawyer said, "Yes or no to the plea offer? FYI, the judges assigned to this division are named Shapiro, Hoffman, and Nussbaum. It doesn't matter which one we draw. They're all ballbusters."

Fuck me sideways, Figgo thought dolefully.

"Just do the damn deal," he huffed at Webster.

"I will. And you're welcome."

"Get over yourself, dude."

"You were looking at serious time, Mr. Figgo. Agg assault or possibly attempted homicide. Throw in the whole hate-crime scenario, and it's not a rosy picture. Those flyers you threw from your truck would have pissed off the jury—not to mention that J6 video that you so brilliantly posted on the internet."

Figgo reddened. "I took that video down the day I got back from D.C."

"Not fast enough."

"I put shit on the wrong statue. So what? I thought it was U. S. Grant."

"But why shit at all? That's what the jurors would be wondering. What kind of degenerate does such a thing?" Webster said. "Of course, I'd try my best to keep those images out of evidence, but these days no one can predict how a judge will rule."

"Whatever. They're all crooks."

"Somebody made a phone call to the prosecutor on your behalf. I'd love to know who."

"I got high-up friends," Figgo said.

"Anything's possible."

"Can I go now?"

"Please," said Webster.

The ten grand he'd been paid had not come from Figgo's private bank account, but rather from a sketchy-sounding trust up in Bonifay County. Webster truly had no curiosity about the source of the money; it was a relief to be done with the case.

He stood at the office window watching as the Capitol shitter got on the battered bicycle, took out his phone, and, while texting, pedaled directly into the side of a speeding termite truck. Webster thought he was daydreaming again until he heard the sirens.

Viva grew tired of waiting for Twilly to call back. She drove to his apartment, where he appeared in the doorway wearing gray boxers and the dingy arm sling. She did a mock hair flip and said, "May I come in, sir?"

"It's not a good time, Viva."

"Why not?"

"Then give me a minute to clean up. Sorry."

She prepared to spin on her heels and walk away.

"Is there a woman in there?" she asked.

"Not in the conventional sense."

"What does *that* mean? Let's have a peek, shall we?"

She swept past him and saw an empty cardboard box on the kitchen counter. Next to the box, poised upright, was a fleshy, anatomically accurate replica of a female torso. It was the approximate size of a basketball.

Viva pressed a fingertip to one of the butt cheeks and said, "Nicely toned. Pardon the pun, but does she come with batteries?"

"Lord, I hope not."

"No judgment here. The singles life takes a toll. We all deal with the loneliness in our own way."

Twilly said, "For what it's worth, my honor remains intact. But here's what I was thinking: Somewhere in China there's a sweltering hot factory that punches out these things by the truckload. Then the workers go home to their families and sit around the dinner table talking about their jobs as if everything was perfectly normal, like they're making Game Boys or Jordans. 'Hey, Mom, how was work today?' 'Great, son. We shipped off eighteen dozen fuck toys!'"

Viva examined the lurid facsimile from all angles.

Men are so odd, she thought. The congressman with his ermine bondage collar, Twilly with . . . whatever this creepy object was called.

"Does it have a name?" Viva asked.

"Does your vibrator?"

Viva blushed, then recovered. "Which one?"

Twilly smiled. "That would be Darcy you're staring at. Darcy's Dream Booty."

"So Nineties," Viva said.

"It's my initiation gift from the Strokers."

"Get out."

"Swear to God," Twilly said. "Your landlord gave it to me."

"Dale? Yuk."

"He swore it's never been used. I think he swiped it from his jobsite."

"That lying perv," Viva said. "He told me his warehouse distributed party supplies like magic tricks and kites. He never mentioned—"

"Masturbation accessories? Maybe he thought you'd be offended."

"Right. Because a latex rump is so much worse than the horrid neo-Nazi ravings he leaves lying around the apartment."

Twilly took off his sling. Viva said she couldn't be romantic as long as the Dream Booty loomed in plain sight. Twilly led her to the bedroom and closed the door.

"Have you even been to New York?" he asked.

"No. But I bet lots of people who read the magazine haven't gone."

"Including me," Twilly said.

"Well, look at us two dumb yokels." Viva took off her shoes. "Are you thinking about a trip? We should fly up together. See a Broadway show."

"For sure," he said. "An old-fashioned, rip-roaring musical that leaves the audience cheering for more."

"Did you just side-eye me? You side-eyed me!"

"Never."

"The only reason I came here," she said, "was to tell you something important."

"Understood."

"Clure Boyette admitted that the Wee Hammers is a front, and that the money's being funneled to white Christian warriors."

Twilly sat down on the bed and said, "No shit?"

"Oh, and I found Dale Figgo's cell number on Boyette's phone."

"Outstanding!" Twilly pulled Viva close. "You know what that means, if we can tie the congressman to the Strokers? Huge, as they say. No, humongous."

She sat down beside him. "I got all of Boyette's contacts after he passed out."

"The spy who roofied me. May I take a peek?"

"No roofie," Viva said. "He got shitfaced all on his own."

She swiped through her screenshots of the congressman's phone list. When she got to Barry Martino's name, she told Twilly that Martino had been on the phone with the Minks that morning, all of them raging about Lewin Baltry and the stymied Bunkers project.

"Pure gold," Twilly said. "Martino is a player, a big-time lobbyist. He's probably the one who negotiated the payoff for Baltry's vote. Unfortunately for him, the commissioner experienced a belated pang of conscience and decided to abstain."

"Was that your doing?"

"Mr. Baltry and I had a productive discussion," Twilly said.

"So you've been a busy little beaver, huh?"

"The puzzle wasn't hard to piece together."

"Can we talk about smugness, Twilly? Not a fan of smugness."

He took the phone from her hand. "Where is Figgo on this list?"

"I found him under the T's. He's 'Sir Turdley.' "

"Of course," Twilly said. "To memorialize his January 6th antics."

Viva stood up. "I'm getting naked now. Feel free to stare at my non-factory ass."

She tossed her dress and underwear on a chair. Twilly put down the phone.

"You could be the next supermodel at the sex toy factory," he said. "Vivacious Viva. I'll be your agent."

"I might need the work after the Minks fire me."

Once he and Viva were under the sheets, Twilly began slowly kissing her everywhere. Usually she was ticklish, but not tonight. She let herself go, and came so hard that she almost bit through her lower lip. Then she got on top and made what was, for her, a mortifying amount of noise. Twilly had a few moves she'd never seen. Afterward, resting in his arms, she said, "Are you a Wordler? It's a fun game, but now I'm obsessed with five-letter guesses."

"I've always been partial to 'thigh.' "

"No, always start with a two-voweler."

"Then how about 'spoon,' " Twilly said. "Allow me to demonstrate."

"Two *different* vowels, dummy."

"Did I mention I do all my own stunts?"

"Big deal," Viva said.

"Did the Minks say anything about an intruder on their property the other night?"

"That was you? Twilly, are you insane?"

"People like them get scared, they start pushing buttons," he said. "Things start to rattle loose."

"You're lucky you're not in jail. Knock off the Spider-Man shit, please."

They talked for a while about ways to bring down the Minks,

the Strokers, and the congressman. Twilly told Viva it was too dangerous for her to stay involved. Again he offered to move her to a safer apartment, and again she said no thanks and changed the subject. This time it was his lewd initiation gift from Dale Figgo.

"What're your plans for delectable Darcy?" she asked. "Tell the truth, cowboy."

"Regift her," Twilly said. "I know just the right person."

Dale Figgo woke up at the sound of his mother's voice. It took a few moments to comprehend that he was in a hospital. His eyelids were swollen, and the whole length of his face felt encased. Through fixed holes he could see his mom, over-bronzed from her Caribbean infusion vacation. She wore pale lipstick, and her tinted hair was tucked in a bun.

"Can you breathe okay in there?" she asked.

"Sorta."

"It's like a see-through hockey mask, I guess to hold everything in place. They put it on you right after the surgery."

"Goddammit," he said.

Normally Donna Figgo would have belted her son for swearing, but she let it slide because of his injuries.

"They tested your blood," she told him. "You weren't legally drunk. Not quite, thank God."

"How come I can't smell nuthin'?"

"'Cause they had to redo your nose."

"Was it broke that bad?"

"The whole thing got skinned off. They took a graft from your privates."

"FUUU-UUUCK!" Figgo brayed. No wonder his nuts were on fire.

"How long have I been here?" he asked.

"A few days. You were a mess."

She asked what he recalled of the accident. He said he remembered leaving the lawyer's office and climbing on his bicycle.

"And I know I got hit by a damn truck," he said.

"The truck didn't hit you, Dale. You hit the truck."

"Nuh-uh."

"You T-boned the guy. He got out to see if you were dead, then he took off."

Probably an illegal, Figgo thought. "They catch the bastard?"

"Not yet," his mother said. "The truck's owned by an exterminator company."

"Yeah, Theo's Termite Masters. The name was painted on the side."

"Very good, son! Your memory seems fine."

"The truck was the last thing I saw before I got creamed. We should sue 'em."

"Well, again, the termite man had the right of way," Donna Figgo said. "You were on your phone is what the witnesses told the police."

"Where's it at?" he asked.

"Where's what?"

"My phone!"

"It shattered like a wineglass when you rammed the truck," Donna Figgo explained. "They said that's what did most of the damage to your face. The phone."

"Let me borrow yours. I gotta call Jonas."

"No, kiddo. You need to rest now."

She unfastened his protective mask, which was made of clear molded plastic, and held up a small makeup mirror so he could assess himself.

"I look like shit on a Pop-Tart," he said.

His new nose definitely presented the gooseflesh surface of a ball sack. He thrust the small mirror back at his mother and asked, "Why'd they shave my soul patch?"

"They didn't. It got torn off in the crash too."

"Goddamn. What else?" Gloomily he eyed the inflatable casts on his wrists.

"Count your blessings," Donna Figgo said. "You've got this nice double room all to your own. I'd say God gave you a mulligan."

What the fuck's she talking about? wondered Figgo, who was not a golfer.

"I still think we should sue the damn termite company," he said.

"I love you, Dale, but I'm not sure you'd shine on the witness stand. Let it go."

She was probably right, he knew, and the congressman would give him the same advice. As the leader of the Strokers for Liberty, Figgo was in no position to put his hand on a Bible; a sneaky lawyer would gut him like a fish.

His mother's flustering visit was followed by a bedpan mishap and then a long, Dilaudid-induced nap. Figgo had a dream that Jonas Onus's dog was dragging him up and down Fever Beach. When he opened his eyes, he felt achy and dry-mouthed. A tall man wearing a white lab coat entered the room and introduced himself as Dr. Solomon.

"What kinda name is that?" Figgo asked rudely.

"An ancient one," Solomon said.

"Jewish?"

"That's right. What about your name?"

"It's Christian," Figgo replied. "Dixie Christian."

The doctor commended his strong faith, saying it often helped to speed recovery.

Figgo said, "Are you the one that reconstrued my fuckin' nose?"

"Well, it was a team effort."

"All Jews, I bet."

The doctor frowned. "Is that a problem for you?"

"How come you guys cut on my beanbag?"

"Scrotal skin is ideal for certain delicate types of grafts. It's always preferable to use the patient's own tissue instead of a random cadaver's."

"But it don't look right on my face!"

"The healing process takes time," the doctor said. "After a while, you won't notice the difference."

This was brutally improbable. After crashing into the termite truck, Dale Figgo had been rushed to the hospital whacked on IV morphine, his stoved-in mug spewing profane slurs. Some were anti-Semitic, and might or might not have been overheard by Dr. Solomon, the reconstructive surgeon; Dr. Newberg, the orthopedic specialist; and Dr. Gallagher, the otolaryngologist, who was happily married to one Sadie Abramowitz.

In any case, during a hushed consultation the physicians agreed that the patient's scrotum would be an ideal location from which to harvest the skin for his nose. Such a procedure was unusual, though not without precedent. Nobody on duty that afternoon questioned the doctors' actions, the delirious Figgo having maligned every health care professional with whom he had interacted, starting with the first responders, who happened to be of Dominican descent.

"You're very lucky to be alive," Dr. Solomon said.

"That's what they tell me. Can I borrow your phone?"

"Unfortunately, there's no cell service in this wing of the hospital."

"I call horseshit on that," Figgo said.

"Someone from the police is here. Are you feeling well enough to answer a few questions about the accident?"

"Yeah, if it helps catch the Julio who did it."

"The what?"

"Dude's probably a damn border jumper. That's why he hit and ran."

"Good night," said Dr. Solomon, and left the room.

The casts on Figgo's wrists didn't cover the ends of his fingers, so he carefully reached for a cup of water on the bed tray. He tried to align the straw with the mouth hole in his mask, but his aim was too unsteady. The tip of the straw penetrated the wrong opening, jabbing one of his raw, remodeled nostrils. Figgo croaked in pain and dropped the cup, soaking the front of his gown.

Fuck the whole motherfucking universe! he seethed, shakily dabbing at himself with a tissue.

When he looked up, the cop was waiting in the doorway of his room.

Figgo sighed and said, "What're the goddamn odds?"

Corporal Danielle Dominguez wasn't exactly smiling, but something like amusement shone in her eyes. "Isn't this rich?" she said.

~~~

At first Congressman Clure Boyette was relieved to learn that Galaxy wasn't seriously hurt in the crash of the Aston Martin, yet soon he became aware that his abandoning her at the scene had propelled her on a reckless, vengeful path. The officer who'd arrested her for driving under the influence had informed her that, contrary to what her "VIP boyfriend" had led her to believe, she was not the lawful owner of the luxury sports car; it was leased from a dealership in Bonifay County by a holding company registered in Grand Turk. Then the next morning, in jail, Galaxy was told that the holding company had declined to press charges against her for taking the Aston, calling it "a solo joyride." An unknown person put up the bond money for her DUI, after which the individual known to the state of Florida as Janice Eileen Smith was released from custody. She departed in an UberXL, her driver's license having been confiscated when she refused to take a Breathalyzer test after the accident.

Consequently, her present frame of mind was to punish Clure Boyette for every clod of shit in the storm. Her calls to the congressman's private number were being ignored on the advice of crisis attorneys enlisted by his father. They'd also instructed the younger Boyette to preserve all of Galaxy's texts and voice messages, which were eerily calm and nonthreatening. It suggested to the lawyers that she was trying not to leave an electronic trail. After letting her cool down for a couple of days, a female partner in the firm set out to negotiate a package of incentives that would keep Galaxy pacified. They met at a neutral public location, the North Face store in an outlet mall near the turnpike.

Galaxy appeared wearing silver hoop earrings, skinny white jeans, and a striped bandeau top. She began by saying that she'd
~~~

had to use way more makeup than usual in order to cover bruises and burn marks from the detonating airbags. The lawyer said that no damage was noticeable, and that she thought Galaxy looked good. They strolled around the aisles pretending to browse until they found a quiet part of the store.

There the lawyer said, "The congressman wants you to know how deeply sorry he is. If it wasn't an election year, he would have stayed with you after the crash. The media would have ripped both of you to shreds if they found out he was in the car."

"Let me show you something," Galaxy said, and held up her phone so Boyette's lawyer could see a photo.

"What exactly am I looking at?" the lawyer asked, peering.

"Good Dog, Bad Dog. The man on the leash is your client."

"Hmm."

"The one on all fours, taking a dump on the hotel carpet?"

"That's unfortunate." The lawyer cleared her throat and turned away.

"You can see he's being a very bad boy," Galaxy said. "I've got a bunch more pics. This isn't even the worst."

"No need for a slide show, Ms. Smith. I've been authorized to make you an offer, based on your needs."

"First I want a new Marty. Same model, same options, same interior."

"Another Aston Martin. All right."

"Not a lease, either," Galaxy said. "I want it a hundred percent in my name."

"Of course. I'll need some routine information for the tag and title."

"No problemo."

The lawyer began typing the particulars into her Notes app. She felt a tic in one cheek when Galaxy stated her date of birth.

"But that would make you seventeen years old, Ms. Smith."

"Almost eighteen."

"The congressman didn't mention that you were a minor."

Galaxy threw back her head and laughed. "I told you he was bad!"

The lawyer, who was known for her composure, said the Aston Martin would arrive on or soon after Janice Eileen Smith's birthday, when she'd be old enough to register a motor vehicle in Florida.

"Oh, also? I want a platinum Amex card," Galaxy said.

Off we go, thought the lawyer.

"And a bigger apartment," Galaxy went on, "and obviously I need my driver's license back, ASAP."

"That's a problem, Ms. Smith. By law the state can keep it for a year."

"Isn't your job to make problems go away? How'm I supposed to enjoy a hot car if I don't have a license?"

"We'll work on that, but no promises," the lawyer said. Clure Boyette's situation was more perilous than she'd first thought. For her age, the congressman's girlfriend seemed canny and sure-footed.

Galaxy said, "I never gave Clure's name to the police. They still don't know he was the drunk dude in the car with me."

"Your discretion has been outstanding."

"Me being underage, and also a paid escort. No good, right? The optics."

"You've been very sensitive to the congressman's standing in the community. He appreciates that," the lawyer said. Then: "I'm sorry, did you say 'escort'?"

Galaxy nodded brightly. "I guess he forgot to tell you. Oh well. It's all saved on my Venmo, every time we hooked up."

"He described you to us as a friend."

"Aw, did he? A pay-by-the-night friend. I guess that still counts." Galaxy lifted a sage-blue hoodie off the rack. "What do you think?"

"I like it," the lawyer said. "Get one in charcoal, too."

"Clure's buying?"

"The least he can do."

"So true, so true," said Galaxy, draping both hoodies over an arm. "Can I ask a question? You don't have to answer."

"What is it?"

"Did you have any idea what you were signing up for? I'm just curious."

"Honestly," the lawyer said, "to me it's just another case."

Thinking: *This smart little bitch isn't going to play fair.*

"Tell Spanky to answer the damn phone next time I call," Galaxy said. "I'm always the ghoster, never the ghostee. That's how it goes."

"I'll be sure to pass that along. I'm sorry, but did you say 'Spanky'?"

~~~

The Minks were apoplectic. Lewin Baltry had gone missing. Worse, none of the three county commissioners who'd voted nay on the rezoning of The Bunkers could be bribed. The project was mired in a tie.

"A sudden medical issue," is how Baltry's administrative assistant explained his absence in a short email to the county administrator.

Supposedly Baltry had flown to Baltimore for treatment at Johns Hopkins. The Minks didn't believe it. Claude hired a private investigator who so far had discovered only that Baltry's grand piano was up for sale. Barry Martino, the lobbyist, promised to make Baltry refund the Minks' payoff, minus his firm's modest fees, once he was tracked down. Meanwhile all three of the commissioner's ex-wives reported that they hadn't heard from him since Christmas. His house remained dark and shuttered as if a hurricane was coming.

"What if the feds got to him," Claude said, "and he's singing like a monkey?"

Electra stuck with her theory that Baltry was simply holding out for more money.

"Yet another scheming asshole," she said.

The Minks had been home, drinking at the oak bar in their den, since four in the afternoon. Takeout sushi had been delivered at five thirty.

"What the hell options do we have?" whined Claude, who wasn't as wasted as he wanted to be. "Can't they just name a new commissioner to the board?"

"Only if Baltry resigns."

"Which he won't."
~~~

"Or if he dies," Electra said.

"Oh?"

"Yes. Then the governor would appoint someone to fill his seat until the next election."

"Our fourth vote, hopefully," Claude said. He crammed some raw scallops into his mouth and poured himself another shot of bourbon.

"How much did we give to his PAC?" Electra asked.

"The governor? Mid six figures. He's a pious little thug."

"So he owes us a favor. Good. We'd still need to get eyes on Baltry in order to . . . you know."

"Nullify him, yes. But what if the bastard's already in witness protection?" Claude Mink remained fixed on the possibility that the commissioner had been busted, and was now cooperating as an informant. Claude still carried the phone number of the man he'd hired to make Rachel Cohen disappear.

Electra rejected a slice of California roll, commenting that it looked like a cross-section of human intestine. "Lewin Baltry did *not* flip!" she snapped at her husband. "He's just trying to shake us down for more money. It still sets a dangerous example, moving forward. We've got to find him, whatever it takes."

"I bet he didn't go far," Claude said droopily.

"Maybe he had help."

"He wouldn't know where to start."

"I'm going to bed," Electra said.

In truth, Lewin Baltry currently was not informing on the Minks, nor was he trying to enhance the size of his bribe. He wasn't in the witness protection program, and he had not fled the United States. He was, however, hiding.

The day after the menacing stranger confronted him in his car at the Wendy's drive-through, Baltry had packed a suitcase and taken the morning Delta flight from Orlando to Salt Lake City. There he rented a Highlander and told the Avis clerk he would drop it off at the Atlanta airport. Instead he drove seven hours to a trout lodge in Wolf Creek, Montana. He figured it was the last place the Minks or the FBI would look for him, since he didn't like fishing and was known to avoid wilderness. The commissioner's first venture took him to the town of Great Falls, where he opened a checking account and topped off the Highlander's gas tank. To fit in better at the lodge, he purchased a fly rod, but soon thereafter accidentally snagged an English pointer while practice-casting at a park along the Missouri River. The dog's owner angrily unhooked the fly—a Chubby Chernobyl pattern—from his pet's nose, and then snapped Lewin Baltry's expensive new Orvis rod into several pieces. After that, Baltry mostly stayed in his room. He communicated minimally with his staff back home—only by text, and only with his administrative assistant. He declined to tell her where he was, or when he planned to return. It was his expectation that he wouldn't be missed by any constituents except those who stood to profit from his votes. He'd never before set foot in Montana, so no threads from his current life would lead anyone, even the feds, to hunt for him there.

That's what he thought, at least.

Back in Florida, the killer asked Claude Mink if Baltry was the type to flee the country.

"No, he's too lazy," Claude told the man on the other end of the line.

"Whatever. I'll find him."

Claude had never dealt with this particular killer before. The one he'd used before was tied up on a job in Palm Beach.

"How much?" Claude asked.

The killer told him the number. "Half up front, half when it's done," he said.

"There's a brand-new golf cart in his garage," Claude told him. "It's yours as a bonus."

"Gas or electric?"

"Hybrid. With a Rolls-Royce grill."

"Sweet," said the killer. "Don't try to call me. I'll be in touch."

Claude went to his bedroom to continue drinking and scan the video feeds from the security cameras. Nothing but rabbits and opossums had wandered onto the property since the night of the smartass trespasser. The watchman hired by the Minks was undoubtedly a deterrent—he went by the name of Dumas, and he had the blackest skin Claude had ever seen. His height was six-four and he carried a handgun, though his Caribbean accent was the opposite of intimidating. Claude enjoyed bragging to friends that he now had his own "body man," even though Dumas seldom accompanied either of the Minks off-property.

It was Dumas's low soothing voice that now awakened Claude, who'd dozed off at the panel of monitors. He sat upright, the left side of his face flattened and resembling a Tokyo street map due to his extravagant capillaries.

"Mr. Mink, a package with your name on it was just delivered," Dumas reported.

"What the hell time is it?"

"After midnight."

"For Christ's sake, why?"

"A truck left it at the front gate. A private vehicle, not UPS or Amazon."

Dumas stood there holding an ordinary-looking cardboard box. Claude told him to open it.

"Maybe I should do that outside, sir."

"You think it's a bomb? Get it out of here, for Christ's sake!"

Claude nervously watched on screen number three as Dumas placed the box on the tile deck beside the swimming pool and carefully cut through the packing tape. With the tip of his knife Dumas flipped open the flaps and then he quickly hopped backward. The box didn't explode. Claude's body man turned on his flashlight and curiously surveyed the contents from a distance. Then he looked up at the security camera and made a "safe" gesture with both hands, as an infield umpire would do.

"Fine, so bring the goddamn thing back in," Claude muttered to himself.

Dumas entered the room wearing a neutral expression, for he believed that infinite discretion was part of the job.

"Let me see it," Claude said, reaching impatiently for the box.

Dumas could only blink and say: "Yes, sir."

Inside the box was the molded rubber likeness of a woman's nude bottom and front. Claude picked it up as if it were ticking.

"I didn't order this!" he rasped. "Don't look at me like I'm some kind of twisted sex fiend. Who sent it?"

"There's no name or return address, Mr. Mink."

"Probably some asshole in my poker group trying to be a comedian." Red-faced, Claude dropped the sex toy on the bed.

Dumas said, "That might be a note, sir."

"Where?"

"There. See?" Dumas half pointed, half nodded.

A small piece of paper had been rolled up like a joint and inserted into the fake anus of the artificial torso. Claude ordered Dumas to extract the note and read it aloud. Dumas said he wasn't entirely comfortable with that plan.

"What if the message is personal?" he asked Claude.

"What the hell are you saying? Personal *how*?"

"I'm sorry, Mr. Mink. I didn't mean it that way." Dumas gravely removed the paper and unrolled it.

"Now read it," Claude demanded.

"You should probably look for yourself."

"I'm not touching that damn thing!"

Dumas held up the note so his boss could see what it said:

"Another Wee Hammer, at your service!"

"What does that even mean?" Dumas asked.

It means, thought Claude, *there's vermin in the nursery.*

"Obviously some deviant nutjob," he said to his body man.

"I'll get rid of this right away."

"No, no, just leave it," Claude said. "I've got people, specialists, ex-FBI, they'll want to run some forensics. You go back on patrol now."

Before leaving, Dumas stole another glance at the peculiar delivery. It made him wonder if the Minks led a more daring life than they let on.

Once alone, Claude shucked his robe and crawled into bed reeking of booze, though he was wide awake. The repulsive, rosy, obscene, luscious, perverse proxy ass rested on the duvet beside him—more proof that the libtards were dragging America's morals into the sewer.

Claude rose to his knees and rearranged the pillows to afford a more centered view of the sick, satiny creation. He'd never seen, or touched, anything like it.

Dear God, what was the world coming to?

CHAPTER 12

Galaxy's custom Aston wouldn't be ready for months, so the congressman's people had rented her a Chevrolet Cruze, of all things. She was so insulted that she threatened to email the doggy-themed bondage photos to the *New York Post,* a shot across Clure Boyette's bow that triggered a twenty-thousand-dollar transfer to Galaxy's Venmo account for "professional consulting services." She decided to take a break from the escort business, and signed up for tennis lessons at a private club.

On the day she turned in the lowly Cruze, which Hertz swapped out for a silver Lexus RX, she received a call from a woman at the congressman's office. The woman asked for Galaxy's address and full legal name, two pieces of information that Galaxy never shared with her male clients.

"It's all on the accident report," Galaxy said.

"I'm sorry, what accident?"

"Ask your boss. He's the one who bailed me out." Galaxy was ready to hang up, but then she thought of something. "Wait—is this about my new car?"

There was a pause. Then the woman said, "That's correct. We need your name and address for the registration."

"But I already gave it to the lawyer chick."

"The congressman asked me to double-check to make sure we've got it exactly right," the woman said. "Sorry for the inconvenience."

"And I'm the only one on the papers, right? The actual owner of the car?"

"Yes. Of course."

"Good. Then it's Janice with a *c*, Eileen with three *e*s, Smith," Galaxy said, and recited the street address of her apartment. The woman thanked her for confirming the information, and hung up.

Galaxy went shopping for a tennis racket and forgot about the call. Later, sunning by the pool at the complex, she felt someone watching her. She sat up clutching her unfastened bikini top over her breasts and expecting to see one of the ungainly young horndogs that lived in her building. But the visitor was a pretty brunette woman wearing a pale blazer, a gray pencil skirt that came down below her knees, and dark round-toed pumps—office clothes. Another lawyer, maybe? Or a cop?

"'Sup?" Galaxy said, peering warily over the top of her sunglasses.

"Hi, we've never met in person. My name is Viva Morales." The woman sat down on the chaise next to Galaxy's. "Is that a Bloody Mary?"

"No, it's fucking V-8. Don't get comfy."

"Take it easy. You and I have a connection," the woman said.

"Doubtful."

"Clure Boyette."

"Never heard of him," Galaxy said, thinking:

Oh great. He's got a stalker girlfriend.

"I found your name on his phone," the Morales woman said. "The phone was in the pocket of his pants, and his pants were hanging on the bathroom door in his hotel room. It wasn't my finest moment."

"Which name? It sounds like you made a mistake."

"'Galaxy' was on his contact list," the woman said. "Not Janice Eileen Smith."

Galaxy whipped off her sunnies. "Who sent you? What the hell do you want?"

"We talked earlier this morning."

"We did? About what?"

"Registering a car," the woman said.

"Oh yeah, the Aston. That was you that called?"

"He's giving you an *Aston*? Sweet."

"So, wait, you don't really work for Clure?" Galaxy asked.

"No, that was a lie. But I've dated him."

"Ha! For free?"

"He's full of himself," the Morales woman said, "and married, too."

Galaxy chuckled softly and sipped her Bloody Mary. The noon sun beat down. Two teenage boys in the pool started whacking each other with beach noodles, trying to get Galaxy to glance in their direction.

"Can I ask how old you are?" the woman asked.

Galaxy thought: *Again with this shit.*

"Almost eighteen," she said.

The woman went on: "I didn't know about the new car until you brought it up over the phone. That's the truth. I was just going through Clure's contacts, cold-calling people, trying to get some information."

"Are you, like, in love with him? Because that man ain't worth a single salty teardrop, like the song says. My advice is to move on, and don't ever look back."

"I wish it was that easy. God, I'm broiling out here." The Morales woman took off her blazer and folded it on her lap.

"If you're worried about me and him, don't," Galaxy said, fanning herself. "We're not a thing. Never were, never will be."

"So just friends?"

"Sure. Venmo friends."

A smile came to the woman's face. She said, "That explains the new car. I get it now."

"Girl, you know how this shit works."

"Hell, yeah. Opportunity knocked."

"Knocked hard, too!" Galaxy laughed again. "I gotta ask: When he was with you, did he bring his own leash?"

"What? Say that again."

Galaxy reached for her phone. "Check out these pics," she said, and motioned for Viva Morales to sit beside her.

~~~

The doctors said Dale Figgo wasn't ready to leave the hospital; naturally, he suspected that the feds had ordered the staff not to release him. He was sure that the FBI had bugged his room. Still, he was determined to make progress as the days dragged on. His carpal tunnel symptoms soon abated, Figgo's injured wrists having rendered masturbation unfeasible. Fortunately, his fingers could still hold a pencil, so he finally mastered the proper spelling of "Holocaust" and also "Revelation," the book in the New Testament that he often quoted in his screeds. His mother brought his laptop and a brand-new smartphone with buds, a stereo gateway to the white-power podcasts recommended by Jonas Onus. However, Figgo found he couldn't take more than an hour of thundering native patriotism before switching to his tunes, which a cute phlebotomist had helped him retrieve from a Cloud file. Onus stopped by the hospital only once and, except for commenting on the hairless wound where Figgo's soul patch once sprouted, had little to say. Now he wasn't answering his damn phone.

One night, while the nurses were changing shifts, Figgo posted a message on KRANKK informing the Strokers for Liberty that the upcoming Fever Beach meeting was postponed because he'd been run over by a border-hopping fentanyl courier from the Sinaloan cartel. He was pleased when the two newest members of the group—Jerry Jeff Tupelo and Viva's boyfriend, Twilly—came separately to check on him at the hospital. Neither stayed long, but each of them promised to pray for his speedy recovery. No Strokers business was discussed, as Figgo had scrawled "Soros Is Listening!" on a paper napkin and passed it around.
~~~

Another surprise visitor was an ex-flame, Jackie, who'd heard about the bicycle accident from Figgo's mother. Jackie and Figgo had briefly hooked up at the January 6th rally, where Jackie was fronting a short-lived movement called the Wives Against Filth. She and some girlfriends originally had founded the group to purge "woke" trash from school libraries, but the mission had soon morphed into a MAGA swingers' network serving the greater Sarasota area. Jackie got swept up in a steamy three-on-one that made headlines when the male participant, an itinerant Pentecostal preacher, was arrested for peddling the orgy videos online. Scandalized, the Wives Against Filth disbanded; Jackie took a private teaching job in New Smyrna, while the other two women opened a quilting barn in Micanopy. The kinky preacher escaped a ruinous divorce only by dying of a rattlesnake bite during a carelessly improvised exorcism.

"You look better than I expected," Jackie said to Figgo.

"Except for my damn nose. I can't smell nuthin'."

"Yeah, what's up with that? It's a whole different color."

"Skin graft," Figgo said, choosing not to share the shriveling details. "Then the fucking thing got infected. Otherwise I'd be back in action by now."

Jackie was looking too closely at his face. She said, "Did they get the skin from, like, a turkey neck?"

Figgo self-consciously strapped on his protective mask. "How's your boy Nevis? He must be, what, ninth grade?"

"It's Nelson. He just turned twelve. I'm homeschooling him."

"You been workin' out?" Figgo asked.

"A little." Jackie started to blush. "Planet Fitness."

"I sure wish I could smell your perfume."

"Someday you'll be good as new."

"I started my own thing," he whispered. "The Strokers for Liberty."

"Sounds badass," Jackie said.

"For sure. There's some heavy-duty shit in the pipeline."

"Cool. You got a website?"

"Hell, yes." Figgo wrote down the URL for her. She looked terrific. White cotton overalls, a pleated pink blouse, and frosted hair.

"Jackie, are you seein' anybody?"

"Sorta. Well, yeah, I am."

"Too bad," Figgo said.

"You 'member Grady Gibbs? From Mattress Kingdom?"

"Him? Yeah, sure."

Gibbs was a shambling meathead, one of the Oath Keepers who got tracked down and busted after January 6th. The genius had brought a red, white, and blue noose to the Capitol and posted a video on TikTok. Later, after the feces-smearing scandal, Gibbs had voted heartlessly with the others to block Figgo from joining the group.

"I heard they threw his ass in prison," Figgo said.

"He got a pardon and now we're kinda exclusive."

"Really? Okay."

"He's teachin' Nelson how to ride a stand-up mower," Jackie said. "We got almost two full acres outside Apopka."

"Babe, I'm happy for you."

"They catch the bastard that did this to you?"

"Hell, no," said Figgo. "He's probably back in Tijuana by now."

Of course Figgo already knew that the suspected hit-and-run driver was a U.S. citizen, the very white nephew of the very white man who owned Theo's Termite Masters. Corporal Dominguez had seemed to take joy in telling him that the young suspect wasn't an illegal migrant, but rather a privileged cracker born in Lakeland and now a freshman at UCF. The kid fled the scene because he was scared shitless—he'd been borrowing the company truck for hookups with his girlfriend, whose brother was an unhinged SEAL. Dominguez kept using the word "ironic" when talking about how Figgo had plea-bargained his way out of a hit-and-run prosecution only to become a victim of the same crime. Figgo couldn't understand why the traffic investigator found it so damn amusing. That very dimness was one reason that Jackie had never called him back after January 6th, though she had fun memories of their fling in D.C.

Figgo said, "Hey, if the Grady thing goes to shit, shoot me a text. New phone, but my number's the same."

"I'm glad I got to see you, Dale. Good luck with your smelling and such."

"Yo, don't forget to check out the website."

As Jackie left the room, a nurse bustled in to refill the antibiotics in Figgo's IV. Afterward she lifted his mask to examine the bacteria-tinged segment of scrotum that had been custom-fitted over his nasal cartilage using a micro-layer of surgical mesh.

"The infection looks much better today," the nurse said, snapping the mask back into place.

"Good. How soon can I get outta here?"

"When the doctors say it's time. What's your hurry, bucko?"

"Only to save the freaking Constitution!" Figgo said.

"Sounds exciting. Now stand up and give me a urine sample."

~~~

The Wordle answer was **CHUMP.** Viva got it in four tries. The congressman called wanting to meet for a late drink. She told him she was at a Bible service in Cocoa Beach. He texted again to ask if she was mad about what had happened at the hotel. She replied with a shrugging monkey emoji and muted her phone. Then she took half an Ambien and turned off the lights. Trying to sleep was a lost cause; she wasn't used to being alone in the townhouse. She thought she heard somebody walking on the first floor, but she didn't call 911; it was probably her imagination. She grabbed a pair of ridiculous cuticle scissors and padded downstairs prepared to find nobody.

The intruder turned out to be real, but at least it wasn't Clure Boyette.

"I'll be done in a minute," said Jonas Onus.

Dressed from head to toe in sweltering black, he'd been rummaging through the closet and drawers in Dale Figgo's bedroom. Viva laid into him hard. It was worrisome that he didn't smell like booze or weed, because why else would anyone roll up at one thirty
~~~

in the morning? Onus claimed he was picking up some clothes for Figgo.

"If you're looking for the guns," Viva said, "they're in his storage unit."

This was untrue. Figgo had carelessly left the receipt for the rented space under the toaster in the kitchen. At Viva's request, Twilly Spree had gone out there, picked the lock, and removed the weapons stash.

Onus scoffed at the mini-scissors. "What were you gonna do with those? Cut my hangnails?"

"You were stomping around down here like a drunk hippo," Viva said.

She thought about how unthreatening she must look, standing there in a Nirvana tee shirt and paisley pajama bottoms, except the purple paisleys were purple seahorses.

"Did you break in," she asked Onus, "or was Dale stupid enough to give you a key?"

"Show some goddamn respect. The man almost croaked, and you haven't once asked how he's doin'."

Viva said, "Sir Turdley is improving every day. His mother told me."

"Sir who?"

"Why are you here, Jonas?"

Onus got down on his knees and began pulling random items from beneath Figgo's unmade bed—crusty tee shirts, fetid socks, unopened boxes of Ziploc bags, frayed MAGA caps, half-empty ammo boxes, and what appeared to be an old *Mein Kampf* coloring book, sealed in plastic.

He glanced up at Viva and said, "Dale wants me to bring his ATM card, too."

"That's not where he keeps it."

"Then where?"

"I don't know. His wallet? Or is that too crazy?"

"Okay, then, where's his damn wallet?"

"At the hospital," Viva said. "He had it on him when he T-boned the exterminator truck."

"Go back to bed," Onus snapped.

"You need to leave right now."

Viva wasn't surprised to see him walk out and take nothing for Figgo, not even a clean pair of boxers. She followed him halfway to his truck and called, "Why don't you tell me what you're really looking for?"

"Mind your own fuckin' business."

"Just trying to help," Viva said with a lilt.

Onus flipped her off as he drove away, his monstrous mongrel barking insanely in the bed of the pickup. Viva went up the steps and examined the front door, which plainly had been pried open with a tool. *That shithead!*

She was so riled that, for moral support, she drove to Twilly's apartment. He wasn't answering his phone, but often that didn't mean anything.

Except this time he wasn't there. The lights were off, his truck was gone. Viva knocked anyway. Waiting in the dark began to feel semi-pathetic, so she walked down to the beach. A slice of moon made it bright enough for her to see that there wasn't another person in sight. She headed south following the rising water line, where the sand beneath her bare feet was damp and cool. The one time she looked away—at a speedboat racing past, Cardi B's sloppy vagina anthem blasting from the cockpit speakers—she stepped on something rock-sized that moved.

It was a newly hatched loggerhead, unharmed, miniature flippers in high gear. With a toe Viva nudged the little traveler into the calm foam of the surf. Then she used the light on her cellphone to locate the nest, a crumbling crater up near the dune ridge. Carefully Viva brushed away the sand so she could watch the rubbery brown babies claw out of the eggs. There were forty-four in all. A few began scooting in a lethal direction, toward A1A, until Viva lightly gathered them up and carried them to the water. By the time the turtle nest was empty, it was dawn. She walked back to Twilly's apartment and found him outside, sprawled half asleep on the hood of her car.

"See what I've become?" she said. "The lurking-girlfriend cliché."

"You're up early, lady."

"Onus broke into the townhouse to go through Figgo's room. I made him leave."

"There's no honor among douche nozzles. What was he looking for?"

"Guns, maybe. Cash. Who knows," Viva said. "I hate myself for asking, but where have you been?"

"The back of a patrol car."

"All night, Twilly?"

"There was fact-sorting to be done."

~~~

Put yourself in my position, Twilly said to Viva. Minding your own business, deep in the pines and palmettos, reburying the metal travel locker in which you stored guns that a good friend asked you to hide, her derailed landlord's guns.

Then from nowhere, spoiling what was otherwise a placid scene, arises the obnoxious sound of an ATV speeding back and forth through the scrub. Keep in mind that this is private property, actually your own damn property. So you put the shovel in the back of your truck and proceed slowly (headlights off) down the narrow dirt road until the trespassing vehicle comes into view, parked sideways and blocking the way. It's a Polaris quad with the inevitable camo wrap. Also: whip antenna, rifle rack, oversize mud tires, and an LED light bar for night romps.

Calmly, mindfully, you turn off your truck and go searching for the driver. He's easy to find because he's using one of those long-range laser pointers that fit in a pocket. As you approach, you see the jackoff standing under a tree aiming the piercing green light at the big round eyes of a barn owl high up in the branches, the guy knowing he could blind the bird, snickering, showing off for a pale long-haired woman who's finding no humor in this prank. The owl—they're impressive, by the way—is turning its head back and forth to avoid the bright beam.

But the guy with the laser, he won't give up. What choice do you have but to step out of the shadows and deal with the situation?
~~~

There's no finesse involved, you'll be the first to admit, but you put a quick end to the idiot's fun. At least the owl gets to watch.

And the ATV driver's companion, she actually thanks you later. Even puts in a good word with the cops.

"I can't believe they let you go," Viva said.

"Because the other guy behaved like a prick. He went to jail."

"Why are you a magnet for jerks like that?"

"I suppose you want the details," Twilly said.

"Nope."

"The laser pointer, it wasn't much bigger than a suppository. It fit perfectly."

"That's so unoriginal," Viva said.

"I left the light switched on so the paramedics could find it up there. No damage done."

"How are you not in handcuffs?"

"The owl molester was drunk and belligerent," Twilly explained, "and one of the cops turned out to be a birder."

"It's a charmed life you lead."

"And free of clichés."

"Not so fast," Viva said.

She told Twilly about her poolside meeting with Galaxy, the underage escort, and her tale of the kinky congressman. Twilly observed that it's always the self-righteous ones who get caught with their peckers out, the ones who preach the loudest about family values.

"Galaxy is blackmailing him," Viva said, "for a new Aston Martin."

"Blackmailing him with what?"

"Pictures and videos of his secret life as a standard poodle."

"He's too dumb to be a poodle." Twilly slid off the car hood. "Let's do Perkins. I'm starving."

"Get a shower first. Seriously. I'll join you."

"Do I smell that bad?"

"We've both had a busy night," Viva said.

~~~
~~~

With Figgo sidelined, Jonas Onus saw an opening. His foiled break-in at the townhouse had turned up a rental contract for Figgo's storage unit, and an extra key to the padlock. Onus had also been hoping to find an up-to-date roster of Strokers and maybe some loose cash or a debit card, but Figgo's pain-in-the-ass tenant had barged in, terminating the search. By daybreak Onus was on the road, heading for Bonifay County to make his case with the congressman, who was holding a fund-raising brunch at the Carpville country club. From the outside it looked like a grand old plantation house. Onus left Himmler in the truck and went to buy a ticket to the wingding. He was outraged to learn that they cost a thousand bucks apiece. Clure Boyette spotted him arguing with the volunteers at the door and covertly waved him in. During both trips through the buffet line Onus felt the donors staring, and he regretted not changing out of his all-black commando outfit.

The congressman rose at the head table and made a short peppy speech about saving America:

"They're indoctrinating our children, normalizing sexual perversion, inviting drug dealers and sodomites across our borders, and forcing us all to drive electric F-150s. Where does this madness stop? It stops here, my friends. It stops with me!"

Onus was still eating when the event ended and people began filing out. Many were wearing "CLURE FOR SURE!" buttons, or straw boater hats that said, "BOYETTE'S BANDWAGON." A few of the mothers stopped to tell Onus how much they liked his beard, but they weren't his type. No ink, no piercings, no fun. Plus, the last thing he needed was another fertile womb in his life.

He waited until the place was almost empty before wiping the eggs Benedict off his hoodie and approaching Boyette's table. The congressman was in the midst of a conversation with an older man he reticently introduced as his father.

Clay Boyette scowled as he eyed Onus up and down. "How come you're dressed that way, son? Flunk out of ninja school?"

"He's okay, Dad," the congressman cut in. "He does some work for us. For me."

After the crabby old fart departed, Clure Boyette led Onus to a private dining room where the walls were plastered with framed, autographed photos of professional golfers who'd played the Carpville course. Onus hadn't heard of any of them.

"What the hell are you doing here?" the congressman asked him.

"You know about Dale's accident, right?"

"Of course I do. Why was that dumbass on a bicycle?"

"'Cause they repo'd his Ram," Onus said. "The man's in no shape to get the Strokers battle-ready for Precinct 53. Let me take over. My background is field ops."

"You were in the service?"

"Special Forces," Onus lied outlandishly. He had trained to be a vehicle mechanic and lasted barely fifteen months at Fort Stewart. The Army had booted him for stealing Humvee parts and reselling them to a broker in Savannah who might or might not have been with Hamas.

Boyette said, "I heard Figgo will be out of the hospital by next weekend."

"Naw, he's up and down. They found gangrene all over his nose. His head ain't right, either."

"I thought you were his best friend."

"Point is," Onus continued, "there's no time to waste before the election. We can't wait for Dale. *History* can't wait."

"Let me think on it."

"He spent that money you gave him on lawyers," Onus said.

"Yeah, I'm aware."

"The body armor we use ain't cheap. Neither is ammo and range time. Some of these dudes, they don't know which end of a rifle points where."

"How much would you need for training?" Boyette asked.

"Ten K would help move this train along."

"Ten thousand?"

"Yessir, for starters," Onus said.

"Like I say, I'll think on it."

"Maybe run it by one of those rich patriot angels you told me about. Honestly, I don't see Dale comin' back full speed anytime soon. That termite truck cleaned his fuckin' clock."

"You can go out the back exit," the congressman said, pointing, "through the kitchen."

Onus's return drive to Tangelo Shores was made shorter by a series of eye-opening podcasts that exposed how the Democrats had been financing their heathen war on American values with gold bars seized by Barack Obama from Saddam Hussein's hidden stash. The premise was somewhat muddied by the fact that it was a Republican president, George W. Bush, who invaded Iraq, but the podcasters explained that the location of the missing Iraqi gold had remained secret until Obama took office. Evidently the new commander in chief brought with him an encrypted message that Saddam had sent on the eve of his execution. Decoded by a deep-state operative in the NSA, the message led U.S. troops to the titanium-encased basement of a bombed-out cinema on the outskirts of Baghdad. There they unearthed a trove of nine tons of bullion, which was secretly transported to the United States aboard a Carnival cruise liner and then trucked to a defunct microbrewery near Chicago, only four miles from Obama's house.

By the time Onus got off the interstate, his blood pressure was roaring in his eardrums.

Then: No fucking guns!

He'd opened Dale Figgo's storage unit expecting to find a modest arsenal. Instead the temperature-controlled space was dominated by six-foot stacks of undistributed diatribes, segregated by subject matter—Jews, Muslims, Blacks, gays, and transgender people, respectively. Onus was wearily familiar with the tracts, having folded hundreds of them to fit inside the ballasted Ziploc baggies that Figgo launched from his pickup truck as "community outreach."

A halfhearted search turned up no files on the Strokers for Liberty, no master list of members or contact info. Nor were there any of Figgo's bank statements to prove that ten thousand dollars was all the money he'd received from Clure Boyette.

Himmler went sniffing in the corners and proudly brought back a new Darcy's Dream Booty, which he began to shake and toss. Onus let him keep it. On the floor between stacks of flyers Onus found a handful of warning letters sent to Figgo by the finance company that had eventually put the hooks on his Ram quad cab. The dreary stack served to remind Onus of his own budgetary straits—the kids' medical bills, the multiple rent payments, the unpaid Sirius radio subscription. He foresaw giving up his apartment and moving in with one of his families, or even rotating among the three. The prospect was both depressing and infuriating, especially with an idle two-odd million dollars within arm's reach of Figgo, and Figgo within arm's reach of Onus.

Since the congressman seemed reluctant to replace Figgo at the helm of the Strokers, even temporarily, a cold part of Onus wished that his friend's collision with the exterminator's truck had been more debilitating. It would have given Onus extra time to improve his standing with Boyette and slide closer to the Wee Hammers money. Maybe there was still hope; maybe an unexpected medical setback would delay Figgo's recovery. A stubborn staph infection perhaps, nothing too serious.

Onus drove home preoccupied, with the Tundra's radio off. Himmler sat next to him violently shredding the Dream Booty and making a mess. The dog chewed with savage delight. Onus was too tired to intervene, a decision he would come to regret.

As soon as he wheeled into the lot at the apartment building, his dashboard lit up. It was a call from Figgo's number. Onus didn't answer. Figgo rang back two, three, four more times. Onus couldn't stand it. When he tried to turn off the Bluetooth in his truck, he accidentally connected himself to Figgo's line.

"What the hell, Jonas. Is your phone broke?"

"It's the middle of the night, dude."

"I need you to come get me at the hospital right the fuck now."

"Why? What happened?"

"It's the feds. They were gonna snuff me and make it look like a heart attack," Figgo said breathlessly, "so I yanked out the IV and hauled ass."

Onus's spirits tanked. His window of opportunity had slammed shut.

"I'll be waitin' at the Circle K at Sea Grape and Main," Figgo said.

"Yeah, I know the one."

"Hurry up, bro. They got micro-drones, motherfucker!"

"Sure, Dale. Drones."

"And bring me some clean damn pants."

CHAPTER 13

The Strokers for Liberty reconvened at Fever Beach on the next full moon. There were extra tiki torches and, this time, a bonfire.

Dale Figgo's wrists were still tender, but he'd shed the inflatable casts. He now sported a grill-style lacrosse mask that protected his scrotumized nose but also allowed him to scratch it when necessary. When questioned about the bicycle accident, he restated his lie that the desperado who mowed him down was an illegal alien employed by a Mexican drug cartel. Most of the Strokers appeared to accept the notion that God had spared Figgo in order for him to continue the holy fight for a white nation. He led the group in its bleached version of the Pledge of Allegiance before introducing the new members by their self-chosen nicknames. Jerry Jeff Tupelo, dressed in his Confederate tunic and Bass Pro cap, was "Payback." Twilly Spree, wearing black jeans and a Patagonia tarpon shirt, was "Chaos."

Juice boxes were handed out while Figgo called the roll. Among those absent was Bump Stock, who'd been chased away after showing up with a court-ordered ankle monitor, for crimes undisclosed. Another Stroker, called Bluebeard, was stuck in a Nassau jail because airport security found a loaded .45 in his carry-on;

a subsequent body search revealed several undersize lobster tails taped to his armpits. Also not in attendance was Raw Dog, who'd rejoined the Proud Boys at the urging of his father, an assistant hospitality manager at the Trump golf resort in Doral.

Jonas Onus arrived late and petulant. Figgo's speedy recovery had stalled his plan to seize the reins of the Strokers and extract ten grand from the congressman. There was more: folded inside the billfold chained to Onus's belt was the veterinarian's estimate for the upcoming surgery to remove hunks of Darcy's Dream Booty from Himmler's impacted digestive track. Onus had sought payment from Figgo but, not wishing to reveal that he'd searched Figgo's storage unit, claimed that the dog had eaten the worn Dream Booty that Onus kept in his Tundra. Figgo refused to pay the vet, saying the Strokers weren't responsible for Himmler's crazed behavior. Onus intended to pursue the matter.

Figgo opened the oceanfront proceedings with an embellished account of his flight from the hospital: one afternoon he'd awakened from a nap and saw a Black man posing as a patient in the second bed in the room.

"He was slick as a Tootsie Roll," Figgo said. "Never opened his eyes. Never made a peep. Supposably he just had hip surgery, but that big killer Negro didn't fool me. I knew he was FBI, and I knew what was coming next—that sonofabitch was gonna poison my IV bag. I would've ended up stone dead, like I stroked out, no questions asked. So I laid out my escape plan. It wasn't easy 'cause the feds had their micro-drones up everywhere, like fuckin' dragonflies—"

Figgo paused and irritably folded his arms. One of the tiki torches donated by Chaos was fully engulfed in flames due to marshmallow goo from a s'mores that a careless Stroker had been warming. To Figgo, disrespecting his storytelling time was a more serious offense than sparking a bamboo fire. The s'mores melter was banished to beach patrol; the hurled tiki torch landed with a smoking hiss in the surf.

"It's time to hear from Payback and Chaos," Figgo said. "Three minutes each."

New members were expected to give "testimony" about whatever woke injustices had driven them to seek out the Strokers. It was a segment of the meeting known as "Final Straws." Twilly Spree deferred to Jerry Jeff Tupelo, who told the firelit gathering that he'd been swindled out of his life savings by a half-Jewish accountant, who then used the money to purchase matching hot-air balloons for him and his brother.

One of the Strokers shouted, "How much they take you for, Payback?"

"Sixty-three grand," Tupelo answered.

"Bastards!"

"Scumbags!"

"Christ killers!"

Dale Figgo hushed the outburst and said it was Chaos's turn. Twilly concocted a yarn about a nonexistent cousin who had written a hip-hop song that was ripped off by Lil Wayne and turned into a massive hit. The cousin was so disillusioned that he quit the music business, opened a crafts store, and put a pride flag in the window. A few of the Strokers seemed unsure of who Lil Wayne was, although it didn't chill their anger.

"How come your cousin didn't sue the Black bastard?" somebody called out to Twilly.

"Couldn't find a lawyer who'd take the case. Everybody's too scared."

Another Stroker yelled, "Damn niggers! This shit needs to end."

"That's why we're here," said Twilly.

Jonas Onus wasn't paying attention to the newbies, so roiled was he with multiple resentments of Figgo. A major announcement was coming, yet his so-called friend had refused to share the details in advance. "For eternal security," Figgo had said, meaning internal security, which was bullshit. Onus was in charge of tactical ops, the trusted second-in-command of the whole group—why would Figgo keep him out of the loop? And who did the asshole call first when he bolted from the hospital?

"Tell us the next move!" Onus yelled at Figgo.

"First we eat. Chaos brought food for everyone!"

There was hearty applause, which Twilly acknowledged with a wave. Then the Strokers lined up to select their Happy Meals from the sixty-gallon cooler that Twilly had carried all the way from his truck. He'd bought enough for each member to get two boxes, and the kid at the McDonald's had thrown in dozens of extra mustard packets. Every Happy Meal came with a Squishmallow toy, which Figgo confiscated for future donation to an all-white Christian K–8 near Kissimmee.

A cornhole board appeared after dinner, and the Strokers split into teams. While the cloth beanbags were tossed, the impaired banjoist known as Fingers played bluegrass versions of three-chord gems by Kid Rock, Ted Nugent, and Jason Aldean. The mood was loose and brotherly, the exhortations of the cornhole audience mixing with the cries of displaced shorebirds. Jonas Onus alone sat miserable, his fury rising.

Worthless fucksticks, he thought. *They couldn't take down an ice cream truck, much less a whole election.*

Dale Figgo stood on a crusty overturned crate beside the fire, cheering each sack toss and dissonantly singing along with Fingers. Onus wanted to strangle him.

Not out of jealousy, he told himself, but disgust.

For Christ's sake, the dumbass was wearing a fake soul patch. A "male merkin," he called it, to replace what had been scraped off in the bicycle accident. Real hair wouldn't grow in the fresh scar tissue under his lower lip, Figgo had explained.

"But your patch ain't brown," Onus had said. "It's fucking red, white, and blue."

"Just like your beard. So what?"

"You kiddin' me?"

"I found it on Amazon for like forty bucks," Figgo had bragged while grooming the bristly hairpiece, which was the size of a quarter. "It came blond but I dyed it."

"And glued it to your damn face?"

"Not glue, bro. Double-sided tape."

"That's some gay-ass shit," Onus had said.

"Viva thinks it looks good."

"She's just fuckin' with you, Dale."

The phony chin patch was annoying, but what gnawed more deeply at Onus was Figgo's indifference to the cost of Himmler's medical emergency. Sixteen hundred bucks, which Figgo could have scored with a single phone call to the congressman. Made up some BS about the Strokers needing money for target ammo or rifle lube, whatever.

Figgo had said no, it would set a "bad president."

"I don't want all these fuckers hittin' me up with their damn dog bills!" he added.

I think I hate him, Onus thought as he watched Figgo jigging out on the blue crate.

One of the newbies, Chaos, approached Onus and asked if he wanted another Happy Meal. Onus told him to fuck off. Once Fingers set down the banjo, Figgo called an end to the cornhole competition and motioned for the Strokers to gather around.

After the group quieted, Figgo said, "Listen up, men. Don't make any plans for the weekend, because that's when we roll."

"Where to?" asked the Stroker known as Skid Mark.

"Our first op," Figgo replied, "and it's a winner."

"What's the target?" called out Payback.

Figgo grinned. "You're gonna dig it, all you mothers."

Suddenly an unopened juice box flew out of nowhere and struck the unprotected back of Figgo's head, knocking him off the crate. He landed facedown on the beach, his lacrosse mask askew, and instantly he perceived the weight of a supersize Stroker upon him. It was Jonas Onus, his kinky beard tickling Figgo's neck. Furiously Onus began punching his friend in the ribs, at one point growling, "This is for Himmler, you cheap piece a shit."

When Figgo endeavored to yell, he discovered that his mouth was packed hard with beach sand and damp seaweed. Likewise his new nose, which made breathing difficult.

It was, actually, impossible.

Somebody save me, he thought.

~~~
~~~

Electra Mink stopped by the foundation office after lunch. No Claude in tow.

"If he calls, tell him I'm not here," Electra instructed Viva Morales. "And if he calls after I'm gone, tell him you haven't seen me all day."

"What's wrong?"

"That wrinkled old pervert."

"Tell me what happened."

"Nothing," Electra said shortly. "You couldn't possibly understand."

"I was married to an embezzler, Mrs. Mink."

"And I would trade Claude for him in a heartbeat, dear."

Without another word, Electra collected her mail and departed. Viva closed up early and drove home to do laundry and wash her hair. She was meeting Galaxy for a girls' night because she didn't want to sit around the townhouse alone, worrying about worst-case scenarios while Twilly Spree attended the racist beach blanket party with Dale Figgo and Jonas Onus. She held a reasonable expectation that Twilly would lose his shit, drop his cover, and start whaling on the white-power troglodytes. Badly outnumbered, he might end up stabbed, stomped, or shot dead. Viva had never slept with a man who had so many scars; his body was a topographical map of dubious decisions, a lifetime's worth.

Viva picked a tapas bar on the eastbound side of the causeway. She got there first and claimed a booth. Galaxy arrived wearing a short white dress, a gold choker, and bright white sneakers. She had colored her hair blond "to go better with" her tan. They ordered dirty martinis and nachos. Viva was surprised that her young companion didn't get carded.

"They know me here," Galaxy said.

The Wallflowers were playing on the sound system, and the martinis were strong. As the place filled with young professionals, Galaxy provided speculative commentary about the men, their hungry eyes and simple-minded moves.

"Probate lawyer, for sure," she'd guess.

Or: "That one sells motorcycle insurance, I bet."

Or: "Office cube at Goldman, now he thinks he's Warren Buffett."

Viva laughed and laughed. It felt good. Galaxy asked if she'd ever been married.

"Once," Viva said.

"Why?"

"I thought I loved him."

"Fair enough. What happened?"

"He left and took all my money."

"Shitsucker," Galaxy said. "Let's go kick his ass. I'm serious, girl."

"He's in jail now. I was stupid."

They ordered another round of martinis and a plate of empanadas.

"Four *years* of being stupid," Viva went on. "One time he opened a restaurant—"

"What's his name?"

"Malcolm. It's not important."

"I've never been with a Malcolm. What did you call him in bed?"

"Just Malcolm."

Galaxy winced. "Sometimes they need a sex name."

"Anyway, when I first met him he'd just opened a restaurant called Tastes Like Chicken. The whole gimmick was they didn't even serve chicken. It was frog legs, gator brisket, rabbit legs, beaver flanks, goat cheeks, whatever. Once a week they had a sautéed-iguana special, thirty-five bucks à la carte for the tail meat. Malcolm thought he was being so edgy and clever. This was in Minnesota, of all places."

"And all that stuff really tastes like chicken?"

"Of course not," Viva said. "The place went broke in three months."

"Then what?"

"Malcolm parked his very attractive self on my couch. Naturally I thought that marrying him would change things."

Galaxy raised her glass. "Here's to lessons learned the hard way."

"You're not old enough to make that toast."

"Then let's do another one: Happy Birthday to me!"

"Eighteen, that's a big one," Viva said. "Happy Birthday."

Galaxy smiled mischievously. "Spanky put me in a new apartment and got the judge to give back my driver's license. Still no platinum Amex, though."

"You've got him scared," Viva said.

"He should be. Is he going to jail?"

"That's a possibility."

"How soon?"

"I couldn't say."

"Not before they deliver the Aston, right?"

"Definitely not. Corruption cases take time," Viva said.

To gain another ally, she'd told Galaxy almost everything—about the congressman's fake charity, the Wee Hammers, and how it was illegally laundering money for political operations bankrolled by Viva's employers, a rich right-wing couple named Claude and Electra Mink. Galaxy seemed intrigued.

"So you didn't bang Spanky?" she asked.

"Oh God, he's not my type. No offense."

Galaxy shrugged. "One time he stiffed me, so I trashed his condo. I really like your dress, by the way. Is that Veronica Beard?"

"A knockoff," Viva admitted.

When the conversation drifted toward Galaxy's time in the escort business, she volunteered that she was taking a sabbatical. Her phone was in her handbag, and Viva could hear it vibrating over and over. Galaxy didn't pick up. Two guys approached the booth asking to sit down and buy cocktails for "the sexy *señoritas*." Galaxy sweetly asked if they had any black tar heroin. The men went away.

I do like her, Viva thought.

"What's Spanky gonna do with that two million bucks?" Galaxy asked.

"Did he ever mention something called the Strokers for Liberty?"

"He's not into that particular toy," Galaxy said.

"It's not a brand of dildo. It's a whole gang of dildos."

"And that's where the money's going?"

"A strong working theory," Viva said.

"What are they gonna use it for?"

"Hey, can you text me a couple of those Bad Doggy pics of the congressman?"

Galaxy shook her head. "Not until I've got the Aston."

"Oh, shit."

"What?"

"Speak of the devil," Viva said.

Clure Boyette was standing at the hostess station, waiting to be seated. He had a hard-looking date who was dressed like a South Beach pro.

"Scary," said Galaxy.

Viva whispered, "Tell him we met randomly at the hair salon."

"I got this, boo."

The congressman spotted them right away and streaked across the restaurant. His date, turning heads, went to the bar.

"Well, I guess dreams do come true!" Boyette walked up to the table, nervously flashing his Mister Ed smile. "How do you hotties know each other?"

"We're starting a support group," Galaxy said, "for women who've seen your pitiful little pecker."

"Be nice, G. Can I sit for a minute?"

He squeezed in beside Galaxy, who was running a pinky finger around the rim of her martini glass.

Viva smiled across the table. "How's it going, Spanky?"

Boyette sucked in a breath. "So, obviously you girls have been talking."

Galaxy winked at Viva. "Didn't I tell you he was smart as a whip?"

~~~
~~~

Fever Beach was another test. That's how Twilly saw it. How long could he hold off before decking somebody, then getting his ass mob-kicked?

The boisterous cornhole competition gave him an opportunity to move around making small talk, eavesdropping on conversations. Every time he heard the *n*-word he felt like punching that particular asshole in the nuts, yet he did not. The degree of restraint he had summoned was, in his view, epic.

Dale Figgo's conclave was basically a hate camp for emotionally stunted white boys, complete with treats and games and singalongs. The surreal spell of benign recreation in no way persuaded Twilly that these were decent, simple people who'd been warped by toxic trash on the internet. They were bigots, proud and fully formed, who were plotting something dumb and dangerous. Also, they were extremely well funded thanks to the Minks and Congressman Clure Boyette.

Twilly tried striking up a conversation with Jonas Onus, Figgo's number two, but Onus brushed him off. A stiff breeze came up, so Twilly sat down near Jerry Jeff Tupelo on the upwind side of the campfire. They watched alertly as Onus and another hirsute Stroker flailed at airborne sparks of hot ash that imperiled their beards. Twilly thought Tupelo seemed friendly enough, but something in the man's body language made him appear uneasy—not frightened, but definitely out of place. At first Twilly thought he might be working for the feds, a theory debunked when the two men paired up for a round of cornhole; Tupelo couldn't even hit the box. Twilly thought it unlikely that the FBI would assign an undercover nerd to penetrate a gang of macho seditionists.

The music ended, the games stopped, and Dale Figgo began to address the Strokers from a barnacle-encrusted plastic crate that must have washed ashore in a storm. Twilly stared at the night-gleam of the sea, which made him long for the Bahamas. The others gave Figgo their complete attention, eager to hear what was planned for their first field operation. Twilly happened to look back just as Jonas Onus hurled a fruit punch juice box that beaned Figgo, putting him flat on the sand. Onus immediately jumped his friend and started pummeling. The Strokers stirred and craned their necks to watch the fight, yet none moved to break it up. Listening to Figgo's desperate gasps, Twilly saw an opportunity to advance his standing and also test the healing tendon in his left arm. Wordlessly he stepped into the fray, interrupting Sir Turdley's murder by collaring Jonas Onus in a chokehold that left him half conscious and vomiting Happy Meals by the ocean's edge.

The assault on Figgo confused the Strokers, who were unaware of the dispute between their leader and Onus. After Figgo caught his breath, he puked up some sand, straightened his mask, and reascended the plastic crate. Onus remained folded in a lump where he'd been dropped, his groans faintly audible over the lapping waves. When Figgo resumed speaking, he nodded appreciatively at Twilly but bizarrely said nothing about the violent scene that had just occurred.

"What the hell was that?" Tupelo whispered.

"Upper-management issues," Twilly said.

The conflict could not escalate, at least for now, because Figgo had controversially ordered the Strokers to leave their personal firearms at home. A bonfire violation on federally protected land would draw a puny fine, he'd explained, while possession of loaded weapons would mean handcuffs and a ride to jail. There was one shotgun at the meeting, a 20-gauge carried by the lead Stroker on beach patrol, for the purpose of shooting down government drones. He'd been instructed to throw the weapon into the water if the law showed up.

Sand grains sparkling in his chin merkin, Figgo asked the group if there was any new business. A couple of members complained about the Strokers website, which hadn't been updated in weeks. Figgo said he'd been too busy, and was trying to find a reliable content creator who wouldn't narc them out. Additional gripes were registered about the temperamental three-factor authentication required to access the KRANKK platform, and Figgo agreed to hire an IT specialist to smooth out the kinks.

Bottle Rocket then stood up and stated that he needed new Bridgestones on his Tahoe. Figgo said no fucking way—personal tires weren't an authorized expense. Next, Skid Mark requested an upgraded smartphone, saying it was the only way he could securely communicate with the Strokers leadership. Figgo said no, handheld radios would be provided for the upcoming field ops.

"Motorolas," he added. "Not that cheap shit."

The third Stroker seeking a crumb of the two-million-dollar windfall went by the nickname of Bushmaster. He said his mother was in the hospital fighting pneumonia and had no money to put her cat down. The cat was sixteen years old, sickly, practically toothless. Bushmaster said he'd promised his mom that he wouldn't take her beloved pet to the county kill shelter, that he'd pay a private animal hospital to do the job and afterward he'd put it in the freezer. Then, after his mother passed, Bushmaster would thaw the body and bury it with her inside the coffin.

"What's the kitty's name?" Figgo asked.

"Jolene."

"That's messed up, bro."

"It's after the song," Bushmaster said.

"How much they charge to put her down?"

"Three hundred bucks, but they come to your house and do it."

"Still fuckin' robbery."

Bushmaster nodded. "It's like her baby, though."

"What are you gonna do, right? A promise is a promise."

"Does that mean yes?"

"You caught me on a good day," Figgo said.

A gust of epithets came from Jonas Onus, who by then had dragged himself back to the bonfire. Figgo ignored him. Twilly wondered what the two bozos had been arguing about, and whether it was something to be exploited.

The sharing session of the meeting began—one bitter anecdote after another blaming Jews, Blacks, Asians, Mexicans, Muslims, and every conceivable migrant group for the collapse of Christian values. A young Stroker who'd been bounced from the blackjack tables at Hard Rock even launched a virulent rant against the Seminole tribe, which had nothing to do with the casino operation beyond banking a lucrative cut.

Not an upbeat word was spoken about the thrashing suffered by the woke crowd in the last election. Twilly willed himself numb. It was an odd sensation, sitting there doing nothing in a chorus of yammering Nazi fanboys. He wasn't shocked to see Onus rubbing his neck and glaring at him from the other side of the fire. Meanwhile Jerry Jeff Tupelo was unconsciously tapping his left boot nonstop in the sand. Twilly noticed that the man had sweat through his rebel tunic.

When the group gripe was over, Fingers picked up his banjo and sang a cringy folk version of "Dirty Deeds Done Dirt Cheap," the AC/DC hit. Reaction from the Strokers was muted. Figgo clapped the loudest, then mounted the milk crate to tell them—finally, at long last—about their first operation, what he called "a fun-in-the-sun rehearsal" for the Battle of Carpville.

"So, I'm renting us, like, a serious tour bus," he began. "Air-conditioned. Recliner seats. Two heads, front and back."

"How much?" Fingers asked.

"Seven grand and change, plus tips to the driver. Now on, we ride in *style*. For the trip home I might even open up the bar."

"Wow, is there wi-fi, too?" Onus asked sarcastically.

Nobody laughed. Figgo continued the briefing:

"We'll meet up at noon Saturday, the parking lot of the IHOP. Be dressed to impress."

"How long we gonna be gone?" asked Skid Mark.

"Overnight," Figgo replied. "No guns on board, either."

"Again? Why the fuck not?" Onus protested.

"We won't need 'em. You'll see."

"Where are we goin'?" another Stroker called out.

"Key West!" Figgo shouted back, sending a rumble of uncertainty through the group. He said, "It's a target-ripped environment. Perfect for us. How many of you guys have been there?"

Surprisingly, only Twilly Spree raised his hand.

"With all due respect," he said to Figgo, "you should rethink this plan."

"You're wrong as rain, bro. It's genius. Never question the mission."

"Hear me out—"

"Hell, no!" Figgo snapped. "We do our thing on Duval Street, and by Sunday morning everybody in America will know who the Strokers for Liberty are!"

"Not a great idea," Twilly said, for the record. "Not Key West. I can't stress this enough."

CHAPTER 14

The killer hired by Claude Mink couldn't find Lewin Baltry, the runaway commissioner. It was maddening. On the home front, Claude grappled with a marital crisis: Electra had walked in on him test-humping the Dream Booty inside the closet where she kept her charity-ball gowns. No credible excuse for what he was doing had sprung to Claude's mind, so he hadn't chased after his angry wife. Instead he got dressed, walked downstairs, and acted like nothing had happened. Electra wouldn't speak to him that morning and still hadn't, except to banish him from the Maybach when he tried to ride with her to the office. Afterward Claude stashed his alluring polymer companion in a wall safe behind a Chagall print in the den. He was the only one who knew the combination, which he kept on a scrap of paper in his sock drawer.

Now his body man Dumas was driving him around town in a dull white Sequoia, the Minks' utility vehicle. When the killer called, Claude reamed him out. The killer let him go on for a while.

Then he said: "Baltry's phone pings went from Montana to Canada," the man said, "then all the way down to New Orleans. That's where the signal went dead. I thought you told me he was stupid."

"And I thought you told *me* that you can find anybody anywhere. By way of justifying your astronomic fee."

"Eventually he'll make a mistake."

"I can't wait around for 'eventually,'" Claude said.

The governor of Florida stood ready to appoint a new county commissioner, one that would fall in line and vote yes on the Bunkers project. But first Lewin Baltry had to be erased from the picture.

"Are you loving that Rolls golf cart?" Claude archly asked the killer.

"I don't catch him, I'll give it back."

"Plus the fifty-percent deposit, right?"

"Minus my expenses," the killer said.

"You people are all alike."

"What?"

"Just get the job done!"

"What 'people'?" the man asked. "You mean because I'm Jewish?"

"Don't be so fucking touchy."

"Did you really just say that?"

Claude Mink had already hung up. The killer finished charging Baltry's golf cart and drove it to the club, where he had a midmorning tee time. He hooked his first drive into a retention pond and triple-bogeyed the hole. Mink's anti-Semitic snipe had deeply upset him.

Twenty-six hundred miles away, Lewin Baltry was organizing the contents of the refrigerator in the house he'd rented in Wolf Creek, Montana. The fugitive commissioner had felt conspicuous staying at the fishing lodge. Dinner conversations with the flycasters had been painful, as Baltry didn't know the difference between a rainbow trout and a barracuda. The two-bedroom rental was crazy expensive, but what price—Baltry had rationalized—can one put on blessed solitude? He paid for three months with cash using the name Donnie Lee Estefan. The owner of the house, who was dodging bed taxes, didn't ask for an ID.

Barry Martino, the fixer-lobbyist, called repeatedly from Florida. Baltry wouldn't answer, and soon stopped listening to Martino's baleful messages. One afternoon he drove to the I-15 rest stop near a town called Dearborn and placed his cellphone inside a spare tire under a tractor-trailer rig that was—fortuitously for Baltry—heading first to Alberta and then back to the port of New Orleans.

Baltry bought a new phone in Cascade and began mulling his next move. Montana was a good place to hide, but he didn't want to stay much longer. There were grizzlies in the mountains and cougars in the canyons. The river water was too cold for swimming, and sometimes at night he smelled skunk on the wind. His neighbor up the road had shot a muskrat in his pond and asked Baltry if he wanted the pelt.

The options, in Baltry's view, were few. He could stay lost and ultimately burn through his money—or return to Florida, vote to approve the Bunkers project, and pray he didn't get indicted for bribery.

There was also a third, more daring course: Go to the FBI and make a deal to testify against the Minks, Martino, and the other corrupt commissioners. They were, after all, scum. And the witness protection program didn't sound so terrible; certainly it was better than prison, or being murdered by operatives of the Minks. Baltry could picture himself tending a modest tract house in a drab but quiet neighborhood, like the one where Ray Liotta's character ended up in *Goodfellas*.

As long as there was a decent golf course nearby.

With a driving range.

Baltry thought about the phone number given to him by the menacing stranger at the Wendy's drive-through. The scrap of paper was still tucked with the cash in his billfold. There was no cell service at the house, but Baltry got two bars at the gas station in Wolf Creek. When he dialed the stranger's number, the call went directly to voicemail. Baltry didn't leave a message. He wasn't sure that two time zones away was a safe enough distance.

Assuming that the Minks had already hired someone to track him, the commissioner drove the rented Highlander all the way to

Portland, turned it in, and bought a used Outback on Craigslist, one hundred and nineteen thousand gritty miles on the engine.

Baltry didn't look in the glove compartment until he got back to Montana. Immediately he phoned the seller and said, "You forgot something in the car."

"Damn," the man said. "Oh well."

Guns made Baltry nervous.

"I'll send it back to you," he said to the man.

"Nah. Keep it."

"Really?"

"Yeah. It was never my fave."

"Okay," Lewin Baltry said. "Can I ask you something?"

"I guess."

"Is it loaded?"

The man chuckled. "Very funny."

"No, I'm serious," the commissioner said.

⩘⩘⩘

Twilly's father was called Little Phil and his mother's name was Amy. They took him to Paris when he was thirteen with a game plan to do all the museums, the Eiffel Tower, Notre Dame, the works. During their first full day in the city they went for a cruise on the Seine. As the tour boat approached the first bridge, Twilly's mom started freaking; she was terrified that a pedestrian on the span would spit down on them. Where such a disgusting idea sprung from, Twilly couldn't imagine. Little Phil dropped his voice and told Amy to quit making a scene. Although she had many eclectic phobias, Twilly had never seen her unravel in public. He tried to hold her hand, but she shook free and shielded her head with both arms as the boat passed slowly under the bridge. Nobody honked a gob on the cruise passengers. However, there were other bridges over the river, and then there was the return trip, so Amy Spree's drama repeated over and over. She spent the rest of the France trip meditating at the hotel while Little Phil halfheartedly hauled their only son around to see the famous sights. Twilly recalled admiring the van Goghs at the Musée d'Orsay but nearly suffocating on human body odor at the Louvre, where the tourists had packed in like squirming garfish to see the listless Mona Lisa.

That was, unsurprisingly, the Sprees' last family vacation. Twilly's parents stayed married for five more years, until Little Phil—a diehard real estate man—ran off with a clerk from the title-and-escrow company. By then Amy Spree was well down a transcendental path, incapable of resentment or jealousy. Nonetheless, she hired a tough lawyer and ended up with the family house, the Nissan coupe, and both WaveRunners. Twilly himself was newly independent thanks to the unsought inheritance from Big Phil, his mountain-plundering grandfather. At the time, the value of the trust was approximately five million dollars. Although Twilly was only eighteen, he devised a budget that allowed him to live off the interest and dividends. He steered clear of the principal, and over the years his net worth wealth grew vastly. When the trust expired, on Twilly's fortieth birthday, he immediately converted the portfolio to tax-free bonds. His only extravagance was anonymously bankrolling environmental lawsuits against out-of-state developers or sugar companies. More often than not, these cases withered in court. Twilly Spree didn't discuss his wealth with Viva, or anyone in his past.

"Other than your mom's panic attacks, how'd you like Paris?" Viva asked.

"Too crowded."

"You *always* feel crowded."

"Not here," Twilly said.

They were lying in bed at his place. It was seven thirty in the morning. Clothes and sheets lay in a riot on the floor. Viva was propped on one elbow with her hair pulled back. She'd been entertaining Twilly with the story of her bachelorette party in Nashville, where her best friend had gotten buzzed and toppled off a party bus on Broadway only to be scooped up and adopted by another rowdy female armada—competing bachelorettes from Philadelphia. It had been the last time Viva ever saw her friend, who stayed in Nashville, skipped Viva's wedding, got her boobs done, and moved in with a nightclub bouncer.

"Six years later they're still together, still deliriously happy," she said to Twilly. "Wouldn't you call that amazing? She picked the right man, obviously."

"Are you envious?"

"A little. She's an ER nurse at Vanderbilt hospital."

"Probably treating the drunk bozos that her husband beats up."

"Only you would think of that," Viva said.

"Speaking of which, did you see your landlord last night?"

"Yeah, he could barely limp in the door. What happened?"

Twilly told her about the brawl at Fever Beach, and Figgo's bird-brained Key West plot. "He's got something big and stupid planned on Duval Street. He won't say what."

"Why'd Onus beat him up?" Viva asked. "They're like besties."

"Unclear."

"Yet you stopped it."

"For now. What did Figgo tell you?"

"That he hurt his ribs when a bunch of rastas tried to mug him, but he John Cena'd the shit out of them and they ran away."

"Marvelous," Twilly said. He stood up and pulled on his jeans.

Viva warned him to be careful dealing with Jonas Onus. "You embarrassed him in front of the whole tribe. He'll want revenge."

"I'd think even less of him if he didn't."

"You know another place besides Paris that I've never been? Key West."

"Also too crowded," Twilly said. "But you'll like it. Best grouper sandwiches on the planet."

"So I'm going with you? I mean, I *want* to."

"Of course you're going, Viva. I see you as playing a key role."

"What role? Can we not get carried away?"

Twilly took a pressed white tee out of the drawer. "I'm hungry," he said. "And you've got to go home and get ready for work."

"Has anyone ever counted all your scars?" Viva asked.

"That's your pre-breakfast move? Seriously?"

"Don't you put that shirt on, mister," she said, scooting across the bed. "Not just yet."

~~~
~~~

Donna Figgo was at the gym, pounding the heavy bag, when a tall, pretty African American woman walked up and said, "May I have a word?"

"Sure."

"Your son ran down my husband with his pickup truck."

The woman was calm and firm. Donna kept punching the bag. "Sorry," she said. "Dale didn't tell me."

"About the hit-and-run?"

"No, that he ran over a Black man."

"My husband's white."

"Oops. My bad." Donna was sticking left jabs, keeping to her rhythm. "The lawyer said it's all been taken care of."

"We accepted the settlement, yes, but my husband's not getting better. Far from it. Emotionally, I mean."

"So, bottom line, you want more money."

"Not a dime," the woman said. "I know conversations like this aren't easy. I'm a mother, like you."

Only I doubt your kid's a moron, Donna thought, ending her workout with a brisk right-left-right combination. She took off her boxing gloves and said, "Well, I guess we can chat. I owe you that much."

"First, can I try the bag?"

Her name was Mary Kristiansen. It was her husband, Noel, who'd been hit by Dale Figgo's Ram 1500 in front of their home in Sanctuary Falls. The experience had profoundly affected him, Mary said, and it wasn't just the head injury.

Donna Figgo listened courteously as she helped the woman lace on a dry pair of gloves. She agreed that her son's actions were inexcusable, especially him fleeing the scene and all. Mary stepped out of her flats and started hitting the bag, hopping from side to side, barefoot in her red shift dress. Her form was free-swinging and unschooled, but she could punch hard.

"I don't see how I can help. What's done is done," Donna said.

"You could talk to Dale."

"He and my current significant don't get along. Are you lookin' for him to come over and apologize to Neil?"

"His name is Noel. But that's not what—"

"Dale's folded-up brain don't work like that. He'd only make things worse."

Mary Kristiansen did three full minutes and stopped. She was breathing hard, the slope of her neck damp with sweat. The gym was warm. She removed the boxing gloves and smoothed back her hair. Donna Figgo handed her a towel and a bottle of water.

"I understand why people get into this. It feels great," Mary said. She took a small baggie from her purse and handed it to Donna. "Here's what started everything."

Donna opened the baggie and stared at the headline on the flyer: "EVERY SINGLE ASPECT OF THE EVIL COVID AGENDA IS JEWISH."

"What is this crap?" she said to Mary.

"That's what your son was throwing in people's yards. Noel got furious when he read it. That's why he confronted Dale."

"So you're Jewish, then."

"We're not, but that doesn't matter."

"Christ on a Triscuit, is that thing supposed to be a swastika?" Donna was upset to see that Dale had taken things so far.

"Ever since Noel got home from the hospital, he hardly sleeps," Mary went on. "Sometimes he goes out late and lies about where. The all-night bowling alley where he supposedly plays in a league went out of business two months ago—there's one example. Now he's bought a gun. This is a man who couldn't hit a Greyhound bus with a fire hose, and suddenly he's taking shooting lessons with an AR-15. A man who once got his finger stuck in an electric pencil sharpener!"

"What Dale did was mean and shameful," Donna Figgo said. "I hope your husband can work through it."

"Think about everyone else who got one of these messages, how much hurt and fear were caused. Did you have any idea your son felt this way?"

"He wasn't always hateful. What happened is he got turned the wrong direction by some bad eggs way back in high school. Since then I've heard plenty of ignorant shit come out of his mouth. These days he'll get a right cross that puts him on the damn floor. I've been hoping it would knock the poison out of his soul, but I guess not."

"There's got to be another way," Mary Kristiansen said.

"Dale's not slow. He's just empty." Donna paused to read the printed diatribe to herself, line by line. "I got three other boys that turned out good," she said quietly. "Not a racist hair on their heads. Solid, decent young men. One's datin' a Jewish girl, and he's lucky to have her."

Mary Kristiansen felt somewhat sorry for Dale Figgo's mother, and it showed. She said, "Maybe if you sat down and spoke with him alone, he'd quit this nonsense and steer his life back on track. Otherwise he's going to end up in prison, or worse."

Donna peered more closely at the flyer. "Who the hell are the 'Strokers for Liberty'?"

"Exactly who you think. There's even a website. Dale's their leader."

Donna swore under her breath. She slipped the flyer into the Ziploc and asked if she could keep it. Mary said of course.

"Can I ask how you tracked me down?" Donna asked.

"Court." Mary shrugged. "Property records."

"I get it. My name's on Dale's townhouse."

"The mailing address for the property tax is your home," Mary said.

"So you went there first?"

"And met Breck. He's the one who told me where to find you."

Donna laughed ruefully. "You'd never guess he went to Stanford, would you? Not in a million years. Be honest: You want more money, right?"

"I do not. All I want is for this to end," Mary said.

"Because I wasn't in on the payoff, however much it was. I don't even know where it came from. If Dale's got insurance, that's news to me."

"We were told a friend of Dale's put up the settlement money. They wouldn't give us the name. Some VIP is all they said."

Impossible, Donna thought. *Border-line hilarious.*

"Smithfield Semiconductor finds out about this Stroker group," she said, "they'll fire his dumb ass."

Mary looked down and away.

"What?" Donna asked. "Sister, you did everything but roll your eyes."

"It's none of my concern. And it's got nothing to do with what's happened to Noel, and the reason I came to see you."

"Dale doesn't really work at Smithfield?"

"He should tell you these things himself."

"So, wait—the useless sandbagger is out of work?" Donna erupted.

"Oh, no, he's got a job."

"Where? Doin' what?"

Mary Kristiansen put her shoes on. "I'm sorry, Donna, I have to go now."

"Wait. Tell me whatever else you know."

"You're his flesh and blood," Mary whispered, tucking her handbag under her arm. "Please do something, before it's too late."

Donna Figgo watched her visitor walk out of the gym, and turned back to the heavy bag. No gloves, this time, just bare knuckles.

~~~

The meeting was painful. Nicki Boyette wore a short silk dress that had been proven to drive her future ex-husband crazy. Harold Fistman chose a tailored gray suit but no necktie, unbuttoning his shirt just enough to flaunt a retro gold chain nestled in his silver chest hair. The congressman's attorney was Chip Milkwright from Milkwright & Menser in Fort Lauderdale; he specialized in divorces involving unfaithful professional athletes. He'd taken the congressman's case as a favor to Clay Boyette, who years ago had cut him in on a lucrative land swap involving a phosphate mine.

They gathered in the long cold conference room at Fistman's office. Nicki and Fistman sat on one side of the mahogany table, the congressman and his attorney on the other. In the middle was a
~~~

pewter pitcher of ice water and a dozen blue ballpoints that nobody touched. The lawyers all came armed with laptops.

Clure Boyette's mood was impatient and downcast; seeing Galaxy and Viva Morales together the night before had floored him. His date, a seasoned escort from Boca Raton, took home a thousand bucks for doing nothing except wolfing a four-star meal. Naughty leash play had been the last thing on the congressman's mind. That Viva and Galaxy were sharing notes about him was now the source of a dyspeptic ache.

The viper Fistman started the mediation by swinging for the fence: "My client wishes to keep the marital residence and the vacation condo in Park City. Also her SUV, the jewelry, the art, the snooker table, and sixty percent of all bank and brokerage accounts controlled by Mr. Boyette."

"Some of those assets predate the marriage," Chip Milkwright said.

Fistman chuckled. "What a quaint concept."

Florida being a no-fault-divorce state was true only in the abstract. Nicki Boyette had the names of sixteen women—not all of them prostitutes—who had slept with her husband during the marriage. It was combustible information to possess in the midst of a tense re-election campaign. The loyalty of the congressman's conservative base would be strained by revelations of double-digit adulteries, and possibly appalled by the cringy details of his cosplay preference. By and large, his voters were dog lovers.

"Sixty percent ain't happenin'," Chip Milkwright asserted.

Harold Fistman winked at Nicki Boyette, who nodded.

"In that case," said Fistman, "we intend to subpoena all documents relating to a 501(c)(3) nonprofit that your client recently set up. The Teeny Weenies, I believe."

The congressman blanched. "It's the *Wee Hammers,*" he said. "And what's that got to do with the divorce?"

Fistman explained that Mrs. Boyette wanted to be sure no joint marital funds were tapped to fund the entity if it was, in fact, a legitimate nonprofit.

"The money came from outside donors. Every damn penny," Boyette said indignantly. "We're already building our first house."

Chip Milkwright spoke up: "No need for a subpoena, Harold. We'll provide copies of all the relevant paperwork."

Queasily Boyette turned and whispered into his lawyer's ear: "Fuck this shit, Chip. I can't afford to have anything blow up on me right now."

"But sixty percent is robbery," Chip Milkwright whispered back.

"Dad wants this settled fast. Offer her fifty and everything else she's asking for."

"Plus a joint statement saying the divorce was a mutual decision, and that the two of you will always remain close friends."

"I like that," Clure Boyette said. "Pals forever."

Early polling showed that the congressional race was closer than expected, Boyette's constituency having tired of him voting every few months to shut down the U.S. government. A major employer in his district was an Air Force base where four hundred–plus civilians worked, most of them registered voters who didn't enjoy biannual drama involving their paychecks. Many no longer viewed Boyette as a principled young budget hawk; they saw him as an attention whore rapidly approaching asshole status. His Democratic opponent was a schoolteacher and twice-divorced mom nobody had heard of a year ago. Yet now, somehow, she hovered within ten points of the incumbent. Her yard signs were sprouting all over the place, even on the lot across from Clay Boyette's gated estate. He told his son to wake the fuck up and start kissing babies.

Harold Fistman and his client were aware that the congressman was highly motivated to expedite the divorce and seal the court file. They countered at fifty-five percent but added one more high-end demand:

"The Aston Martin," Nicki said.

Boyette bristled. "You told me you didn't want it!"

"She had a change of heart," said Fistman.

"It got totaled. Sorry."

Nicki lightly drummed two fingers on the table. "Then buy me another one just like it."

"But it was a *lease,*" said Boyette, boiling on the inside. The new car had been promised to Galaxy, and there was zero chance that his old man would pay for two of them. None of this was known to the congressman's divorce attorney.

"You're not getting an Aston," Chip Milkwright said to Nicki.

She asked Harold Fistman to read the list aloud.

"What for?" her husband snapped.

"What list?" asked Milkwright.

Fistman began reading out the female names his IT ace had screen-grabbed from Boyette's unprotected Venmo account. He made it only as far as number five before the congressman cut in:

"Stop. I'll get you the car, Nicki."

"Why, thank you, Clure."

"It's a custom model, so you'll have to wait a few months."

"No problem. The Carrera's running fine."

"Nice to hear," Boyette said thinly.

The Boyettes departed within two minutes of each other. Milkwright shut his laptop while griping that nobody had told him there was a fucking Venmo list.

Fistman shook his hand, saying, "This was too easy, Chip. No blood on the floor. We must be losing our edge."

"Harold, I have a feeling we're not done yet."

"Really? Don't tease me, you bastard."

After the meeting, Clure Boyette hurried out of the building and phoned his father, who called him a pathetic fucknoodle and refused to order a second Aston. One was enough, Clay Boyette snapped. But he would come around, the congressman felt sure; his father was all about tying up loose ends before the election. He was more worried about the narrowing poll numbers than his son was, because Clay Boyette didn't know that the once-problematic Precinct 53 was a lock. He'd never heard of the Strokers for Liberty and was unaware that Clure was summoning an armed force to Carpville as "citizen poll watchers" on voting day.

The old toad will be impressed, the congressman thought confidently.

He was wrong, but that would turn out to be the least of his troubles.

~~~

Unlike many white supremacists, Dale Figgo wasn't addicted to the internet—just the opposite. He avoided the dark web because groups such as the Proud Boys and Oath Keepers—corrupted with informants since the original January 6th prosecutions—continued to maintain a loud, oversize presence. It irked Figgo to see their frequent posts and the blind fervor of their followers, as if nothing out of the ordinary had happened that day in Washington. He feared that impressionable Strokers might defect, as Raw Dog had, in hopes of a larger social profile and a benefits package that included future legal fees.

Figgo had conceived the Key West mission not only as an easy practice but also as a morale booster. In advance of the trip, his touchiest dilemma was deciding what to do about his former number two, Jonas Onus. Figgo had expected him to resign from the Strokers after his drubbing at Fever Beach, but Onus remained silent. Figgo's first impulse was to expel the hotheaded goon from the group, but Twilly Spree advised him to hold off.

"But I don't want to look weak," Figgo said. "The asshole attacked me in front of everybody!"

"Unfortunately, he knows too much. What if you kick him out of the group and he runs all butt-hurt to the feds? Down goes the congressman, down go you, and down go the Strokers."

"So what do I do? I'm between a rut and a hard place."

"Meet with the man," Twilly said.

"One on one? Fuck no."

"I'll come along, too."

"Yeah?"

Of all the Strokers, it had been Twilly alone who had rushed to Figgo's aid when Onus jumped him on the beach. And, even out-
~~~

weighed by twenty-five pounds, Twilly had kicked Onus's ass. It had been over so fast you couldn't even call it a fight.

"Okay, I'll set a meeting," Figgo said. "But you ride with me."

"One more thing, Dale."

"What's that?"

"Pay for Himmler's vet bill," Twilly said.

"Are you crazy? No fucking way."

"You want Jonas to stay pissed? Or settle down and get with the program?"

Figgo said, "That damn dog is insane. It's not my fault he'll eat everything."

"Just pay the veterinarian," Twilly said.

"But then all the other guys—"

"No, they'll respect you for it."

"You mean respect me *more*."

"Yes. Exactly."

"Hell," sighed Figgo. "Fine, I'll reach out to the dude."

He and Twilly were having beers in the kitchen at the townhouse. Twilly was waiting for Viva to get home from work. He'd given up trying to talk Figgo out of the Key West trip; from now on, it was damage control. Figgo was scrawling out a budget for the mission so he could hit up the congressman for a cash advance. He'd felt comfortable enough to remove his postsurgery mask in front of Twilly, who refrained from commenting on the peculiar texture of Figgo's rebuilt nose.

Yo, let's meet up, Figgo texted Onus.

Already on my way, Onus texted back.

Figgo was surprised. **I meant tomorrow,** he typed.

Nothing.

"Don't go anywhere," he said to Twilly.

Ten minutes later, the Tundra rumbled into the driveway. It was pouring rain outside. Figgo, watching from a window, reported that Onus looked pretty rough.

Twilly was reading one of Viva's *New Yorker*s. He glanced up and said, "Open the door, Dale. You got this."

Onus walked in with a labored, bent-legged waddle, as if a freezer was strapped to his back. His clothes—the same ones he'd worn to Fever Beach—were wet and dirty. The Chris Stapleton–style beard had been rinsed of its patriotic hues and hacked to a sagebrush stubble. Through puffy slits, Onus glowered at Twilly, who put down the magazine but remained seated.

"Hello, Jonas," Twilly said.

"What the fuck are *you* doin' here?"

"Waiting on my date."

Figgo shut the door. "I asked Chaos to hang around, dude."

"So he's your bodyguard now. That's cute," Onus said.

"If you came over here to tell me you're quittin', don't. The Strokers need you."

"I didn't come here to quit. I came here to kill you."

"Not today." Figgo drew a pistol from his waistband and pointed it at Onus's gut.

Twilly rolled his eyes. "Give me that thing, Dale. Yours, too, Jonas."

Matching Glocks, of course. *Douche v. Douche*. Twilly popped the clip from each gun and checked the chambers.

He said, "You boys have some major shit to sort out. Dale can go first."

Figgo sneered. "Me? Uh, I don't think so."

Onus hungrily eyed his empty Glock on the counter where Twilly had placed it.

"Sit down, both of you," Twilly said. "I can't let you blow up the biggest thing that'll ever happen to us."

Neither of the men would sit.

"Dale's got something important to tell you," Twilly said to Onus.

"I've got somethin' to say, too."

Figgo frowned, fidgeted, then: "I've been thinkin' about it, dude. Let me take care of the damn surgery bill for your dog. I'll get the money lined up today."

Onus responded with an odd, desolate grin.

"Fuck you, Dale," he said.

Figgo looked coldly at Twilly. "Told you this was a stupid idea."

Twilly said, "Come on, Jonas. The man's trying to do the right thing."

Onus threw up his hands. "Too goddamn late! Himmler's gone."

"He ran off again?" Figgo asked.

"No, motherfucker. Gone as in croaked. Dead."

The air in the room turned heavy.

"What the hell happened?" Twilly asked.

"What happened is he ate the sex booty that Dale gave us and it killed his ass. The vet said there was, like, five pounds of rubber pluggin' the poor guy's gut. It wouldn't pass natural and the operation was sixteen hundred bucks, which I didn't have. *Don't* have. So I tried everything else I could think of. By the way, good luck stickin' an enema tube up the butthole of a hundred-and-twenty-pound pit mix. They do *not* fucking dig it, bro. Meanwhile, First Lieutenant Dipshit here, he's sittin' fat and happy on two million dollars."

Figgo shoved his hands in his pockets.

"Himmler swallowed that whole thing?" he said. "Damn."

"How about you're sorry for my loss, shithead?"

"That's what he means," Twilly cut in. "Both of us feel awful about your dog."

"But then he gives Bushmaster three hundred bucks to put down his mother's damn cat!" Onus was practically yelling.

Weakly, Figgo said, "That was different. The cat was like a hundred years old."

"Fuck you, Dale," Onus snapped again. "Himmler was in his prime."

A key clicked in the lock, and the front door opened.

Viva walked in with a dripping umbrella and muttered, "Hello, gentlemen."

Immediately she read the room.

Please don't say it, Twilly thought.

But she did.

"Jesus, who died?"

CHAPTER 15

It was a legit rock-star bus. Dale Figgo had rented it with seventy-two hundred dollars from the congressman's secret fund. Clure Boyette knew nothing about the Key West operation, and he seemed to believe Figgo's story that the money would be spent on deodorizing body armor for the Strokers for Liberty.

The bus was a Van Hool Astromega, top of the line. It had tinted windows, premium air-conditioning, wi-fi, and an entertainment system featuring a video screen on the back of each seat. There was also a wet bar and two toilets. The charter company advertised that it had been Morgan Wallen's favorite tour bus before he bought his own.

Figgo was so excited that he arrived at the IHOP an hour early. The bus driver was standing in the parking lot smoking a vape pen. He wore a short-sleeve uniform but no hat. His name was Fournier, and he pronounced it twice as he shook Figgo's hand. He had very dark skin, which put Figgo on edge, knowing the general outspokenness of the Strokers. The last thing they needed was trouble on the long ride to the Keys.

KRANKK had crashed again that morning, so Figgo had been

forced to text each of the members individually. **Don't forget the barbecue** was one of his self-coded messages. **See you at mass**, said another. **Bring my worm pills** was a third choice, and so on. In the end, fourteen unarmed Christian white nationalists showed up at noon wearing street clothes and carrying duffels filled with black tactical wear. Jonas Onus wasn't among them, to Figgo's relief.

At half past the hour, the bus departed from the IHOP. The new guys, Chaos and Payback, sat near the front. They were one row behind Figgo, who'd left his postsurgical mask at home, assuming that Key West was one place where a ball-sack nose would draw little attention. Once the bus was on the interstate, Figgo handed a pair of Beats to Fournier, who took the hint, fit the cups over his ears, and dialed up the playlists on his phone.

Standing in the aisle, Figgo faced the rows of Strokers and began reviewing the conduct rules. Das Regulator cut him off with a shout: "Not in front of *him*!"

Meaning the driver, who had professionally fixed his eyes on the highway.

"He can't hear a word," Figgo said, pointing to Fournier's headphones.

"The hell he can't!" another Stroker yelled.

Bottle Rocket stepped forward to ask how come there wasn't a white driver. Figgo explained that the Black dude came with the bus; he was employed by the charter company. The *n*-word began to ricochet around the bus.

"Fucker might be a fed," Bottle Rocket whispered.

"No way," Figgo said. "He smells like weed."

"I don't trust him, dude. None of us do."

To avert another blowup, Figgo sat down, saying, "Whatever. I'll wait and do the briefing after we get there."

Head bobbing behind the wheel, Fournier gave no sign of hearing anything but his tunes. Bottle Rocket was scowling as he returned to his seat. Figgo felt a tap on his shoulder and turned around.

Twilly Spree, aka Chaos, leaned over and asked, "What about the radios?"

"They didn't get here in time. Fucking Bass Pro."

"Where's Jonas?"

Figgo shrugged. "Good question."

"Call him."

"I tried, like, a hundred times."

"You think he quit?" Twilly asked.

"Probably one of the kids got strep. That happens a lot."

Meanwhile, Payback remained silent. He was looking at Dale Figgo in a strange, unblinking way, and tapping one of his boots.

"You okay, bro?" Figgo asked him.

"I'm fine. Why?"

"Payback's cool," Chaos said. "We're all cool."

Wait'll they find out I forgot the beers, thought Figgo.

He took out his phone and called up an Apple map of the Old Town district in Key West. Surely there was a special parking lot for luxury buses.

~~~

Viva was placing her travel bag in the car when Figgo's mother drove up in her boyfriend's Volvo. The coupe was a vivid custom shade of green, somewhere between shamrock and parakeet. Donna Figgo wore a denim bucket hat, white tank top, and Dior sunglasses the size of tea saucers. The window rolled down, and Viva could see the bunched muscles of Donna's bare left arm.

"Is Dale here?" she called out.

"No, he's southbound."

"Where he's going?"

"All the way to the end of the road."

"Damn fool," said Donna. "Hop in. Hurry up."

"We can take my car."

Donna chuckled. "Why?"

Viva fit her small suitcase in the back seat of the coupe and belted herself into the passenger seat. The interior of the Volvo was sportier than its lines. Donna said she'd never made the drive to Key West.
~~~

"Me, neither," Viva said, "but I hear it's basically impossible to get lost."

By the time they reached the turnpike, Viva was digging her fingernails into the upholstery. Donna drove like an experienced maniac.

Viva said, "I read there are forty-two bridges on the Overseas Highway."

"So?"

"You ever see *Thelma and Louise*?"

"Nope." Donna was weaving through a gauntlet of eighteen-wheelers. "But didn't one of those gals get to bang Brad Pitt?"

The speedometer hit ninety-four miles an hour. Viva put on her own sunglasses to hide the fear that must have been showing in her pupils. A radar detector on the dashboard was no consolation. Getting pulled over by the police wasn't what Viva worried about; it was dying in a flaming high-speed wreck.

Donna asked her to find some good road music on the radio.

"Breck's stations are all yacht rock," she added. "We need the hard stuff. No Hall. No Oates."

"Will Zeppelin work?"

"Yes, ma'am. I cross-train to *Houses of the Holy*."

Viva found a classic rock station. Donna smiled and nonchalantly stated that she was going to knock her son unconscious when they caught up with him.

"It won't take but a second. I know what I'm doing," she said.

Twilly Spree had texted Viva a picture of the tour bus that Dale Figgo had chartered for the Strokers. Viva held it up so Donna could see. The bus was jet black with faux-mica flecking. The words "CORBETT'S RUM TOURS" were painted in gold script on the side.

"Dale's cover story is they're doing a bachelor party," Viva said.

"But what are they really planning?"

"Some stupid white-power spectacle on Duval Street. Dale wouldn't spill any details in advance, in case the group had been 'infellated.' His word, not mine. Twilly asked me to be the undercover videographer. None of the other guys know I'm coming, not even Dale."

"Why didn't you tell me about the Strokers? The sickening leaflets he's been spreading?"

Viva said, "I wasn't sure where you stood. Or whether you already knew."

"I did *not*." Donna shook her head emphatically. "I also found out he doesn't really work at the semiconductor plant."

"Lord, no. Was that the story he told you?"

"But he is employed somewhere, right?"

"He is," Viva said. "At a packing hub for adult merchandise."

"By 'adult' you mean beyond the risqué?"

"Way beyond, I'm afraid."

"No son of mine," was all Donna Figgo said.

"Kashmir" came on the radio. Donna cut her speed to eighty-five. The traffic had gotten heavy, so she was using the emergency breakdown lane to pass other cars. Every so often the Volvo would run over a traffic cone or an orphaned hubcap.

"Is that creepy Jonas traveling with Dale?" she asked Viva.

"No, they had a falling-out."

"I'm glad. That oaf is a terrible influence."

Viva said, "His dog died, and he blames Dale. It's a long story."

"Hey, isn't that them up ahead?"

Viva said no, it was a Disney tour bus. "Can we stop for a bathroom break?"

"Hold on till Florida City," Donna said.

But she didn't stop there. In Homestead the Strokers' black bus came into view, and Figgo's mother dropped back half a dozen car lengths. Viva agreed that the Volvo's unusual color could be problematic if Dale was on the lookout. They maintained a chill gap all the way down the Eighteen-Mile Stretch and into the Upper Keys. Finally, in Tavernier, the bus pulled over at a gas station. Donna sped past and parked a half mile down the road. Viva dashed inside a Wendy's to pee. She texted Twilly from the restroom but got no answer. When she returned to where the Volvo was parked, she saw flashing police lights and Donna standing beside the car talking animatedly with a sheriff's deputy. The deputy was writing a ticket.

"I don't have my insurance card," Donna explained to Viva.

"Or her driver's license," the deputy noted.

"And I didn't tell Breck I was taking the Volvo," Donna said, "so he called it in as stolen. You believe that?"

"Get him on the phone," Viva said.

"I tried. He must be on the damn golf course. No, wait, I remember. He's getting a treatment."

"Chemo?" the deputy asked, on the verge of sympathy.

"No, it's a facial. Avocado paste."

"It was me," the deputy said, "I'd bring a bag of chips."

Donna showed him a screenshot of her and Breck entwined on a water slide as evidence of her connection to the car's legal owner. The deputy wrote her the ticket anyway.

Viva saw the Strokers' tour bus reentering the highway. She ducked behind the police car and told Donna to do the same thing. The deputy didn't bother asking why.

He grabbed the Volvo's key fob and radioed for a tow truck. Donna glumly ordered an Uber. By the time the driver arrived, the Strokers were long gone. Donna and Viva climbed into the minivan, which smelled like spearmint and spoiled artichokes. The Uber driver mumbled his first name, but they couldn't understand it.

The trip to Key West was slow due to the weekend stampede of day-trippers from Miami. Donna ate a Xanax and dozed. Viva counted the bridges—she couldn't get over how much bluer the water looked on the Atlantic side compared to the Gulf. Twilly still wasn't picking up his phone, which was annoying. There was no music in the van; instead the driver was listening to a podcast called *A Drug-Free Path to Conquering Narcolepsy*. It made Viva think about Malcolm, who'd routinely slept about thirteen hours a day. She wondered how he was doing in prison, sharing a cell and so forth. Early on, he'd written to her sister Maya, of all people, claiming he had found Jesus Christ the Savior and, P.S., what is Viva's address in Florida? Maya had wiped her cockatoo's ass with the letter and mailed it back to Malcolm. That seemed to do the trick.

Donna's phone started jangling. Viva nudged her awake. It was Breck, highly pissed off about the Volvo situation. Donna put him on speaker.

"The impound lot's all the way in fucking Hialeah!" he was hollering. "They want six hundred bucks!"

Donna told him she'd borrowed his car because hers was low on gas.

"I hope you filled it up," she said.

"Where the hell are you?"

"On the way to Key West. Dale's fixin' to get himself into a situation."

"Loser," said Breck. "Don't you dare bond him out."

"I'll be home tomorrow, honey."

"Who's that riding with you? I hear a guy talking."

"It's only a podcast," Donna said.

"Don't lie."

"I'm with my friend Viva. Say hi to Breck, Viva."

Viva was trapped. "Hello, Breck," she said. "I've heard so much about you."

There was, on the other end, the proverbial stony silence.

Then Breck's voice: "Donna, I can't do this anymore."

"Of course you can, baby. You can and you will. Call me later."

She hung up smiling warmly. "He's just a boy. Simple and adorbs."

"Not all of them are," Viva said.

"Our relationship is very organic."

"I'll have to try that approach."

Traffic congealed in Marathon, where the Uber got stuck behind a deafening swarm of bikers riding three and four abreast. They had just exited a bar where the roadside sign said, **WELCOME POKER RUN. BEERS $3!!!**

Viva asked Donna if she'd ever been on a Harley.

"Not while it was moving," Donna said.

No sooner had the narcolepsy podcast ended than the Uber driver started getting groggy. Donna reached over the seat and pinched one of his earlobes. He let out a grumpy cry as he straightened behind the wheel. They persuaded him to stop at a Dunkin' Donuts for a cup of hot coffee, which turned into two. Donna and Viva each had a French cruller. Donna warned the driver that she would Tase him in the neck if he nodded off. He promised to remain wakeful the rest of the trip.

Yet, halfway across the Seven Mile Bridge, his head drooped again, and he was out like a bear. Being only two lanes, the span would have been a dangerous place to electroshock a sleeping motorist. Instead Viva one-handedly kept the wheel steady while Donna yanked the man aside and vaulted into his seat. He was agape with his eyelids half open, so Viva checked his pulse to make sure he wasn't dead or dying.

Twilly finally called. Viva told him she was accompanying Figgo's mother to Key West via Uber.

"How the fuck did that happen?" Twilly asked, but didn't wait for a reply. He sounded tense.

"Have the driver bring you to Mallory Square," he said.

"You okay?"

"I'm fabulous. Everything's wonderful."

"Tell me what's going on," Viva pressed. "Are things getting chippy between Dale and the membership?"

"It's a goddamn goat wedding."

"Worse than you predicted?"

"The night is young, unfortunately," Twilly said. "Stay out of sight when you get here. Figgo will freak if he sees you."

But by the time Donna and Viva made it to Mallory Square, the black tour bus was empty and the Strokers for Liberty were gone. The bus driver said the crazy white fuckers had gone marching up Duval.

Trauma Queens was on upper Duval, not far from the iconic buoy at the Southernmost Point. Billy Butterneck had worked at the club for five years, six nights a week. He opened his show as Marilyn Monroe and ended as Taylor Swift. In between he cycled Cher, Beyoncé, Liza, Dolly, and (weekends only) Gaga. One night a VIP requested Condoleezza Rice, a character not in Billy's wheelhouse, so he did the former secretary of state à la Tina Turner in gold lamé culottes. The show scored unexpectedly big laughs, though not enough to add Condi to the rotation.

Billy had met his life partner and husband-to-be at the Queens. Chester ran a lobster boat out of Stock Island. One late summer night he came into the club and sat alone at a two-top in the back. Billy, who was working the audience as Cher, whooshed up to Chester's table singing "Gypsies, Tramps & Thieves." Chester turned crimson in the spotlight. Billy put an arm around him, pecked him on the cheek, and moved on. Chester stayed until closing time. The next morning Billy went out pulling traps with him in the Gulf, and they'd been together ever since. They had a big wild wedding on the beach at Ballast Key officiated by the mayor of Monroe County.

From May until August, between lobster seasons, Chester did handyman jobs at the club. On Barbie Nights they needed an extra bouncer, so Chester was on board for that, too. Tonight he was upgrading the light bulbs on the dressing room mirrors when the manager came back and said a bachelor party of ninja rednecks was causing trouble. Chester picked up his baseball bat and walked to the main room. There, in front of the stage, Billy Butterneck had shed his Marilyn wig and was beating the crap out of some wheezing cracker while holding off like a dozen others. Clearly the intruders hadn't expected a drag queen to know martial arts. Chester joined the melee and wasn't surprised to learn that the blood on Billy's silver gown belonged to someone else.

The men had swept into the club wearing all-black tactical outfits topped with blaze-orange trucker hats identifying them as "STROKERS," the name underlined with a blue lightning bolt. Their aim apparently was to close down the show and chase off the customers—a misbegotten display of force against the LGBTQ movement, it turned out. Scattered all over the floor were flyers that said **GOD HATES HOMOZ.** Printed on the other side of each paper was a URL, strokersforliberty.org.

The crowd was rooting boisterously for bald Marilyn. Upon Chester's arrival, other members of the redneck crew entered the fight but were quickly driven back, taking heavy blows from Chester and several of the other stars, including a diminutive Black man boldly dressed as Diana Ross. A more willowy performer, who did a midnight sketch as Gwyneth Paltrow, made efficient use of a fiberglass scepter by skull-thumping one of the intruders dressed in a Confederate-style tunic. The man had been standing away from the tumult frowning but holding both hands behind him, as if he had a weapon. He did not.

Tourists from the street were pouring into the Queens to see the action, so the manager waited to dial the police until all their drink orders were taken. Meanwhile, one of the white gang members began removing the injured from the club. A few had to be carried fireman style, while others limped or crawled on their own. The group's leader—a dull-eyed slug with a cheesy sack face and a melted-looking nose—had been hogtied with red mesh stockings by the performers and placed on his belly under the spotlight onstage.

"Chaos! Payback!" he yelled, perhaps as a rallying cry. Then: "Get me outta here, goddammit!"

A wiry blond woman who identified herself as the bound homophobe's mother dragged him out the rear exit. A younger civilian wearing fake Billie Eilish hair and tortoiseshell sunglasses stood off in a corner, recording videos on her phone. The club manager gave her his card and asked her to AirDrop the best clips to him; he planned to post them on the website of the gym where all the performers trained.

Billy Butterneck retrieved his Marilyn wig and disappeared backstage with the others. Chester began sweeping up the leaflets and broken glass while the bouncer touched a mop to the blood spatters. The first wave of cops arrived, followed by EMTs. Gwyneth had a black eye and Diana Ross had suffered a nasty scratch on one arm, but nobody at the club needed an ambulance. Outraged patrons lined up to offer witness statements and moral support for the performers. The cops said the assailants must have split up and scattered; none were in custody so far.

Chester went back to the dressing room to check on Billy, who had changed into a fresh gown and was sitting at the makeup mirror redoing his candy-red "Some Like It Hot" lipstick.

"I think those dudes were Nazis," he said. "Or nouveaux Nazis, at least."

"Who threw the first punch?" Chester asked.

"That would be me."

"I knew it. Good."

"They jumped up on the stage! What would Keith Richards have done?"

Chester whooped. "Keith in the old days? Are you kidding? How about a Telecaster in the balls!"

Billy smiled and put on his wig. "Those guys seemed completely blown away, didn't they? Like, 'What in the *fuck* is happening here'?"

Chester handed him one of the flyers. "Check out this shit."

Billy looked at it and blurted, "The Strokers for Liberty? Oh my God!"

"How're you feelin'?"

"Lucky, I guess, that they didn't stroke all over me."

"But you didn't get hurt is what I'm askin'."

"No, totally fine. Broke a couple nails, that's all." He held up his right hand to show Chester. "I'll pop on some new ones, then on with the show!"

"The cops want to talk with you."

"Of course," Billy said, "but not till after my act."

"So I guess I'll go home and start dinner."

"What's on the menu, Chef Hot Stuff?"

"Hearts of palm, grilled Blue Points, and fresh mahi."

"Awesome!" Billy pumped both hands in the air. Then he blew a kiss at the mirror and cooed, "Happy birthday, Mr. President."

"Nailed it," Chester said proudly. "Just like always."

~~~

After helping the battered Strokers reboard the bus, Twilly Spree counted heads. Three men were missing—Skid Mark, Jerry Jeff Tupelo, and Dale Figgo. The driver, Fournier, refused to leave Key
~~~

West without them. It was a strict company policy, he explained, stemming from a lawsuit filed by a female passenger who'd accused a driver of abandoning her alone on a charter trip. In reality the woman was stoned to the gills and had boarded the wrong bus, which is how she'd ended up at Busch Gardens instead of the Kennedy Space Center.

Das Regulator, who had painfully tweaked an ACL in the brawl, volunteered to wait for the waylaid Strokers while Twilly and Fournier conducted a street-by-street. They flagged down a stretch golf cart, Twilly offering a hundred dollars to the honeymooning couple who'd rented it. The pair was from Little Rock and couldn't have been nicer. Twilly told them the cart would be left beside the Mile 0 road sign, near the Green Parrot. The couple said that would work out perfectly; the beginning of U.S. Highway One (or end, depending on your situation) topped their list of must-see sights. Fournier informed them that replicas of the street sign were available in many of the souvenir shops on Duval.

The foot search of Old Town turned up none of the missing Strokers. On Fleming Street, Twilly and Fournier ran into Viva Morales, who told them Dale Figgo had been whisked away by his mother. Still wearing the Billie wig she'd lifted from the drag club's dressing room, Viva accompanied Twilly and Fournier to the hospital on Stock Island. There Skid Mark was being treated for a fractured jaw and contused testicles. Jerry Jeff Tupelo, aka Payback, was being wheeled to surgery.

After the ER team finished with Skid Mark, Twilly walked him outside and propped him up in the golf cart. Fournier secured the injured man with an extension cord, and they sped off toward Mallory Square.

Viva and Twilly sat together holding hands in the ER. An hour passed.

"This would be romantic," Viva said finally, "under different circumstances."

Twilly stared at the floor wearing an expression that Viva couldn't read.

"It's loud here," she said.

"Too many fucked-up drunks."

"Of all shapes and sizes."

"They fall down stairs," Twilly said. "Stab each other. Shoot each other. Grab the wrong guy's fiancée."

"Are you all right?" Viva asked.

"Not really."

"This isn't your fault. You warned Dale not to bring his troop of troglodytes down here."

"Because I knew something like this would happen," Twilly said. "A total goddamn goat wedding."

He went to inquire about the condition of Jerry Jeff Tupelo. A gray-haired Cuban man at the admissions desk asked if he was related to the patient.

"He's my brother," Twilly said.

"Are you on his HIPAA list?"

"Next of kin. Same difference."

The man, who was wearing green scrubs, a stethoscope, and Apple buds, identified himself as the triage nurse. After a minute or so at his keyboard, he looked up and stated that no one named Jerry Jeff Tupelo had been admitted that night.

Twilly said, "But I was standing right here when they took him to surgery."

"Spell the last name again for me."

"T-U-P-E-L-O. Like the town in Mississippi."

"I don't see him on the patient list."

"Then try it with an *a*. Tup*a*lo." Twilly was guessing.

More tap-tap-tapping on the computer. Then: "Sir, he's not here."

"Well, shit," Twilly said. "Is there a back door?"

The triage nurse arched an eyebrow. "Not in surgery."

"You think this is a joke, amigo?"

Viva put her hands on Twilly's shoulders and steered him outside, where another ambulance had arrived—some genius from Biloxi had gotten his face raked open by a rooster he'd tackled and tried to kiss in front of the Hemingway House. A lost barroom bet was Viva's guess.

Still another ambulance pulled up, and Twilly started pacing in the parking lot. When he called Dale Figgo's cell number, Figgo's mother picked up, mad as a hornet. Twilly passed the phone to Viva. The conversation was short.

"Dale admitted it was all his idea," Viva told Twilly afterward.

"Attacking a drag show."

"Because they're a symptom of 'immoral turpentine.' His words."

"Not just any drag show, a *Key West* drag show," Twilly said.

"His mom's still furious. She kicked his lumpy white ass," Viva reported. "Her words."

"All of 'em got their asses kicked."

"It wasn't your job to stop it—as if you could."

"I'm worried about Jerry Jeff." Twilly turned and walked back into the ER, Viva on his heels. They were told to have a seat; the staff was busy treating new patients.

Viva took off the wig and tied her hair back in a ponytail, a style she'd been told suited her. "Cute but not wholesome," had been Galaxy's comment. "Also super practical. Doesn't get in the way while you're giving head." Viva was okay with the "cute but not wholesome" part. She started reaching for Twilly's hand but changed her mind. He looked like he was about to go off. There was already a fair amount of blood, vomit, and moaning in the room.

Malcolm would have fainted by now, she thought.

Twilly grumbled, "I can't sit here doing nothing."

"Pretend you're somewhere else. A beach in the Bahamas."

"Sure. A beach that smells like puke and ammonia."

A female nurse approached them and said she was looking for a person named Mary Kristiansen.

"That's her," Twilly said, nodding toward Viva. "I'm the brother."

Now what's he doing? thought Viva. She shook out her hair and fitted Billie Eilish on her head again.

The nurse said nothing except: "Both of you come with me, please."

"But—"

"Finally!" Twilly boomed.

The nurse led them down a brightly lit hallway to the recovery unit. Twilly lay back a few steps, peeking briefly into each of the rooms to see if Payback was there. Viva was mentally concocting a story for when they got caught in the lie.

"The procedures went fine," the nurse was saying. "Your husband should be waking up soon."

"Will he even know who I am?" Viva asked, thinking: *Because I won't know* him.

"One step at a time," the nurse said quietly, and opened the door to Room 107.

Viva expected to see a stranger, but the man lying in the bed was Jerry Jeff Tupelo. His eyes were closed, and he was breathing oxygen through a canula. Viva counted a dozen shiny surgical staples in his bruised forehead. She stepped close enough to see the ID on his baby-blue wrist tag: "KRISTIANSEN, NOEL."

What a name! she thought. *Where did old Jerry Jeff come up with that one?*

"How's our guy doing?" It was Twilly, standing beside the nurse in the doorway.

She said, "Somebody cracked his head open, as you can see. He'll stay with us a couple of days for observation. I think he'll be fine."

"How did he get here?" Viva asked.

"He took a cab on his own, Mrs. Kristiansen."

"That is *so* Noel."

Twilly said, "We should probably let him rest."

"Wait—who did this to him?" Viva demanded, warming to the role.

"He told us somebody named Gwyneth," the nurse said skeptically.

"Who?"

"The Goop lady."

"Oh dear," said Viva.

"Obviously he suffered head trauma, Mrs. Kristiansen. Our priority was to do a scan and stitch him up."

Viva whispered, "What else did he say?"

Tupelo/Payback/Kristiansen opened his eyes and blinked once, like a stoned salamander. He seemed confused by Viva's shiny multicolored wig, but he smiled blearily when he recognized Twilly Spree.

"Yo, Chaos," he murmured.

"Yo, Payback," Twilly said.

With the nurse watching, Viva sweetly touched the man's cheek, called him "darling," and told him to get some rest. She was gambling that he was too drugged to remember her from the night he first showed up at Figgo's door. When she left the hospital room, Twilly was close behind. They hurried through double doors to the hospital's main lobby, where Viva called another Uber. It was the world's smallest EV driven by the world's hairiest, sweatiest man. Viva boosted herself into the back seat while Twilly squeezed up front and told the driver to haul ass.

"I've got a bus to catch," he said.

CHAPTER 16

Jonas Onus had gotten up before dawn to go bury Himmler in a Jewish cemetery, an act of subtle desecration that, once completed, left Onus feeling unfulfilled. The makeshift grave marker—an Iron Cross made from rusty scraps of aluminum—succumbed to a gust of wind before Onus made it back to his truck. By then the cemetery's landscape crew had arrived, so there was no going back. Onus fled the scene.

He made brief stops to visit his children, and all three times he was cornered by their mothers. They needed more money, or claimed they did. Onus told them to be patient, because he had a plan.

Which was true, though it was a plan starving for details. If Figgo (and Twilly Spree, his shady body man) were removed from the picture, Onus would be the next Stroker in line to manage the congressman's top-secret white vigilance fund. All two million bucks of it, minus whatever the Key West mission had cost. Onus's strategy was to discredit or even eliminate Figgo and Twilly without drawing suspicion to himself and stoking more dissension within the group. Already he was at risk of being ostracized for starting the fight on Fever Beach.

Due to a fierce aversion to mainstream media, Onus didn't hear about what had happened on Duval Street until the next morning as he listened to podcasts in his Tundra under the big special oak. Steve Bannon was hailing the drag-club mission as a bold, righteous attack on wokeism, and several times he mentioned the fucking Strokers for Liberty by name. This was huge. Dale Figgo, that back-stabbing bastard, had done it. The Strokers were officially in the national conversation.

Onus was now too perturbed to enjoy an interlude with his Dream Booty. He capped the bottle of baby oil and thought: *Skipping the Key West trip was a big goddamn mistake.*

Overnight the Strokers had been legitimized and Congressman Clure Boyette would undoubtedly view Dale Figgo as a natural-born mastermind. Onus felt sick. He had no Plan B except to back off and wait patiently, agonizingly, for Figgo to fuck up—and to hasten that outcome when an opportunity presented itself. He drove home in a gut-sour funk. He hadn't felt so helpless and bitter since the day Tucker got canned by the pussies at Fox.

There was a six-pack of Modelo in the refrigerator and Onus drank every bottle. Later he heard somebody knocking, fished the Glock out of his right boot, and flung open the front door. The visitor was a pleasant short-haired woman wearing a tan shirt bearing the logo of the county animal shelter. She was carrying a plastic crate.

"Are you Mr. Onus?" she said. "This is for you."

"What the hell is it?"

"Just a puppy."

"A mistake is what it is." Onus shoved the Glock into the waistband of his pants.

"He's only seven weeks old," said the woman, who plainly was accustomed to seeing firearms during pet adoptions.

"I didn't ask for another damn dog!" Onus snapped.

"He's a rescue." The woman opened the crate and took out the brown-and-white pup, which had fluffy curled hair.

Onus said, "When's the last time he ate? He's so runty."

"That's because he's a mini-mix."

"Mix a what?"

"Oh, a variety of fun, feisty genes," the woman from the shelter answered cheerily. "If I had to guess, I'd say toy poodle, Yorkie, and golden."

"So, mixed *race* is what you're sayin'. He's a mixed-race canine."

"Mr. Figgo picked him especially out for you." The woman handed the puppy to Onus. "Don't worry, he's been dewormed."

"Dale did this?" Onus was surprised, and ruffled.

"He said you'd recently lost a cherished dog."

"Well, I don't want this nappy little turd."

"Keep him tonight and call us tomorrow if you still feel that way."

"I damn sure will. What time do you open?" Onus said.

But he woke up from a nap with the friendly little hairball in his arms and said what the hell. He named it Goebbels and luckily it liked Himmler's dog food, because Onus still had a thirty-pound bag in the pantry.

After dinner, when he took the puppy outside to poop in the neighbor's flower bed, he saw that his muted phone had been blowing up. Friends were texting viral videos of the scene at the Key West drag club, and it looked nothing like Steve Bannon's glory-filled account. There were no citizen heroics by the Strokers for Liberty. No political statement was made, no ground held, no honor preserved. It was a fucking rout, an old-fashioned stomping. Onus was ashamed to see Skid Mark, Das Regulator, and the others being pummeled by female impersonators in high heels. He felt embarrassed for the group though he held zero sympathy for the responsible party, despite his gift to Onus of a replacement pet.

The drag performers had trussed Dale Figgo with sheer red leggings and left him bleating pathetically on the stage. The memes being posted by gay-loving libtards were freakin' clever, Onus had to admit. He couldn't help but chuckle. It was awesome how fast his prospects had changed.

Then the congressman called.

~~~~

Viva rented a car at the Key West airport and beat Twilly back to his apartment in Tangelo Shores. He had given her a key. She lay in his bed posting reels of video she'd recorded at the Trauma Queens, and she was still awake when he walked in at two something in the morning. He described the bus ride home as somber and uneventful; he'd tipped Fournier a couple hundred bucks to help him hoist the banged-up Strokers into their cars and pickups at the IHOP. Viva told him she'd scouted for the name Noel Kristiansen online and learned he was a registered Republican and former high-level executive at a pharmaceutical company.

"I have a street address, too," she said.

"Local?" Twilly asked.

"Only two zip codes from mine."

She took a long shower. Afterward she wiped the steam from the mirror and stood there dripping, looking at herself.

"I wish I could be a hot mess for a day," she said. "Or at least a smoke show."

Twilly peeked into the bathroom. "Hon, you're already a smoke show."

"*Not*. But I know when it's being blown up my ass."

Twilly grinned. Viva wrapped herself in a towel and said, out of nowhere, "Malcolm hated my hair in a ponytail. He said it made me look like a waitress."

"I'm a huge fan of waitresses."

"*Servers,* Twilly."

"It's late. You're a zombie."

"He also wanted me to get new boobs. Gravity-defying boobs. I said no."

"Take a gummy," was Twilly's advice. "Malcolm was a fool."

While Twilly was in the shower, Viva opened the *New York Times* app on her phone and tackled an in-depth story about the Federal Reserve. She was sound asleep by the time Twilly came out of the bathroom, and she didn't wake up until she heard him mov-
~~~~

ing around the next morning. He was sipping coffee and pressing a collared white shirt.

She said, "Is this a dream? You own an iron?"

"I didn't sleep much. I feel shitty about what's-his-face."

"Payback. The nurse said he'll be okay."

"He wasn't into it at the drag club. He was just standing there watching when they clocked him," Twilly said. "The others deserved what they got. Not him. He looked like he wanted to crawl down a hole. What did I do with my damn keys?"

"On the counter next to the coffee machine. Where might you be going?"

"To check out a theory."

"I'm too tired for theories," Viva said.

"Go back to sleep. I got Claude Mink's cell number off your phone. Clure Boyette's, too. Is that okay?"

"Did you talk to them?"

"Claude and I chatted for a time," Twilly said. "The congressman received a text. I represented myself as a concerned earthling."

He put on the collared shirt and buttoned it up. Then black jeans. Viva told him he looked good.

"FYI, I counted eleven," she said.

"Eleven what?"

"Scars. From your neck to your kneecaps."

"That's not so bad," Twilly said. "I would've guessed more."

"Why won't you tell me where you're goin'?"

"Later, Smoke Show."

Viva got up at noon. The packaging from Twilly's new burner phone was on the kitchen counter where he'd opened it. Viva made some toast and did the new Wordle. The answer was **POLYP**, and she nailed it in three tries. She put on her clothes and went to turn in the car. The rental company tried to gouge her for a full second day and she ended up behind the counter, arguing with an assistant manager who didn't look old enough to drive. He had no chance.

Dale Figgo wasn't home when Viva arrived at the townhouse. His duffel lay open on the kitchen floor beside a damp black tactical outfit, turned inside out except for the body armor vest. She poked through the bag and spied nothing of interest. When she entered his room she saw that the bed had been slept in. A glass of flat cola was on the nightstand next to an open bottle of Tylenol. In the drawer were loose bullets, empty Ziplocs, and a AAA street map of Bonifay County, Florida. Viva unfolded the map and noticed that someone had used a red pen to circle the intersection of Beet Boulevard and 17th Avenue, in the municipality of Carpville. Viva remembered that it was Clure Boyette's hometown. She took a picture of the map, returned it to the drawer, and went upstairs to read.

At lunchtime she ordered a Cuban sandwich on DoorDash, and it showed up at the same time as her landlord. Figgo was in a rotten mood, pale and more paranoid than usual. He refused to speak out loud, setting the television to a deafening volume and lowering all the shades in case the feds were using directional mics. Then he took out a ladder and covered all the smoke alarms except Viva's with duct tape, saying they contained miniature cameras monitored by Homeland Security. He looked like he'd been pushed down an escalator.

Viva pretended not to know where he'd been the previous night, or what had gone down. Clearly he hadn't recognized her in the blue Billie wig at the Trauma Queens—if he noticed her at all during the scuffle. Citing Viva's exemplary record as a tenant, Donna Figgo had promised to keep her name out of it when she confronted her son, a chat that obviously had been punctuated with left-right combinations.

"ICE!" Dale wrote on Viva's Pollo Tropical bag and thrust it at her. Then he unzipped his hoodie and collapsed on the sectional.

The icemaker in the refrigerator was broken, so Viva brought him four bags of frozen broccoli, which he gingerly arranged across his midsection.

"What happened?" she wrote on another part of the bag.

"NEVER MIND."

"But you're hurt."

"NO SHIT!" Figgo scribbled back.

Damn, Viva thought. *This man's momma did a number on him.*

When she motioned that she was going upstairs, Figgo shook his head and continued writing. The Sharpie had a large tip, and he was running out of space on the bag. Viva saw that his words were getting smaller and smaller. When he was done, he emphatically jabbed a finger at the message:

"ONUS SHOWS UP, TELL HIM I WENT TO MIAMI FOR A FUNEREL. DON'T LET HIM IN!!!!"

The last part was underlined several times. Viva shrugged and mouthed the word, "Okay."

But later, when Jonas Onus appeared at the door, she couldn't say no. She had a soft spot for puppies.

~~~~

"I wanted you to hear this from me," Clure Boyette said to the Minks, "not the fake news."

Ripped on coke, he'd driven to their house first thing in the morning responding to a furious phone call. Claude and Electra had learned about the Key West brawl from *Fox & Friends,* where the story had been twisted into a dire warning about the mental instability of cross-dressing performers. Meanwhile the Strokers for Liberty had been described by one of the Fox hosts as a "peaceful organization dedicated to protecting family values by confronting perversion in all its forms." The Minks didn't approve of drag shows, but they weren't weirdly obsessed, as some politicians were. Claude and Electra thought gay marriage was a much bigger threat to the country's tender youth, followed by non-European immigrants, hip-hop music, and the novels of Judy Blume.

One of Claude's MAGA friends sent a link to a compilation of TikTok videos from the fight at the Key West nightclub, merrily set to Ozzy Osbourne's "Crazy Train." The black-clad Strokers had obviously misread the room, as not a single audience member rushed forward to help them. It was a shameful showing, the Minks agreed independently. They were unaware that they'd financed the debacle until an anonymous male caller told Claude, in enough detail to be convincing. The caller identified himself as
~~~~

Wee Hammer *Numero Uno*. Clure Boyette had received a similar message on a text that proved untraceable.

Now the congressman was face-to-face with his seething benefactors. Claude sat stubbled and prunish in long loose pajamas, bony elbows planted on the kitchen table. "I can't believe those boobs are your guys!" he railed at Boyette. "I can't believe this is where our money's going!"

Electra was wearing a white bath towel on her head and an alarmingly short breakfast kimono.

"They all look alike," she said contemptuously. "Same beards, same beer guts."

"The lighting in that nightclub wasn't great," Boyette pointed out. "But, hey, I feel you."

"Feel *what*?" Claude snapped.

"I mean I'm disappointed by the outcome, just like you."

Electra cackled derisively. "*Disappointed?* Those clowns got the holy shit beat out of them by a bunch of fairies!"

The Minks weren't podcast-savvy, so they were unaware of Steve Bannon's positive spin on the event. Boyette had heard about it, but the videos didn't lie.

"Don't worry," he said. "Nobody else is aware of the connection between us and them."

Which, based on the anonymous calls, clearly wasn't true.

"Not 'us,' Congressman. It's *you*. *You* and them." Claude's voice was ice.

"We never heard of these people until today," Electra added pointedly. "We believed our donation was going to fund the Wee Hammers. Teaching valuable construction skills to children is what you said. Kids in underserved communities."

The old hag's talking like the place is bugged, Boyette thought. *She knew exactly where the money was going.*

He smiled valiantly. "The Wee Hammers are very real, and they're doing inspirational work. Next week the trusses go up on the first house. Would you like to have a look at the pictures?"

"No, I would like you to leave now and come back with some answers. *We* would like you to leave."

Boyette noticed that Electra hadn't once made eye contact with her husband. There was tension in the room that had nothing to do with the disaster on Duval Street.

"Go out the back door," Claude barked at Boyette, "so nobody'll see you."

"But I'm parked out front."

"Vamoose," Electra said.

The congressman stood to leave. "What happened in Key West won't ever happen again, you've got my word. Next time the operation will be flawless and professional."

"Screw next time." Claude struggled to his feet. "We want our two million back right now."

Electra snorted. "And do what with it, Claude? Buy another MRI for the hospital, so all the rapists and dope dealers sneaking across the border can get a free scan when they show up? It's real Americans we should be worried about. American culture, American principles, American blood. We'll give Clure another shot. The stakes are too high to quit now."

Boyette said, "Thank you, Electra, I won't let you down."

"But if one dime of our 'donation' gets traced back to these baboons—"

"Or the name 'M-I-N-K' shows up in the *Times*—" Claude cut in.

"Then you're the one who's going down, Congressman." Electra chomped into a scone, spraying crumbs. "And I'll make sure it happens before Election Day."

"There's nothing to worry about," Boyette said, sidling toward the door. "Just wait and see."

He snorted his last two lines while driving to the Denny's where Dale Figgo had been summoned to appear. The man showed up twenty minutes late with a New College hoodie pulled up over his head but bent over and creaking like he was a hundred years old. Bleeding kidneys, he whispered to the twitchy congressman, due to a barrage of rabbit punches. Boyette assumed that the drag performers were the offenders. He never would have guessed that it was Figgo's own mother.

"What'd they do to your nose?" Boyette asked.

"No, that's from the bike accident. Skin graft."

"Christ, it looks like a nut sack."

Figgo flushed. "You sure it's safe to talk here?"

"Safe from what, Dale? Nobody in the FBI eats at a fucking Denny's."

Out of caution, Figgo kept the hoodie on his head, the same as he had during the service that his mother had punitively dragged him to at St. David's that morning. It was the first church she'd spotted on the two-lane into Tangelo Shores. They had sat in the last pew and ducked out after only twenty minutes due to Donna Figgo's long-standing beef with Catholicism. She drove her son back to the townhouse and stayed there, watching a damn golf tournament, until the plumber that she'd made him call showed up to snake his model tenant's shower drain.

"So, what did your patriot angels say?" Figgo asked Clure Boyette.

"They're pissed. They want to pull the plug on your outfit, but I talked 'em out of it."

The congressman ordered the Grand Slamwich. Figgo went for a country-fried steak and an iced tea, sweetened. He couldn't get comfortable in the booth; every joint in his body ached. There were ligature grooves on his wrists from being tied up with the stockings that came from a mothballed Carol Channing act, or so he'd been told by his captors. He had no clue who or what Carol Channing was.

"So, Key fucking West," Boyette said. "Your bright idea?"

"I thought it'd be easy-peasy. I don't know what went wrong."

"Besides everything?"

"Maybe they knew we were coming," Figgo said.

"So, somebody tipped off the drag queens? Seriously?"

"Bro, the target was a secret. Nobody in the group knew except me . . ." Figgo sat back and snapped his fingers. "Maybe the feds put a tracker on the bus! Or they had micro-drones tailin' us!"

"Or they hid a chip up your ass," Boyette said.

"Whatever. All I know is they were bad motherfuckers, those dudes at the club."

"Yeah, the lowlights are all over the internet."

Breakfast arrived, and Figgo attacked it. The congressman narrowly examined his entree. He had many things on his mind, the foremost of which was making sure his father didn't find out that he'd been secretly seeding the Strokers for Liberty.

"It's a miracle none of you Einsteins ended up in jail," he muttered.

Figgo chewed on a strip of bacon. As dense as he could be, he realized it wasn't an ideal moment to ask for a full-time salaried position for managing the group. For now, at least, he'd have to hang on to his line job at Bottom Drawer Novelties.

"Here's what I can do," he said to Boyette. "I'll go on KRANKK and make a statement saying the Key West videos are deepfakes. I'll say the guys who stormed the club were really undercover feds, not Strokers. And then the government edited the videos and put our faces on their bodies with . . . you know, whatchacallit."

"AI?"

"Right. Artificial interference."

"Have you ever been tested," the congressman asked, "by experts?"

"Tested for what?"

"Never mind."

"I'm a hundred percent normal," Figgo said defensively.

"By the way, those caps you wore to the drag show? There's three of 'em up on eBay already."

"Cocksuckers," Figgo sighed. Several of the men, himself included, had lost their Strokers lids during the fight.

"Dale, here's my concern." Boyette took a crisp bite of his sandwich. "It's a management issue. Obviously you've taken on too much responsibility. The kind of shit that went down in Key West cannot go down at Precinct 53. Understand? Basically my whole universe hinges on winning that election, and winning big."

"Totally."

"Your friend Onus—what was his role in the drag club mission?"

"Zero," Figgo said spitefully. "Hell, he didn't even show up."

"I want you to give him a co-leadership position in the Strokers."

"Dude, that'll never work! Too many chefs in the soup."

Boyette said, "I've met the man. He seems capable."

"He's got a shitty temper and no respect for rank."

"Let's try it, okay?" The congressman paused to polish his top front teeth with a forefinger. "I've got a feeling," he went on, "that the drag show operation would've turned out way different if Onus had been there."

"Nobody stopped that puss-boy from gettin' on the bus," Figgo said. "Speakin' of which, the charter company won't refund the damn security deposit."

"How much is that?"

"Three thousand bucks."

"For what?" Boyette demanded.

"Extra cleanup, they said. There was some blood on the seats, yeah, but not three grand worth. No fuckin' way! One of the guys might've pissed hisself on the floor, sure, but that's an easy-peasy deal with a wet vac—"

"Enough." Boyette raised a hand. "Sweet Jesus, no more."

His phone was vibrating. It was Chalk, the salesperson at the Aston Martin dealership.

"Dale, I need to take this call."

Figgo gave a sulky nod and went back to eating. Boyette answered the phone and said, "What's up, my brother?"

"It's about the DB11 we were building for your special friend."

"No more delays. I don't want to hear that."

Galaxy's new Aston Martin convertible. She'd been texting and leaving voice messages on Boyette's phone almost every day, not seeming to comprehend that the term "built to order" meant extra factory time.

"Actually, the car came in yesterday," Chalk said.

"That's awesome! How's she look?"

"Understand that it was my day off."

"Yeah, so?"

"You won't believe what happened," Chalk said, and he laid it all out for the congressman.

The line went dead before Chalk had a chance to apologize.

CHAPTER 17

Lewin Baltry drove miles and miles down a dirt road. In the back of the commissioner's Subaru was a Hefty bag filled with empty Pabst Blue Ribbon cans. When he got out of sight of the interstate, he stopped and set one of the cans on a fence post. Six times he fired the pistol and missed. He stepped closer, reloaded, and tried again. The can didn't even wobble.

Baltry couldn't believe how hard it was to put a bullet in a stationary target at close range. His shooting arm noodled up and down. He tried aiming with his right eye squinted shut, then his left eye closed, then with both eyes wide open. He was standing only eight paces from the beer can when he finally shot it off the post. A pathetic display, as he was well aware.

A gopher, its cheeks stuffed with grass, appeared upright on the dusty road behind the commissioner, and, by God, he fired at that, too. The result was a hole in the left front quarter panel of the Outback. That's how the afternoon went. Baltry returned to the house in Wolf Creek with all but three of the PBR empties and one round in the gun. He'd started with a box of fifty.

His arm throbbed and his eardrums rang. He poured a tumbler of Jack Daniel's and sagged into the recliner, which, although recently reupholstered, smelled like a wet Labrador. He missed playing his piano, a Yamaha grand that had been purchased with proceeds from the first bribe he ever took. Maybe he would donate it to the high school music department, in case he got indicted and needed to impress the judge.

The pistol mocked Baltry from a nearby windowsill. He knew he was supposed to clean the damn thing after firing it; he'd watched the tutorials on YouTube. Still, he saw no harm in waiting until tomorrow.

He drank another Jack, straight, and wondered if he'd ever be able to return to Florida. Probably not. But then what? The one thing he was good at was graft, which worked pretty much the same way no matter where you lived. True, corruption opportunities were less abundant for politicians in Montana, but Baltry could picture himself moving to a boomtown like Bozeman or Missoula and running for a commission seat there. Getting elected couldn't be that hard. Hell, the governor of the whole state was a whackadoodle who believed that Noah brought dinosaurs on the ark.

Baltry tried calling the number given to him by the fake carjacker at the Wendy's back home. He was hoping for an update regarding the feds who were supposedly surveilling him—had they tracked him all the way to Wolf Creek?

The call didn't go through. Baltry's phone showed zero bars.

He told himself it might work in his favor, being so far from a cell tower. That would make him harder to find, he reasoned, oblivious to other trails he had left.

A car drove up to the house—a generic late-model compact, utterly useless as a personal vehicle in the northern Rockies. It had to be a rental, some lost tourist. Baltry grabbed the pistol from the sill and went outside.

The man who got out of the car was middle-aged, short, balding. He had a golfer's tan but wore stiff new Carhartt work pants and a forest-green fleece over a shirt and tie. His wire-rimmed glasses made him look like an auditor, or maybe a jeweler.

"Hello, Mr. Baltry," he said.

The commissioner was stunned. "Who are you? What's your business here?"

"I go by Moe," the man said. "No *Three Stooges* jokes, please."

"My name's not Baltry. You've got the wrong house."

The man walked up to the commissioner and straightforwardly took the gun. He said, "You could easily shoot off your own schlong with this thing."

I'm a dead man, thought Baltry.

"You can have it," he said to the stranger. "It doesn't work right, anyway."

"Are you sure?"

"It aims crooked. The sight must be messed up."

"Hmm." Moe raised the pistol and shot a yapping magpie out of an aspen tree. The bird fell dead onto the hood of Baltry's Subaru.

"Jesus," said Baltry, under his breath.

"Well, now you know why I'm here."

"I don't. What I mean is, hold on. Please?"

"Claude Mink sent me."

"Shit. *Shit.*"

"Yup," the killer said. "Let's go inside."

Baltry thought about running away, but he was barefoot and the chipped rocks in the driveway were sharp. Also, he was out of shape. He calculated that the odds of escaping were lower than the odds of talking Moe out of murdering him.

"How'd you find me?" he asked the killer after they sat down in the house.

"You bought a used vehicle in Oregon and put this address as where the registration should be sent. Don't feel bad about using your own name. If you're not a pro, it's tough to buy a car with fake ID and insurance, even in the secondary market. Most people in my field wouldn't have been able to locate you through a DMV on the other side of the country. I'm not bragging. It's the truth. For a putz, you did a half-decent job of disappearing."

Baltry began to shake; first his hands, then his knees. That the man looked so normal made him scarier.

"Listen, Moe, the feds are after me. That's why I left Florida. I'm totally on their radar."

"Interesting," the killer said. "Who told you that?"

"Someone on the inside."

"The inside of what? A mental hospital?"

"I'm not bullshitting you," Baltry insisted.

"No offense, but the FBI wouldn't waste five minutes chasing a mouse turd like you." The killer said this firmly but mildly, as if speaking to a bartender who'd fucked up his margarita.

Baltry sucked in his breath and tried another approach. "Moe, there's no reason for you to go through with this. Seriously. I won't cause any more trouble for the Minks."

"That's what we need to talk about," the killer said.

"Sure. Okay. I'll do anything they want. Like, what if I resign from the commission? Then they can pick a new guy—their own guy—to vote for The Bunkers. Or gal. Doesn't matter, you get what I'm saying."

"How well do you know Claude Mink?"

"Never met him," Baltry replied, which was true.

"Have you two spoken on the phone? He's quite the crude old prick."

"Oh."

"And, also, prejudiced against Jews," the killer added.

What's that got to do with me? Baltry wondered.

"Tell Mr. Mink I'll give him his money back, all seventy-five thousand," he said. "It's in Bermuda. I'll have it wired to my bank in Great Falls tomorrow. You can come with me."

The killer said he couldn't care less about the terms of the bribe. "Claude isn't paying me to get the money back. He's paying me to erase you from the picture."

"But, see, that's what I'm tryin' to tell you. I'm already out of the picture! I'm gone, Moe, and I promise to stay gone."

"And what I'm trying to tell *you*," the killer said, "is that I don't want you to stay gone, Mr. Baltry. I want you to come back."

~~~~
~~~~

Mary was an angel. Mary was his rock. Could she ever forgive him?

"We'll see," she said, with half a smile.

Noel Kristiansen reached over the rail of the hospital bed to squeeze her hand. His head hurt like hell—again—but the doctors said he'd feel better in a few weeks.

"I lied to you," he said to his wife. "I'm sorry."

"Well, I knew damn well you weren't out bowling."

"I had a good plan," he said. "I can't remember what it was, but I know I had one."

"The main thing is you're going to be okay."

"I have a question." This was Twilly Spree, all dressed up and standing at the foot of the bed. "It's about the name you made up for yourself. 'Jerry Jeff Tupelo'?"

"Wait, you knew it was fake?" Kristiansen said.

His wife gave him a pitying look.

Twilly said, "Jerry Jeff as in Walker, right? And Tupelo because that's where Elvis was born."

Kristiansen was bummed. "I didn't think the Strokers would figure it out."

"Dale Figgo never did," Twilly said, "because he has shitty taste in music."

"So, how'd you come up with 'Chaos'?"

"I've had more than one girlfriend say it should be my middle name."

"'Payback' wasn't bad, either. Right?"

"Very snappy," Twilly said. "But your days as an avenging superhero are over. Go back to your quiet, normal life, Noel. The clock of misery is ticking down for Figgo, don't worry."

Earlier, after Twilly had introduced himself to Mary Kristiansen in the hallway outside her husband's hospital room, she'd told him that Figgo was the Nazi-inspired leafleteer who ran Noel over in front of their home, and that Noel had been bent on justice.

"You gave it a try," Mary now said to Noel. "Time to stand down and let this play out."

"How's that gonna happen?"

"In a way that doesn't endanger our family. That much I can say for sure."

"So, you're tapping me out?"

"As of yesterday," Mary said.

Kristiansen touched the row of stitches on the side of his shorn head.

"I can't believe I got taken down by a drag queen."

"Gwyneth Paltrow," Twilly said.

"I didn't know that."

"From her *Shakespeare in Love* era. She had arms like Travis Kelce, by the way, so don't be too hard on yourself."

Mary said, "Mr. Spree has another question, Noel."

"I'm tired."

"I came to ask if you're with the feds," Twilly said.

It hurt to laugh, but Noel did.

Twilly explained: "They've got informants deep in the Proud Boys, Oath Keepers, White Fists of Doom, all the hate groups. When you backed away from that big fight in Key West, it seemed like something a snitch or an FBI agent would do. They need to be clean as a whistle on the witness stand."

Kristiansen felt flattered that Twilly thought he could be smooth enough—and ballsy enough—to go undercover for the government. He admitted that he was a solo operative, ruefully adding, "I didn't throw a single punch, yet I'm the one that ended up in the hospital."

Mary said, "We power through, and we learn."

"But how do I tell the Strokers I'm quitting?"

"Don't reach out. I'll deal with those dipshits," Twilly said.

In a way, Kristiansen felt he was being cut from the team.

"So, what's *your* real story?" he asked Twilly tartly. "Maybe you're the one with the feds."

Now it was Twilly's turn to laugh.

"I'm not with anyone," he said.

"Then why bother to screw with these maniacs?"

"Reflex, I guess. When you see a cockroach, you step on it."

"Roaches don't carry assault rifles," Mary said.

Twilly shrugged. "The timing was right. I'm between projects right now."

Kristiansen lifted his head. "What exactly do you do in your regular life?"

Twilly coughed once, tightly, and fished the asthma inhaler out of his pocket.

"Excuse me, folks," he wheezed, and stepped out of the room.

Twenty minutes passed before the Kristiansens realized he wasn't coming back.

"What an odd duck," Noel said to his wife.

"He paid for the ambulance that brought you back from Key West."

"Really? I thought it was you."

"I tried to give him a check, but he wouldn't take it." Mary didn't know what to make of Twilly Spree, or of his risky infiltration of the Strokers. He gave the impression of having no sensible fear, or second thoughts.

"The doctors say you've got another concussion," Mary told her husband, "but not quite as bad as the first."

Kristiansen nodded unhappily. "They told me it could've been worse."

"Fred Brillstein wants to sue the drag club, but I said there's no way we could win. Not in front of a Key West jury—and especially with the defendants being icons of stage and screen."

"Ha-ha," Kristiansen said, though it was sort of funny. He liked watching Mary try to keep a straight face when she teased him.

"I got rid of your gun," she said. "That's no joke."

"It was just part of the act."

"And that ratty Confederate coat, too."

Kristiansen had bought the mock tunic online from a costume shop in Atlanta. Only fifty bucks.

"It got ruined by all the blood," his wife said. "Your blood."

"I'm sorry. I really am."

"What life lesson are you taking from all this, Noel?"

"I love you, Mary."

\/\/\/\/

The puppy bounded up on the sectional and squatted. Viva blotted the peed-on pleather with a picnic napkin. Figgo was hunkered down in an upstairs closet.

Jonas Onus was all torqued up after an hour of Alex Jones under the oak tree—the latest COVID booster was actually a government sterilization formula that affected only Caucasians.

"Sounds like you missed quite a show in Key West," Viva said.

"Disaster's more like it."

"That's a super-cute dog, I've got to admit. What's his name?"

"Goebbels," Onus said. "He's all right."

"What mix?"

"He ain't a mix. He's a hundred percent purebred Yarborough."

"What's a Yarborough?"

"From Ireland." Onus felt pretty solid about the story. He got the name Yarborough from a Netflix documentary about the Daytona 500.

"They're pub dogs," he told Viva. "For killin' rats and such."

Thinking: *I'm crushing it.*

"How big do they get?" she asked.

"Not as big as Himmler. Where's Dale at?"

"He went down to Miami for a funeral."

"Really? How'd he get there with no wheels?" Onus took a beer from the refrigerator and planted his mountainous, unbathed self in front of the blank TV.

Viva scooped up the hyper puppy, which started licking her chin and neck.

"If you ever need a dogsitter," she said, grinning.

Onus wouldn't allow himself to be distracted by chitchat, even with a pretty girl. He was dying to ask Viva about her boyfriend, Chaos, with whom he had a score to settle—though not tonight. He was laser-locked on seizing power, Figgo having single-handedly demoralized the Strokers for Liberty.

"I ain't movin' from here till I talk with Dale," Onus said.

Viva told him to hang tight, and, still carrying the dog, she went up the stairs. A few minutes later, Figgo came down alone, holding his Glock.

Not this shit again, thought Onus.

His former friend moved haltingly, taking small cautious steps until he sat down on a facing wedge of sectional. Onus thought he looked awful—gray, drained, downcast.

"We could've used some of your muscle in Key West," Figgo said. "Where the hell were you?"

"Don't blame me for what went down. You guys got stomped by a bunch a queers and now it's all over the damn internet."

Figgo's eyes narrowed. "Those were badass queers, bro. It was a trap."

"Put away the piece," Onus said.

"In a minute."

"I'm not here to kill ya. The congressman called me."

"Why?" said Figgo.

"About my promotion. He told me you'd been briefed."

"There was talk of it." Figgo disconsolately concealed his pistol between the cushions.

Onus said, "The fuck happened to your arms?"

Figgo self-consciously covered the stocking marks on his wrists. "So, what'd he tell you? Congressman Clueless."

"He said from now on it's you and me in charge, fifty-fifty. Co-chairs for field ops, logistics, tactical, budget, everything."

"Co-chairs," Figgo repeated.

"Starting today."

"After you jumped me at the beach? In front a everybody."

"Won't happen again. I was drunk and pissed off."

"You weren't drunk, bro. Don't lie."

Onus told Figgo to grab himself a beer.

"I ain't thirsty," Figgo said.

"We need to tell the others about the new arrangement."

"Your big promotion. Yaay."

"It's important, chain-of-command-wise. We gotta start rampin' up for Precinct 53." Onus watched the reality of the situation sink in. Dale Figgo was a man with diminishing options.

"Whatever," he mumbled. "Back to Fever Beach, I guess."

"When?"

"Next Wednesday night at one-zero-hundred hours."

"You mean twenty-two hundred. Just say ten o'clock." Onus stood up and whistled. Little Goebbels came clambering down the stairs and leapt into his arms.

Onus cleared his throat. The next part wouldn't be easy.

"Another reason I came over," he said to Figgo, "was to say thanks for this cool surprise. 'Preciate the effort, bro."

"Wait—thanks for what?"

"This furry little pisser." Onus patted the puppy's nose. "First I didn't want to keep him, but he's pretty cool."

"That wasn't me," Figgo said sharply.

"Don't try and screw with my head, bro. The chick from the shelter said you picked him out yourself and even paid to get him wormed."

"Bullshit, Jonas. I wouldn't give you another dog! Not after the last one."

"Then what the fuck?" Onus held Goebbels at arm's length for examination. The puppy squirmed and whined and kicked its short nappy legs.

"It's a setup," Figgo whispered ominously. "We gotta X-ray this motherfucker."

~~~

Viva's sister Maya sent her a book called *Digging Up and Digging Out*. It was the personal journey of a twice-rejected TV bachelorette. The jacket flap said that her occupation was "digital strategist" and her story was inspirational. She was twenty-four years old, centered, resilient, and newly married to a Silicon Valley entrepreneur with three challenging teenage sons. Viva threw out the book but saved the Amazon box. She called her parents in Dallas but cut it short when the conversation turned to border politics.

Twilly had invited her on a possible date. For some reason, he'd asked her to meet him in the parking lot at TJ Maxx. With a rare tease of autumn in the air, Viva put on white jeans, a light knit
~~~

pullover, and the simple gold necklace her parents had given her for high-school graduation. She wondered what Figgo and Onus were talking about downstairs, and she was glad not to hear scuffling or gunshots. Twilly had continued urging her to move out of the townhouse, but she couldn't afford to and refused to let him help with the money. Galaxy said she was being stupidly prideful, and there were moments when Viva felt that might be true. Just because Figgo was a bungler didn't mean he wasn't a menace. Viva couldn't understand why she wasn't more frightened of him, though it didn't hurt to have his hard-punching mother as a backup.

He and Onus were gone when Viva went downstairs. She cleaned up an amber puddle of puppy pee in the kitchen, locked the apartment, and drove to the TJ Maxx. The lot was empty. Viva called Twilly from her car. He answered on the first ring and said he was already there.

A sleek convertible with the top down came around the side of the building, Twilly at the wheel. And not just any convertible.

Viva got in and said, "The real you. Finally."

"This is why I couldn't come to the townhouse. Figgo would be all over me."

"Well, sure. You bought a fucking Aston Martin."

"I did, I did," Twilly said. "It's a DB11."

"Stunning. I hear good things."

"Solar bronze."

"My fave. How'd you know?"

"There's a backstory," Twilly said.

"Yeah, this is Galaxy's car. You bought Galaxy's new car."

"These salesmen, Viva, no scruples whatsoever. He told me it was promised to another customer but I made him an offer—twenty percent over MSRP—and he practically came in his pants. Now Clure Boyette's got to tell young Galaxy there's no DB11. I expect she'll be upset."

"Livid," Viva said, smiling in spite of herself. "Out of control."

"She'll need someone to talk to."

"I like her. She likes me."

Twilly pulled into traffic and drove west. Viva's hair was a mess from the wind by the time they got to The Bunkers. Twilly stopped outside the gate and took a pair of bolt cutters from the trunk.

"That is *so* sexy," Viva said.

"Don't be snarky. I want you to see something."

"Isn't it unbelievable that we're both still single? With all we've got going for us?"

"Quiet," said Twilly.

He clipped the padlock off the gate and drove past the contractor's trailer to where the graded road ended. Under a hazy yellow moon, Twilly and Viva had a clear view of the sprawling, scraped vista where citrus groves once stood. She tried to picture bushy rows of orange trees reaching to the horizon, but the dead-gray flatness made it look more like tundra. For dinner Twilly had brought takeout Mexican—quesadillas, chips, salsa—and YETI tumblers filled with an unidentifiable red wine.

Viva heard a muffled rumble of machinery, and Twilly pointed to a distant silvery stripe, moonlight on water. The Bunkers contractor was surreptitiously digging canals despite the fact that the project remained legally in limbo, deadlocked by the shorthanded county commission. Wisps of exhaust smoke trailed from the squat shape of the excavator, though no lights were visible on the cab.

Viva said, "I get it, Twilly. I get why you're mad."

"But the pointlessness is obvious, right? They're not going to suddenly change their minds and turn this place into a nature preserve."

"You're not one to look the other way. This is well documented."

"When all is said and done," Twilly said, "it'll be a slightly smaller version of the same atrocity. The Minks could drop dead tomorrow and not much would change, except for the bankers."

He took out the burner phone to pester Claude. Viva listened to Twilly's side of the exchange as he warned the old toad about dredging illegal canals and matter-of-factly threatened to ruin the Minks' name, undoing decades of image-cleansing philanthropy. Viva was taken by Twilly's expert calm. On the other end Claude mistakenly assumed that his anonymous irritant wanted money and blurted a series of escalating offers that Viva couldn't quite hear.

It was Twilly who terminated the phone conversation: "Like the song says, even a dog can shake hands. Good-bye, Claude."

Viva sipped wine from the YETI and commented on the irony: If Twilly's avaricious grandfather hadn't left him so much money—and Twilly was just a working stiff with a regular job—he wouldn't have time to roam around constantly getting triggered, derailed, and carried away by some naive notion of justice. His mind would be too tired to spark all night. Some random a-hole tosses a cigarette in the road, Twilly would just look away and let it go, like a normal person. He wouldn't have enough energy to chase the guy down and use his ear as an ashtray.

"You might be right," Twilly said. "Big Phil made sure I'd be rich enough to ricochet from one dead-end skirmish to another. Maybe that was the plan, the payback for me scorning his life of proud plunder. He knew I'd never come to terms."

"But what does it say about me that I'm hanging out with *you*?"

"We're not so different, Viva. Where else would you rather be on a lovely Florida night? What's better than eating pepper jack cheese on luxe upholstery?"

Viva traced a fingertip across the leather. "What exactly is this color?"

"They call it 'cream truffle.' I swear to God."

"Fabulous," she said. "I bet Big Phil would approve of this ride."

"No, he was a Cadillac man till the day he died."

Twilly's eyes drifted back to the faraway excavator. Viva changed the subject.

"I found a map of Bonifay County in Dale's room," she said.

"Ah. The Carpville Intercession."

"Fill me in, please."

"The Strokers' final stand," Twilly said. "I'll get all the details at the next beach bash."

"Will you be needing a chanteuse? Or a DJ?"

"Take Galaxy to dinner," Twilly said. "She'll need your brand of cheering up."

Viva noted that the stars looked brighter toward the west. She spotted a small sleek form darting and dipping overhead, and asked Twilly what kind of bird it was.

"Not a bird," he said. "That's a bat."

She threatened to stroke out if it landed on her, but Twilly made no move to raise the top of the convertible. The creature disappeared from the sky as silently as it had appeared.

Twilly said, "I meant to ask—has Dale heard from Onus?"

"As a matter of fact, Jonas dropped by tonight. Suave as ever."

"Did you meet his new bestie?"

"Who are you talking about?"

"The puppy."

"Get the fuck out," Viva said.

"From the rescue shelter."

"That was you?"

Twilly said, "He's pretty cute, right?"

CHAPTER 18

Dale Figgo got called off the packaging line and sent to Pierre's office. He figured that one of his coworkers must have stolen more Darcy's Dream Booties, and that he was being framed for it.

"Wasn't me," he asserted.

"Who did what?" Pierre said.

"Steal more product."

"Shut fuck up."

"But I didn't take nuthin'!"

"Sit fuck down." The Russian was slumped sourly at his desk. His forehead acne had flared.

"Tell me what are Strokers of Liberty," he said to Figgo.

"Strokers *for* Liberty. We're a vanguard of white male patriots."

"What is vanguard? You mean like Sprinter?"

"No, not a van—"

"You went Key West last weekend. Why? To fight homosexuals in dresses? All over internet is memes and reels. Your picture, too." Pierre was aggravated.

Figgo said, "We went to a drag show to defend American family values."

"Such shit you should save for idiots."

"We went there to protect our children from—"

"Now Pierre is so stupid you can lie to his face? Is fucking insult."

"Dude, those memes are deepfakes, all photoshopped!" Figgo protested. "The government, they're tryin' to discreditate us."

It felt like eighty degrees in the shabby little office. The air blowing from the broken AC smelled like a moldy root cellar. Pierre unbent a paper clip and began picking lunch particles from his molars.

"I have no like for homosexuals," he said, "but this I keep to myself. Blacks and Jews, eh, the same. Because we are businessmen, and businesses must keep open doors for all customers. LGBTQs, MAGAs, everybody. Is company rules."

"I got it, I got it," Figgo said. A husky male version of the polymer torso—Dickie's Dream Booty—was a top seller in certain markets.

"You know what is 'facial recognition' software?" Pierre asked.

"Sure. CIA uses it. FBI and TSA, too." That, Figgo had heard, was how they busted all the occupiers after January 6th. *His* people, before they spurned him.

"Who else uses facial recognition is airports, futbol stadiums, casinos, private security contractors. Pissed-off homosexual nightclub owners. Is fucked-up situation, I agree," Pierre said. "No privacy in this country anymore."

Figgo wasn't sure where the cagey Russian was steering the conversation. It didn't sound promising.

Pierre twirled the paper clip in his lips. "They say you are one of Capitol shitters. Is true? They match your January 6th picture with drag club posts."

"It wasn't my shit, bro. It was from a dog."

"And this is better how?"

"I picked it up on Pennsylvania Avenue. Under a tree."

"Then you shmear on statue, yes? There are several videos."

"Congress was stealing the goddamn election!" Figgo yelled. "What the hell's this got to do with Key West, anyhow? Things I do in my free time, places I go, that's up to me."

"Is fallout, unfortunately." Pierre sat forward. "You are done here."

"What?"

"Terminated."

"I thought this was America!"

"Is not coming from me. My bosses up in New Jersey, they said, 'Fire that stupid fuck-o.' "

Figgo was floored. "But why?"

"Company policy. Here, I read slow to you because of my English." Pierre opened an email on his laptop. "Is from Bottom Drawer Novelties, Inc. 'We seek a diverse, inclusive workforce, and will not tolerate displays of prejudice, discrimination, or sexual misconduct from any employees.' You want printout?"

"That's some woke-ass bullshit," Figgo said bitterly.

Pierre shrugged. "Two strikes and out you are."

"No, no, it's supposed to be *three* strikes!"

"Okay, first strike was stealing of product, Dream Booties. Second strike is viral fistfight against homosexuals. Third strike, for me, is shmearing stool on historic relic."

Figgo said, "I told you, the shit wasn't from a human."

"Stool is stool. My bosses, they are sensitive about corporate reputation."

"What reputation? You guys sell pocket pussies and solar-powered butt plugs—"

Pierre raised a hand. "Please not so loud."

"The Prostate Plow! Your company sells the goddamn Prostate Plow."

"Is very successful item, Mr. Figgo. Portable. Discreet."

"You can't fire me, not in Florida. This is where woke comes to die!"

Pierre smiled curiously. "What is meaning? How does woke 'die' in Florida? Alligators? Sharks? COVID? I am only joke making, of course. You Americans and your idiot metaphors. We will mail final paycheck."

Figgo shot to his feet. "You fire me, I'll sue your dirty immigrant ass."

"Sit fuck down."

"Hell, no, I won't."

Pierre took out a small black pistol and placed it on the desk.

"Is Makarov," he said. "Better than Glock."

An icy cramp seized Figgo's bowels. He sat down.

The Russian went on: "My personal opinions, these I do not bring to workplace. Men with cocks should dress like men is my view. But we have good customers not liking at all what you and your Strokers did in Key West. Senior management, they follow Reddit, X, other social media. Is a big backlash, they say. Is that the right word? Some trans podcaster, he also is calling for boycott of Bottom Drawer products. Anyway, my bosses said to fire you, so it's done. Now you go."

"I can't fuckin' believe this." Figgo tried to yank off his carpal tunnel wrist brace, but the Velcro held stubbornly.

"How many weeks' pay do I get?" he asked.

"Pay stops today."

"But I got rent and groceries to buy," Figgo griped. "You guys suck."

"Is only business."

Kiss my white Christian ass! Figgo thought. *This shows exactly what's wrong with the country—when an American worker gets canned by a damn Russian!*

Pierre took the paper clip from his mouth and bent it back to its original shape. He looked up and said, "What if I write letter to help you get new job?"

Figgo was caught off guard. "You mean like a recommendation?"

The Russian nodded. "To prove is no hard feelings."

"Sweet," said Dale Figgo.

~~~

Clay Boyette flew down from Carpville on the Citation, which meant he was taking most seriously the problems that Galaxy, the escort, presented. His useless fuck-doodle spawn was waiting at the FBO when the jet landed. They went directly to the Aston
~~~

Martin dealership, where they were apologetically informed that it would be at least three months before another DB11 convertible could be delivered.

"Let me talk to Chalk," Clure Boyette said gruffly.

"He's off today."

"I bet."

Clay Boyette asked for the name of the person who'd bought the car that was custom-built for his son's "good friend." The manager of the dealership said the buyer's information was confidential. The younger Boyette then demanded to know which salesman had let some rich scumbag jump the line and snag the convertible. Once more the manager declined to divulge any details, though he offered to refund the deposit made by one of Clay Boyette's shell companies.

"I'll take a cashier's check," Clay Boyette snapped.

"No, Dad—"

"Ship's sailed, junior."

"But it's not just Galaxy," Clure Boyette said. "Nicki wants a DB11, too."

"Shit. Of course she does."

The elder Boyette instructed the manager to put the deposit toward another convertible—same trim, same color, same everything—for his son's future ex-wife. The manager said he'd try to move the Boyettes to the top of the list at the factory, but no promises. He made a copy of the sales order for Nicki's divorce attorney, the sulfurous Fistman.

Afterward, the congressman took his father to lunch at one of the country clubs he favored. The Cobb salad was sweaty, and the blackened flounder tasted like asphalt. Clay Boyette scowled, set down his fork, and said:

"Son, your hair looks like a goddamn bird beak."

"It's a style," Clure Boyette said. "Women like it."

"The pussy you chase always seems to cost me a fortune, not that you care."

The congressman said, "We live in a greedy world. Everybody's got an angle."

"The Democrats haven't won Bonifay County since LBJ."

"Relax, Dad. I'm a lock."

"Horseshit," Clay Boyette said. "You're only up by seven points."

"That's fake news from the liberal legacy media."

"The race shouldn't be this close. We're talking about a divorced middle-school teacher with two kids by different husbands."

"Is she hot?"

"The inside of your brain is like a fucking bounce house."

"Christ, Dad, I'm only kidding." Clure Boyette was nursing his second vodka tonic. "Which lame poll has me winning by only seven?"

"Quinnipiac."

"Ha! Fox has me ahead by ten." The congressman continued gnawing on his petrified flounder. He strived to appear stoic and confident in front of his father.

Clay Boyette said, "These days, there's no such thing as a lock."

"Just wait and see, Dad." The younger Boyette was dying to reveal his strategy for securing Precinct 53, but he couldn't risk being shot down and ordered to call off the operation. His father was a proponent of oily behind-the-scenes machinations—not public scenes.

"You should be ahead by twenty, thirty points," the old man grumbled. "You're the incumbent, for God's sake, and this woman hasn't ever run for office until now."

"You gotta quit worrying," Clure Boyette said.

"What about your Venmo girl's sex pictures?"

"Galaxy won't be a problem. I'll find her another cool car, and she'll stay quiet."

"Sure. The same crazy bitch that wrecked the condo."

"This time I know how to handle her, Dad."

He so doesn't, thought Clay Boyette.

"I'm not hungry," he said abruptly to his son. "Take me back to the airport."

Later, alone on the return flight to Carpville, the elder Boyette sipped a gin martini and recalled the summer that he'd sent Clure's DNA for testing to make sure the kid was really his. Clure was then only ten years old but already exhibiting behavior that friends and family members considered to be clinically defective. The boy's mother was his lone defender; tellingly, however, she did not oppose the DNA test. She'd seen stories about hospitals mixing up newborns and saw no harm in ruling out the possibility—not that she would have loved Clure any less, but she might have taken a firmer stance regarding his extracurricular interests, specifically his precocious collection of bondage-themed pornography. The genetic swab had confirmed Clure's lineage, but Clay Boyette subsequently submitted the boy's saliva to two other labs, just to make absolutely sure.

That Clure's rocky and reckless youth didn't prevent him from getting elected to public office was a tribute to his father's political connections. Now, finally, the young chowderhead was in a position to help the family's far-reaching businesses and, for that reason only, Clay Boyette didn't want him to lose the upcoming election.

Having spotted Galaxy's real name on the original delivery order at the Aston Martin dealership, the elder Boyette placed a phone call from the jet.

"Janice Eileen Smith, common spelling," he told the man on the other line. "Eighteen years old."

"Damn," the man said. "That's young."

"Yes or no?"

"I might need to think about it."

"Give me your answer by noon tomorrow," Clay Boyette said.

"I'm out of town for a few more days."

"Then never mind, I'll find somebody else. This is high priority."

"I've got a friend who's good," the man said. "What's the girl's address?"

~~~

Dr. Kim Zhou had been out of veterinary school for six months, and he didn't miss the Gainesville traffic. He was glad to be working at the Tangelo Shores Animal Hospital, where as the new doctor on staff he'd been assigned to the all-night shift. There was
~~~

usually downtime between emergencies, so Zhou brought books to read. James McBride and Margaret Atwood were his current favorites. He owned no pets because he lived in a small duplex and worked crazy-long hours. His fiancée was finishing law school in Tampa, and every night they FaceTimed. Twice a month one of them would make the cross-state drive to hook up. No wedding date had been set. Zhou's parents lived in northern California and refused to come to Florida, fearing red tides, carjackings, and snakes in the toilets.

Zhou had become a vet because, with few exceptions, he liked animals more than people. The saddest part of his job was euthanizing dogs and cats that had been struck on the highway; it was a rare event when one could be saved. Reserved and somewhat halting, Zhou comforted the families as best as he could. On the inside, he was grieving, too. The clinic offered zippered body sacks for all-sized pets, from gerbils to Great Danes. Given the puny average size of residential lots in Florida, Zhou was surprised that so many people wanted to bury their deceased companions in the backyard. He always lobbied delicately for cremation.

It was early in the shift, while his assistant was on her dinner break, when Zhou heard the clinic's door chime. He put down his book and went out front, where two heavyset men were waiting. The tallest appeared to have thinned his beard with a rusty garden tool; the other one had a fake soul patch and an altered nose that reminded Zhou of hog genitalia he had dissected in school.

The men wore military-style boots, faded saggy jeans, and black long-sleeved tees. The shorter one's shirt said "BOMB THE RIO GRANDE!" The bigger one was carrying a poodle-whatever mix that he claimed was "a purebred Yarborough," a breed that Zhou never heard of.

"His name's Goebbels," the bigger man said. "He needs a X-ray."

"What happened? Is he hurt?" Zhou carefully took the drowsy dog from the man's hands.

"He acts fine on the outside," Sack Face said.

"Then why the X-ray?"

"To see if his insides are wired up."

"I don't understand," Zhou said.

"Bugged," Pube Beard explained, "by the government."

"What kind a name is Zhou?" the other man asked. "Japanese?"

"It's Chinese," the veterinarian replied.

"Are you a damn Wuhan?"

"My family's from Hong Kong."

"Hell, that doesn't even count," said Pube Beard.

Zhou had received no training for such a situation—not one, but two pushy, racist, unhinged pet owners. They followed him to an examining room, where he placed the easygoing pup on a steel table and pressed two fingers lightly on its tummy.

"Any vomiting?" he asked.

"Nope," said Sack Face. "Like I told you, he seems normal on the outside."

"Has he been having regular bowel movements?"

"Dude, we're kind of in a rush," Pube Beard cut in.

The veterinarian tried to explain that he couldn't take X-rays if the dog wasn't showing any symptoms.

"We brought cash," Pube Beard interjected.

"When you say 'bugged,' do you mean chipped?" Zhou asked. "Because lots of people's pets have microchips for identification, in case they run away or get lost."

"No, this would be a super-micro microphone," Sack Face said. He put a finger to his lips and mouthed the letters F-B-I. "Signal goes all the way to the space station," he whispered, pointing up.

"Why," Zhou asked quietly, "would anyone put a listening device in your dog?"

"It's deep-state shit. You don't want to know," Pube Beard said. When he leaned over to stroke the puppy, the black butt of a handgun peeked from the frayed waistband of his underwear. Zhou was scared. He asked the paranoid meatheads to wait while he took the dog to the X-ray room.

Without an assistant's help, it was difficult for him to hold Goebbels still and operate the machine. Some of the images turned out blurry, but Zhou took a full set hoping that Pube Beard and Sack Face wouldn't notice. They didn't.

"See, there's no secret microphone, no transmitter," Zhou said nervously as he hung the radiographs on the light board.

"Exactly what're we lookin' at?" Sack Face asked.

"A healthy normal dog."

Pube Beard squinted at the frames. "You checked his brainpan?"

The vet pointed at the first X-ray. "That's his skull right there. Clean as a whistle."

"What about his butthole?"

"This second sequence shows the whole GI tract," Zhou said. "No foreign objects."

Thinking: *Now please take your animal and go.*

Pube Beard, who held the puppy in the crook of his arm, asked, "You ever seen one a these suckers that *was* bugged?"

Sack Face sniggered. "What a dumb question. 'Course he has."

"No, actually, I haven't," Zhou said, adding quickly: "But I've only been in private practice a short while."

"For real?" Sack Face frowned. "How short?"

"I graduated six months ago."

Pube Beard said, "Shit, maybe we should find a grownup vet."

Zhou said he'd understand completely—and, honestly, no hard feelings—if the men wanted to get a second opinion. He was worried about the fat oaf's gun, wondering if he had a carry permit. Like it mattered in Florida.

Sack Face said he had an idea: "Tomorrow we'll take the dog to the airport and walk him through the TSA machines."

"Worth a try," said Pube Beard. He turned to Zhou: "How much we owe you?"

"Nothing. It's on the house." The veterinarian led the two goons out a side exit and waved with relief as their pickup truck rumbled away, into the darkness, with their unwired pet.

Back in the waiting room was another patient—an adult iguana with a lawn dart imbedded in its scaly green haunches. The stoned owner blamed a stoned roommate for the cruel prank.

When Zhou tried to pick up the agitated lizard, it bit him on the forearm and whipped his shins with its long tail. Zhou didn't flinch; the thrashing made him feel alive and reconnected to the natural world.

The night could have turned out much worse, he thought.

~~~~

"What are you reading?" Viva asked when she got out of the shower.

"A poem," Twilly said.

"Let me hear a good line."

" 'I'm no longer afraid to die but is this the guidepost of lunacy?' "

"Yes, it is. Pure lunacy," she said. "Who wrote that?"

"The great Jim Harrison."

"Did he drive an Aston?"

"That would be crushing news," Twilly said.

He had leased a small airplane hangar for the expensive convertible because he didn't want to park it in front of his apartment. The car was as subtle as a burning chandelier. He and Viva had Ubered back to his place.

"Are you like the man in the poem who's not scared of dying?" She wrapped herself in a towel and sat on the corner of the bed. Her auburn hair looked black when it was wet. "Because *I'm* sure scared of that," she added.

"I just act like I'm not. It's a good way to attract brilliant, beautiful women."

"Ah. Because secretly we all seek heart-stopping adventures."

"And, boy, do I deliver."

"Are your mom and dad still alive?"

"My mother's in an ALF," Twilly said. "She thinks it's 1989, but she's cute as a kitten."

"And your father?"

"He drowned in a beach house that was apparently built with popsicle sticks. I forget which hurricane. Florence, maybe? It was up in South Carolina. Anyway, the irony of a real estate salesman falling for his own bullshit about dream locations—we weren't tight, obviously. He lit off and started a new life."
~~~~

"Still, what happened to him is awful," Viva said.

Twilly put down his book and pulled her close.

"I'm dripping all over your pillows," she said.

"Drip away." Slowly, softly, he kissed the top of her head.

"Twilly, are you breaking up with me? Because that's not your regular kiss. That's some sad and wistful shit."

"Not sad. Pensive."

"What's wrong?" Viva sat up. "Tell me."

"Same old thing."

"Uh-oh. Here we go."

"Sorry to bring it up again," Twilly said, "but you need to move out of that townhouse and quit your job at the foundation. These are terrible people. It's crazy for you to be involved."

"I was already involved, pre-you, so get over yourself. Dale was my landlord, the Minks were my employers, and then you entered the picture, just another gentleman caller. Now please take off your pants."

"Later," he said. "Let's go walk the beach."

"You're kidding."

"I need to unwind. My brain's lit up like a damn pinball machine."

Viva said, "But you're crushing it, guy. Adopting that puppy using Dale's name was a masterstroke."

"A modest little mindfuck, that's all."

"He and Jonas must be freaking out. Anything else I should know?"

"The sex toy Figgo gave me for joining the Strokers?"

"How could I forget that perky rubber ass?"

"Well, I sent it to your boss Claude," Twilly said.

"What!" Viva didn't try to hide her delight. "That might be what's causing some friction in the marriage. Diabolical is what you are, Twilly, and usually I'm not a fan. But this is outstanding."

He got out of bed and put on a light sweatshirt.

She went on: "I just washed my hair, Romeo, so I'm not leaving the premises. Go have a good, healthy walk—but no incidents, promise? No altercations. Just chill out and enjoy the sea breeze. Take deep breaths, hum a song, or maybe try one of those mindfulness exercises you never do."

"You'll wait up for me?"

"Unless I hear sirens. Then I'm out the back door."

"First call my bail bondsman," Twilly said.

"When you come back I want to try something super kinky in bed."

"Like what?"

"Eye contact," Viva said.

Twilly smiled. "Are you sure you're ready?"

It was nearly midnight. The beach looked empty. Jogging barefoot along the water's edge, Twilly heard piping gulls and rolling waves and the distant horn of a train. For a while he stopped thinking about the Strokers for Liberty, the Minks, the congressman, and what hell might break loose during the Carpville operation. Instead he focused on his own selfish project. Soon he'd be flying to the Bahamas and signing a deed, the owners of Starfish Point having accepted his cash offer. His first chore would be tourist-proofing the island, starting with the capture and removal of the overfed pigs. The house he planned to build was modestly sized, about twenty-five hundred square feet elevated on heavy pilings. The walls would be concrete block, the windows high-impact glass, and a propane-fueled generator would provide electricity during hurricanes. Twilly had already picked out a geeky telescope for stargazing on the deck.

Building anything in the Exumas could be a slow grind; the nearest Home Depot was in Miami, three hundred miles away. Every nail, truss, and doorknob would have to be delivered by boat. Setting a rigid timetable was folly—the simplest of projects might take years, Twilly knew. And then to live there full-time? The isolation would test him. The calmness, mainly. Twilly wasn't sure he could shut off the adrenaline pump and get by on spearfishing, coconut milk, and books. He hoped that he and Viva would still be close when the house on Starfish Point was finished, and that she would visit him.

He was mentally tweaking the floor plan as he jogged unnoticed past a skinny couple writhing on a blanket. The lovers were gone by the time he came back the other way, and he stopped to pick up several empty Corona bottles they'd left behind. It wasn't easy, but he resisted the impulse to run after the couple and educate them about the low-rent crime of littering. Instead he put the beer bottles in a recycling barrel and trotted lawfully back to the apartment.

The lights were still on, though Viva had fallen asleep. As soon as Twilly lay down beside her, the too-familiar restlessness started buzzing again in both ears. It wasn't an anxiety disorder, or rage at the world, or any of the suppressed childhood emotions cited by his many therapists. It was as simple as metabolically needing activity more than sleep. The beach run had taken the edge off, but only some. A road trip might help him reset.

Gently he tried to wake Viva, saying, "Come take a ride with me."

Her eyes remained closed as she gave him the finger and rolled over. He didn't want to leave her there, but when he touched her cheek, she nipped his hand. Message received.

Twilly set the burglar alarm, locked the place, and drove his Suburban out to the pine woods where he'd buried the metal trunk containing Dale Figgo's weapons. He dug up the trunk and took it to the airplane hangar. It wouldn't fit in the boot of the Aston Martin, but Twilly had to try.

He was always working on fun ideas.

Time for a drive.

CHAPTER 19

Claude Mink was hit hard by the loss of his Dream Booty. One lusty night he'd forgotten to put it back in the wall safe, and Electra found it under the duvet on his bed the next morning. She destroyed it while he was at the endocrinologist, melted it in the granite fire pit by the swimming pool. After Claude returned home from the doctor, Dumas somberly led him to the site, a smoking puddle of flesh-colored goo. When Claude confronted his wife, she smiled coldly and walked away. Later he discovered that she'd also rooted through his underwear drawer and nicked his stash of Canadian Viagra, a thousand dollars' worth of blue magic, which she flushed down a bidet. As the days went by, the woman showed no signs of softening. Claude could foresee himself dying unforgiven, a prospect that didn't bother him as much as the thought of nights without Darcy dearest. He didn't know how to go about finding a replacement; the sensitive task was assigned to Dumas. The note in the doll's rectum had convinced Claude that the sender was the same person making those nerve-wracking calls about the Wee Hammers; Claude's chief suspect was the cocky lawn intruder in the Marlins baseball cap, but his motive was unknown. Dumas arranged for the calls to be traced, only to find that the creep was using burner phones. Notifying the authorities was, of course, out of the question.

On weekdays Claude and Electra traveled to the Mink Foundation in separate cars; if there was a public event, they'd ride together in the Maybach to maintain the appearance of marital peace. No spoken words passed between them. At work Electra communicated strictly by email, and the subject was always business. The stymied Bunkers development was at the top of her list. Claude had assured her that the Lewin Baltry situation would soon be resolved in their favor, though he hadn't shared the details of his plot. When Electra probed for updates, Claude typically responded with the same four-word email: "Still in the works."

Because the Minks had separate offices with soundproofed walls, Claude was able to speak freely on the phone. It was the hired killer who responded vaguely, almost evasively, whenever he deigned to take Claude's calls.

"Where the hell are you?" Claude snapped a few days after his wife incinerated the Dream Booty, when he was in a particularly foul mood.

"On the way back to Florida," Moe said.

"Does that mean it's done?" Claude asked.

"My part, yes."

"I'm confused. Is there more?"

"Not much," the killer said.

Claude didn't love the sound of that. He said, "When and where can we expect the news to break?"

The where being equally as crucial as the when, because Claude Mink had ordered Moe to make sure Baltry's body would be promptly found and identified. Claude had carefully sorted through the options. If Baltry vanished completely, it might be years until a judge declared him legally dead. The swift recovery of his corpse, however, would lead to a death certificate and free the governor to appoint a new county commissioner. The sooner that happened, the sooner the deadlock on The Bunkers could be broken.

"We'll discuss the details when we meet," Moe said.

"What time's your flight?"

"I'm driving."

"What? Why?" Claude practically shouted.

"I enjoy the scenery," the killer said. "The leaves are turning."

"Why are you people so fucking cheap?"

"Excuse me?"

"I'll buy you a goddamn plane ticket!" Claude said.

Moe hung up, turned to his passenger, and said, "Did you hear how that anti-Semitic cocksucker was talking to me?"

Baltry stared emptily out the window. "Why are we in South Dakota?"

"Gorgeous landscape. Birthplace of Tom Brokaw."

"Who's that?"

The killer sighed. "Maybe I should shoot your dumb self after all."

"That's not funny," Baltry said.

"Mount Rushmore?"

"What about it?"

"You've heard of that?"

"Sure. I've seen pictures. Who hasn't?"

Moe nodded. "Well, it's right here in South Dakota."

"Okay, but we're not gonna stop, are we?"

"No, Lewin, it's a bit out of our way."

"What's gonna happen to me?"

"You mean when we get back?" the killer said.

If *I get back,* Baltry thought. "How do I know you're not going to murder me and dump my body out here in the middle of nowhere?"

"Right, because my lifelong dream is to own a used Subaru."

"I'm just sayin'."

"Get some rest," Moe said. "That would be my suggestion."

The killer had plenty on his mind, too. A colleague had contacted him about doing another job that the colleague was too busy to handle. The offer was a hundred grand plus expenses, which was serious money. However, the job was in the town of Tangelo Shores—either a strange coincidence, or the hit was somehow connected to the Baltry assignment.

Another concern: the target was an eighteen-year-old woman, Janice Eileen Smith, aka Galaxy, a professional escort. Moe had never clipped anyone so young, and he couldn't help wondering what the kid had done—or what information she had—that would generate a premium contract on her life.

Moe asked Baltry if he knew any Janice Smiths back home. He said no.

"What about an escort named Galaxy?"

"I'm out of the loop when it comes to that stuff," Baltry said.

"You don't do hookers?"

"Noooooo! Not in my position on the commission."

"But you *will* take a bribe," the killer said.

"That's different."

"Because then you're the prostitute and not the john."

"I don't think of it that way," Baltry said.

Moe smiled. "There are all kinds of whores, is my point. One's no better or worse than another."

Baltry resented getting a morality lecture from a hit man, but he was in no position to stoke an argument. Moe was jacked up on Red Bull and driving the old Outback ninety miles per hour. Also, he was armed.

So Baltry said he was going to take a nap.

"First you've got to close your eyes," the killer said.

Baltry nodded. "I can do that."

But he couldn't.

~~~

The congressman reserved a back booth at the only restaurant in Tangelo Shores that served Wagyu beef. Galaxy was her usual half hour late but she looked awesome, which he mentioned several times.

Finally she said, "Chill out, dude. This skirt was only eighty bucks."

"Are you working?" Clure Boyette had iced champagne waiting in the "Dylan Cash" junior suite.
~~~

"No, I'm on a sabbatical," Galaxy said.

"Ah. Good to know." Boyette had already sucked down two double vodka tonics, which deadened the sting of rejection.

"So what's new, Spanky?"

Boyette perked up. "I'm co-chairing a big hearing in D.C. in a couple weeks. I'll be on C-SPAN live for like, four hours."

"God, why?"

"My subcommittee subpoenaed the CEOs of the three top U.S. billiard companies. I'm going to find out if it's true they're canceling black eight balls. Those woke snowflakes will be under oath, too!"

"Dude, you're still hung up on the stupid pool balls?"

"C-SPAN is like a pre-audition for Hannity. It's mega."

But not to Galaxy, apparently.

She shrugged and said, "I didn't see my new Marty in the parking lot."

"Yeah, we need to talk about that. But first let's do a toast to pre-celebrate my C-SPAN premiere."

"No, first we talk. Then, maybe, one drink."

The congressman had his story polished and ready: "It's not great news, G. They just announced a massive recall of all late-model Aston Martins, so production is delayed indefinitely. The assembly lines are down."

"What's wrong with the fucking cars?"

"Sometimes the seats explode when you turn on the butt warmers. I think you should go ahead and pick out something else."

"I don't want to," Galaxy said.

"How about a Corvette?"

"Gross."

"Lambo?"

"Ew."

"Porsche?"

"Do I look like I'm missing a penis?"

"Hey, the Carreras are hot," Boyette said. "I can get you a pre-owned that's basically brand new." His future ex-wife's car. He wasn't quite drunk enough to spill the gory deets.

Galaxy stared at him like a bored cat. "All I want is a DB11. That was our deal."

"What can I do, G? It might be months before it's delivered. Maybe longer. The Brits are totally OCD about auto recalls."

Galaxy picked up her purse and said, "I've gotta pee."

While she was gone, Boyette ordered another drink and a bottle of Cristal for the table. Things were going pretty well so far—no yelling, no meltdown, no blackmail threats. The server was being extra nice.

Galaxy returned but didn't sit down.

"There's not a recall on Astons, and the seats aren't spontaneously exploding. I Googled it in the bathroom." She held up her phone to show him. "So, which of your bitches got my car?"

"That's not what happened, I swear." Boyette patted her empty chair. "Please sit."

"Not till you tell me who's driving my Marty."

Her voice was unnervingly calm. The congressman had braced for fireworks.

He said, "Some rich prick went to the showroom and bought your DB11 the same day it came off the truck. Paid twenty percent over retail. By the time my salesman called me, it was too late."

"You're lying. You gave it to one of your nasty girlfriends. Just grow a pair and tell the truth."

"But I am, luv! I am!"

The server appeared, popped open the champagne, and poured two glasses. Galaxy, who remained standing, reached for one and drained it.

"So, what's the rich prick's name?" she asked Boyette.

"The dealership wouldn't say."

"That's so weak, bro. You make up this whole lame story except for the guy's name?"

"You can ask my dad! He was there."

Galaxy downed Boyette's glass of champagne and said, "I feel sorry for you, Spanky."

"Don't say that. Why would you say that? Where are you going?"

She glided out of the restaurant without so much as a wave. For a moment, Boyette felt sick to his stomach.

Who says no to a free fucking Porsche? he wondered.

After dinner, he called his father to report that Galaxy was still fixated on the Aston. "She'll come around," he added. "I just need more time."

It was late, but the old man was still very much awake. "Did she say anything about your X-rated pictures?"

"Not. One. Word. *Nada*."

"Good. Let it go," Clay Boyette told his son. "Don't talk to her again. Or text, either. No goddamn contact whatsoever."

"Okay, but why?"

"Never mind why," Clay Boyette said. "You sound drunk. Are you in the car?"

"Yeah, but it's cool. A friend's driving me to the hotel."

The upbeat young server from the restaurant. She was studying for a teaching degree at the local college. Her first name began with either an *E* or an *A*, and her mom had been active in Wives Against Filth.

"Did you put me on speaker?" Boyette's father asked angrily.

"Of course not."

There was a heavy pause on the other end.

"Oh, Dad?" the congressman said.

"Where are you right now?"

"There's nothing to worry about. She's an excellent driver."

"Listen to me, you hopeless jerk-off," Clay Boyette said to his son. "When you get to the hotel, say nighty-night to the girl and go straight to your room."

"Aw, come on," the congressman whined.

"Alone!" his father said.

"One drink, that's all."

"No! Fistman's probably having you followed."

"Sorry, Dad, I'm losing the signal . . ."

Boyette turned off the phone, in case the old man was steamed enough to call back. Tomorrow he would tell him that the battery went dead.

"You all right?" the young woman asked.

"It's just, y'know, my dad. The doctors say it's postnasal dementia. Some nights are better than others."

"God, that must be so tough."

"Breaks my heart," Clure Boyette said. "Wanna do some blow?"

~~~

Tomas De Leon was the general contractor on the building site in Carpville. The floor plan was super basic and the house on Watermelon Way was small, but the job had turned into a shit blizzard. Tomas had never heard of the "Wee Hammers," and he'd sure as hell never heard of kids that age working construction. On most days they scampered heedlessly throughout the site, and Tomas had been ordered not to take his eyes off of them. Usually there was a sub or two present who could help supervise, but it was almost impossible for two grownups to keep track of so many brats. They were thrilled as fuck to have day passes from school. Every time Tomas turned around, they were throwing their little orange work helmets at each other.

After four, when the kids were gone, Tomas would bring in his regular crew to fix what was fixable, which wasn't everything. The code inspectors who were usually crawling up his ass were nowhere to be seen, leading Tomas to suspect that somebody with clout had a stake in the house.

One morning a tall, odd-looking politician arrived with a video crew. Tomas quickly got a fistful of nails started in the doorframe of an interior bathroom. Then he rounded up a few of the kids, placed various styles of hammers in their hands, and watched apprehensively as they pounded like tweaked-out chimps on the two-by-fours. Finally, blessedly, the camera guy said he had enough footage. The politician then struck a pose in front of the foundation slab, ostensibly the future front yard, and planted a sign that said: "Designed and built by the Wee Hammers—Don't Be Fooled By Our Size! *Small Bodies, Big Dreams*."

Some stiff in a striped necktie stepped out of a TV van and began interviewing the politician, who had teeth like roof tiles and
~~~

a face that could chop a block of ice. Tomas told one of the adult electricians to disarm the Wee Hammers while he edged closer to the TV setup. The politician's name was Boyette, and Tomas heard him say that a new charity was paying for the house, which upon completion would be donated free and clear to a needy family. It would be the first of many such residences, the politician bragged, from the Panhandle to Key Largo.

That's insane, thought Tomas. The house on Watermelon Way was being built of wood. A hurricane would flatten it like a goddamn billboard.

Tomas was proud of his tradesman skills. A decade earlier, after wading the Rio Grande with nothing but a box of stale Triscuits and a backpack, he'd determinedly made his way from south Texas to north Florida. In the town of Gulf Breeze he'd connected with a Hispanic construction crew, and learned to mix cement and even hang windows. Every month he wired money to his older sister back in Guatemala. She and her children now lived in a home that wasn't made of corrugated tin.

Tomas worked his tail off and earned a reputation for being sharp and conscientious. His GC license was legit, even though the paperwork documenting his citizenship had been forged by a gifted pro in Corpus Christi. Tomas felt he'd come a long way since arriving on American soil. He couldn't let his success be jeopardized by one flaky, dangerous job—a charade conceived by some greasy politician.

The money is what had lured Tomas off course. For unexplained reasons, he was being paid double the going rate, twice as much as he'd made on his last project. The checks rolled in from the Wee Hammers Fund, an entity about which Tomas had expressed no curiosity and asked no questions. He should have. It was now apparent that finishing the simple two-bedroom house would take his crew months longer than usual. Even with serious tools in their paws, the kids were not dependable followers of instructions. They weren't good listeners, period.

The worst by far was Egregio, a boy whose mother had enrolled him in the Wee Hammers because she thought it would look good on future college applications. Egregio was eleven years old. His first day on the site, the surly psycho tried to shoot a blue jay with a nail gun, puncturing the grill of Tomas De Leon's F-350. No remorse, insincere or otherwise, was expressed.

Egregio was a hulk for his age, simultaneously a momma's boy and a bully, though oddly deficient in the simplest of motor skills. He couldn't be trusted to walk a bucket of drywall mud fifteen feet without dropping it on somebody's toes. Then he would laugh and run off. The kid singularly had done more damage to the construction site than all the other Wee Hammers combined. In Egregio's hands, the most innocuous device could be a weapon; Tomas had once caught him lashing another child's bare shins with a steel tape measure.

Although the words were never spoken aloud, Tomas hated Egregio—his meanness, his disrespect, his gleeful ineptitude. Tomas had no children of his own, and no experience dealing with boys; his exposure to Egregio had poisoned him against the idea of starting a family, possibly forever. It seemed like a crapshoot. He'd spoken with Egregio's parents, both of whom heatedly claimed that they didn't recognize the reckless young monster Tomas was describing.

The monster, who was now wearing his scuffed orange helmet to pose for a photograph with the tall politician—a U.S. congressman, according to the TV guy. Congressman *Clure* Boyette. What kind of name was that? He stopped to shake Tomas's hand before departing in a black SUV with tinted windows.

Moments later, a high wail rose from a corner of the site—Egregio had yanked the Barbie-themed Crocs from the feet of a Wee Hammer named Cynthia and fed them to a circular saw from which he'd been banned since day one. When Egregio tried to run away, Tomas grabbed a handful of the kid's tee shirt, snatched his cellphone, and hauled him to the reeking Jiffy John out by the road. Bracing the door shut, Tomas kept one eye on the time. Nine minutes passed before Egregio quit swearing and kicking the plastic walls.

Then, from inside the fetid chamber, a smaller voice: "Mr. De Leon?"

"What."

"Lemme out. Seriously."

"That's all you've got to say?"

"Okay. I'm sooooo sorry. Now open the damn door."

"You're too young to talk like that," Tomas said.

"I can't breathe! Lemme out, or I'll tell my fucking mom!"

Tomas opened the door. Egregio emerged, gasping, and called Tomas a cocksucker.

That night, during dinner, Tomas told his wife what had happened. He wasn't proud of what he'd done, and he blamed it on extreme workplace stress. She warned him about losing his temper.

"Don't get yourself fired, Tommy."

"It wouldn't be the worst thing."

"What do you mean?"

"These damn kids are too much. They think everything's a play toy. I mean, they're *kids*. Somethin' bad's gonna happen on this job."

"Don't talk like that. It scares me."

"I need another beer," Tomas said.

~~~

The TSA officers at the Daytona Beach airport wouldn't let Dale Figgo and Jonas Onus pass Goebbels through the checkpoint metal detectors or the backscatter screening machines. Instead the men and the puppy were escorted from the facility. On the drive back to Tangelo Shores, a decision was made: Goebbels had to go.

That the sender of the dog still hadn't revealed himself could only mean that there was sinister intent behind the gift. Figgo remained sure that a tiny listening device or at least a tracker had been planted inside the animal. Onus's chief complaint was the puppy's attitude—sweet, approachable, cuddly with strangers. Such qualities were the opposite of what a para-militant patriot sought in a canine companion. Himmler had been a frothing gargoyle that would rather have dismembered another dog than sniff its ass. Savage, Onus reflected wistfully, and irreplaceable. Himmler's choke chain weighed more than Goebbels. Onus was embarrassed to be
~~~

seen thundering through town in his jacked-up truck with the mutt's perky doodle face in the window.

"Himmler, he was my spirit animal," Onus said. "He would literally kill for me. This little butt-licker wouldn't hurt a flea."

"Least he don't shed." Figgo wondering, *What the hell's a spirit animal?*

Onus said, "We can't take him to Carpville to guard the ballot boxes."

"True. There's no way."

The solution turned out to be simple. Custody of the puppy would be rotated among Onus's three families; all the boys had been begging for a pet with fur. If indeed the dog was electronically bugged, the eavesdroppers would hear nothing but Super Mario and kiddie farts.

While Onus delivered Goebbels to one of the baby mothers, Figgo waited in the Tundra. He felt like he'd been rolled down the John Glenn Bridge in a barrel; every joint in his body throbbed. The radio was tuned to a rebroadcast of an Alex Jones rant that made Figgo's palms itch. Worthless college-diversity programs were the topic, and Jones boomed with scorn until it came time to peddle his toxin-flushing, testosterone-boosting supplements. Figgo turned off the show. Through the open windows of the apartment he could hear Onus holler at Goebbels for peeing on the sofa.

Figgo dreaded sharing the leadership of the Strokers. He could never trust Onus again, not after the cheap-shot ambush at Fever Beach. Then, unforgivably, Onus had gone around Figgo's back to lobby the congressman.

Is it the two million bucks? Figgo wondered. *Or just his big fat ego?*

Figgo was aware that, after all this time, Onus remained bitter about missing the January 6th siege. The man often spoke of being "blood ready" for the next uprising, whenever that might be necessary. He had repeatedly vowed to stand front and center, loud and proud, locked and loaded, whatever.

And maybe that's what the power grab was about—redemption. Figgo wasn't interested in digging any deeper. Like it or not, he was shackled to the Strokers' helm with an unstable cockhead who'd assaulted him in front of his men. The stakes were high. The Battle of Carpville couldn't be a repeat of the high-profile fuckage that had occurred on Figgo's watch at the Key West drag club—the congressman and his behind-the-scenes money angels wouldn't stand for it.

Meanwhile, thanks to the woke policies of Bottom Drawer Novelties, Figgo was out of a job and running low on cash. Pierre's so-called reference letter had worthlessly been written in Russian. For all Figgo knew, the jerk could have outed him for stealing those Dream Booties off the packing lines.

Not for the first time in his life, Figgo felt like he was balls-deep in bad luck. His once-soaring hopes for a paid position as leader of the Strokers had crashed due to the congressman's surprise promotion of Jonas Onus. Figgo did *not* want to split a salary with his friend-turned-archrival.

"Yo, where's my boy Alex?" Onus asked when he climbed back into the truck.

"Off. He was doing that ten-minute boner-pill commercial."

"Someday we'll be on his show. After Precinct 53, I guarantee we get the call."

"That'd be awesome," Figgo said tepidly.

"We'll wear black ski masks. Hang a big Strokers flag in his radio studio. How sick would that be? Fuck the Proud Boys, right?"

"Only we don't have a flag."

"Not yet," Onus said, "but I got an idea."

"Me, too," Figgo lied.

Onus made a left turn out of the apartment complex, tucked a nicotine pouch under his top lip, and hung one thick arm out the window. Figgo blinked tiredly and stared at the road ahead.

"A snow-white king cobra was my idea for the flag," Onus said. "Hood spread wide. Fangs out. The tongue would be a bright orange flame. For the motto, somethin' like, 'I Dare You Pussies to Tread on Me!' "

Figgo said, "You'll need a big damn flag to fit all that."

"Who cares?"

"A mongoose would be better."

Onus chuckled derisively. "A *what*?"

"They're badass critters. They *eat* fuckin' cobras."

"Dale, you're fulla shit."

"It's their favorite food," Figgo said. "You don't believe me, look it up on YouTube."

And they both knew that this was how things would be going forward—each of them distant and distrustful, automatically shooting down the other's ideas. Onus would always blame Figgo for Himmler's death, while Figgo would never forgive Onus for jumping him at Fever Beach and trying to "mutinize" the Strokers. There was no easy pathway to fix the friendship, and neither man saw a benefit in trying.

CHAPTER 20

Dumas found a website that sold Darcy's Dream Booties and ordered a new one for Claude Mink, overnight delivery. At first Claude flipped out when he opened the shipping box because the color of the sex torso was mocha brown, not Caucasian. Dumas said the company screwed up, and he offered to send back the toy. Claude said don't bother, and gruffly waved Dumas out of the room. Wary of Electra and the housekeepers, Claude took the doll to his office and locked it in a deep desk drawer. He had never been with a woman of color, or a polymer partial replica of a woman of color. To his surprise, the idea aroused him.

Some dolt from the governor's office called to remind him that Lewin Baltry couldn't be removed from the commission simply for taking off personal time. There was no alleged malfeasance, no evidence of illegal actions.

"But what if he never comes back?" Claude said.

His partners in the Bunkers development were getting jumpy about not having the county's final approval. Claude feared they might walk away from the project and let the banks bury him.

"As you know, there's a process for replacing public officeholders," said the empty suit from the governor's office. "It takes a while. We've talked about this before."

Claude hung up and called the killer's number. Baltry should be dead by now. Moe didn't answer his phone, and Claude didn't leave a voice message.

"Slippery kike," he groused.

Viva knocked and Claude called out for her to come in. She said the door was locked. Claude shuffled over to open it.

"What's so damn important?" he asked.

Viva said the local United Way wanted fifty thousand dollars from the Mink Foundation for its annual fund-raising drive.

Claude made a sour face. "How much did we give 'em last year?"

"I don't know. I wasn't here."

"Then go ask my wife," Claude said.

A minute later, Viva returned with a number.

"Electra says fifty," she said.

"Then make it forty-nine. Close the door on your way out."

Viva came around the desk and straightened Claude's necktie, which usually was Dumas's responsibility. "Do you mind if I leave a little early today?" she asked.

"Better clear it with Electra," Claude said, flustered by Viva's perfume. "Hell, you know what? Just do it."

After she left he wanted to get up and lock the door, but his legs ached too much for the effort. He called Clure Boyette, who claimed to be in the middle of an important meeting. Claude said he didn't care; he wanted an update on the new Strokers operation.

"No more surprises, and no more fuckups like Key West," he warned the congressman.

"Claude, I told you how many times not to worry? All the wrinkles have been ironed out. Everybody's on the right page."

"I saw a thing on TV about the Wee Hammers. Pretty good. You were in it."

"Hey, I *arranged* it," Clure Boyette bragged.

"How much of our two million is left?"

"Most of it, Claude. Almost all of it. I've really got to hop off now."

Claude lowered his trousers and underwear to his ankles. Then he removed the smooth brown Dream Booty from the drawer and positioned it on his hairy marbled lap. Nothing started happening except in his imagination. Still he was breathing heavy when the killer returned his call.

"Are you on a treadmill?" Moe asked. "Or having a heart attack?"

"Where the hell's Lewin Baltry?"

"Dead in a ditch. Self-inflicted gunshot is what the coroner will say."

"But where?" Claude noticed that his palms were damp. He wiped them on his tie.

"Outside Memphis," said Moe the killer.

"Has the body been found yet?"

"I don't think so. I'll text a picture."

It was a middle-aged man sprawled on his back, his head and face covered with blood. Claude grimaced, deleting the photo immediately.

He said, "This doesn't do me any good until somebody finds the bastard."

"They will. I left him and the pistol lying right near the interstate. His driver's license is in his pants."

"I'll wire the rest of your money after the body's been positively identified."

"You'll wire it to my account by noon tomorrow," the killer said, "or I'll go collect Mr. Baltry and make sure no piece of him, not even a toenail, is ever recovered."

Asshole! Claude thought.

"Exactly where are you now?" he asked.

"North Carolina," Moe the killer lied. They were back in Florida, Lewin Baltry at the wheel of the Subaru. He had dirt and grass on his clothes, and he smelled like Heinz ketchup. Moe sat beside him on the passenger side with Baltry's handgun wedged under one leg.

"While I've got you on the phone," Moe said to Claude Mink.

"Ever heard of a hooker named Galaxy? She works for an escort service down your way."

"I don't need to pay for hookers," said Claude, patting the velvet curvature of the Dream Booty.

Moe said he would be contacting his bank at noon sharp the following day to make sure the balance of his fee had been deposited. Claude snorted and slapped away his phone. He closed his eyes, bunched his shoulders, and resumed his feeble humping of the rubber torso until Dumas and Viva ran in, having misinterpreted his warthog grunts as sounds of a grand mal seizure.

"For fuck's sake," Claude wheezed. "Doesn't anybody in this office know how to knock?"

That night, he took the Dream Booty back home and smuggled it into his bedroom.

~~~

For dinner, Viva and Galaxy chose a casual seafood joint in Satellite Beach, where there seemed little chance of seeing anyone they knew. Viva arrived early and ordered a Diet Coke. Outside, a storm rolled in—lightning, high winds, and sideways-blowing rain. Viva texted Twilly telling him to be careful, like she was a wife or a girlfriend. The Strokers for Liberty were meeting at Fever Beach and, based on what had happened the last time, Dale Figgo had designated Twilly his de facto bodyguard. Viva couldn't imagine that tonight's summit would be peaceful, and Twilly was amped. He'd been gone all night and half the morning. She didn't ask him where, but with a wink he'd told her that he was road-testing the Aston Martin.

Galaxy hurried into the restaurant with wet hair and closing a golf umbrella borrowed from some country club. She was wearing pressed jeans, flats, and a plain sage-blue hoodie. No makeup, no jewelry, no ink on display—yet still she drew randy stares from the men.

"Simple creatures," she said as she sat down.

Viva ordered mango margaritas for both of them. A server
~~~

brought a basket of hot rolls. Galaxy asked Viva if she was still having coyote dreams.

"Last night it was a chinchilla," Viva said. "Same English garden, though."

"Long as he didn't bite you."

"It's weird. They never bite. They just talk."

"Keep a journal. That's what I do," Galaxy said.

"Just your dreams?"

"No, I journal everything. I like to write."

"Excellent," Viva said. "Does the congressman know?"

"I might've forgot to tell him."

A young man with a fastidiously groomed two-day growth approached the table and wanted to know if Galaxy remembered him. She said of course. When he asked if she was still working, she shook her head and said she was on sabbatical, taking care of an ailing aunt—long COVID was the sad diagnosis. The man turned his gaze to Viva, who shut him down with a high-speed ramble in Spanish, basically: "Who do you think you are? You're wearing a wedding ring and your nose hairs need trimming."

The man shrunk away. Galaxy recalled that his name was Ronnie and he was heavy into rope play. "Not Western knots. Boat knots. Ever heard of an icicle hitch? I got pretty good at it."

Then her tone changed: "Spanky gave away my new Aston Martin. Can you believe that two-faced shitsucker?"

"Gave it to who?" Viva could not, of course, reveal Twilly's role.

"One of his skanks, no doubt. Now he's telling me to pick out another car, but that's not the point. It's the disrespect, right? The assumption that one bright shiny thing is as good as another—like I'd be caught dead in a fucking Lambo."

The margaritas were delivered. Galaxy managed to lick the salt from the rim of her glass without looking like a cruise ship touron. Thunder rattled the windows near their table.

Viva said, "You've got every right to get mad about the car."

"I'll be fine. Not him, though."

"What've you got in mind?"

"Check your phone," Galaxy said, sipping her drink. "I Air-Dropped you something."

It was a photo of the congressman that Galaxy hadn't shown her before.

"Wow," Viva said. "Is that a dog cone he's wearing?"

"Stay tuned. I'll be sending the whole bunch soon."

"What would you like me to do with them?"

"They say democracy dies in darkness."

"I believe that's true," Viva said.

"Leave me out of it, if you can."

"Is that cocaine on his cheeks?"

Galaxy laughed. "You have to ask? That's actually adorable."

"And what's with the leash and snowshoes?"

Galaxy was studying the menu. "Honestly, I never act too interested. Then you hear their whole life story, which is usually a drag. I mean, you can't blame your parents for every shitty little thing that happens. I don't. By the way, the dates on the pictures will match up with my journal entries."

Viva said, "I've got to ask: Did he know you were seventeen?"

Galaxy opened her purse, took out her driver's license, and put it on the table in front of Viva. She said, "Don't look at my hair in that picture. The night before was Mardi Gras."

Viva's eyes had already locked on Galaxy's date of birth.

"Wait, this says you're twenty-five." Viva was dumbfounded.

"You and me went out on my birthday, 'member?"

"But I thought you just turned eighteen!"

Galaxy vampishly stroked one of her own cheeks. "It's all about skin care."

"The congressman didn't know?"

Galaxy slapped down a Louisiana license that showed she was seven years younger. It was a good fake. Viva didn't know what to say. Galaxy told her to breathe, reset, and listen.

"The young ones are Spanky's thing," she said, lowering her voice. "Not just him, either, there's plenty of Epstein wannabes out there. But I know how to handle 'em, I really do, with or without a leash. Better me in their hotel bed than some clueless high school girl. That's one way I look at it. The other is the money, I won't lie."

"Why'd you pick seventeen for your age?" Viva asked.

"Because I knew I could pull it off. Fooled your ass, didn't I?"

"And now you're taking a break, right? That's what you said."

"Might be forever. We'll see."

"I hope so." Viva had more heavy questions, but she didn't want to sound like her mother. The woman never knew when to back off.

"So tell me what's next," she said to Janice Eileen Smith.

"Oh, I'm moving to Atlanta."

"Family up there?"

"Nursing school, actually. That's the truth," Galaxy said. "I'm not just making up a fairy tale I know you'd like to hear. Kennesaw State. I want to do trauma."

Viva said, "That's smart. You're still young."

Galaxy peeked over the top of the menu. "Don't worry, I'll be gone when poor ole Spanky's world blows up."

"He is *not* a good guy. The people he's tight with, they're worse. Watch out."

Galaxy said there was an old green Subaru with Oregon plates parked near her apartment that afternoon. An ordinary-looking middle-aged dude was sitting in the driver's seat reading a newspaper, which, where can you even buy one these days? Galaxy said she walked over to the car and the man said he was waiting for his aunt, who lived in Building G.

"When I told him there's no such building, he folded up his paper and drove away. It was semi-sketch."

"Did you recognize the guy?" Viva asked.

"Nah, and he had one of those totally forgettable faces. Maybe we went on a date sometime and I just don't remember."

"Stay with me at the townhouse tonight, just in case."

"Thanks, but no," Galaxy said. "I'm super careful. He wouldn't be my first crawly creeper."

Raindrops drummed on the metal roof of the restaurant. Outside, the wind was shaking the palm trees like pom-poms.

Galaxy said, "I don't mind a good storm. Aren't you hungry, girl?"

"I'm glad you're getting out of Florida. Seriously."

"What are you starting with?"

"Wedge salad," said Viva, "and one more margarita."

Galaxy grinned. "Yeah, momma."

Viva's phone vibrated—a return text from Twilly Spree on Fever Beach.

You were right, he said. **Another goat wedding**

U ok? she asked.

This group is only about three teeth shy of a biker gang

Time to call cops?

Under no circumstances, Twilly replied.

Viva returned the phone to her purse.

"I want to meet this guy," said Galaxy, who'd read the text exchange upside down. "I think *you* think he might be the one. You're crushing on him, dude."

"God, no, he's trouble," Viva said. "Delicious trouble, but still."

Divorce cases rarely went to trial if a couple was wealthy. Mediation was the battlefield, and Harold Fistman loved it because he loved being feared. Overtly he wasn't a classically loathsome presence; he dressed expensively but not flashy, he always had minty breath, and he never raised his voice. The many crude nicknames attached to him had originated with sore losers, mostly future ex-husbands on the opposite side of a case. Fistman preferred to represent future ex-wives because it was easier to keep them focused on the big picture. Also, they were more keen to refer their restless married friends to him afterward.

Fistman himself had never experienced divorce, having been with the same wonderful woman for thirty-one years. He didn't share that with clients because he needed them to believe he understood their pain. Similarly, he never told his clients (or, especially, colleagues) that his hobby was building dainty hummingbird feeders; it was better to be pegged as a big-game hunter or a ringside fan of cage match wrestling. The appearance of nurturing a blood lust was good for Fistman's business.

He flung an arm around Chip Milkwright and said, "I've been watching the polls. Your client seems to be headed the wrong direction against a total nobody."

They were standing outside the mediation room. Milkwright slipped free, shuddering reflexively.

"Don't threaten us, Harold," he said.

"Not a threat. An observation. The congressman must be under a lot of pressure from the party. His old man, too. Nobody expected the race to be so tight. Even a faint whiff of scandal might swing the needle, no?"

Despite his reputation, Fistman always tried to be civil with opposing counsel. Many of them, like poor Milkwright, were stuck with clients they abhorred. Fistman had been there many times himself. He wasn't fond of Nicki Boyette, nor did he dislike her; she was along for the ride. Fistman was all about the kill shot.

Milkwright said, "I can't believe we're still arguing over a goddamn car."

"There are new developments, Chip."

"The factory says three months' assembly time, minimum. What're we supposed to do?"

"Let's sit down and get this case worked out," Fistman said. "Come on, man. Have faith in the system."

"Not funny, Harold."

Fistman and Milkwright reentered the mediation room, where the Boyettes sat in silence across the table from each other. The soon-to-be-divorced husband and wife were riveted to their smartphones, messaging more significant humans in their current lives. Clure was in a dark blue suit, as usual, and Nicki was dressed like the president-elect of the Junior League.

As soon as the attorneys seated themselves, Milkwright began:

"Mr. Fistman, my client and I are confused. At our last meeting, Mrs. Boyette indicated she wouldn't mind waiting a few months for the Aston Martin, a vehicle she previously rejected."

Nicki set her phone on the table. "Clure promised me it was one of a kind, but there's another DB11 exactly like it. Same color, trim, top, everything. Brand new. I saw it drive by my house."

Milkwright cut his eyes toward the congressman, who vehemently shook his head, saying, "That's impossible."

Fistman cut in. "Bottom line: my client is no longer interested in owning the convertible in question. Consequently, the divorce settlement needs to be restructured. Shall we get to it?"

Milkwright stiffened in his chair. Clure Boyette said, "This is total bullshit."

Again Nicki offered to recite a list of her husband's Venmo hookups. Fistman mentioned that some of the young women seemed willing to sit for depositions. The congressman glared venomously.

Fistman didn't take it personally. Fresh out of law school he'd been hired by the Public Defender's Office in Pasco County. His first client was a fifty-year-old woman who'd strangled her sleeping husband with the tube of his CPAP machine. It was Fistman's baptism in the sewer of domestic tumult. He pled his client down to involuntary manslaughter after digging up records of a Visa card used by the husband exclusively to purchase barnyard pornography. At one point the dead man's brother had threatened to disembowel Fistman, who decided it was time to pursue another field of law. In a divorce practice, at least, one got well paid to be despised.

"In lieu of the car," Fistman said to Milkwright, "my client would like a boat."

Nicki's boyfriend, the retired pole vaulter, was learning to water-ski.

"How big a boat?" Clure Boyette asked. "And what's it go for retail?"

Fistman's answer made Milkwright suspicious. The ski boat cost half as much as an Aston Martin DB11.

"Deal!" said the congressman.

Fistman wore the neutral expression of a python. "We're not quite finished, Chip."

"Of course we're not. That would be too reasonable."

"Congressman, your father owns a jet," Fistman pressed on. "Is that correct?"

"He's got a fractional share of a PJ," Boyette said. "Not the same thing as owning."

"My client would like fifty hours of flying time."

"Ha! Me, too."

"A year," said Fistman. "Fifty hours a year."

Boyette sneered. "Nicki, are you out of your fucking mind?"

Milkwright said, "We can't possibly make that happen. That asset doesn't even belong to my client."

Fistman was in heaven. "Aw, Chip, let's get creative."

Nicki spoke up. "FYI, guys, this is a deal-breaker."

She truly hates my guts, Clure Boyette thought.

Fifty hours on the Citation was what—three, four, five hundred grand? Boyette didn't know because he never saw the bills. His father did. The father whose aorta might blow out when Clure told him what Nicki was demanding. Fifty hours a year was ludicrous. Yet what choice did they have? One lurid press conference by Nicki could detonate Clure's re-election campaign and, even in Florida, drive him out of politics. He would never be governor. His dad would give him a phony job and ignore him for the rest of his life.

Milkwright turned his chair away from the table, leaned closer to Boyette, and whispered, "Counter with forty hours on the jet?"

"Okay, but not for life."

"Until she turns sixty?"

"Or remarries."

"That goes without saying," Milkwright said.

The congressman grabbed the lawyer's shoulder. "We're still getting plowed, Chip. Tell me I'm not wrong."

"You want to keep fighting, we'll fight. My advice?"

"I *know* your advice," said Boyette.

Nicki said yes to the deal. Fistman was radiant; he shook Milkwright's hand twice.

Milkwright drove straight back to his office to draw up the settlement, and an invoice. Boyette went to tell his father, who said he hoped the ski boat crashed and sunk with Nicki and the pole vaulter aboard, before they had a chance to fly on the Citation.

The congressman said, "Well, at least we got the divorce wrapped up before the election."

Clay Boyette frowned. "Yeah, another masterful piece of negotiating. Before you go, could you please pull Harold Fistman's foot out of my ass?"

"Since Nicki changed her mind about the Aston Martin, we can give it to Galaxy when it's ready. That'll solve *that* problem."

"The girl's not getting a car," said the congressman's father, "and the problem's been taken care of."

The wind began to rage. Down like dominos fell the tiki torches and Confederate flag, interrupting the pledge. Dale Figgo canceled the sharing portion of the meeting as the Strokers shielded their faces against the salt spray and flying sand. It seemed as if all of Fever Beach was swirling airborne, pelting the hunkered men. Then came a hard cool squall, drowning what was left of the bonfire. The storm lasted a solid hour and ended with a wild lightning show over the Atlantic.

Twilly Spree was the only one who'd brought weather gear, the only one to stay dry. The other Strokers huddled wretchedly in clusters, arms clamped around their heads, spitting curses and wet sand. As soon as the rain quit, Jonas Onus beat Figgo to the overturned Publix crate that served as a dais. Somebody had brought a battery-powered microphone and amplifier, neither of which survived the downpour. Onus was left to shout:

"First order of business is I got promoted!"

A few men chuckled because they thought he was joking. Others sat there confused or suspicious, plucking grit out of their beards, eyebrows, and hair.

Onus said, "Now on, it's me and Dale together, fifty-fifty on every big move we make."

"How's that gonna work?" Bottle Rocket asked.

"Twice as good as before."

The Strokers one by one started clapping and Figgo felt obliged to join in, though sardonically. In a way, he was relieved that Onus had decided to announce his own promotion; Figgo would have had to fake his way through it, pretending he approved.

But Onus wasn't finished. "Second order of business, fuck this weather and fuck Fever Beach. We're like sitting ducks out here. What we need is a covered, guarded compound all our own!"

What the hell? Figgo thought. Originally it had been Onus's idea to meet at Fever Beach, isolation being one of its selling points. Now Figgo listened fitfully as Onus, hogging the spotlight, promoted the idea of a walled, climate-controlled meeting place with bunks, flat-screens, a recreation room, and an aboveground swimming pool. Ten, fifteen acres minimum.

It was a goofy brainstorm, and Onus had no authority to add it to the agenda. He kept yakking even as Figgo elbowed his way onto the crate.

"The Proud Boys don't have a compound!" Onus was saying. "Neither do the goddamn Oath Keepers!" Then he reeled off a litany of complaints about Fever Beach—the sargassum weeds, the sea lice, the stinging jellyfish, the crabs, the sweaty hike from the parking area, and the threat of being surveilled by government submarines and satellites.

"Pointed order!" Figgo hollered through cupped hands. "Everybody knows old business always comes first. This ain't old business."

Onus tried hip-checking Figgo back off the crate, but Chaos intervened and it was Onus who got removed. Unwisely he threw a punch and went down hard, reminding him how much he resented Twilly Spree. He grabbed Twilly around the knees, triggering a short struggle that ended unfavorably for the putative new coleader of the Strokers for Liberty.

Nothing about the meeting was going smoothly. They had gotten a late start because the KRANKK platform had crashed again, forcing Figgo to communicate the travel details using self-encrypted texts that stymied many of the members. At some point Twilly loaned Figgo a burner phone so he could call every Stroker, a time-consuming task with which Onus declined to assist. Then, during the drive to the pre-meet, Figgo ordered Onus to detour through a neighborhood of old condominiums so they could distribute the last batch of pro-Nazi, anti-vax flyers, Figgo's mother having threatened to evict him from the townhouse if he didn't get rid of them. Though of course she'd meant for the material to be destroyed, not disseminated.

As Figgo tossed one weighted baggy after another from the truck, Onus acidly scoffed that it was a fool's mission.

"How do you know any Jews live here?"

"Who else buys a condo in Florida?" was Figgo's response.

The pre-meet had been set at a Buc-ee's near an interstate exchange in Daytona. Figgo and Onus were the first to show up, followed by Chaos in his dusty Suburban. They waited out front as other Strokers arrived, some still hobbling from the Key West brawl—Bushmaster, Komodo, Bottle Rocket, Das Regulator in a knee brace, and Skid Mark with his busted jaw wired shut and dinged testicles cosseted by a contoured Kevlar truss. Latecomers included an imbecile named Quake, who got spun around and marched back to his van because he'd charged the entrance wearing a ski mask, riot helmet, black commando jumpsuit, and gold Trump high-tops.

The rest of the group followed Figgo and Onus into the store and gathered near the jerky bar, where Chaos broke the news that Payback was out of action indefinitely because of head trauma suffered at the Key West drag show. Figgo solemnly declared that the Strokers would dedicate the upcoming Crapville mission to their injured brethren.

"Jesus Christ, it's *Carp*ville," Onus said.

The men fanned out to stock up on kettle corn and Buc-ee's famous beaver nuggets. By the time they checked out, the sky was turning purple. Figgo, foraging for gum, found an Apple AirTag concealed inside a pack of breath mints in the console of Onus's Tundra. Rattled, both men assumed that the FBI was following them, when in fact the device had been planted by Donna Figgo. Onus dropped it down a sewer grate and, moments later, saw Figgo's phone light up.

"What's your mom want?" he asked testily.

"Who knows," Figgo said. He let it ring and ring.

The harrowing storm had struck soon after the group made it to the beach. Then, once the weather had rumbled away, Onus presumptively stepped up on the crate to pitch his plan for a gated, roofed compound where the Strokers could meet safely, and in comfort. Figgo stood grinding his teeth as Onus described a ranch property in Mims that was on the market for six hundred grand. It needed some work, of course. Onus offered to contact the seller, and none of the men objected.

Mad disrespect, Figgo fumed, and that's when the trouble started.

⩘⩘⩘

Twilly hadn't slept in thirty-five hours, but he enjoyed the road trip. Traffic was light, and the Aston Martin's sound system was superb. He stayed alert all the way to Carpville. There he cruised back and forth past the house of Nicole Grace Boyette, the congressman's wife, easily identifiable from a pre-estrangement photo on the campaign's website. On the fourth pass Twilly spotted Nicki in the driveway, tanned fists on her hips, sourly watching the convertible go by. She was wearing lavender workout tights and carrying a rolled-up yoga mat. Twilly beeped the horn and stomped the gas pedal. Later, southbound on the interstate, he lowered the top and punched up Radio Margaritaville. Once he got back to Tangelo Shores, he stopped at the Baptist cemetery, where a feral tabby had been picking off mockingbirds. The cat, plump but flea-bitten, was sulking in the second of three live-catch traps that Twilly had set. He got scratched on both arms while attaching the bell collar before taking the tabby to the free spay clinic. Then he went to the hangar and swapped out the Aston Martin for his Suburban, which he drove back to the apartment. There he showered and shaved and packed a small handgun for the big night.

The Strokers' first stop would be a Buc-ee's, then on to Fever Beach. In Twilly's mind, being surrounded by burly white bigots wasn't necessarily a triggering scenario. Therapists had wasted innumerable hours of anger-management counseling on him because they'd had so little experience with the unusual nature of his anger—he was able to do furious-seeming deeds without ever losing his shit. His default approach was calm and methodical, which to his way of thinking was how anger ought to be managed. In a jam, disorganized hotheads had a tendency to wave pistols; the one that Twilly was carrying had never been fired except for a hundred times on a closed range.

Viva texted on her way to meet Galaxy for dinner. She told him to be careful at Fever Beach. Dale Figgo and Jonas Onus were half-cocked troglodytes, she said, more reckless now that they were feuding. Twilly didn't want Viva to worry, but knowing she cared enough to nag wasn't a bad feeling.

Besides the two bickering dipshits, Twilly counted eleven other Strokers in the convoy to the meeting. He attributed the low turnout to the bad weather or possibly the dispiriting aftertaste of Key West. As usual, a couple of the men had shown up half drunk or high, which, after the storm, added unnecessary risk to the task of relighting the tiki torches. While none of the members had publicly aligned themselves with either Figgo or Onus, Twilly knew that maintaining order would be a chore. The men were sopping wet, sand-blown, and cranky. No sooner had the meeting started than Figgo and Onus began battling over the crate, forcing Twilly to step in. He wasn't at all surprised when Onus tried to slug him, whereas Onus seemed genuinely perplexed to find himself doubled over, dripping blood and mucus on his boots. Gloating, Figgo kept pumping his right fist in the air until an undeclared supporter of Onus lobbed a Red Bull at his noggin.

Twilly pulled Figgo and Onus aside and advised them to chill out and take turns addressing the group. Onus was still trying to clear his windpipe, leaving Figgo to ascend the crate armed with an agenda he'd typed on his phone.

Item one, he began, was "re-brandifying." He said the Strokers for Liberty had been threatened with a name-infringement lawsuit by a male rowing club in Rhode Island called the Strokers Liberati. An attorney for the oarsmen had contacted Figgo using the information provided on Figgo's white-power leaflets, one of which had improbably found its way to Providence. Figgo told the beach assembly that the "patriot angels" who were funding the movement wouldn't want the expense of litigation, or the publicity. Figgo's solution was to change the group's name to "Strokerz for Liberty," the *z* adding to the brand a hint of both Nazi tribute and death-metal flair. Everyone seemed okay with the idea except Onus, who, despite a bleeding tongue, objected emphatically.

"This is horseshit! This is cancel culture!"

Komodo spoke up, noting that there was no extra cost to the group because its current logo—designed by Figgo using a cock-eyed swastika for the capital *S*—hadn't yet been placed on any decals, ramblers, or outerwear. Another Stroker agreed, saying the merch would look cooler and sell better with a *z* in place of the final *s*.

Figgo called for a voice vote, and the rebranding motion passed easily. Onus snarled at Figgo and tried to kick the crate out from under him. Once again Twilly put Onus on the ground, this time with an elbow to the sternum. Reaction to the disturbance was mixed; the drag club beatdown plainly had cost Figgo some loyalty.

Onus struggled to his feet in time for his next turn. His voice sounded raw, and the proposal seemed relatively innocuous.

"Neck hair," he said.

"Speak up!" shouted Skid Mark through his wired jaw.

"Neck hair!" Onus said louder. "The vibe is savage caveman. Scares the hell out of illegals. Blacks, too."

The Strokerz who had beards, which was the majority, tentatively agreed to let their neck hair grow, front and back.

"That won't scare the Jews," Figgo piped up.

Onus flared. "Hell it won't."

"Look at the Sids, bro. They rock those manes," Figgo needled on. "They got girly curls all the way down to their ass cracks."

Twilly couldn't let it pass. "You mean the Hasids," he said.

Nobody was listening.

"Bin Laden had neck hair," Figgo continued. "So does El Kado and ISIS."

"Dale, you're full a shit." Onus was getting torqued up again.

Figgo asked of the group, "You guys really wanna look like Moose-lims?"

Das Regulator pointed a grimy finger at Figgo and said, "Bro, you're just jealous." It was a dig at Figgo's frayed soul-patch merkin and sparse facial hair. Some of the Strokerz were caught snickering.

"You assholes shut the fuck up," Figgo barked.

"Show of hands," Onus said to the group. "All in favor?"

The neck hair mandate passed nine to four. Twilly alone abstained.

Once more it was Figgo's turn on the crate. His next agenda item was the big one: Precinct 53. He said he'd spoken with the congressman, who green-lighted the Election Day operation. Street maps of Bonifay County would be distributed at the end of the meeting. A timetable was in place, and assignments were ready to be handed out.

Onus wore a fiery scowl while the others murmured eagerly and bumped knuckles.

"Yo, Strokerz, everybody listen up good!" Figgo said.

Nobody was listening more closely than Twilly.

~~~

Jonas Onus didn't need a map. He was the only Stroker who'd scouted Precinct 53 in person. It was the softest of targets, a rest home for old folks. A slam dunk compared to the drag club, Onus thought. He was enraged that Figgo had gone ahead and plotted out the Election Day operation by himself. The congressman had
~~~

made it crystal clear: Figgo and Onus were supposed to consult together on all decisions. Figgo wasn't a detail guy. He had no grasp of logistics or tactics, as evidenced by the calamity in Key West. Watching him exhort atop the crate restoked Onus's secret ambition to take over the Strokerz and capture sole credit for the Carpville occupation. He viewed the congressman's voter-integrity op as a stepping stone to the white-supremacist big leagues and a guest spot on Alex Jones, putting him high on the call list for the next January 6th.

Still squarely in Onus's sights was the Wee Hammers Fund. He wanted control of it or, at least, access via Clure Boyette. Spread among three young families, Onus's firefighter pension was gone by the twentieth of every month. None of the mothers of his children had jobs, and Onus had been eyeing a new lift kit for his Tundra. He calculated that the siege of Carpville wouldn't cost much beyond snacks and gas money. Minus the Key West expenses and Figgo's legal fees, the bulk of the two-million-dollar bonanza should be available.

Unless Figgo or the congressman had been dipping into the pot. One of them was newly unemployed, and the other was an experienced slimeball.

For those concerns alone, Onus was in a hurry to make his move. He would have been stupefied to learn that a chunk of the Wee Hammers money was being spent constructing a real house using real children for labor. He'd assumed the project was nonexistent, a PR ploy by Boyette for laundering purposes. Onus was plotting to skim a portion of the fund for personal lifestyle expenses and use the remainder to buy and upgrade a legit headquarters for the Strokerz for Liberty. The latter notion had come to him while parked beneath his serenity oak listening to Charlie Kirk retell the violent saga of the Branch Davidians in Waco. Obviously that bunch had lacked adequate fortification; Onus did not intend to scrimp. The Mims spread was heavily wooded and out of view from the only dirt road leading to the gate. He imagined the final upgrade as a paramilitary command post with first-class amenities, including central air. It would, he believed, secure for him the full allegiance of the Strokerz and thereby the authority to expel Dale Figgo for life—payback for what had happened to luckless Himmler.

Twilly Spree would remain a problem, though, unless Onus could win him over.

Or, better yet, get rid of him.

Neither would be easy. Onus bitterly wished not to be beaten up again in front of the men; currently he had what felt like a bruise the size of a dinner plate on his sternum. A few inches to the left, and the blow might have stopped his heart. That none of the other Strokerz had swarmed to his defense was disappointing. Were they afraid of Twilly, undecided about the power struggle, or just lazy fucktards?

Figgo's Carpville briefing was winding down, and Onus realized he'd missed most of the critical details, including the date. That meant relying directly on Figgo, who would treat him even less like an equal.

The wind freshened again, and the Strokerz anxiously eyed a fresh line of rain clouds edging over the starlight. Cheers went up when Figgo announced that it was time to eat, and the men noisily attacked their Buc-ee's takeout. Juice boxes and bottles of Powerade in many hues were handed out.

Standing beside one of the tiki torches, Twilly twirled a piece of jerky in his mouth. Onus walked over and woodenly apologized for the punch. Twilly nodded but didn't inquire how Onus was feeling after the body slam.

"What'd you think of Mims?" Onus asked.

"The clubhouse idea?"

"Ain't a damn clubhouse. It's a compound."

Twilly said, "I prefer the beach."

"Are you kiddin' me?" Onus chuckled scornfully.

"It's dark and peaceful out here. No traffic noise, no light pollution."

"No electric outlets, no AC," Onus said. "Come on, bro. Get on board with this thing. Dale listens to you."

"This beach is a calm place. The Strokerz, as a group, would benefit from calm."

"That's so gay, dude."

Twilly began chewing the stick of jerky.

"So, I can put you down as anti-Mims," Onus said.

"Pro-beach is what I am. The dunes, the birds, turtle nests. Who needs Netflix, Jonas?"

"Oh, now you're one of those snowflakes who hate TV?"

"I don't own one."

"That's fucked up," Onus said.

Un-American, he almost added.

Twilly said, "One thing, though: Don't mess with Dale."

Onus's blackish little rat eyes narrowed. "Or what?"

He couldn't stop himself, no matter how many times he got laid out. Something about Twilly lit his fuse.

Behind them the Strokerz were loud and laughing, heady with macho talk about the Precinct 53 operation. Figgo was passing out Little Debbie shortcake rolls. One of the stoned attendees tried to shake the beach sand from the downed Stars and Bars and, with the flagstick, clocked the guy sitting next to him. The dazed Stroker was Bottle Rocket. Figgo filled a bandanna with ice and placed it on the man's head.

Twilly told Onus, "You were a paramedic. Go take a look at your pal."

"I was a firefighter."

"With no EMT training? Give me a break."

"He'll be fine. It's just a bump," Onus said. "You didn't answer my question. What're you gonna do about it if I've gotta take Dale down?"

"Come in hot," said Twilly.

Onus slipped a greasy hand into his jeans, where he kept a folding knife with a fake-bone handle. He didn't know about Twilly's gun until he felt the barrel pressed against his junk. Interestingly, it was the same move he'd planned to make with the knife.

"It's against the regs," he protested hoarsely. "No firearms at meetings."

Twilly, still working on the jerky, said, "This can't be fun for you, Jonas. Over and over again, yet the outcome never changes."

A sweet-smelling gust blew down the tiki torch beside them. The flame went out in the sand.

Onus said, "You ain't gonna shoot me. These dudes would kill you in five seconds."

"How can you not like this place? Listen to the waves. Look at the whitecaps on the water."

"So fucking gay," Onus muttered.

Twilly had him positioned with his back to the others, so none of them could see the handgun.

"I got promoted, don't forget," Onus whispered. "You don't give me orders. I give *you* orders!"

Twilly said, "Pretend that's true if it makes you feel better."

He lowered the pistol, spat out the gnawed nub of meat, and brought up his right knee hard. Onus let out a long, slow squeak, like the door to a haunted basement in a movie. Cupping himself with both hands, he hobbled crookedly toward the dunes.

The rain arrived in cold slanting volleys. Twilly pocketed the gun and pulled up the hood of his rainsuit. Hollering back and forth through the wind, the Strokerz scrabbled wildly to gather their shit and flee the downpour. Dale Figgo, still creaky from the whupping given by his mother, struggled to keep up.

Alone in the dunes knelt Jonas Onus, furiously blinking the raindrops from his eyes.

CHAPTER 22

Donna Figgo was waiting at the townhouse when her son returned from Fever Beach looking half drowned. He dove outstretched onto the sectional before she could throw a punch.

She jumped on the cushions and briefly stood over him, glaring like Cassius Clay over Sonny Liston.

"So you found my AirTag, woo-fucking-hoooo," she said. "Now you think you're James Bond, 'cept I know exactly where you went tonight, and who you met up with—those white-power Neanderthals. Viva told me."

"Don't listen to that bitch," Figgo said, muffled by the pleather.

Viva was upstairs in bed with her Death Cab for Cutie playlist cranked up loud on her headphones; she didn't want to hear Figgo's head hit the floor when his mother popped him. Viva was slightly drunk and melancholy from her night out with Galaxy, who at least had a solid life plan. Nursing school, for God's sake. Nurses helped to heal the sick. Nurses saved lives. The whole human race needed more nurses. How was Viva supposed to get psyched up about a corporate HR job?

Unless something good came open in New York—that would be hard to refuse, if she could screw up the courage to go. Twilly

Spree was no help, muddling her aspirations by being so decent and interesting, and also, if she was being honest, hot.

God, I need to sleep, Viva thought. She sprawled on the comforter and closed her eyes. Soon the talking dwarf coyote was back.

"You need an oil change," it said. "Make sure they rotate the tires, too."

"What are you?" Viva asked. "And where are we?"

The coyote growled.

"Really?" Viva held out her hand. "Go ahead and bite me, fleabag."

"Guess what," said the coyote. "I ate that fucking chinchilla."

Then it dashed between Viva's legs and disappeared into the tall ferns of the dream garden. She opened her eyes and removed her headphones. She could hear shouting on the first floor, which meant that Donna Figgo hadn't yet knocked her grown son cold. Viva got out of bed and took a shower. It was quiet there, and she was happy not to be standing in clammy water; Dale still griped about his mother forcing him to pay a plumber to fix the drain. The next tenant would benefit from Viva's tenacity on the issue.

Downstairs, Donna had been joined by her boyfriend, Breck. He and Dale detested the sight of each other.

"Get outta my house," Figgo said to Breck.

"It's not *your* house, Sir Turdley."

"What did you say?"

"Your mom owns this place," Breck said.

"No, before that. What'd you call me?"

Donna said, "Sir Turdley. That's your nickname on the congressman's phone."

"It's pretty damn funny," said Breck, grinning.

Figgo was livid. He rolled off the sectional and snapped, "Now you're just makin' up stuff."

"Not true," his mother said. "Viva said she saw it in the congressman's contacts."

"Christ, I can't believe she told you about him."

"Of course she told me. She's worried," Donna said.

Breck continued smirking, him with his candy-ass golf tan. Figgo could visualize beating him with a claw hammer.

Donna continued: "I'm worried, too, son. You need to quit these losers before you end up dead or in prison."

"The Strokerz? How 'bout endin' up a hero is more like it. Famous as fuck, too. You wait and see. History will be the final jury."

"The final judge, you mean."

"Back off, Mom."

"Whatever you've got planned," Breck interjected, "is going to break your mother's heart. Obviously you don't care about that."

"And obviously *you* don't care about the future of this country. I believe I was put on this earth to warrior for God's chosen race."

"And I was put on this earth," Donna said, "not to raise a brain-dead bigot."

Figgo didn't see it coming—a lefthanded slap to the right side of his head.

It was, emotionally, worse than a punch. He would rather have gone down unconscious and not see his mother see the look on his face. For a moment he considered taking a dive, but she and Breck wouldn't have bought it. All he could think to do was point at the door until they walked out.

Viva came barefoot down the stairs wearing a long terrycloth robe, her wet hair brushed back.

Figgo looked up coldly. " 'Sir Turdley'? What the fuck?"

"The congressman, your good buddy? That's how he thinks of you, Dale. You're the bozo who left a turd on the wrong statue."

"Did you tell my mother about that? Swear to God, if you did—"

"I did not."

Viva happened to have her phone in one hand. She showed Figgo the screenshot of the second page of Clure Boyette's "S" contacts. Angrily he asked how she'd gotten access.

She said, "Doesn't matter. The point is the low opinion he has of you."

"Is Jonas's number on there?"

"I didn't see it, but maybe Boyette gave him a mean nickname, too."

"Not worse than mine, I bet. Christ, what's that smell?"

"My shampoo," Viva said. "It's geranium leaf."

Figgo pretended to put a finger down his throat and stalked to the refrigerator for a beer.

Viva maturely changed the subject. "How was the beach shindig?"

"It rained like hell, duh. Didn't your boyfriend tell ya?"

"He hasn't called yet."

"Is he comin' over tonight? Me and him gotta have a word." Figgo was squeaking around the kitchen in his sandy wet boots and soggy black commando outfit. He pulled out his own phone and shot a text to Clure Boyette:

This is SIR TURDLEY we need to meet ASAP

"Stand up for yourself," Viva said.

"Don't talk to my mother no more!"

"We're friends, Dale. Friends share."

"She ain't your friend. Now on, don't tell her a goddamn thing. Not if you care about this country and the whole big picture."

"Key West was tough on her."

Figgo cackled bitterly. "Tough on *her*?"

"The fact it was your idea, her own flesh and blood, to go after female impersonators. She's bummed and pissed off, and you don't even get it."

"No, I'm the one that feels like that. She's the one that don't get it."

"See you in the morning, Dale." Viva grabbed a can of LaCroix from the refrigerator door and headed up the stairs.

Figgo heaved himself onto the sectional and stared grimly at his phone on the coffee table. It took more than an hour for the congressman to reply.

I'm in DC, he texted. **We'll tlk tmw**

No apology for the insulting nickname, no mention of it.

What a prick, thought Figgo, struggling out of his rancid boots. *Soon I'll be bigger and more famous than him.*

The killer named Moe drove to the headquarters of the Mink Foundation. He walked past Viva Morales and knocked on Claude Mink's door. No response. The door was locked. The killer walked back to Viva's desk and asked for the key.

"Do you have an appointment with Mr. Mink?" she said.

"I don't need one."

"I'll let him know you're waiting," Viva said.

"Give me the key or I'll break off the doorknob."

"You must be stronger than you look."

"I won't take much of his time. That's a promise."

Viva said, "I wouldn't go in there right now if I were you."

"The key, please."

"All right, but don't say I didn't warn you."

Claude Mink was hunched in his desk chair strenuously using both hands to maneuver a pliable sex toy on his lap.

He looked up and yelled, "Get out of here! Go!"

The killer saw that the toy was a molded replica of the lower female torso. Nutmeg was the color, if he had to guess.

"Put that thing away," he said to Claude.

"How'd you get in? Who the hell do you think you are?"

Moe closed the door behind him. "I'm the one you hired to deal with Commissioner Baltry. I checked with the bank. You still owe half my fee."

Claude's hands were shaking more than usual as he sheepishly stowed the Dream Booty beneath the desk.

"You'll get the money," he said to the killer, "when the body is found."

"That wasn't our agreement."

"Oh yes, it was," Claude said, without much starch.

Moe sat down in an oversize armchair. He said, "I texted you the picture of Baltry by the road."

"Yes, but a picture won't get us the death certificate we need."

" 'We' being who else?" Moe asked. "Never mind, I'm on a tight schedule. Just give me the rest of my fee."

"That's crazy. Would you pay your tailor before you even tried on the suit?"

"Did you pay up front for your burial plot?"

"I don't own a burial plot," Claude rattled back. "I own a mausoleum."

"Good," said Moe. "If you end up in pieces, there'll be a cubby for all of them."

"That's a sick thing to say," Claude said, but he gave up on arguing. The killer was annoyed, and acted like he was fighting a headache.

He said, "Transfer the balance by the time I get to my car, which is three blocks away. Understand? The bank app's on my phone, and it only takes me a minute to check my balance. Don't ask what happens if you jerk me around again, because you know what happens. Do you want to hear Baltry's last words?"

"No! Fuck, no. You'll get the damn money, but this is no way to do business."

"No pouting, Mr. Mink. You're loaded, you and your wife. I've seen your house, or should I say your McMansion?"

"*Mansion*. Our architect is world famous."

"You got ripped off," Moe said. "Either that, or you've got heinous taste."

Claude was thrown. "Were you staking out my property? Why?"

"Relax. Have a drink of water."

"I got cameras everywhere outside the house. Front, back, poolside."

"Yes, I noticed," the killer said.

There was a copper water pitcher on the credenza by the window. Moe got up and poured a glass for Claude, who looked rocky.

"Something's been bothering me," Moe said.

"Bothering *you*?"

"Yes, I have a feeling you don't care much for Jews."

Claude fidgeted, moving an ivory paperweight from one side of his desktop to the other and back again.

"Uh, look. It's nothing personal," he said.

"No?"

"Absolutely not. I'm a businessman. Over the years I've had a few run-ins, that's all."

The hit man said, "You knew I was Jewish. How? Did someone tell you?"

Claude almost smiled. "Nobody told me anything. It's simple intuition. I pick up on little things."

Unbelievable, Moe thought.

"Like now, for example," Claude bumbled on, "you asking for your whole fee all at once."

"That was the deal, Mr. Mink."

"Not as I remember it."

Moe looked around the office, a predictable overload of tropical hardwood and dark leather. A potted bird-of-paradise plant occupied a corner that received zero natural sunlight. In another corner was a fifty-gallon aquarium featuring the obligatory clownfish, a pale anemone, and a trio of listless seahorses. Meanwhile the broad picture window behind Claude's desk inflicted a soul-deadening view of shopping mall rooftops, traffic jams, and a cellphone tower. Displayed on the walls were at least a dozen plaques honoring the Minks' philanthropy and all-around saintliness. Also: framed fund-raising party photos of the couple posing with Ted Cruz, Newt Gingrich, Aaron Rodgers, and a random country music star who clearly had no fucking clue who Claude and Electra were. There were a few recent pictures of Claude shaking hands with Donald Trump, two crusty iguanas in tuxedos.

Moe rubbed his throbbing forehead and said, "Get on the phone to your banker, Mr. Mink. I'm leaving now, so you've got five, maybe ten minutes."

"Jesus, you people are worse than the Mafia!"

Wow, Moe thought. *This asshole's making it easy.*

~~~

Put yourself in my position, Twilly would say to Viva later. The stupid bastard is supposed to be miles away, safe and sound, and then he calls you from the CVS parking lot. Scared shitless, of course.
~~~

"Lewin, why the hell did you come back?" you ask.

"It's a long story," he says. "You probably won't believe it."

And since you'd given him your phone number, which he actually saved, there's a sense of responsibility even though he's a crook. It's not like you feel sorry for him; it's that you know what would happen if he got himself murdered right now. The governor would appoint a new county commissioner and The Bunkers would get approved four to three.

Baltry is pacing in front of the CVS when you pull up. He smells awful, his clothes are filthy. You roll down all the windows and drive back and forth across town while he yammers out this story about hiding in the mountains of Montana until a hit man hired by Claude Mink tracked him down.

"I don't understand why he didn't kill you," you say.

"I think maybe because Claude Mink is an anti-Semite."

"What?"

"He made some remark on the phone and the guy was very offended."

"The hit man was offended?"

"That's my impression," Baltry says. "I slept on a school playground last night, in a damn kiddie crawl pipe."

"At least you weren't out on a beach in the rain."

"Are the feds still after me?"

"For sure," you say, knowing he'll believe you.

"Can we swing by my house so I can get some clean clothes?"

"Do any of your neighbors have Ring cameras?"

"Yeah, of course."

"Then no," you tell him. "Don't go anywhere near the house. I've got a shirt and pants you can change into. Getting back to the hit man—"

"What about underwear?"

"Lewin, I'll *buy* you some goddamn underwear. Now, this supposed hit man—"

"He didn't give me his name. But I don't know yours, either."

"If you interrupt me one more time," you say, "I'm leaving your dumb ass on Claude Mink's doorstep."

"Sorry, sorry."

"So, did this professional killer drive you all the way back from Montana and let you go purely out of the goodness of his heart? Or is there something specific he told you to do?"

"Yes," Baltry says.

"Yes, what?"

It was like talking to a mulch pit, Twilly would say to Viva, but somebody's got to keep him safe from the Minks, right? Baltry has no experience at being on the run. Viva had remained skeptical until Twilly told her what the hit man had ordered the commissioner to do. Then it started to make sense.

"Holy shit," she'd said.

Which had been your exact words, too, when you heard it.

Baltry's incisive remark, sitting next to you in the Suburban is, "Weird, huh?"

"Mind-boggling, actually. What else does he want from you?"

"That's all."

"No money?"

"He said he's keeping my Rolls golf cart. And, well, now my car."

You ask for the make, model, and color. Baltry says it's a 2016 Subaru Outback. "Dark green," he adds. "I found it online out in Oregon."

"Did the hit man change out the license plates?"

"Nope. But don't ask me the tag number. I didn't memorize that because I didn't plan on having the car stolen."

"Is he still here in Tangelo Shores?"

"The hit man?"

"Yes, Lewin."

"No idea," Baltry says, and you can almost hear the gears in his thick head slowing to a grind.

"What's the last thing he told you when he dropped you off?"

" 'Stay alive, Lewin. Don't let me down.' "

"He said that? The hit man?" You're drumming your fingers on the dashboard, thinking about the killer's extraordinary change of plans.

Baltry says, "The whole thing, it's freaking me out. I don't know where to go, but I sure don't want to get shot."

"Does Claude Mink think you're dead?" you ask.

"The guy made me lie down by the side of the highway with my eyes wide open like a zombie. This was someplace in Tennessee. He squirted Heinz ketchup all over my head and took a bunch of pictures."

"Which he sent to Claude."

"At least one," Baltry says.

"I know a place for you to stay where they'll never find you."

Baltry stammers out a thank-you.

"There will be rules, Lewin."

"Long as I'm safe."

"That you'll be," is what you tell him, basically a promise.

Put yourself in the same spot, Twilly had said to Viva later. Baltry wouldn't last a day on the street once the Minks found out he was alive and back in town. This isn't Bumfuck, Montana, where it's easy to lie low. If I got him a hotel room, he'd be lined up in plain sight at the nearest Dunkin' Donuts the next morning—

"Twilly, whoa, back up," Viva had interrupted. "Baltry's car, the one that the killer's driving—it's an Outback?"

"That's what he told me. Green. 2016."

"And definitely Oregon plates?"

"Yeah. Why?"

"Holy shit," Viva had said for the second time in the conversation. "Galaxy."

~~~

Moe had lucked out when he went to buy Gas-X; the drugstore sold day-old editions of the *New York Daily News*. He'd been skimming the sports section when the target surprised him by walking up to the car. It had been sloppy and unprofessional of him not to know that the rental complex where she lived didn't have a Building G, but she acted more amused than suspicious.

And at least he'd gotten an up-close look at Janice Eileen Smith, aka Galaxy. Her face had sharper features than he'd anticipated,
~~~

and she dressed older than most eighteen-year-olds. Moe was fairly certain he hadn't spooked her; she likely thought he was a lost vacationer sent to pick up his retiree aunt. So many Florida apartment complexes looked identical, as if designed by the same prison architect.

Moe returned on foot the next day after wiping down Baltry's Outback and abandoning it at an Olive Garden. Janice Eileen Smith wasn't home, so Moe sat in an unlocked Comcast van and waited. He should have been in a better mood, having opened his banking app and confirmed that Claude Mink had deposited the rest of his money. But Moe couldn't shake a clinging unease about this new assignment; for once he wished he knew the personal background of the target. It wasn't long before she pulled up driving a light-colored Lexus RX that had a rental company bar code on one of the windows. Carrying two grocery bags, she entered the apartment in a manner that Moe would have described as peppy.

He stayed in the van a few more minutes before approaching her door and knocking. When Janice Eileen Smith asked who was there, Moe the killer said he'd been sent by the power company to check the fuses in the breaker box.

"It's outside," he heard her say from behind the door.

Shit, Moe thought.

"By the electric meters," she added.

Of course the main electrical box was mounted on an exterior wall. Moe felt like a rookie for using that line. On a male target, he wouldn't have tried it.

"There should be a smaller one in the closet," he said.

"Uh, I don't think so."

Shit.

"Okay, ma'am. Sorry to bother you."

As Moe turned away, the door unexpectedly swung open. There stood Janice Eileen Smith in a plain bra, fashionably torn jeans, and no shoes. It appeared that she'd been taking off her makeup when he knocked.

She said, "I never forget a voice. You're the dude in the Subaru from yesterday."

"That wasn't me. I work for City Electric."

"You were reading a newspaper with your sunglasses on. You asked me for directions to Building G, which doesn't exist. Why lie about it? Everybody makes mistakes."

Moe, who was experienced at keeping a blank face, said, "Sorry, ma'am, but you've got me confused with someone else."

"Come on in," she said. "Whoever you are."

"Sure?"

"Look at you all shy."

"It'll just take a second to check those fuses," Moe said.

"Right. In your new electrician onesie that's big enough to fit the pope."

Moe tried to appear self-conscious. "We don't get a choice of sizes," he said.

And as soon as he took a step into the apartment, Janice Eileen Smith, aka Galaxy, jumped him from behind.

CHAPTER 23

The killer perceived himself horse-collared and facedown on a stale pile carpet, immobilized by a girl he outweighed by at least eighty pounds. She smelled like mountain wildflowers, which made the situation even more surreal. Where her knife came from he didn't know. He felt the tip of the blade pressed keenly to the side of his neck, the girl's calm breath on his ear.

"Did the congressman send you?" she asked.

"Take it easy, Janice."

"You just answered my question. Spanky's the only client who knows my real name, because of the car. Did he tell you about that, too?"

"Never met the man. Swear to God," Moe said. "Did you say 'Spanky'?"

Janice Eileen Smith reached her free hand into the waistband of his pants and found the wire garrote he'd planned to use.

"I'm sure every electrician carries one of these," she said. "For what—strangling squirrels on transformer poles?"

She tossed the garrote across the room. Moe grew increasingly concerned about the knife. If she stuck him too deep, even by accident, he would quickly bleed out. It seemed, moreover, that she was fully aware.

"I'll cut a boy," she said. "So be good."

Moe told her that he didn't know who booked the job, adding, "It was a blind referral from another provider."

"Why do they want me dead?"

"We never ask the reason, Janice. That's rule number one."

"Dude, I'm only eighteen. How am I already worth killing?"

"I wondered the same thing," Moe admitted.

He couldn't get over her wiry strength. He might be able to shake her off his back, but not without risking a fatal puncture.

"How much're they paying you?" she asked.

"One hundred thousand."

"Bullshit."

"I'm serious."

"*Fuck!*"

"Yeah, it's a lot," Moe said.

"I guess I should be flattered. How does it work—you get the money up front?"

"Fifty percent is standard, the rest when it's done. Be careful with the knife, okay?"

"What're you supposed to do with my dead body?"

"Make it disappear. They don't care how," Moe said.

He actually didn't mind her perfume. It was light, not overpowering.

"They told me you're a prostitute," he said. "Nothing personal, but how did someone like you get into a business like that?"

She chuckled. "I could ask you the same question."

"True. Am I bleeding?"

"Just a tad. FYI, I'm on a sabbatical from the Venmo dating scene. Thinking about a new career path."

"Smart," Moe said.

"Yes, I am. What did you do before you became a hired 'provider'?"

"Twenty-one years on Wall Street."

"No shit?"

"Ever heard of BlackRock?"

"I loved their first album," Janice Eileen Smith said.

"That's a joke, right?"

"Yeah. Sorry."

"I got laid off after the '08 crash," Moe said. He blinked a few times. "Damn, something weird's going on with my eyes."

"Perfectly normal. No circulation."

"They didn't tell me you trained in martial arts."

Again she laughed. "Right, I'm a blond belt. Tell the truth: Would I be the youngest person you ever killed?"

"By many years, yes."

"How do you feel about that?"

"Not great," Moe said.

"Especially now that you're getting to know me."

"I didn't feel right about it to start with."

Moe saw a drop of his own blood fall on the carpet. Then another. The girl had him in a terrible pose. He felt like a goddamn amateur.

"You play golf?" she asked.

"That's right."

"The white man's burden. I could tell by the tan line from your shirt collar."

"How about you? I'm guessing tennis."

"On nice days I lie out by the pool," she said. "And I like to shop."

"Please put down the knife."

"You aren't enjoying our convo? I've been told I'm good at small talk."

Moe said, "It's important in your line of work, I'm guessing."

"So true, so true. But, like I told you, I'm presently on sabbatical."

"Paid or unpaid?"

"Paid," she said. "I'm no fool."

Moe watched another drop of his blood fall. It felt like the knife tip was about a millimeter away from popping a gusher. He could hear his breathing get faster.

Janice Eileen Smith asked for the name of the bank that had wired the fifty percent deposit.

"Some mail drop in Lichtenberg. Doesn't matter," he said. "A shell company for a shell company. I couldn't trace it if I wanted to, and I'm a pro."

"I bet it's the congressman."

"Why would he want you dead?" Moe asked.

"He's got some kinks that won't win him any votes."

"So you're blackmailing the guy."

Janice Eileen Smith said, "It's not only the money. It's his attitude. If you met him, you'd understand."

"I get it. He's a dickhead."

"Major." She eased off a touch with the knife and told the killer about Clure Boyette's insulting Aston Martin switcheroo, the secret pictures of him dolled up for Westminster, his Wee Hammers fraud that she'd learned about from Viva, and his two-million-dollar pipeline to some rich old farts who fronted a Hitler-loving white-power gang.

"That's a lot to process," said Moe, "especially Nazis."

"Now you know why I'm taking a leave."

"Who are the rich farts?"

"My friend told me. Let me think," she said. "They've got an animal name. Fox? Wolf? No, it's Mink. That's a high-end weasel, right? A mink."

"Yes, the mink." Moe the killer smiled to himself. He felt another warm droplet roll slowly off his neck. He started laughing.

"Oh, Janice," he said. "This is funny."

"What's funny about bleeding?"

"No, not that."

"Then what?"

"Let me buy you dinner."

"That *is* funny," she said. "Actually, I could go for a pizza."

The Wee Hammers were corralled and lined up for a group photo wearing their new matching tee shirts. A raspy old lady from the Bonifay County Chamber of Commerce was having them pose in front of the far-from-completed house on Watermelon Way. She made Tomas De Leon squeeze into the picture with the kids. Egregio stood beside him deliberately passing gas. That morning, Egregio had assaulted one of the other Wee Hammers using a power drill fitted with a Phillips-head attachment and a two-inch flathead screw. Just for laughs, Egregio had fastened the smaller boy's hand to a sheet of plywood subflooring. The paramedics wanted to call the police, but the victim insisted it had been his idea. He feared retribution from Egregio.

That was the last straw for Tomas. He'd stripped Egregio of his tee shirt and sent him home in a cab. Soon thereafter he got a call from his friend Rocky, the vice president of the construction company. Rocky said that Tomas wasn't allowed to ban Egregio from the jobsite, because the kid's parents had donated two thousand dollars to the re-election campaign of Clure Boyette.

"Not that guy," Tomas said disgustedly.

"He's the one who came up with the Wee Hammers. You met him at the house."

"I remember. The congressman. *El Dildo Pomposo.*"

"Here's the deal: Egregio's mom and dad want him to keep working on the site. They say he needs structure in his day, along with—these aren't my words—'task-building skills.' "

"That's what school's for," Tomas said.

"No, see, they're homeschooling the kid."

"But they don't want him at home."

"Basically, yeah."

"Because he's psycho," said Tomas.

It was the second time Tomas had faced questioning about his treatment of Egregio. Rocky had also called him in on the day the boy got trapped in the Jiffy John. Knowing their son was both a putz and a liar, Egregio's parents had believed Tomas's story that Egregio had accidentally locked himself in the portable commode.

"The kid he screwed to the subfloor," Rocky said, "his folks don't want to make a federal case out of it. All we've gotta do is cover the medical bills. The kid's embarrassed, is what it sounds like."

Tomas said, "That was more than a prank. It was agg assault."

"I heard there was another incident today. Is that true?"

"She's in stable condition. I drove her to the ER myself."

Rocky sighed glumly. "Tell me what happened."

"She was doing pull-ups and all this crazy gymnastic shit on a scaffold and, surprise, it came apart."

"How old is this one?"

"Nine," Tomas said, "but not a string bean. A big girl."

"She hurt bad?"

"Broken collarbone. Dislocated elbow. She wasn't wearing her helmet, so, gash on her scalp. I want off of this job."

"Not yet," Rocky said.

"Put me on the Osprey Mall project. Get someone else over here."

"No other GC will touch the Watermelon house. You're it."

"What kind of fucked-up parents would let their child work construction?"

"The kids can't all be bad," Rocky said.

"They're not, but there's no safe job for them here. What if one of 'em gets crippled or killed? We'll get our asses sued and then we're out of business."

"Hang in there, amigo. It's not a forever scenario."

"Then how much longer?"

"November 4th, no more kids on the job. They're done," Rocky said.

Tomas chuckled bleakly. "Okay. Now I get it."

Within the hour, Egregio reappeared at the Wee Hammers house. Tomas handed him a can of white paint and pointed him toward a pile of lumber scraps. The kid called Tomas an old dick-brain, and Tomas numbly let it slide.

That night his wife fixed a buttery roast chicken for dinner, but Tomas had no appetite. She asked what was wrong, suspecting it was another crisis at 545 Watermelon Way. Tomas told her about Egregio's latest power-tool crime, and about the girl who brought down the scaffold pretending to be Simone Biles.

He added, "They won't let me off this job, so I think I might quit the company."

"Tommy, no. I'm sure they've got plenty of liability insurance."

"I don't care. A kid dies, it's on me."

"Don't ever talk like that," his wife implored. "You're the best they've got."

Tomas loved her like crazy. She poured him a drink from a bottle of Jack Daniel's they'd had for years, an anniversary present from her uncle.

She said, "So, when's the house of horrors supposed to be finished?"

"The date keeps changing. But here's my one and only piece of good news: Rocky says the kids will be out of there on November 4th."

"Baby, that's fantastic! You can hang on till then, I know you can." She was glowing with relief.

"I'm not sure I can make it," Tomas said, staring deep into the glass of whiskey. "Each day gets worse. They're like hyenas on Molly."

He sat there finishing his drink while his wife cleared the dinner dishes. Afterward she came over, kissed the top of his head, and asked, "So, why are they letting the little brats hang around until November 4th?"

Tomas looked up at her and smiled helplessly.

"Because November 3rd is Election Day," he said.

~~~

One thing that Jonas Onus learned the hard way on Fever Beach: It's not like the movies or television, where a guy gets kneed in the nuts, rolls around moaning for a minute, then pops to his feet and starts punching again. In real life the pain keeps you down. Also, your balls swell up so much they don't even *look* like balls—more like weird raw plums, blackish and purple. And they hurt so fucking bad you almost wish they'd fall off.

Onus stayed in bed all the next morning. At noon he went to the Winn-Dixie, where he walked the aisles at toddler speed with his knees pinched together. He picked up a twelve-pack of Budweiser, a bottle of Advil, and a bag of ice. He paid with three tens
~~~

that he wrestled from his homemade duct-tape wallet. The wallet was indestructible as advertised but Onus had misread the online instructions, leaving the sticky side of the tape exposed in the fold where he kept his money. The checkout kid helped him so as not to tear the cash.

When Onus got to Elm Street, he saw that the oak tree, *his* oak tree, was gone. He parked in his usual space staring in confusion at the fresh stump. Other trees had been chopped down, too—so many that the street looked totally different, bare and void of shade. Onus delicately fit the ice bag beneath his scrotum and a numbing relief commenced immediately, even through his jeans. He saw a paper notice on a lamppost saying the city was widening Elm and apologizing for the temporary inconvenience.

It's not temporary for the damn trees, Onus thought.

He turned on the radio and heard a commercial for "Stop the Next Steal" mouse pads endorsed by the wife of Supreme Court Justice Clarence Thomas. All of Onus's favorite pundits were predicting a chaotic midterm election with vengeful ballot fraud by border jumpers, college radicals, and urban agitators. Onus himself planned to vote for the first time ever but by mail, because on November 3rd he would be in Carpville, defending Precinct 53. The race between Congressman Clure Boyette and some liberal schoolteacher had become unexpectedly tight, making it one of the most important contests in the country. Laura Loomer was warning that a loss by Boyette could tip the balance of power in the House of Representatives, dooming Americans to a squalid future of unisex bathrooms, pornography-packed libraries, and weak shower nozzles.

The higher the stakes, the better, thought Onus.

He was excited at the prospect of having a national stage upon which to shine as a white patriot—a long-awaited opportunity to make up for his absence from the Capitol on January 6th. He couldn't wait to lead the Strokerz for Liberty into Bonifay County, Florida, and do it alone, without Dale Figgo and his asshole bodyguard. All that Onus needed was a plan, an alibi, and healed testicles.

He was fumbling under the bottom of his jeans, repositioning the ice bag, when somebody tapped sharply on the passenger window. It was a cop. He told Onus to get out.

Onus wasn't worried. The cop was white, and looked about the same age as he.

"What's up, bro?" Onus asked.

The cop motioned for him to turn down the radio. Onus complied.

"Exit the vehicle," the cop said, "and keep your hands where I can see 'em."

After Onus got out of the truck, the cop asked if he had any weapons. Onus said there was a Glock in the console and a Chinese throwing star under the passenger seat.

"I need to see some ID," the cop said.

"Why? What'd I do?"

It turned out that a pedestrian on Elm Street had complained about a possible pervert in a light-colored Tundra. Onus insisted he wasn't doing anything wrong.

"Then what's all over your pants?" the cop asked.

"Just water. I was sittin' on a pile of ice."

Onus showed him the bag on the front seat. The cop told him to keep his hands still.

"Sir, why were you sitting on ice?"

"Groin injury," Onus said.

"Is there more to the story?"

"Some big Black dude kicked me in the *cojones*."

"Why?"

"He was tryin' to jack my rims."

"Mind if I look in your truck?"

Onus bristled. "I *do* mind. I know what the Constitution says."

The problem was that his Dream Booty lay in plain sight behind the front seat. It looked so realistic that the cop, thinking Onus had dismembered somebody, hurled him to the pavement and locked him in handcuffs. The cop had no luck trying to extract Onus's ID from the duct-tape wallet.

Soon many backup officers arrived, along with an unnecessary contingent from the medical examiner's office. It was a long, humiliating afternoon.

In the end, Onus wasn't arrested, although the police seized his gun and, of course, the Dream Booty. He drove off in a murderous mood. The seat of the Tundra was wet and cold from the melted ice.

~~~

Galaxy texted Viva back to say everything was fine. Viva and Twilly rushed to her apartment anyway. The lights inside were on, but nobody answered the door. Twilly looked in the windows and didn't see any signs of a struggle. No green Outbacks were in the parking lot, but neither was Galaxy's rented silver Lexus.

Viva and Twilly went back to sit in the Suburban. A message on Twilly's smartwatch confirmed that Lewin Baltry had not left the house where Twilly had deposited him, and that he was behaving himself except for hogging the TV remote.

When Viva called Galaxy's phone, it went directly to voicemail.

"Maybe she's on a date," Twilly said.

"Let's wait here for her," she said. "Do you mind?"

"I don't like waiting."

"Why not? We can make out and fog up the windows."

"Maybe later," Twilly said absently.

"I'm done with you. Who turns down an offer like that?"

"We'll come back in a while and see if she's home."

"Fair enough," Viva said. "Meanwhile we should go get a drink somewhere quiet. Snuggle in a booth and plan our life together."

"Sure, maybe later."

"You've left the planet, haven't you, Twilly?"

"There's something I have to do. Want to ride along?"

"Right now?"

"Yes, right now," he said. "I need to blow up something."

Viva couldn't read his expression because it was dark outside and this impossible man was sitting behind the wheel wearing aviator sunglasses. She sensed that he was strung tight as a bow.

"Blow up what?" she asked. "You mean, like, our relationship?"
~~~

"I've got a box of Unigel in the back."

"Is that a lube? Gross, Twilly."

"No, it's dynamite," he said. "Old-school shit."

"So you were being literal."

He nodded and turned the key in the ignition. "You don't have to come. I'd understand completely."

"Are you kidding?" Viva heard herself say. "*Vamos ahora!*"

"Sweet," said Twilly.

Viva thinking: *Who* am *I?*

"I brought ear protection," he told her.

"Good, because I left mine at the artillery depot."

He drove west out of town to the perimeter of the Bunkers project, where he cut through a chain-link fence and handed her a set of military-grade earmuffs. Then they blew up a twenty-ton excavator. The tank was full of diesel, and drivers could see the flames all the way from the turnpike.

On the way back to Tangelo Shores, Viva counted six fire trucks speeding the other way on Grissom Boulevard. Twilly was like a different person—upbeat, animated, cracking jokes. He got excited when he found a radio station playing *Quadrophenia* from beginning to end. Viva, still dazed, confessed that she'd never heard of the album.

"You're in for a treat," Twilly said, "you gorgeous little monkey wrencher."

Viva shook her head. "All I did was light the fuse."

Thinking:

Holy shit. I lit the fuse.

CHAPTER 24

The congressman flew straight from D.C. and gave Dale Figgo fifteen minutes at the small municipal airport outside of town. Figgo had never been invited aboard a private jet before. The pilots kept the engines running so the cabin would stay cool. Figgo resisted an urge to sneak a picture and text it to his mother down in São Paulo, where she and Breck had gone for stem-cell facials and nude ziplining.

Clure Boyette was on his way to Carpville and dressed for schmoozing at a farmer's market—flannel shirt, blue jeans, and stiff new cowboy boots. He gave Figgo a cold Pepsi in a plastic go-cup.

"Your guys are ready for Election Day?" he said.

"Yessir, they are."

"Why'd you want to meet up? I assume there's a problem."

"It's Onus. He's mutinizing," Figgo said.

The congressman snorted crossly. "I already told you both to get along."

"It don't work with two chiefs in the tepee."

"Make it work," Boyette snapped.

"He shows me no damn respect."

"Clean this up, Dale. There's only seventy-two hours before go-time."

"He's tryin' to overtake the whole group. Can't you talk to him?"

The congressman shrugged and raised his hands. "Campaigning's a full-time job. Wet babies to kiss, dirty hands to shake, smelly old ladies to hug. Plus there's media out the ying-yang—Fox, Newsmax, podcasts I never even heard of. Give me a break, dude."

Figgo listened, fidgeting with the Velcro strap on his wrist brace. His carpal tunnel issues had flared due to a jerk-off marathon that he attributed to stress. The KRANKK platform had crashed again—permanently, according to Figgo's new IT guy. But his other problem was much more serious.

"Jonas is outta control," Figgo said to Boyette. "He could incapacerate the whole fuckin' operation. The entire future of America!"

"Okay, Dale. I'll call his dumb ass and tell him the same thing I'm telling *your* dumb ass."

"Good. He might listen to you."

Figgo looked around, admiring the jet's cabin—polished wood paneling, a push-bottom snack drawer filled with Reese's Peanut Butter Cups, plush armrests on every seat, and a flat-screen that featured live mapping of every flight. The safety belts had a shiny gold finish, lap-and-shoulder style for extra safety.

Meanwhile the congressman had been distracted by Figgo's ball-sack nose. It was the freakiest skin graft he'd ever seen.

He said, "We done, Dale? There's only, like, five hundred registered voters waiting on me at a rally back home."

"One more thing: Could you change my screen name in your contacts?"

Boyette was caught by surprise. "The Sir Turdley thing? Who told you about that? Did you look through my goddamn phone?"

"Hell, no. I got sources."

The congressman didn't have time to cross-examine the nitwit. He said, "So, what's the big deal? Everybody on my private list has a funny code name."

"Ain't funny to me." Figgo was getting riled again, in spite of the intimidating surroundings. "What code name did you give Jonas?" he asked.

Boyette didn't hesitate. " 'Bebe Daddy,' " he replied.

"On account of all his kids."

"Obviously."

"Change mine to somethin' better," Figgo said. "I hate 'Sir Turdley.' "

"Okay, how about 'The Evacuator'?"

Figgo wasn't sure what it meant, but he liked the way it sounded. "That'll work," he said.

"Right?" The congressman smiled and fastened his safety belt. "Time to get my white butt airborne. We'll be in touch."

"There's one other thing: my Ram quad cab."

"What about it, Dale?"

"I need some money to get 'er out of repo."

"Now, hold on—"

"I ain't ridin' in the same truck with Jonas," Figgo declared. "We'll shoot each other 'fore we get to Carpville."

Boyette's phone started ringing on the tray table. He turned it over and saw Claude Mink's name, for which he had no amusing code.

"Who's that?" Figgo asked.

"A friend and supporter. One of many."

"Take the call if you need to. I won't listen in."

Boyette shook his head, thinking: *This guy's thick as a brick.*

Once the phone stopped ringing, he said, "Fuck it, Dale. How much to get your pickup truck back? I'll put it in your bank account by the end of the day."

Figgo told him how much and said thanks. He added: "Don't worry about next Tuesday. You're gonna mop up."

"The other side's putting out fake polls to make me look bad."

"Just wait. Precinct 53 is gonna be a blowout."

"I'm counting on your guys," Boyette said. "And remember: No matter what happens, I don't know you and you don't know me. Same goes for Onus."

"You mean 'Bebe Daddy.' Don't forget to call him and tell him to back off."

The congressman laughed drily. "He's a piece of work, that dude. Know what he said the other day? That you're a snitch."

"What?"

"For the FBI is what he said."

"Lying motherfucker!" Figgo felt like kicking out one of the aircraft's cool little windows.

"I told him he's losing his shit," Boyette said. "You'd never work for the feds, not in a million years." Thinking: *And they wouldn't touch you with a ten-foot pole.*

Figgo croaked, "Anybody's a snitch, it's him!"

"Chill out, Dale. Let's keep our eyes on the prize."

Figgo deplaned clutching his empty go-cup and trembling with fury. Ever since his rejection by the Proud Boys and other groups, he was hypersensitive to the false charge of being a government informer.

He hung around the airport to watch the congressman's jet take off. The noise was awesome. Minutes later a blue-striped crop duster touched down and taxied off the runway to refill its pesticide tank. Next was a small plane towing a banner that said VOTE TO BAN FAKE MEAT. Figgo felt himself begin to calm. Soon the feverish pounding in his temples stopped.

He drove back to the townhouse with a thought that Jonas Onas, once his best friend, was now a mortal enemy. Onas looked at him the same way, to a degree that would have shocked Figgo.

⩘⩘⩘

Viva felt guilty about making love to Twilly and then sleeping so untroubled. She felt guilty about jumping him again at five in the morning. Guilty, too, for fixing a tall stack of pancakes and two mimosas, and bringing them up to her bedroom.

The source of her guilt was lack of guilt. She wondered if she had sociopathic tendencies. She was now a criminal, after all. A bomber. Her sister Maya would have a field day.

Twilly said, "If it makes you feel better, the developers have tons of insurance. They'll haul another excavator out there by lunchtime."

"Then what was the point?"

"The concept is to get ahead of one's anger before it boils over. That's my current path of treatment."

Viva sat up. "This is crazy. I should've stopped you."

"It was a hunk of steel. Nobody got hurt. Baby steps, is what they preach in therapy. Avoid confrontation with others whenever possible. Lately, as you know, I've been slipping."

"Both of us could wind up in jail."

"Don't worry. I'll testify that I forced you to do it," Twilly said. "Anyway, I scouted the place first. There are no cameras on that section of the property."

He and Viva were done with the pancakes and back under the sheets. Dale Figgo had left the townhouse early, but they kept their voices down, anyway.

She said, "What if somebody saw us driving away? The police—they've got tag readers and street cams all over the place."

"That's why I switched license plates on the Suburban."

"You did what now?"

"In addition to the ludicrous Maybach, your boss owns a straight-off-the-lot Sequoia," Twilly said. "Yesterday afternoon he sent his driver to that big liquor store on Hickory. While he was inside, I switched out the Sequoia's tag with mine. Claude and Electra seriously pound the hooch, by the way. The driver came out with five cases."

"Unreal," Viva said, not in reference to the alcohol purchase.

"I probably shouldn't have taken you with me last night."

"No, this is how you're wired. You've been honest from the start."

"Futile gestures that feel good at the time. That's my weakness. Was blowing up a piece of machinery an original idea? Not at all. Did it change anything? Not one bit." Twilly put his arms around her. “Same as sinking the councilman’s party barge. He never even went to prison for taking all those bribes. Before the trial, he skipped off to Costa Rica.”

“So when you commit these . . . ‘gestures,’ ” she said, “it’s a high?”

“Well, that slimeball *loved* his stupid boat. So, yeah, I do enjoy ruining a bad guy’s day. Sometimes you’ve got to take whatever you can get. Were you scared last night?”

“Not really,” said Viva. “That’s why I’m scared today.”

“It was all me. You’re the impressionable one.”

“Lame is the word for it. The arc of my serious relationships goes from a thief to an arsonist. What the hell?” She groaned and put a pillow over her head. “Men who read *The New Yorker* aren’t supposed to know how to rig dynamite.”

Twilly agreed that he skewed wide of the usual demographic.

Viva peered out from under the pillow and asked, “Anyway, what’s so fucking great about orange groves?”

“For starters, they’re not concrete. They’re trees.”

“It wasn’t a real question, Twilly. I’m just mad at myself.”

Immediately after the bombing they’d returned to Galaxy’s apartment building. Her Lexus was parked out front and they found her at home, safe, happily watching Colbert. She said that she and the killer had a nice chat at dinner. He ordered pizza with a gluten-free crust, which she thought was hysterical. She said his name was Moe and he had four kids, three already in college. Coincidentally, he knew the rich old farts who funneled all that money to Clure Boyette. The Minks, right? The killer said they were bad news and told Galaxy to steer clear of them. He wouldn’t reveal who’d hired him to murder her, but he said he was dropping the contract. It would be wise for her to leave Florida, he advised, at least for a while. He offered to help if she needed a fake ID, and Galaxy said she was covered in that department. When she admitted her true age, Moe the killer seemed relieved. What’s more, he voiced support for her sabbatical from the escort business. Viva and Twilly weren’t sure if they believed all of Galaxy’s story, though they wanted to. They didn’t bring up their vandalous visit to The Bunkers. As Janice Eileen Smith walked them to the door, she told Viva to be on the lookout for a "blockbuster" email the next morning.

So that was on Viva's mind, too.

"What about the election?" she asked Twilly.

He was getting dressed for a quick trip to the mall—new clothes for Lewin Baltry.

"Don't worry about Carpville," he said to Viva. "Honestly, you don't have to go."

"Oh yes, I damn sure do!" She hurled the pillow at him. "Don't be a dick. I just need to know what to bring."

"A pair of running shoes," Twilly said. "Oh, and scrubs."

Viva could hear her sister's snippy voice: *Why can't you find somebody normal?*

It wasn't an outlandish question.

~~~

The polls were not fake news. A divorced eighth-grade teacher named Deborah Eden had improbably pulled to within striking distance of Clure Boyette. The incumbent congressman had outspent his neophyte opponent ten to one, yet he seemed to be losing ground every day. Smug pundits blamed the most recent government shutdown, initiated by Boyette and other unhinged jackasses in the so-called Free Will Caucus. Every civilian in Bonifay County who was employed at the Air Force base had come to think of the congressman as a serial job killer. His overhyped investigation into rainbow-colored eight balls was also backfiring, now a regular topic of ridicule by late-night comics. "FLUSH BOYETTE!" bumper stickers could be seen around town, even on a few pickup trucks. As his son disintegrated into a political caricature, Clay Boyette felt exasperated and slightly tainted.

"How is this even happening?" asked Barker Drane, the CEO of M'Noor. The phosphate-and-fertilizer conglomerate had sunk a small fortune into a PAC funding the congressman's re-election campaign.
~~~

"The whole country's in a shitty mood. Everyone hates Washington," said Clay Boyette.

He and the chubby young executive were lunching at a restricted country club that employed only young white eastern Europeans. Seasonal work visas got handed out by the bucket since a complimentary club membership had been given to the former secretary of Homeland Security. That had been Clay Boyette's idea.

Barker Drane, attacking his salad like a starved hare, said, "A Democrat hasn't won this district since I don't know when."

"I do. Johnson was president."

"Andrew?"

"Lyndon," Clay Boyette said dully. He wasn't hungry.

"Still, Clay, what the fucking fuck? I don't get it. Your boy should be ahead by miles!" Barker Drane was spraying bits of arugula. "Have you seen the woman who's running against him? No makeup. No boobs. Two kids, two exes, and she dresses like she's in line at the DMV. How's Clure not stomping her by double digits?"

"Just a few more days. He'll hang on."

"He'd damn well better," said Barker Drane. His breath reeked of blue cheese. "We haven't seen much of him around town."

"He flew back from D.C. this morning. He's got a rally at the 4-H fairgrounds."

"Fox is saying we might lose the House if he doesn't win."

Clay Boyette sneered at the comment. "Jesse Watters can blow me."

In truth, though, the old man was worried. His son was skilled at coasting and preening, but not much else. Never in his life had Clure been made to battle for something he desired, forced to dig in and focus. Whenever he stepped on his own pecker, which was frequently and occasionally scandalous, the cover-up was left to his savvy but beset father.

And now this shit.

"Well? You guys in?" Clay Boyette pressed Barker Drane.

"Where exactly will the money go?"

"Radio ads and social media. We're doing a big buy tomorrow."

The CEO nodded. "I guess we can bundle another fifty, but you need to have a come-to-Jesus with the boy."

"Amen." Clay Boyette signaled with an invisible pen for the server to put the tab on his account. "Sorry I've got to cut and run," he said to Barker Drane.

"Tell Clure not to miss church again this Sunday. It would be a good look, right before the election."

"I'll bring him myself," lied Clay Boyette.

"Can't hurt. You know, people are talkin' about the divorce. The usual nasty rumors." Barker Drane used a corner of his napkin to wipe a driblet of dressing from his chin. He added: "Being a churchgoer always plays well in this county. The schoolteacher, she's just a Methodist."

Clure Boyette's father said, "See you Sunday."

A black Navigator was waiting in front of the clubhouse to take him to 545 Watermelon Way. A couple of television news crews from Pensacola were already there, scrambling to go live while the smoke was still thick. The police refused to let any media past the yellow tape. One of the sergeants recognized Clay Boyette and escorted him through the ladder trucks and ambulances. The first thing he did, with the sergeant's help, was pull down the Wee Hammers sign bearing the grinning muley face of his son. Besides the concrete foundation, the sign was all that had survived the fire. The wood frame of the house was down, smoldering in pieces.

Clay Boyette was introduced to Tomas De Leon, the contractor in charge of the project. De Leon was being treated for burns on his legs. He explained that the blaze had been ignited by a boy using an oxyacetylene torch like a toy lightsaber, slashing wildly at the other kids. During the fantasized swordfight, the cutting head of the torch made contact with two other Wee Hammers and an uncapped container of halogenated solvent, which exploded. The children suffered only minor wounds, and everyone was able to get away from the house.

The torch boy's name was Egregio, and he sat handcuffed in the back of a police car. Clay Boyette had no interest in speaking to the little pyro.

De Leon, downcast, said, "I tried to stop him, sir."

The legs of the man's work pants were blackened up to his knees. Clay Boyette told him to go straight to the hospital.

"I'm putting in my notice," Tomas De Leon said.

"You're in shock, buddy."

"No, sir. I quit."

"Wish I could help," said Clay Boyette, "but I'm not your boss."

As he trudged back to the Navigator, one of the TV reporters thrust a microphone in his face and asked for his reaction to the fire.

"Sing praise to our Lord and Savior that no one was mortally injured," Clay Boyette said.

"What do you say to the child-safety advocates who've been criticizing the use of minors on this site?"

"I'm not sure what's going on. I've never been here before."

For better or worse, both statements were true. Clure Boyette had told his father very little about the project on Watermelon Way, except that he'd agreed to endorse a home-building charity modeled on Habitat for Humanity. Clay Boyette had barely tuned in to the conversation, though it surely would have grabbed his attention if his son had mentioned that the construction workers were young kids in hard hats. The term "Wee Hammers" never came up. An upbeat article and photo in the Carpville newspaper never reached the desk of Clay Boyette; he was boycotting the rag due to a feud with the editorial board, which had published a savage cartoon depicting his son as a braying "nepo baby" wearing a diaper made of hundred-dollar bills.

From the beginning, the Wee Hammers house had sparked controversy of which Clay Boyette remained unaware. No one informed him when community leaders signed a letter to the editor warning that the use of child labor around building equipment was extremely dangerous and likely illegal, even if the kids were volunteers. Not for a moment did the senior Boyette believe that his son had protectively kept him in the dark in case of a PR disaster, such as was currently unfolding. Clay Boyette would have shut down the Wee Hammers before the first nail got pounded, which was why Clure had withheld the details of the project. There was one thing of which his old man was sure: it damn sure wasn't a charity.

But then what was it?

Clure Boyette was abruptly extracted from his second campaign rally of the day, at a VFW hall, and delivered to his father's office. A whiff of corn dogs from the fairgrounds event followed him through the door. He settled in the high-backed leather chair on the other side of Clay Boyette's desk.

"What's up, Dad?" he asked, as if inconvenienced.

"I can't keep doing this. I'm running out of goddamn miracles."

Clure Boyette looked perplexed. "Can't keep doing what?"

"Tell me everything I don't know about the Wee Hammers."

Instantly the congressman's expression changed and he broke off eye contact. His father was familiar with this reaction. He informed his son that the fake-charity house on Watermelon Way had burned to the ground.

Clure Boyette emitted a slow gasp. "What the hell happened?"

"One of the little fuckers went Darth Vader with a welding torch. That's a straight quote from the fire marshal. Nobody died, in case you give a shit, but a couple of kids went to the ER. The timing couldn't be worse."

Clay Boyette's tone of voice reminded Clure of the time his father caught him lobbing raccoon droppings into the family Jacuzzi.

"Is there a numbnuts universe," the old man said, "where you imagine this fiasco winning us more votes?"

"It's not a nuclear moment, Dad. I'll just put out a statement saying the fire was political sabotage. The schoolteacher, what's-her-face, did it."

"Son, if I had a two-by-four in my hands right now—"

"No, wait—it was antifa! That's who we blame."

"Obviously you're back on the cocaine."

Clure Boyette shook his head. "No way, Dad. Come on."

Jangled with fury, the old man leaned back in his chair. To

avoid looking at his dullard offspring, he stared out the window at a manmade lake stocked with bass and bluegills. The dark water was flat as glass, and in the middle lay a dead log that Clay Boyette fantasized was an alligator large enough to devour a one-hundred-and-ninety-five-pound idiot, cowboy boots and all.

His gaze glided back toward his son.

"Where'd you get those fancy shitkickers?" he asked.

"The boots? There's a new Western shop on K Street."

"In Washington?"

"Yeah, so? *I* didn't pay for 'em. Some Boeing lobbyist did."

"You're a cocky little shitweasel, aren't you?"

"How come you're so pissed? I'm not the one that burned down the house."

"Listen, son, I know the Wee Hammers is a front."

"Not true!" Clure Boyette protested. "That's a damn lie."

"Tell me where the money came from, and how you're moving it."

"Dad, there's no reason to freak. I got this. I really do."

Clay Boyette and his late wife had occasionally wondered if they should shelve their disappointment and have one more child. What were the odds of two in a row turning out like Clure? Ultimately they chose not to risk a repeat, a decision that Clay Boyette at no point regretted.

His son said: "I set up the Wee Hammers as a legit nonprofit. My two donors are concerned mega-patriots who want to protect American values. Protect and defend."

"Give me their names."

"Can't do that. All I can tell you is they're loaded as fuck—the kind of dough that guarantees I'm gonna win this election. One hundred and ten percent. It'll be a textbook show on how to stop a steal."

Clay Boyette was more worried than before. "What the fuck are you up to?"

"You'll love it, Dad. This is next-level shit."

"Pull the goddamn plug."

The younger Boyette laughed mordantly. "I couldn't do that if I wanted. All the pieces are already in motion."

His father sighed. "Son, you've become a permanent affliction. Like plaque psoriasis, or pubic rot."

"Mom would raise hell if she heard you talk like that."

"Her suffering is over, thank God. Mine isn't."

A man knocked on the door and, without waiting, entered the office carrying an open laptop. The man was Sanford, one of Clay Boyette's assistants. Without a word, he placed the laptop on his boss's desk. Then he stepped away.

Clay Boyette's ruddy cheeks went gray. He turned the laptop around so his son could view what was on the screen.

"Oh shit," said the congressman.

"There's video, too. Explain the goddamn coke and dog leash."

"Nobody was supposed to see these!"

"That's all you've got to say?"

"You told me you'd taken care of it!"

"I thought I had." Clay Boyette thinking: *The whore is supposed to be dead.*

His son said, "We should've got her the damn Aston like she wanted."

Clay Boyette closed the laptop with a slap.

"Thanks for your input, Fido," he said. "Does she also have pictures of you licking your own balls?"

CHAPTER 25

None of the videos and only three of the photographs distributed anonymously by Viva Morales were suitable for mainstream media. The others showcased the be-leashed congressman in a state of florid verticality. Even the perviest of online gawkers found the snowshoes inexplicable. In one eight-second clip, a young woman's voice could be heard addressing a muzzled Clure Boyette as "Spanky." It went viral immediately.

The speaker of the House, himself no stranger to bondage-themed intimacy, brusquely announced that Boyette's "Woke Eight Ball" hearings were postponed indefinitely. Dead was his scheduled star turn on C-SPAN, as was his dream of a prime-time appearance on Sean Hannity's show. Meanwhile, Boyette's election opponent put out a statement denouncing his hypocritical depravity and warning the parents of her students to closely monitor their internet activity, lest they stumble across any of the "disturbing images."

By noon the Boyette campaign had settled on a response: The lurid photographs and videos had been altered by political enemies using AI technology. According to a press release, the congressman's face had been digitally overlaid on the images. No evidence was offered to support this defense, and nobody who knew Clure Boyette believed he was framed.

High on that list were Claude and Electra Mink. Although barely communicating, they agreed over breakfast that Boyette was a colossal fuckstick in danger of losing his House seat and hastening the country's doomsday slide toward socialism. Electra Mink summoned the Maybach and went to the hair salon while Claude returned to his bedroom and decrepitly humped the polymer Dream Booty until chest pains put him on the floor. He had recovered by the time Dumas walked in announcing that a police detective was at the door.

The detective told Claude that he was investigating an arson. A license-tag scanner mounted on a utility pole had tracked the Minks' white Sequoia speeding from the scene of the crime, a construction site on the western edge of the county. While Claude fumed, Dumas led the detective to a bank of security monitors and dialed up a time-stamped video loop proving that the Sequoia was parked at the Mink residence all night. They went outside to confirm that the license plate was on the vehicle, unaware that someone had reattached it that morning after tailing Dumas to the Walmart Supercenter. That person was Twilly Spree.

The detective apologized to Claude Mink and said the roadside tag reader must be defective.

Claude cocked his knobby head. "Know what else is defective?"

Dumas cut in and offered a cup of coffee to the detective, who declined and departed. Minutes later, Viva phoned Claude on behalf of Electra:

"She wanted you to know there was a fire at The Bunkers."

"What kind of goddamn fire?"

"Vandals blew up a machine."

"You mean like a bulldozer?"

"Mrs. Mink called it an excavator," Viva said.

"What kind of dumb pricks would do that?"

"I don't know. Kids maybe?"

"Border monkeys," Claude grumbled. "Gangbangers."

"How do you know the bombers aren't white?" Viva asked.

Claude scoffed at the question. "Wake up, young lady. This isn't your mommy and daddy's America."

Viva's tone seemed to change. "Mrs. Mink wanted you to know the police are working on some solid leads."

"Like what?"

"They got the license plate of a suspect from a tag-reading machine."

"No, honey, they don't." Claude laughed bitterly and handed the phone back to Dumas. Then he made his way upstairs, where he peeled off his sweaty pajamas and arduously changed into one of his vivid golf ensembles. What were the odds of breaking 90 on a day that started so badly?

It only got worse. The next call came from Clure Boyette. He said one of the Wee Hammers had accidentally burned the charity house to the ground.

"I wanted you to hear it from me, not the fake news," the congressman said.

"But it really happened?"

"Yes, unfortunately."

"So then it isn't fake."

"Not this time," Boyette allowed.

He started giving more details of the mishap, but Claude cut him short. Claude's chief concern was dodging liability. Boyette assured him that the Mink Foundation was shielded from any lawsuits.

"The kids' parents all signed releases," he added.

"On toilet paper? Because that's what they're worth in court." Claude paused for a wet cough. "Speaking of getting shit on your fingers, who leaked your porno slide show?"

The congressman said, "That wasn't me in the photos. That was AI."

"Which stands for what—'absolutely incompetent'?"

"Don't believe everything you see, Claude. Tuesday's a lock. My team is ready to rock the shit out of Carpville."

"Same boobs that fucked up Key West?"

Clure Boyette moved on, saying, "If any reporters contact you about the Wee Hammers accident, no-comment the bastards. You've got nothing to say, okay? Be sure and tell Electra, too."

"So, the house is completely gone?"

"Ashes," said the congressman.

The whole damn world's on fire, Claude thought as he clicked off.

He told Dumas to take him to the golf course, where, on the driving range, he powered off his phone. "More bad news might put me in the ICU," he joked with his playing partners, who thought he looked terrible.

There was one more unpleasant bit of news that Claude was ultimately doomed to receive. Barry Martino, the powerhouse lobbyist, tried calling several times during the afternoon, while Claude was busy shooting 107.

Martino didn't leave a voice message because he feared it might come back and bite him on the ass. He wasn't supposed to possess the information he needed to drop on his client: the Bunkers development had unexpectedly reappeared on the agenda of the county zoning board, which was scheduled to meet the day after the election. It would be the last item up for discussion, added with no public notice.

For once, Martino was caught unprepared. He'd worked hard on each of the development's opponents in the 3–3 deadlock; all had politely but firmly refused to be bribed. If one of them had changed their mind, Martino should have been the first to know. He was wondering if the Minks had gone behind his back and hired another lobby firm to fix the Bunkers vote.

The answer would have to wait. Claude, who was leveraged to the gills on the deal, had turned off his fucking phone.

Slimy old prune, Martino thought.

His wife came into the den with a message. According to their son, a divinity major at Duke, the explicit cosplay images of Congressman Clure Boyette were already trending on Pornhub and DoodleTinder.

"You think that schoolteacher can beat him?" Martino's wife asked.

"Who cares," said Martino. "He's not a client."

~~~

Viva didn't post—or even read—the entries in Galaxy's private journal. She trusted that the fallout from the photos and videos would be enough. Janice Eileen Smith was already gone when she and Twilly went to the apartment. The place stood vacant except for the tatty furniture that came with the rental. Afterward Viva went with Twilly to check on Lewin Baltry, whose hosts described him as whiny though resigned to what lay ahead. To Twilly the commissioner articulated a well-founded fear of violent harm, including death. Twilly gave him some new clothes and promised a future plane ticket to wherever he wanted to go.

The next few hours were spent in front of a floor fan at Twilly's un-air-conditioned storage unit. Viva finished the daily Wordle (**GRIME** was the answer) and did her nails. Her sister had mailed her another book, *The Ten Golden Rules of Life Partnering*, which for laughs Viva started reading aloud to Twilly. He sat on the concrete floor taking apart each of the guns in Dale Figgo's weapons cache and disabling them in a way that was invisible upon reassembly. Figgo's favorite AR-15 now had a trigger, but no spring for it. Twilly told Viva there was an interesting piece about urban coyotes in the latest *New Yorker.*

"The dreams don't bother me anymore," she said.

"Last night you were barking in your sleep."

"Is that true? I hate you."

Dale Figgo wasn't home when Viva and Twilly returned to the townhouse. Twilly neatly arranged the weapons on the grungy sectional in the living room and stacked the boxes of ammo in the garage. Viva led him upstairs, sat him on a corner of the bed, and made him listen to the Arctic Monkeys, Larkin Poe, and Kendrick Lamar while she washed and dried her hair. When she came out of the bathroom, Twilly was standing at the window.
~~~

"What are you looking at?" she asked.

"A situation." He motioned for Viva to come see for herself.

Jonas Onus was sitting alone in his white pickup, parked on the road. He was squinting at the townhouse and picking at his resurgent beard.

"He's after Dale," Viva said.

"I guess it's showtime."

"What should we do?"

"Lock the door," said Twilly.

"I already did."

"No, *this* door." Twilly started unbuttoning his shirt.

"Wait, really?" Viva said.

"Why not?"

"You want to do this right now, while that lunatic's lurking outside?"

"I feel like Kendrick would give it a shot."

"A hundred percent."

Viva locked the bedroom door, tossed her hairbrush, and took off her panties.

Twilly yanked the comforter off the bed. "One way or another," he said, "this will be memorable."

It was.

Top five, Viva thought afterward.

Twilly was still breathing hard, flat on his back, when she got up and crept to the window. The white pickup truck was parked in the same spot, but the driver's seat was empty.

~~~

Jonas Onus wanted his hatreds to be authentic, as were his father's, but he couldn't obsess as purely as other men in the movement. Onus believed fervidly in white supremacy yet he had a Black friend, a fellow firefighter with whom he'd stayed in touch. Sometimes they got online late at night to play *Call of Duty,* a fact that Onus kept secret from Dale Figgo and the other Strokerz. Similarly, he was privately ambivalent about Figgo's Nazi-inspired driveway flyers; Onus's favorite teacher in high school was a Jew, Miss Blau,
~~~

who'd taught algebra and had a rocking bod. Occasionally Onus found himself wondering whether she'd retired or was still teaching in the same classroom, a dingy FEMA trailer where he had often imagined her seducing him.

Then there was Enrico, the little gay dude who detailed Onus's pickup truck once a month. Enrico was from Honduras, a border crosser waiting for his asylum claim to reach a judge. Nice guy with a quick sense of humor—and he made the Tundra's chrome rims shine like new. It would suck if Enrico ever got deported.

Despite such anomalies, Jonas Onus adhered to the ethos of racial superiority and social intolerance. He remained confident of his capacity for cold hatred—surely that's what he felt toward Figgo and Twilly Spree, who were scheming to thwart his rise as co-leader of the Strokerz and block access to the Wee Hammers jackpot. Onus hated those two men as much as he'd ever hated anybody, including the Houston district fire chief who'd challenged his fictitious disability claim and cost him nearly eleven hundred bucks in lawyer fees.

Sitting in the truck was murder on Onus's hemorrhoids; he was fairly sure that the melted suppositories had leaked into his boxers. One of his baby mothers texted him a reminder to stop by the store and get more kibble for Goebbels.

Give him a slider, Onus texted back. He turned off Bongino's radio show and fitted the always-loaded Glock under his belt. Where the hell was Figgo?

Onus decided to break into the townhouse and wait. He got down from the truck and painfully waddled around to the back of the building. The rear door of the townhouse was unlocked, which seemed unusual given Figgo's paranoia. Onus stepped inside and noticed the guns lined up on the pleather sectional. He grinned at the sight and shut the door behind him.

"You could ring the bell," a voice said from across the room, "like a normal person."

It was Viva. She wore brown-rimmed glasses and a long black Metallica tee shirt that Onus did not recognize as ironic. He assumed she was a fan.

He said, "It looked like nobody was home. Where's your car?"

"I park it on a different street now. Can you blame me?"

"I'm waitin' on Dale."

"Does he know that?" Viva asked.

"Stay out of it. This is between me and him."

"Battle of the titans. I get it."

"Is anybody else here?"

"No, I'm alone," Viva said.

Her hair was mussed and her cheeks looked flush. In a letchy voice Onus asked her if he'd interrupted something private.

"My workout," she said.

"That's a hot look. Seriously, I like the glasses." Onus had just thought of a way to piss off both Figgo and Twilly. He drew the Glock and unbuckled his belt.

Viva said, "Well, dude, you've lost your marbles."

"Dale's bed, you and me. Let's go."

"I'm not a fat shamer, Jonas, but I can't help but ask: When's the last time you even saw your cock?"

Onus was scorched by the dig. His initial response was to fire a bullet into the television. He was pleased to see Viva jump at the noise. Still, she wouldn't go down the hall to Figgo's room until the gun barrel was poking her in the back.

The bed was a mess, and eye-watering fumes rose from soiled laundry heaped on the floor. Onus himself was grossed out. With his free arm he swept the gnawed pizza crusts off the bedsheets.

He ordered Viva to remove her tee shirt. Underneath was a plain tan bra.

"Take that off, too," he said, waggling the pistol. "And your panties."

"Nah."

"Nah *what*?"

Onus wasn't sure if he could get hard after Viva's vicious remark about his belly fat. It had been a while since he'd had sex with a real woman, so he hurriedly composed a mental fantasy featuring his impounded Dream Booty. That seemed to work.

"I said take off your damn clothes," he barked at Viva.

"No, Jonas."

"You don't put out, you're dead!"

"The show's over," she said.

Is the bitch smiling? Onus wondered incredulously. *Does she think this is a joke?*

It was the last thought to form before the screen in his brainpan went blank. He awoke several hours later seasick on a paddleboard literally without a paddle, floating on a rolling sea somewhere offshore. Under a heavy midnight sky he could make out the fuzzy distant glow from the lights on the coast. Shakily he sat up to puke before unhooking the bungee cord that bound his ankles to the board. His entire marine attire was a crimson MAGA hoodie showing Donald Trump nailed to a cross and sporting a crown of gold-leaf thorns.

Otherwise Onus was naked, his jeans, underwear, and boots having been removed by Viva Morales and whoever had struck him from behind. He guessed it was either Dale Figgo or Twilly Spree, the traitor who called himself Chaos. Unconscious before he hit the floor, Onus didn't know how he'd been transported out to the open Atlantic and launched on the paddleboard. No boat lights were visible in any direction.

His head still pounded from the unseen blow. That and his greasy bulk made for a precarious balance. He'd always been a mediocre swimmer, and a second factor threatened his survival: fear. Years earlier, on a warm spring day in Galveston, he'd witnessed a spinner shark take two toes from a teenage surfer. Since then, Onus had dodged all saltwater recreation. His dread of being mauled at sea had worsened to the point where he blocked the Discovery Channel on all his cable boxes, even when it wasn't "Shark Week."

He managed to roll onto his belly and began cautiously paddling with his arms. Every now and then he would pause for a dry heave and to catch his breath. Time passed, yet the shore glow appeared farther away than ever.

Am I stuck in the fucking Gulf Stream? Onus wondered. He couldn't remember which direction the powerful current went.

At daybreak the wind kicked up hard, and Onus felt as helpless as a cork in the rough waves. The bruise on the side of his skull was now the size of a radish, and his eyes watered whenever he glanced up toward the sun. At midday a sheath of gray clouds brought a calming squall that saved Onus from heatstroke; he fell asleep licking raindrops off the paddleboard, and awoke to the sound of a foreign language, rapidly spoken.

He wasn't sure if it was day or night, his eyelids having swollen shut. He felt himself lifted by several strong sets of hands and placed into a boat with soft sides, like inflatable canvas. Jarringly it sped across the wavetops to the shade of a large ship, where Onus was wrapped in a scratchy towel and hoisted on a cargo net up to the deck. There he was able to stand. Someone gave him water and guided him to the ship's small *clínica*. He was helped onto an examination table, where his sun blisters were treated and a cool cloth was placed over his eyes. When the voices stopped, Onus knew he was alone in the room. The steady rumble of the engines meant the vessel was underway.

"Can you take me back to Florida?" he asked whenever he heard passing footsteps.

Eventually someone spoke to him in English. It was the medical officer.

"How are you feeling, *señor*? What is your name?"

"Jonas," he said.

"Oh, like in the story of the whale."

"No. It's Jonas, not Jonah."

He felt the pinch of an IV needle in the crook of his right arm.

"Where am I?" he asked.

"You are on board the commercial vessel *Carib Global*. It was only by God's mercy that we spotted you in the water. The captain radioed the Coast Guard for an airlift, but all their assets are busy taking passengers off an infected cruise ship. Norovirus, again. *Muy malo*. It looks like you will be our guest until we reach port."

"And where's that?"

"Veracruz."

"What time do we dock?" Onus asked.

"A few days." The medical officer chuckled gently. "Veracruz is in Mexico."

"You're shitting me."

"I am not, *señor.*"

In a flood of despair, Jonas Onus realized that he was doomed to miss the democracy-saving mission to Carpville, just as he had missed the January 6th storming of the Capitol. While Dale Figgo and the other Strokerz for Liberty were securing Precinct 53 and the political fate of the country, Onus would be far, far away, surrounded by Mexicans speaking Mexican.

If the cartels didn't get him, the fucking chili peppers would.

At four a.m. on Election Day, the Strokerz for Liberty swarmed Buc-ee's for coffee, breakfast jerky, and rhino tacos. The place was packed with buoyant retail pilgrims in the spirit of an all-night flea market. Security cameras recorded the arrival of the white supremacists, all but two of them sporting wraparound sunglasses, bushy beards, and random thatches of neck hair. They didn't bother the other customers, nor did they draw as many stares as they might have at other chain outlets. One of the unbearded Strokerz, wearing an old Marlins cap, never raised his face to a camera. The other unbearded one paid for the entire group, after which store videos showed him chugging a sixteen-ounce can of Red Bull and wiping a drop from his red, white, and blue soul patch.

It was Dale Figgo. Happily reunited with his Ram quad cab, he called roll outside in the parking area, near the runway of gas pumps. A couple of men were absent from the convoy: Jonas Onus and an elderly Stroker known as Smeg, who'd been busted hours earlier with a bag of benzos at a gentlemen's bottle club near Bithlo.

The rest of the patriots departed Buc-ee's in high spirits and made it to Carpville well before dawn. They gathered at the Little

League complex beside the city park and belted on their body armor; most of them also donned black or camo sun buffs to hide their mugs. Some wore trucker caps bearing a lightning-bolt Strokerz logo with an improved swastika for the *S*. Other members had invested in police-surplus riot helmets. Figgo handed out firearms to those who hadn't brought their own. When questioned about Onus, Figgo truthfully answered that he'd heard nothing from the man and didn't know where he was. He failed to conceal his elation.

Divided in their loyalties, some Strokerz surmised that Figgo had eliminated Onus because he didn't want to share his top-dog role in the group. On the other side, Figgo's supporters speculated that Onus had pussied out of the op and run to the feds—or, more likely, had been working as an informer all along. Doubts or no doubts, all of the men reiterated with a show of hands their commitment to the current mission.

At sunrise the Strokerz descended on Serene Transitions, the designated voting site for Precinct 53. Figgo posted a line of men in front of the assisted-living facility, while armed pairs guarded each corner of the intersection at Beet Boulevard and 17th Avenue. Other Strokerz fanned through the town to sabotage ballot drop boxes, wreathing them with crime-scene tape and sealing the slot trays with Gorilla Glue.

Inside Serene Transitions, a floor volunteer saw the commotion through a window and reported it to the intake manager, who happened to be Black. He hurried to the front door, peered outside, and said, "It's the Hells Angels!"

Quickly he closed the door. Election workers had been busy setting up folding voting booths and check-in tables. The certified poll watchers were due any minute. A wall-eyed old crank in a wheelchair rolled past yowling about an abscess on his butt. An elegant-looking matron pushing a walker complained about weighted dice in the mah-jongg room. Another silver-haired woman, ambulatory and unstooped, paced through the day room humming "Stairway to Heaven" with tears in her eyes.

Somebody started knocking heavily on the front door.

"Aw, fuck," whispered the intake manager, shaking. He asked the volunteer to call 911.

"Maybe you should talk with them first," she said.

"Did you see those crackers? Have you seen *me*? They don't want to talk, they want to hang my Black ass from that magnolia tree."

"Okay, I'll handle this."

"Are you crazy? It's your first day on the job!"

"Don't worry," said the volunteer, whose name was Viva.

She eased past the frightened man and opened the door.

There stood Twilly Spree, suited up in black.

"Nice vest," Viva said.

"Thank you, ma'am." He lifted his aviator shades and smiled. "Please tell the residents not to worry. We're here to save America."

"Come back when you're done," she said. "I'll give you a sponge bath."

∿∿∿

A loosening of laws had made Florida second only to Texas in the push to make firearms more readily available to the impaired, incompetent, and unstable. The Carpville police chief personally wasn't enthusiastic about this legislative trend, but for political reasons he'd raised no objections with the governor. Now his town had been overrun by an armed horde of white shitkickers calling themselves the Strokerz for Liberty. The chief had never heard of them. Based on their early interactions with voters, the intruders appeared to be castoffs from the Proud Boys and other supremacist groups, or perhaps grandstanding wannabes. Regardless, their presence at Serene Transitions was baffling and unwelcome. The police chief reached out to the Bonifay County sheriff, who offered to send reinforcements. It was agreed that, due to Florida's toothless gun laws, disarming the Strokerz should be a last resort.

Sign-waving supporters of both congressional candidates were gathering at opposite ends of the senior facility's sidewalk, one hundred and fifty feet from the voting site as required by law. The polls opened at seven sharp, and soon afterward Clure Boyette stepped out of a black Navigator to modest cheers. Before entering the ALF and casting his ballot, the congressman was observed scowling at one of the Strokerz, who wore a "CLURE FOR SURE!" tee shirt stretched over his bullet-resistant chest protector. Boyette spoke sharply to the man, who took an asthma inhaler from his pocket and turned away.

The congressman had departed by the time his opponent—schoolteacher, mom, and Cinderella candidate Deborah Eden—pulled up in a faded blue minivan. Her rooting section was louder, but she found her path inside blocked by a Stroker who presented himself as a "citizen poll watcher" and demanded to see identification. The taut exchange was captured by an ABC affiliate and broadcast nationally on *Good Morning America,* a network program that vexingly scored higher ratings in Precinct 53 than its Fox counterpart. Exit surveys would later confirm that many Carpvillians who hadn't planned to vote were galvanized by watching Deborah Eden's confrontation with the menacing thug.

A total of 1,725 voters were registered at the precinct. In all, a record sixty-eight percent of them—exactly 1,173—would cast ballots, only a fifth of those by mail. The rest would show up in person at Serene Transitions, including many bringing photos of vandalized ballot boxes in their neighborhood.

Preventing a high turnout was the main reason that Clure Boyette had recruited the Strokerz for Liberty, and such was his hubris that he spent the rest of the morning shooting clays at a quail ranch owned by his benefactors at M'Noor Mining Resources. Consequently, the congressman wasn't seeing what the rest of north Florida, and eventually the nation, saw.

For example: An immense Stroker who gave his name as "Das Regulator" hectoring a ninety-pound voter of Vietnamese descent. The woman happened to be a U.S. citizen whose naturalized parents owned the town's leading RV dealership. She was also the longtime girlfriend of a well-liked Carpville police sergeant, who raced to the polling site armed with an AR-15 that was, unlike Das Regulator's, in perfect working order.

Also: A Stroker who called himself "Skid Mark" cornering and berating a rail-thin voter who'd arrived at Serene Transitions wearing a yarmulke and a KN95 medical mask. Skid Mark denounced the man as a "fake COVID actor" before yanking off his mask and skullcap. It turned out that the bewildered voter wasn't working undercover for the CDC, and had been covering his nose and mouth for an excellent reason—his immune system was being ravaged by ongoing chemotherapy for advanced lung carcinoma. The man's condition was brought to light when CNN interviewed his brother, who'd tried to push Skid Mark away and gotten a rifle butt to the gut. A masked health worker recovered the cancer patient's yarmulke and brought him a new KN95. As she escorted him inside Serene Transitions, she declined to speak with reporters.

And more: Two helmeted Strokerz roughly pulling from the line a tall Hispanic man named Tony whom they accused of being an illegal border jumper. The man produced his voter registration, driver's license, and even the most recent pay stub from his employer, the Committee to Re-Elect Clure Boyette, for whom he was a billboard installer. Nonetheless, the Strokerz decided that the man's ID papers were fake, zip-tied his wrists, and attempted to turn him over to the fast-growing contingent of local law enforcement. A sheriff's deputy recognized Tony as the father of the All-Star catcher on his son's Little League team, and cut him loose. A shouting match with the black-clad militants commenced, during which the deputy was called a "gay Spic lover" and threatened with "doxxing," which he misconstrued as some sort of biochemical attack. Backed by other officers, he ordered the two Strokerz to drop their weapons and raise their hands. Moronically, they chose to run.

Blocks away, in his Main Street office, Clay Boyette watched the debacle at Precinct 53 unfold in real time on television. He sat alone, icy sober, oppressed by events that he had not foreseen and could never fix. His witless son could possibly have eked out a win in spite of the kinky porn leak and Wee Hammers blowback, but to unleash a gun-waving militia on an assisted-living facility was political suicide, even in Florida. One of the dolts was actually wearing a "CLURE FOR SURE!" tee shirt.

So, as the younger Boyette obliviously sipped bourbon and blasted clay pigeons at a sporting retreat, the elder Boyette was reaching out to his pilots. He told them to fuel up the jet.

~~~~

Too slowly it dawned on Dale Figgo that the Carpville mission was unspooling. His game plan had hinged on the idea that using force would be unnecessary, that the formidable comportment of the Strokerz for Liberty would be enough to intimidate nonwhite, non-Christian undesirables from approaching the polling site. Yet the line outside Precinct 53 kept growing before Figgo's eyes, and skirmishes were breaking out between his men and would-be voters. Fearing another Key West fiasco, Figgo unimaginatively tried firing a couple of rounds into the air to settle the crowd. Yet when he squeezed the trigger nothing happened, not even a click.

Two Strokerz in crooked riot helmets dashed past, pursued by uniformed cops with guns drawn. Seemingly within moments, the entrance to Serene Transitions was occupied by law enforcement. Metal barricades appeared out of nowhere. On a smaller scale the scene reminded Figgo of the Capitol building on January 6th, except for the lack of a supportive mob. His suspicion naturally turned to the missing and unaccounted-for Jonas Onus. Had he ratted out the Strokerz? It damn sure looked that way. Meanwhile, Figgo's handheld radio was spitting only cross-talk and static, leaving him to communicate by shouting. Police on both sides of the walkway had linked arms forming a human corridor to give voters (and worried family members of residents) safe access to the senior-care campus.

An attractive woman in blue scrubs stood on the top step taking video of what was degenerating into another public humiliation for Figgo's group. When the woman in scrubs lowered her smartphone, Figgo recognized her face and swore loudly.

It was his tenant, Viva Morales. She waved at Figgo and gave a thumbs-up.

"What the hell are you doing here?" he yelled over the throng.

"This is history!" she called back. "The world needs to see!"
~~~~

Indeed, the world *was* seeing—on TikTok, Instagram, and Facebook, where Viva was currently live-streaming an interview with a tall, broad-shouldered Stroker. His back was turned to Figgo, but Figgo recognized the Marlins cap. It was his body man, Twilly Spree.

Why was he so far out of position?

"Yo, Chaos!" Figgo hollered angrily.

When Twilly spun around, Figgo's heart sank.

"Take that damn thing off!" he screeched.

Twilly responded with a quizzical shrug.

In a panic, Figgo clumsily struggled to breach the line. The cops easily held him back. It was a nightmare—Twilly was wearing a loud Boyette campaign tee shirt for the whole internet to see: "CLURE FOR SURE!"

Figgo knew the congressman would go ballistic. Before the end of the day he would claim he'd never heard of the Strokerz for Liberty, and condemn their tactics.

"Take off that fucking shirt!" Figgo yelled at Twilly across the crowd. "Dude, I'm serious as a dick blister!"

Twilly ignored him and turned around to face Viva, who was still taking video. His thinking fogged by the dire turn of events, Figgo struggled to understand what the couple was doing. He would have been interested to learn that the Boyette tee shirt didn't belong to Twilly; originally it had been given to Jonas Onus when he stopped at the congressman's campaign headquarters during his scouting trip to Carpville.

Twilly had spotted the shirt crumpled behind the seat of Onus's Tundra while driving the unconscious bonehead to the Wally Schirra Marina. There Twilly shot him up with feral-cat tranquilizer, dragged him aboard a friend's twenty-eight-foot Cobia, ferried him out near the Gulf Stream, and bound him to a secondhand paddleboard, ensuring his absence from Precinct 53.

The details of Jonas Onus's kidnapping would never become known to Dale Figgo. He swayed in a curious haze in front of Serene Transitions while his Strokerz—jolted by their unfriendly reception—scattered like cockroaches.

This, as registered voters of assorted colors, religious beliefs, ethnicities, and sexual preferences continued filing in and out.

Figgo understood that his dream of white-power stardom was crumbling to ashes. Someone tapped his shoulder. Clenching the AR-15 to his chest, he turned slowly.

"Hello, again," the man said.

"Payback?"

"Big time," said the man. "This is my wife, Mary."

She was a beautiful, stern-looking Black woman. Figgo, shaken, mumbled hello. He couldn't recall Payback's Christian name. Jerry Joe Tarantino? Tupelo? Tripoli? Figgo thought back to the first time the man had shown up at the townhouse wearing a Confederate coat. It seemed impossible that he could be married to a Negro.

Payback said, "Mary wanted to meet the criminal who ran me down."

"Uh?"

"The hit-and-run," Payback explained. "She wanted to meet the creep responsible for throwing that vicious garbage in our driveway."

Figgo blinked. "Yo, I . . . seriously, I got no clue what you're talkin' about."

"The baggies stuffed with hate preaching," said Payback's wife.

Figgo's mind was spinning, so it took a moment to put the pieces together.

"Wait," he said to Payback, "are you the dickface who spit on my truck?"

"Oh, that part you remember."

"You're lucky I didn't shoot your ass."

Payback's wife asked: "How do you live with yourself, Mr. Figgo?"

How do you not see this gun? he thought.

The couple seemed unafraid, as if they knew the trigger was broken.

"Why the hell are you even here?" Figgo demanded.

Payback pointed at a Liberty Bell decal stuck to his shirt. "We signed on as poll watchers," he said.

His wife placed her right hand over her heart. "It's a patriotic privilege. How about you, Mr. Figgo? What's your reason for being here?"

"THIS IS A DEEP-STATE MINDFUCK!" he raged.

Then, gutsick, he bolted.

Noel and Mary Kristiansen went back inside Serene Transitions to observe democracy in action.

Viva had called in sick and driven up to Carpville the day before the election. The senior residence facility, always understaffed, was happy to welcome a new volunteer. Twilly Spree had recruited the Kristiansens, who also arrived twenty-four hours in advance. They brought a houseguest, who remained in his room at the Bonifay Lakes motel on Election Day while the couple monitored the voting machines.

The polls closed at seven sharp. Long gone were the Strokerz for Liberty. No serious injuries had been suffered; no arrests had been made. Earlier, when Dale Figgo had fled the scene, nobody even bothered to pursue him. At first he'd ditched his rifle and ran as frantically as if bloodhounds were on his trail, but gradually his pace through the streets of Carpville slowed to a bitter, lonely walk. He stopped briefly in the city park before jumping the fence of the Little League field and retrieving his beloved Ram quad cab from the lot. Pickup trucks belonging to his brothers-in-arms were peeling out left and right.

On the way out of town Figgo spotted a pride flag, of all things, flying in front of a neat two-story home. Incensed, he braked to the curb. The wood house looked old enough to be historic, though freshly painted—white, with dark blue shutters. There was an open porch, a thriving green garden, and even a picket fence. It was, in Figgo's malign view, a mockery of the American dream.

He hopped out of his truck, kicked open the wooden gate, and pulled the knife from his boot. He wasn't planning to cut the flag down; he aimed to shred it, and send a message.

Later, after Figgo's motive became apparent, authorities would wonder why he hadn't simply lowered the flag to deface it, instead of trying to shimmy a slick fifteen-foot pole. No witnesses saw what happened; the gay couple who owned the place wasn't there at the time. They were in line at Precinct 53, waiting to cast their votes for schoolteacher Deborah Eden. Upon returning home, they found a stranger in black hanging frog-eyed from the pole, his meaty neck entangled in both the halyard rope and the pride flag that he evidently was attempting to destroy. A cap on the ground bore the swastika-bearing logo of the "Strokerz for Liberty," which a detective joked must be a Gestapo softball team.

The deceased vandal's ill-advised ascent of the flagpole had also involved a knife, which the Bonifay County medical examiner later extracted from the man's discount body armor. The blade's tip had pierced his perineum or, in street parlance, gooch. In the medical examiner's description of the body, he noted that the victim's nose appeared to have been radically reconstructed, and that skin from his scrotum had been removed in a surgical manner consistent with donor graft tissue.

Dale Figgo didn't live long enough to see the outcome of the election: Congressman Clure Boyette lost by four percentage points. Fox News called it for Deborah Eden at eleven p.m., an hour after CNN and MSNBC. The lopsided margin in Precinct 53 proved to be pivotal—Boyette received only 172 votes there, compared to 1,001 for Deborah Eden.

A post on X, prepared a week earlier by the congressman's campaign director, blared that the election was "ONE HUNDRED THOUSAND PERCENT RIGGED!" It called for a speedy recount, the impoundment of ballot-counting machines, and the empaneling of a grand jury to investigate rife voter fraud by the teachers union in collaboration with federal agents. The lawsuits would sputter along for months, delaying the seating of a new Congress.

Clure Boyette's father was already down in Turks and Caicos by the time the polls had closed in Florida. He tracked the vote results on his phone while drinking Painkillers at a resort tiki bar at Grace Bay, on Providenciales. The woman on the stool next to him asked why he was laughing. Clay Boyette said it was a long story. Mopping up after his fuckwit son had ground the old man's nerves to pulp, and now he felt a lifting of this burden. The Washington lawyers he kept on call were no longer needed. Clure was being sent home.

"Where you from?" the woman asked.

"Florida," Clay Boyette said.

"Are you retired?"

"No, but I'm warming to the idea."

"How long are you on the island?"

"Until Sunday," Clay Boyette said.

"Me, too."

"Maybe Monday."

"Me, too," the woman said.

She was on vacation, she added. Her job was doing physical rehab at Johns Hopkins in Baltimore. Divorced almost two years, no kids, no pets, no roommate.

"Can I get another drink?" she asked.

"Absolutely," Clay Boyette said. "Tell me your name again."

CHAPTER 27

On the day after the election, a Carpville municipal employee messaged his supervisor to report that an unknown individual had smeared poop on the statue in the city park. Testing subsequently determined that the fecal matter was human, and that its origin was Dale Lincoln Figgo, a white male, age thirty-seven, who had accidentally hanged himself on a private flagpole in a nearby neighborhood. Figgo was identified as a leader of the out-of-town militia that had accosted voters in Precinct 53, but his motive for targeting the statue of Clay Boyette was unknown. No connection could be established between the dead Stroker for Liberty and the elder Boyette, a white philanthropic pillar of the community. After a jogger's photo of the defiled statue appeared online, an attorney for John Malkovich contacted the Carpville city manager stating that the famed actor had not consented to such use of his image or likeness, and requested that the statue be removed. Clay Boyette, who'd always hated the stone piece, raised no objection.

On the night of the day after the election, Claude Mink collapsed, wriggled briefly, and died. He'd been seated beside the lobbyist Barry Martino in the front row of public seats in the chamber where the zoning board had convened. Claude's keeling coincided with the surprise reappearance of Commissioner Lewin Baltry, whose tie-breaking vote against the Bunkers project was delayed by a flurry of paramedics. They tried their best to revive Claude. When notified of her husband's death, which left her stuck as the sole surviving signee on an eight-figure construction loan, Electra Mink seemed more grief-struck by the likelihood that her investment partners would bail. With his usual condescension, her husband had repeatedly told her not to worry, Baltry would never return. He couldn't have known that Moe the hired killer, disgusted by Claude's anti-Semitism, would spare the corrupt commissioner and spitefully bring him back to Tangelo Shores for the rezoning vote; or that the cocky trespasser who'd taunted Claude about the Wee Hammers—and later made harassing phone calls about The Bunkers—would recruit upstanding citizens Noel and Mary Kristiansen to feed and shelter Lewin Baltry until the big night; or that the Kristiansens had a personal beef with a xenophobic hit-and-run driver named Dale Figgo, and by default those who had bankrolled the Strokerz for Liberty, namely Claude himself and his now-widow. The morning of the funeral, after Electra's personal shopper arrived with a black veil for her, the watchman Dumas discreetly entered Claude's bedroom and removed the lust-scuffed Dream Booty, which he heaved into a drainage canal behind the Minks' office.

Two days after voting to block the Bunkers development, Lewin Baltry voluntarily spent several hours being interviewed at the FBI field office in Miami. Because of his close call with Moe the killer, Baltry was placed in a witness protection program and, at his request, relocated to Pebble Beach, California. Months would pass before the three other crooked county commissioners, along with Electra Mink, Barry Martino, and half a dozen developers, would be indicted on a slew of seamy bribery counts. By then the Mink Foundation was dissolved and the family name stripped from all buildings except the shingles research center in Ocala. Electra would cut a deal and eventually testify against ex-congressman Clure Boyette, who would be charged with fraud, embezzlement, and a score of child labor violations stemming from the Wee Hammers house scam. The foreman on the site, Tomas De Leon, would be found to have committed no crimes. However, one of the underage Hammers, Egregio Luhan, would the following summer be convicted in juvenile court of crashing a stolen Rivian into a drive-through cannabis dispensary after the cashier declined to accept a bag of baby bird skeletons as payment.

Three days after leaving Florida, Moe the killer checked into the Beau Rivage Resort & Casino in Biloxi, Mississippi. He was not a gambler and hated the smell of cigarettes, so he stayed in his room, called Grubhub, and ordered a pepperoni-and-pineapple pizza with a gluten-free crust. It wasn't as good as the one he'd shared with Janice Eileen Smith in Tangelo Shores. Moe spoke to his wife and then to his youngest son, who was studying to take his SATs for the third time. The kid was obsessed with scoring a perfect 1600, and Moe was worried about him. By the time the prospective client called, Moe was deep into a streaming documentary about Jimi Hendrix at Monterey. He put on his jacket and his Rockports and drove to a boat ramp in Gulfport, where he met the man who wanted to hire him. The man was a fishing guide in his early thirties, and he took Moe out on his skiff in the dark. Miles away they could see the brash lights of the Beau Rivage and, next door, the Hard Rock. A westerly breeze kicked up a chop, but the skiff was a dry ride; Moe liked that the Gulf air tasted saltier than the air on the East Coast. The young guide cut the engine and nervously offered Moe ten thousand dollars to kill another guide who was screwing his wife and, worse, poaching his customers. Moe said he couldn't take the job for less than fifty, which of course the guide did not have. Moe mentioned that he'd always wanted to learn how to cast a flyrod, and the guide offered to teach him. Moe presented himself as a slow learner, which the guide understood to mean that free casting lessons and fishing trips would cover the balance of payment for the contract murder. The following summer, after many long days on the water, Moe the killer caught a twenty-eight-pound jack crevalle on a Clouser Minnow fly in the Chandeleur Islands. His wife shipped the catch to a taxidermist and presented the finished mount to Moe on the first night of Hanukkah.

Four days after Dale Figgo's death by flag, the freighter *Carib Global* docked in Veracruz. Having arrived with no passport, no cash, and one outstanding bench warrant from an old hit-and-run in Houston, Jonas Onus decided to jump ship rather than risk being hassled by Mexican immigration officials. Wearing flip-flops and floral beach baggies loaned to him by a tubby deckhand, Onus stole a motorbike from the port and sped north until it ran out of gas in Poza Rica. There he swiped a Vespa, spent the night in a culvert outside Tampico, and was back on the road at daybreak. After the scooter lost a tire, Onus hopped on a box truck filled with migrants headed for the U.S. border. It felt like the sweet hand of fate; being so unmistakably Caucasian and American, Onus was confident that he'd be waved across the Texas line, no questions asked. However, the hot cramped truck ride brought near-smothering claustrophobia. Not a word of English was being spoken, and Onus had never felt so out of place, outnumbered, and self-conscious about his whiteness. It occurred to him, with gaseous regret, that he'd forgotten to mail in his ballot for the big election. Among his forty-odd traveling companions were teenagers and small children, one of whom offered him a drink from a warm bottle of Sprite. Onus swatted it away because the runt was sweaty and grimy, probably crawling with lice. When the box truck stopped in Matamoros, across the border from Brownsville, the driver ordered everyone to get off. The group milled around until dusk and then quietly reorganized. Because of his size, Onus's silhouette stood out dramatically as the migrants continued on foot through the mesquite. His right flip-flop blew out, and soon afterward he was bitten on his bare heel by a striped bark scorpion. Although the insect's painful sting is seldom fatal, some people report serious reactions that include muscle spasms, abdominal cramps, and shortness of breath. Scorpion-wound victims experiencing such symptoms would be wise not to try crossing the Rio Grande at night. This would be especially true for weak swimmers. Jonas Onus was wading last in the line of exhausted migrants when he tipped sideways and went under, tumbling unnoticed downstream. His body later turned up in the nets of a Brownsville shrimp trawler, and would forever remain unidentified. Back in Tangelo Shores, the three mothers of his children unanimously concluded that the cowardly bastard had flown the coop.

A week after Clure Boyette's indictment, Harold Fistman met Chip Milkwright for drinks at a quiet bar near the Bonifay County courthouse. The two lawyers toasted their good fortune in settling *Boyette v. Boyette* before the feds moved against the ex-congressman. At the time, all his assets had been intact and unseized, leaving plenty to be liquefied for attorneys' fees. That Fistman had ended up with more than Milkwright was a given; both of them did just fine. Fistman said Nicki Boyette and her pole vaulter beau were having fun times in her new ski boat, which had been exorbitantly modified for towing parasails. Nicki had already burned through all forty hours on Clay Boyette's private plane, enjoying it so much that she signed up with NetJets and purchased a fractional share of a Phenom 300. Fistman himself preferred a Lear 60, for the headroom.

Three weeks after the ex-congressman's arraignment in the Wee Hammers case, he was arrested by the state for paying prostitutes on his public Venmo account. The judge would call it "the stupidest crime ever to come before this court." Because none of the young women who'd had sex with Clure Boyette wanted to testify, he was allowed to plead guilty to misdemeanor charges and sentenced to four years' probation. Then, a few nights before the Wee Hammers trial was set to begin, Boyette would go missing on a family hog hunt in deep timber near Pensacola. All that the searchers would find were bloody chewed-up brush pants and a full scalp of black hair, thick as epoxy and glistening with product.

Boyette's death was of interest to many in Washington, D.C., and Florida, but to only one person at Kennesaw State University in north Georgia. She was registered in the nursing program as Janice Eileen Smith, and she owned a West Deck parking permit for her solar-bronze Aston Martin convertible with cream truffle upholstery. It was the only DB11 on campus. One afternoon after class, as Janice Smith got in the car and put down the top, a male student walked up and asked if it was hers. She said yes, a friend had given her the Aston, which she'd nicknamed "Martina." The student, a midfielder on the lacrosse team, condescendingly asked if the "friend" who gave her the convertible was more like a sugar daddy. Janice Smith pressed the ignition button, revved the engine, glanced in the rearview to check her hair, and said no.

The lacrosse player smirked. "Damn, girl, I bet you had to smoke some serious pole to score this ride."

"But then it wouldn't be a gift, would it?" she said, and backed over the asshole's foot.

~~~

Viva and Twilly spread a towel on the warm sand and sat down. She'd just learned that Twilly Spree had given the Aston Martin to Galaxy. Viva was surprised.

"It didn't fit my style," Twilly said. "Yours, either."

"I would have changed my style! Are you kidding? My style sucks."

Twilly knew she didn't care about the car, which she'd labeled a dickhead magnet. He laughed and lay down. Fever Beach was, once again, wondrously free of tourists. Gentle sets of sun-tipped waves cozied up to the shore, and there wasn't a boat in sight all the way to the horizon. A light rain had fallen during the trek from the parking lot, but now the sky was deep azure strung with little popcorn clouds.

Propped on her elbows, Viva looked around and marveled at the quiet, the air, and the incongruity.

"Of all places," she said, "this is where they hatched their big plot?"

"Right here. A confederacy of bumblefucks."

High tides and a late-season tropical storm had washed away the remains of the bonfires, but trash had been pushed up along the dune line, including a blue plastic milk crate and a handful of faded juice boxes. A pair of laughing gulls stood shredding an empty bag of Buc-ee's sea-salted caramel beaver nuggets.

Viva wore a new tan two-piece swimsuit under a cotton coverup
~~~

with spaghetti straps. For Twilly, it was black gym shorts and a gray Last Mango tee shirt. The cooler he'd brought held a six-pack of Stella and turkey wraps from a Winn-Dixie deli.

Viva said, "Dale's mother called. She put the townhouse up for sale. They scattered his ashes at a gun range in Titusville."

"Did David Duke fly in for the eulogy?"

"I feel sorry for her, Twilly."

"Raising kids is like roulette, except you can't just cash in and walk away. That's a quote from my dad. I was a disappointment to him, no surprise."

Viva stood, took off her coverup, and executed a campy twirl.

"Are those new sunglasses?" Twilly asked.

"Ha-ha. Do you like it or not? I almost bought a one-piece instead."

"You look amazing. Let's go for a swim."

"In a minute." Arms at her side, she was looking out across the water. "Don't you ever wonder what happened to Jonas?"

"I do not," Twilly said.

The memory kept rewinding in Viva's mind: Onus coming at her, undoing his pants—and the next instant he was crumbling, almost in layers, like a glacier. Twilly had knocked him out with a single punch to the head. Right hand, left hand, Viva couldn't say. She'd been stunned that it happened so fast and one-sidedly.

"You told me you left him out by the shipping lanes," she said. "Is that a long way back to shore?"

"Without a boat? Yeah." Twilly dug two beers out of the ice and popped the caps. "How's the job hunt going?" he asked.

Viva took one of the beers thinking: *Here goes.*

"Funny you should ask," she said. "This morning I got an offer from a company in New York."

"City?"

"Correct."

"In HR?"

"Yeah, at Macy's. The main office."

"Awesome. Why are you not turning cartwheels?"

"It's a cubicle job," Viva said, "with 'opportunities for advancement.' "

"Which you will."

"Believe it or not, I considered staying here with you."

"Thank God the drugs wore off," Twilly said.

"Seriously. Can you imagine?" She had, in fact, imagined it. He was a self-tuned mess, not quite what she needed. "I start in two weeks," she said.

They stripped down and got in the water. Viva rode on his back, her arms around his neck and legs around his hips. She asked for a progress report on his future island retreat in the Bahamas. Twilly said the first barge was being loaded with construction materials at Port Everglades. The work crews would come from George Town and Nassau, and he was refitting an old seventy-foot Hatteras for them to stay on. Still, he said, it would be a miracle if the house on Starfish Point was finished in two years.

"What are you going to do with yourself until then?" Viva asked.

"Float. Cope. Try to stay out of jail."

"And avoid getting triggered."

"Immmmpppppppossible," Twilly said while blowing bubbles.

When a small lemon shark swam by, Viva let out a cry. Twilly told her to relax, she wasn't on the menu. Next they spotted a pod of dolphins, which kept their distance but thrilled Viva nonetheless.

"Question," she said to the back of Twilly's head. "Torching the excavator, bulldozer, whatever—that wasn't just a move, was it?"

"Actually you're the first date I ever brought along on a property crime." He reached back and pinched her butt underwater. "But I knew you'd be cool."

"Dynamite and futile gestures? That's not me." She returned the pinch.

"Felony mischief would be the charge," he said, "if we'd gotten caught."

"Thanks for the Steve McQueen getaway. Macy's isn't advertising for arsonists."

She swung around so that she was facing him, her arms still

around his neck. He kissed her and then, because he couldn't yet clear his mind, brought up the demise of The Bunkers: "Some other shitty project will get built out there, the usual Florida monstrosity, but at least the widow Mink will be spending her sunset years in bankruptcy court. See, I do try to look for the silver lining."

Viva said, "It would be dickish if you didn't come see me in Manhattan."

"Maybe after New Year's."

"Why so long? What's going on between now and then?"

"Another project. I'll get you a plane ticket." When Twilly started telling her about it, she pretended to choke him.

"Damn, lady," he said, "those are strong thumbs."

"Promotes lymphatic drainage."

"And mindfulness?"

"You're fine," she said.

Twilly let himself fall backward, underwater, pulling her along.

Later, after lunch, he ambled up to the dunes to collect the woeful Stroker debris—the juice boxes, nugget wrappers, cigarette butts, waterlogged cornhole bags—until he'd filled the plastic crate that the late Dale Figgo once used as a rostrum. Walking a few steps behind, Viva spotted something unusual protruding from the sugary sand. Twilly stopped to help her dig it out.

A tiki torch, the bottom half of the stem snapped off by a storm.

Together they toweled off the grit and dead seaweed. The lamp oil canister looked rusty, but it felt half full. Twilly tore a thin strip from his shirt and twisted it into the shape of a wick. In Viva's bag was the Bic lighter she'd used for scented candles in the townhouse to neutralize Figgo's body odor. Twilly steadied the torch head while she fired it up. The flame smelled like citronella.

"Can I keep this thing?" she asked. "It's like a silly piece of history."

"It's definitely a piece of *something*."

"I want it for my new apartment."

"You can't go wrong with bamboo," he said, "especially in New York."

Viva twirled the lit torch on her shoulder as they walked down the beach. Twilly lugged the cooler, balancing the crate of litter on top.

"You'd better call me," she said.

"Count on it." He nudged her with his hip. "You're hooked now."

The End

A NOTE ABOUT THE AUTHOR

Carl Hiaasen was born and raised in Florida. He is the author of many previous novels, including the best sellers *Bad Monkey, Squeeze Me, Nature Girl, Razor Girl, Sick Puppy, Skinny Dip,* and *Star Island,* as well as seven best-selling children's books, *Hoot, Flush, Scat, Chomp, Skink, Squirm,* and *Wrecker.* His most recent work of nonfiction is *Assume the Worst,* a collaboration with the artist Roz Chast.

A NOTE ON THE TYPE

The text of this book was set in Sabon, a typeface designed by Jan Tschichold (1902–1974), the well-known German typographer. Based loosely on the original designs by Claude Garamond (ca. 1480–1561), Sabon is unique in that it was explicitly designed for hot-metal composition on both the Monotype and Linotype machines as well as for filmsetting. Designed in 1966 in Frankfurt, Sabon was named for the famous Lyons punch cutter Jacques Sabon, who is thought to have brought some of Garamond's matrices to Frankfurt.

Typeset by Scribe, Philadelphia, Pennsylvania

Designed by Anna B. Knighton